Hearts of Fire

Luca Duray has been quite happy living a solitary existence for decades. But when a steel trap around his leg catches him when he's weak and hungry, his life is irrevocably changed. He knows the wolf shifter who offers him assistance is more than he appears and immediately makes plans to keep the pup close.

Disowned by his pack for being gay, Tanner McBane is forced to become a lone wolf. While on a hunt, he stumbles upon an injured dragon shifter and provides aid. It's not easy surviving on his own and when money gets tight, he finds himself face-to-face with the dragon shifter once again during an interview. Tanner isn't sure a wolf should be working for a dragon, but he accepts the job and unknowingly creates a bond to his new boss. Soon, Tanner learns Luca isn't just his boss—he's his mate.

The mating of a wolf and dragon shifter is uncharted territory for both Luca and Tanner, but they are determined to make it work despite widespread prejudice, death threats, and the untraditional pack Tanner finds himself leading. Tanner only hopes that the bond he forms with Luca will prove to be unbreakable.

Hearts of Blood

Omega wolf shifter, Vance, and the rest of his small pack have finally found an Alpha willing to take them on and were still trying to regain their footing when the McBane Pack attacked them. When a vampire appears in front of him, Vance realizes he's looking into the ice-blue eyes of his mate, and the fact that his mate is something other than wolf scares him.

Sakima knew the wolf shifter was his destined companion the moment he scented him at Elysium, but claiming the gorgeous young Omega wolf is a dangerous proposition. Vance and his unconventional pack have attracted the attention of the vampire coven. As the owner of Elysium, Sakima has been asked to use the club to gather information on the powerful interspecies pack and its Alpha.

Unfortunately for Vance and Sakima, the vampire coven and the continued attacks by the McBane Pack are only a portion of their problems. Amidst concerns over Alpha Tanner's abilities growing with Sakima's addition to the pack, a spurned ex targets Vance in an attempt to remove him from Sakima's life, and Elysium becomes a hot bed for interspecies mingling where anyone could be an enemy.

Hearts of Magic

A moment of quiet was all Theran was looking for. He was not looking to be nearly decimated when he stumbled across a sorcerer near the pack's hunting grounds. He's certainly not looking for his mate when the pack congregates at Elysium for a meeting, but that's exactly what Theran finds when he runs into the sorcerer a second time.

Colby has been the bartender at Elysium for a year, and he's been relatively happy. He hides his paranormal identity well, flirting for tips while using sarcasm to keep others away. When he first saw the wolf in the forest, he was stunned. Learning the wolf he's been dreaming about is real is only compounded by learning the wolf is his mate.

With the Sorcerer's Enclave now interested in the Chevalier Pack, Colby attempts to protect Theran by kidnapping him, which only results in a deeper involvement with the pack. Despite managing the Enclave, dealing with increasing threats from the McBane Pack, and forging new alliances, Theran and Colby are determined to find their happy ever after.

Hearts of Destiny

Ean and Matthias have known they're mates for a while, but Matthias has been unwilling to claim Ean. He believes his past and age-old secrets are too big for Ean to overcome, so instead keeps Ean away by irritating him.

Depressed and no longer able to be near the dragon-shifter, Ean leaves the pack house and, after a night of heavy drinking, makes a life-changing decision that pushes Matthias into action.

As the blood moon draws nearer, the Chevalier Pack is called before a tribunal of paranormal leaders to assess the Alpha's rumored mysterious abilities. Matthias decides to share his secrets with a little help from Colby. And to top everything off, they face another attack by the McBane Pack, which the Chevalier decide will be the last.

CHEVALIER

Series Collection

Kay Doherty

A NineStar Press Publication

Published by NineStar Press
P.O. Box 91792,
Albuquerque, New Mexico, 87199 USA.
www.ninestarpress.com

Chevalier Series Collection

Printed in the USA
First Edition
March, 2020

Print ISBN: 978-1-951880-80-4

Warning: This book contains sexually explicit content, which may only be suitable for mature readers, homicidal and suicidal ideations, and graphic violence.

This is for every lover who refuses to change, give up, or give in.

Hearts of Fire

Chapter One

TANNER

Tanner McBane ran hard, expertly leaping over rocks and dodging trees as he pushed his body to maximum speed. His paws dug into the ground, kicking up the leaves and dirt of the forest floor behind him. He wasn't on the hunt. He wasn't trying to outrun an enemy. The demons chasing him were internal. Tanner was the McBane-pack-Alpha's son, or at least he was until a week ago.

He had been raised to be the pack's next leader. He had believed the pack would always be there for him; that they'd have his back. He'd certainly expected his mother to stand by him, but the good Alpha mate she was, she'd remained silent about everything as she stood at his father's side. His mother's docile nature annoyed him. Tanner was determined to find a mate who wasn't afraid to speak up.

Pack bond, loyalty, and respect were solid as long as Tanner had remained exactly like them. As soon as he'd stood up to his father, told him he was gay, and he wanted a male to mate, he'd been disowned. The entire pack turned their backs on him. He was hurt, afraid, and pissed as hell. He was also very much alone with no one but himself to rely on. Tanner learned he liked that. He made his own rules, did his own thing, and he was happy. All he needed was someone to share his life with. Now that he was officially a lone wolf, he could search for the mate he truly wanted, not just settle for whomever his father chose.

Tanner's need for a mate had been the catalyst for his disownment. He'd announced his sexuality so his father would stop choosing female shifters for him. His father had wanted to find him a mate the minute Tanner had turned eighteen, but Tanner managed to hold him off for a few years. Apparently, twenty-two years old was the limit his father tolerated. He'd been set up with a new female almost weekly until Tanner finally had enough and announced his homosexuality. He no longer needed to worry about his father's erroneous choices.

A loud, resonating roar of pain ripped through the night. Tanner skidded to a halt, claws digging into the dirt, nose in the air, and ears pricked to the sky. Pinpointing where the scream originated from in the dense forest was tricky. The breeze carried only silence and the faintest scent of smoke and blood. Tanner followed the scent, picking his way silently over the undergrowth, careful not to disturb anything. Heavy breathing interrupted by a growl that rapidly escalated into a roar of frustration once again echoed through the night and led Tanner closer.

Tanner stopped and hunkered down when he came within sight of the scream's owner. A man struggled on the ground with a large bear trap clamped around his calf. A few inches lower and the massive metal teeth might have severed the man's foot at the ankle. The scent of blood was strong, but what was noticeably missing was the scent of fear. The man was angry. He was frustrated. But he wasn't afraid, and that intrigued Tanner. He moved closer, keeping his attention locked on the stranger. His paw landed on a pile of dried leaves, and the man's head swung to face him. Pain twisted the man's handsome features, but his gaze was fierce as he stared at Tanner.

Tanner blinked but remained absolutely still. This man...he wasn't human. He didn't smell human, and he didn't act human, but he was amazingly beautiful. Dark-blond hair hung limply over his tanned forehead and curled slightly at his ears. Dark-brown eyes zeroed in on Tanner and narrowed menacingly.

"Come here, pup," the man growled through elongated fangs.

The man's voice rumbled, coming from deep within his chest. Tanner took a step back. This man shouldn't need his help. He was another shifter, and worse, he was a dragon shifter. From his disheveled, fatigued appearance and the fact the bear trap's teeth were still snuggly buried in his leg, he was a substantially weakened dragon, but still dangerous. Knowing just because the dragon shifter had a steel trap on his leg didn't mean he was helpless, Tanner backed away without breaking eye contact. The dragon slowly disappeared from view as Tanner moved deeper into the surrounding trees. Once out of sight, Tanner turned and ran.

"Come back and help me, or I will hunt you down and eat you for dinner, you pathetic dog," the dragon yelled.

The insult was cut off by an agonized scream that filled the night. The shifter must have moved the wrong way and jarred the trap. Tanner wasn't strong enough in human form to remove the trap, and as a wolf with paws, instead of fingers, he was useless. If the dragon was stronger, he would be able to free himself. Helping a dragon shifter regain his strength was a dangerous proposition. All paranormals knew dragons and wolves didn't get along well. Tanner often wondered why and considered asking his father on several occasions, but he'd never followed through. Ethan McBane was not one who enjoyed being questioned.

Tanner located the herd of deer he'd been following and hunting over the past week. Dragons weren't picky eaters, especially when in such a weakened state. Tanner wasn't all that educated when it came to other shifters, but he vaguely remembered being told dragons preferred their prey be alive until they ate it. With that in mind, he took down a female deer that smelled sick, making sure the wound was debilitating, but not fatal, and dragged her back to the dragon.

Tanner tugged the heavy deer through the trees into the small clearing where the shifter lay. It had been more than an hour since he'd left to hunt for food for the man. The dragon appeared even more weakened by the time Tanner returned, no doubt from the continuous blood loss he was suffering. The man rolled his head toward Tanner and licked his lips as the scent of blood reached him. He pushed up onto his elbows, teeth elongating and eyes swirling gold, as Tanner pulled the still-struggling deer closer.

"You brought me dinner. Aren't you a good pup," the dragon shifter said.

He latched onto the deer's leg with surprising force and pulled the animal closer to himself. Tanner growled, deep and low, baring his teeth as he backed away. Even in a weakened state, this dragon was powerful and dangerous. Plus, Tanner didn't like being called pup. He was a young wolf shifter, twenty-two years old, but he was far from a puppy who needed protecting. The fact he was capable of sustaining himself and feeding an injured, bleeding dragon was proof enough.

The dragon wrapped a strong arm around the deer's body while the other gripped the head. The animal struggled as the shifter sank his teeth into the neck, snapping it in a swift death blow, and then began to feast. Tanner backed away another few feet, well out of reach, and wondered if he should leave now or wait. He knew, once the dragon had fresh meat to strengthen him, he'd pry the metal trap from his leg on his own.

Tanner wasn't sure he wanted to be anywhere nearby when the man was free, especially after seeing him tear into the deer carcass as if it were paper. When most of the deer meat was gone, the dragon pulled away, blood dripping from his fangs and covering his chin and neck.

Tanner watched from his crouched position among the trees as the dragon closed his eyes, turned his face upward, and the blood soaked into his skin. When the shifter's eyes found Tanner, they shined a brighter gold and not a drop of blood marred his perfect skin. The dragon pushed the remainder of the carcass away and turned his attention to his leg. Gripping the thick, saw-toothed edge of the trap, he forced it open as he let out a loud roar.

Tanner jumped to his feet, ready to run at a moment's notice, as the man steadily pulled the sharp teeth from his skin and removed his leg from the iron. He threw the trap into the woods, and Tanner heard the thud as it landed dozens of feet away, testament to the dragon's renewed power. Tanner's gaze was glued to the dragon's leg as the wounds knitted themselves back together. Tanner had an accelerated rate of healing as well, but the wounds the dragon had suffered would have taken Tanner days to heal, assuming he'd been able to free himself in the first place. Tanner lifted his gaze to the dragon's face. His eyes had returned to their deep, rich brown, but his hair was damp with perspiration, the curl more pronounced, hanging wetly around his face. The man had incredible strength, but the effort of removing the trap had taken a toll.

Distant voices floated on the breeze and Tanner's ears pricked. The dragon's acute hearing picked them up as well. He rolled to his knees into a crouch, ready to pounce, his fangs once again elongating, preparing for a fight. Tanner flattened his ears to his head and tucked his tail, his lips curling up to reveal fangs of his own. He bent his knees, the muscles in his legs ready to launch him whichever direction was required. Three men burst through the foliage, rifles in hand.

Chapter Two

LUCA

Luca Duray took one look at the hunters who burst into the small clearing and immediately knew they were human. He rose to his full six-foot-four height and quickly retracted his fangs. He had just feasted on deer, and he wasn't currently hungry, so these men were lucky enough to live out the night. Unless they were the ones who had placed the trap in the first place, and then they would be dead. Luca's keen hearing made him aware of the wolf's subtle movement behind him.

Normally, he never allowed a possible enemy to be at his back, but there was something different about this wolf shifter. This wolf had hunted for him, fed him so he could regain his strength and thereby his freedom, all at an increased risk to the wolf's well-being. No. This shifter was safe enough. Luca straightened his suit coat and brushed off the leaves and debris that had accumulated on the expensive fabric from the recent unfortunate events, then smoothed his drying hair back from his face. He adopted the self-assured businessman persona that was like a second skin to him after so many decades.

"Gentlemen," Luca said as he leveled an intimidating gaze on the hunters.

"Hey," the hunter in the lead said. "We're camping nearby and heard a lot of screaming and roaring—"

"And howling," one of the others murmured as he glanced at the wolf.

"Everything okay here?" the leader asked.

"Yes, everything's fine," Luca said. "I was out for a stroll with my dog when we interrupted something having dinner."

He flicked his wrist dismissively at the deer carcass. The men looked at the deer, and then collectively moved their gazes to the wolf behind him. The hunters were definitely questioning his explanation, but Luca didn't have the inclination to put them at ease. He simply didn't care if these human hunters bought his story or not. In the grander scheme of life, their beliefs didn't matter.

"Awful late for a stroll," one of the men said.

"Insomnia." Luca shrugged as he turned to leave the clearing. "Come boy," he said to the wolf and snapped his fingers.

Luca hoped the wolf understood enough to follow him like an obedient dog following his master. Luca smiled to himself at the thought of this wolf shifter being his to command. A dragon master with a wolf sidekick would certainly stir up the paranormal world. The sleek black-and-white wolf followed as instructed, his intelligent bright-blue eyes taking in the hunters before giving them his back. The animal was beautiful, lean, and powerful—a creature meant to lead.

Luca listened to see if any of the men followed, but all remained quiet. The night became silent, even the breeze taking leave, as they moved through the trees. He was hyperaware of the wolf following at a distance. Once Luca was certain they were alone, he stopped. The wolf paced in a wide arc around him, never getting too close, but maintaining firm eye contact. Luca got the distinct feeling he was being sized up. He lowered himself into a squat, bracing his elbows on his knees. He smirked and glanced up at the surrounding forest.

The night was clear, warm, and dry. The canopy of branches and leaves filtered the moonlight into small patches of luminescence dotting across the ground. Quiet. He lowered his gaze and watched the wolf with a sideways glance. Powerful muscles moved beneath shiny fur and Luca caught himself wondering what the man looked like. Some wolf shifters were attractive as animals but were plain and sometimes hideous as humans. This one was young and smelled uniquely of the forest surrounding them.

"You're a beautiful young pup, aren't you?" Luca asked. The wolf's ears pinned back against his head, and he bared his teeth. Luca chuckled, resulting in a low growl from the wolf. "I meant no offense, I assure you."

Luca stood once again and scanned the area around him. When his gaze returned to where the wolf had stood, there was only forest. The shifter had moved so quickly and quietly. Luca found it a bit disconcerting the wolf was able to disappear like that, despite Luca's enhanced hearing. Feeling eyes on him, Luca smiled.

"Thank you for your assistance...pup," Luca said to the forest, in general. No response came, but he was certain he'd been heard.

Chapter Three

TANNER

Tanner was dressed in his best suit but was still self-conscious. This was his first job interview…ever. Until now, he'd held a position in his father's firm. With his disownment, he had to consider things as mundane as housing, clothing, and food, all of which required income. For the past two weeks, he'd been living off the savings he managed to keep while under his father's thumb. Those funds were now running low and he needed to replenish his account soon.

Breathing deeply, he left the hotel room he acquired the day before. The room was chosen because of its close proximity to the office building where Tanner would, with any luck, be working, starting tomorrow. He walked the short distance, adjusting his tie and suit coat frequently, in a bout of nerves. He hadn't been this nervous in the presence of the dragon last week, though he should have been. The shifter had been in human form, but it would have taken mere seconds for him to achieve dragon form to squash Tanner like a bug. Or perhaps, decide to gore him with a horn or a tail spike many of the more mature dragons developed. No wolf shifter alive had a defense against those.

Tanner shook his head to remove all thoughts of the dragon shifter. He had been obsessing over the man since happening upon him. Every night, Tanner dreamt of brown eyes swirling with gold, wet dark-blond hair, and imagined the shifter appeared that way due to hot and sweaty intimate situations rather than the pain that had actually caused the look. He might have allowed his imagination to run wild and produced a smooth chest and bulging biceps, as well. It was pathetic the most attractive man Tanner had come into contact with since his departure from the pack was a dragon he could never be with and who kept calling him "pup." So damned infuriating.

Moving gracefully through the mass of humans on the street, Tanner made excellent time and entered the air-conditioned building with fifteen minutes to spare. He checked in with reception and took a seat to wait his turn. Several other people, male and female alike, shared the waiting room with him, all impeccably dressed and looking almost as nervous as he was. Tanner used the time to center himself the same way he did when he was about to initiate the change. His breathing deepened, his heart rate slowed, and a calm descended over his mind, silencing his thoughts. Once he was finally called into the office for his interview, he'd appear perfectly calm and completely in control.

A tingle tripped down Tanner's spine, alerting him to the presence of another paranormal. He casually glanced around at the room's occupants, trying to discern who was causing the reaction. No one was looking at him or scanning the waiting area the way he was. The human staff went about their business without the slightest clue a wolf shifter sat in their midst or that another paranormal was nearby. This was why humans made such great prey—they were completely unaware of the predators among them.

A gorgeous man with shoulder-length brown hair and incredibly light-blue eyes exited the hall, catching Tanner's attention. The man stopped outside an office door, looked directly at Tanner, smiled slightly, and then turned to enter the office. Tanner was certain the handsome man was the other paranormal he'd sensed, but he didn't have time to investigate.

A pretty blonde woman in a blue skirt and white blouse stepped behind the rounded mahogany reception desk and spoke in low tones to the clerk. Tanner's hearing picked up every word whispered between the women, and he prepared himself to be called. He slid his hands down his slacks and straightened his suit coat again. The blonde woman walked out from behind the desk and called out to the room in general.

"Tanner McBane."

Tanner pushed to his feet. "Yes, ma'am."

She looked him over head to toe before nodding. "Right this way." She turned and led him down a long hall with glass walls, allowing everyone a view of the offices on the other side. "Do you have a copy of your resume and references?" the woman asked, glancing down at his empty hands. Prickles of anxiety punched holes into Tanner's calm façade.

"No. I sent my resume in with the application, but I didn't bring a copy," he answered. More than a little concerned, he asked, "Will I still be able to interview?"

"Of course, but your chances of being hired are fairly low."

"Why?"

"You came unprepared."

Her tone suggested Tanner was better served not bothering with the interview, but he refused to give in so easily. His resume wasn't fantastic in any way, and he really only had one reference: his father, whom he had no intention of ever using. As they reached the end of the hall, another reception desk appeared, this one of glass and metal, occupied by an average-looking young man. Behind him was an ornately-engraved, opaque frosted-glass door. Upon seeing them approach, the man lifted the phone and announced their arrival. He hung up the receiver with a nod, so the woman opened the door and stepped aside. Tanner smiled at her as he crossed the threshold, but she didn't return the smile. She turned on her heel and left the room, closing the door behind her with a soft click. He took a deep breath to calm his nerves as he stepped farther into the expansive room and froze. His fight-or-flight instinct flared to life, zinging through his system and threatening an uncontrolled shift. His gaze was riveted to the man standing in front of the wall of floor-to-ceiling windows looking out over the city.

Chapter Four

LUCA

Luca inhaled the scent of forest deeply into his lungs and smiled. He kept his gaze on the cityscape beyond his window, though he no longer saw any of it. Every molecule in his body was aware his wolf shifter had entered the room. He had read and dismissed the short, lackluster resume of one Tanner McBane seconds before the applicant was brought to the office. Luca closed his eyes. For the hundredth time in the past week, he pulled the image of the beautiful wolf to the forefront of his mind. Shiny black-and-white fur and brilliant blue eyes had haunted him most of his waking hours since their unfortunate meeting the week before.

Aware any sudden movements might result in an undesirable confrontation given the strong scent of adrenaline filling the room, Luca slowly turned to face the shifter. His breath caught in his chest when he saw his wolf pup was an incredibly handsome young man. Tanner McBane was as gorgeous in human form as he was in wolf form. He had wavy black hair that barely touched the top of his ears in a sexy disheveled look. Bright-blue eyes narrowed in wariness and tracked Luca's every move. Luca chuckled, unsure how to proceed with this meeting since it was no longer a traditional interview.

"Take a seat, Mr. McBane." Luca sat in the plush executive chair behind his desk and quirked an eyebrow. "Or may I call you Tanner?"

"Um...Tanner, please. Mr. McBane brings up unwanted memories," Tanner answered with a shake of his head.

He sat in one of the leather chairs across the desk from Luca. Unlike all the other applicants, whose eyes looked at everything but Luca, Tanner's gaze never left him. Given the chance, Luca would stare into those beautiful blues for the entirety of his eternal life. He wondered what reaction Tanner would have to that news, as he smiled at the young man. Tanner lowered his eyes to his lap.

"Shit," Tanner said under his breath. Thanks to Luca's keen hearing, he heard Tanner's expletive quite clearly. "I wasn't prepared for this."

Luca rested his elbows on the desktop and leaned forward. "You don't need to be prepared for anything. The job is yours."

"You don't know anything about me yet. You haven't asked me anything," Tanner said with eyes narrowed to slits. "I've never done an interview before, but I'm pretty sure that's how it's supposed to go."

Luca leaned back in his chair and gripped the armrests. "I don't need to. The job was yours the moment you walked through my door."

"Why?"

"Because I know who you are, pup. I'd recognize your scent anywhere." Luca smiled broadly as irritation creased Tanner's forehead.

"That still doesn't explain why you'd just give me a job, and don't call me pup."

"You honestly have no idea what you've done, do you?" Luca watched confusion spread across the wolf's face. "You should have left me to die in that trap."

"Why?" Tanner asked softly, revulsion and horror twisting his handsome face.

Luca rose from his chair and walked around the desk. He planted his hands on the rounded edge behind him and leaned back against the glossy wood surface, his leg mere inches from Tanner's knee. He waited until those blue eyes lifted to meet his gaze.

"You hunted for me, you fed me, and then you waited to make sure I got free. Knowingly or not, you submitted to me and elevated me to master. Or in your case, Alpha. That is something I take very seriously. So," Luca said, as he pushed off the desk, "if you are in need of a job, I will provide you one."

Luca walked to the wall of windows and looked out over the city flanked by the distant mountains he had called home for over thirty years. Luca felt Tanner's heat at his side as the wolf shifter joined him in front of the window. Tanner had taken care in his appearance for this interview, probably to make up for his crappy work experience, which was tantamount to none. But Luca knew he was making the right decision in hiring Tanner. The youngster had the countenance and confidence of an Alpha, which made him an important and worthy addition to Luca's business. Luca thought back to the night Tanner had found him in the forest. Tanner had been alone, which, while not unheard of, was extremely unusual and would eventually become dangerous.

"Where is your pack, Tanner? Please, be honest." Luca watched Tanner's reflection in the glass as sadness, anger, and resignation played across his face in rapid succession. Luca wondered if the wolf was aware he was standing slightly behind and to the left of Luca, mirroring the precise positioning of a submissive mate to their more dominant partner. Tanner had obviously been part of a pack at one time and witnessed the Alpha's mate standing in that exact position often enough to now mimic it without thought.

"I don't have one," Tanner said softly. "I was disowned several weeks back."

"That explains a lot. Why did they turn their backs on you?" Luca asked.

He was genuinely curious how this young wolf had ended up on his own, where he could unwittingly bond himself to a dragon. And it was a bond Luca had every intention of strengthening and deepening. Now that he had Tanner within his sphere of influence, he would do whatever was necessary to become Tanner's pack. He refused to risk this beautiful creature's safety and sanity for anything.

"You're a dragon..." Tanner said, and Luca waited for the rest, but Tanner never finished the thought.

"I am. Were you going somewhere with that?"

"Yes, I'm just...not..." Tanner blew out a breath and looked at his shoes for a moment. When he lifted his head to stare out the window, he seemed to have found his confidence again. "Dragons are notoriously sexual, and I'm told, not all that discriminating as to the gender of their mates, so I trust you won't judge me." Tanner held Luca's reflective gaze. "I'm gay. And that's not acceptable, especially from an Alpha's son."

"I see," Luca said.

Dozens of possibilities floated through Luca's mind. The wolves had given him an incredible advantage by ostracizing an Alpha like Tanner. Having a wolf bonded to him was one thing. Having an Alpha wolf bonded to him was quite another. The power Luca and Tanner were going to have over wolves and dragons alike should they bond permanently had incredible potential, especially if they succeeded in bringing more wolves and dragons into their fold.

"No judgment? I still have the job?" Tanner asked.

Luca turned to face his newest employee. "No judgment, my sweet boy. You can start your job now by going out to the waiting area and announcing the position has been filled. Brent, the young man working the desk outside my door right now, will introduce you to your new duties and show you what needs to be done."

Tanner nodded and left the office. No questions asked. Tanner was clearly a man used to being in a position of power, second only to the pack's Alpha, and likely suffered no compunction with issuing orders or following through on disciplinary actions when necessary. He would do well at Luca's side. Luca returned to his chair behind the desk. He rested his elbows on the armrests and pressed his fingers together in front of his lips as he contemplated all the pros and cons of having a wolf shifter close by.

Chapter Five

TANNER

Tanner's first day, or afternoon really, was frustrating. He was the son of an Alpha and accustomed to receiving a certain level of respect. He hadn't made any enemies, but he certainly hadn't made friends when he'd done as Luca instructed and announced to the remaining candidates the position of executive assistant to Luca Duray had been filled. Every one of them had seen Tanner go into the interview, so they were all aware he was the one who'd been hired.

Tanner had felt the mysterious paranormal's gaze on his back as he moved into the waiting room to make the announcement and again when he walked back down the hall to his new desk. He made plans to learn about all possible threats over the next few days to assess his safety. The paranormal might be perfectly friendly, but Tanner was in new territory and he needed to be careful.

Despite the title of executive assistant, which admittedly sounded good, Tanner quickly realized he was Luca's glorified gopher and guard. He managed Luca's many meetings, made phone calls, and played watchdog to Luca's office door. No one got in without an appointment or a damn good reason to be interrupting the dragon. Brent abandoned him hours ago, muttering something about being needed in the accounting department. Tanner shrugged it off and focused on doing his job well enough not to be fired on his first day.

He didn't really think that would happen, considering the way Luca had simply handed him the job, but his perfectionism didn't leave room for failure. Tanner wasn't certain working for a dragon shifter was the best idea, and he didn't know what to expect with having one as a boss. At the end of his workday, Tanner knocked on Luca's door and opened it far enough to stick his head in at Luca's gruff "Enter."

"I don't know if I should offer, but do you need anything before I go?" Tanner asked.

Luca leaned back in his chair and smiled broadly. "You're the first assistant to ever ask me that." Luca motioned Tanner in with a wave. "Come in."

Tanner was reluctant to join the man at his desk, but he did so with a mumbled "Okay." He sat in the same chair he'd occupied earlier. He was hungry and needed to hunt. The past hour had been spent rearranging the desk drawers, file cabinets, and supplies to his liking. Now that he was sitting down, fatigue hit him hard. Hunting when not at full capacity was a reckless idea, so a raw steak from Firestone Bar and Grill, located on the main floor of the hotel, would have to do. Luca's gaze tracked Tanner's every move.

"I was going to ask how your day went, but I think I need to take you hunting first," Luca said.

"I'm not hunting tonight, but even if I was, you don't have to go with me," Tanner said.

"I'm not giving you a choice, pup. You know how dangerous it is to hunt alone. I won't interfere or steal your dinner, but I will be going. Why weren't you planning to eat tonight? Are you unwell?"

Tanner was seriously confused over the dragon's obvious concern for his well-being. "I'm fine, and I am eating. I'm just not hunting. I'll order a few steaks from the restaurant when I get back to the hotel," Tanner told him.

"Not exactly a healthy practice. Wolves need fresh meat as badly as dragons do."

"I know. It's short term."

"Well, my last client angered me, so I flew to his ranch and ate some of his cattle. I wanted to eat him and his asinine little helper, but I'm no murderer." Luca gave Tanner a chilling smile. "I'm full for the night, so I can take you to dinner," Luca added as he rose to his feet.

"You stole from a client?" Tanner asked a bit louder than he planned. Luca shot him a glare that suggested he was crossing a line, but Tanner wasn't one to back down. The trait had earned him several beatings from his father over the years. "You can't do that. It's against the rules." Tanner kept his gaze on Luca as the dragon came around the desk.

"What rules are you referring to, pup?" Luca asked. Tanner looked at him, annoyed and clearly confused. "First thing you need to learn— there are no rules. Not for me. And now that you are no longer part of a pack, there are no rules for you, except those I place on you."

Luca managed to keep himself from smiling in triumph at the fact Tanner paid no attention to the suggestion Luca was the Alpha. Instead, Tanner was oddly focused on the feeding itself, which Luca didn't understand.

"You can't go stealing from your clients because they piss you off. It's bad for business," Tanner said, exasperated.

Luca laughed and shook his head. "They'll assume the cattle were killed by a wild animal. It's not like they know they're dealing with a dragon."

Tanner's distress eased and his muscles relaxed, but he became silent, staring at Luca with lowered brows. He wasn't happy, but he was letting it go.

"Now," Luca said and motioned for Tanner to stand. "Let's get you fed."

Chapter Six

LUCA

Luca leaned against a thick tree trunk, breathed in the cool evening air, and observed Tanner stalk his prey. The wolf looked sleek and powerful as he hunched low, muscles tense and ready for action, as he approached the deer on silent paws. A dragon's feeding style was quite different. Luca typically swooped down from above and snatched up his dinner with sharp talons or let loose a burst of flame to cook it on the spot. Seeing this predator actually hunt was fascinating. It wasn't something dragons typically witnessed because no wolf shifter had ever knowingly turned his back on one. Tanner was different, unique, and something about him spoke directly to Luca's soul.

Tanner bared his teeth and pounced, taking his prey down in one smooth motion and snapping the deer's neck. Luca found such deadly efficiency erotic, and he hardened at the sight. His wolf was absolutely gorgeous. Tanner shook his head, twisting the animal's neck to ensure a swift death, and then took in his surroundings, finding Luca effortlessly. He put a paw on the deer's side and held Luca's gaze for a moment. Luca understood immediately what the pup was doing, offering the Alpha first bite, and it gave him deep satisfaction. He smiled at the young wolf shifter as he shook his head, letting Tanner know he wouldn't be sharing the meal.

Wasting no more time, Tanner tore into the deer hide with gusto. The young wolf was hungrier than Luca had realized, and he wondered how long it'd been since his last meal. Now that he was under Luca's care, Luca planned to feed Tanner on a regular basis. He'd never allow this beautiful shifter to die of starvation, or watch him go insane, which was something else Luca needed to figure out how to prevent.

Wolf shifters without a pack were prone to insanity with a high rate of suicidal and homicidal ideation because the lack of a pack bond left them adrift. From the moment they're born, and some paranormal scholars suspect even before birth, wolf shifters could telepathically communicate with any pack member at will, quickly growing accustomed to experiencing thoughts and emotions not their own. When that connection was severed, the shifter affected couldn't cope and eventually death became preferable to suffering the silence and loneliness. Dragons, on the other hand, were predominately solitary creatures. Some of them lived in communes and took solace from being among their own kind, but when push came to shove, surviving centuries without ever laying eyes on another dragon was an option.

Luca kept his distance until Tanner had decimated the deer, leaving very little meat for the scavengers. He approached slowly and loudly to ensure the wolf knew he was coming. Stomach full, muzzle covered in blood, and clearly re-energized, Tanner crouched into a playful pose with his chest to the ground, ass in the air, tail twitching. Luca pretended to reach for him, and he took off like a shot in the direction of the river. Unsure if he was supposed to give chase or not, Luca decided to give the wolf time to run off his energy. He snapped a leg off the deer, distended his fangs, and snacked on what meat remained until Tanner returned, clean and dripping wet. His arousal increased at the sight of so much slick fur smoothed over hard, powerful muscles. Luca licked his lips and tossed the deer leg away.

"You look good wet, pup."

Tanner pinned his ears to his head and growled. Sexy. Luca dipped his head to look at Tanner through his lashes.

"Want to rumble with me, pup?"

He actually hoped Tanner attacked, because he had serious sexual tension he needed to work off, but Tanner apparently wasn't in the mood to take on a dragon. His ears lifted and he casually walked over to where Luca sat. If Luca thought Tanner had decided to ignore his pup comment, he learned differently when Tanner got right up next to him and shook the water from his fur. Luca closed his eyes against the onslaught, but otherwise didn't react. It didn't matter. His pup would pay for it later, when Luca had time to think of an appropriate punishment, if he even retaliated at all. He loved the comfort and playfulness Tanner exhibited in his presence in so short a time. Becoming Tanner's new pack was going to be easier than Luca had anticipated if Tanner continued to accept him so effortlessly.

They returned to Tanner's hotel the same way they left, side by side as owner and pet. Luca had suggested it would be easier for the wolf to shift in the privacy of the hotel room and leave his clothes there, rather than risk doing it in the forest. After some half-hearted fussing, Tanner capitulated. Other than a few odd looks cast Luca's way for having a large dog in the hotel, the plan worked perfectly. Luca pulled the keycard from his pocket and swiped it, gaining entry to Tanner's room. Tanner shoved past him and Luca watched as he went straight into the bathroom and nudged the door closed with his snout.

Luca stepped into the small hotel room and once again felt cramped. There was a desk with matching chair pushed into the far corner, one queen-sized bed flanked by bedside tables, and an entertainment center precisely big enough to hold the TV and cable box situated at the foot of the bed. The color combination of 1960s orange and green was hideous, and Luca wondered how a wild creature like his wolf pup was able stand being shoehorned into such a tight, ugly space. Luca had just settled onto the bed, his back against the headboard, ankles crossed, when Tanner came out of the bathroom, hair still damp from his dip in the river, and wearing nothing but boxer shorts.

Nothing in Luca's century-long life had prepared him for seeing Tanner in human form with so much skin showing. He had no idea what the hell he'd expected, but a smooth chest, pierced nipples, and finely-honed muscles wasn't it. Amazing, the things a thick coat of fur covered. Luca did his best not to reposition on the bed or reach down to adjust his stiffening erection because he wasn't ready for his wolf pup to know how strongly he was affected by the sight. They were in unexplored territory; as far as Luca knew, a dragon had never mated with a wolf. And that was exactly what he wanted Tanner to become—his mate.

Chapter Seven

TANNER

Tanner left the bathroom and froze when he realized he wasn't alone in the room. He hadn't expected his boss to still be there when he finally got out of the shower, but for some reason, he wasn't surprised by it. Luca was lounging on the bed with the TV remote in his hand, though the television wasn't turned on. The way Luca's gaze moved over his body Tanner decided it might be best to cover up. He went to his travel bag, pulled out a clean T-shirt, and pulled it on over his head. Kicking the old, threadbare bag back under the bed, and uncertain what to do next, he eased himself onto the mattress beside Luca and mimicked his relaxed position, though he was nowhere near relaxed at the moment. Having just fed, he was awake and energized, and he had a sexy-as-hell dragon in the bed next to him. Tanner's legs vibrated with pent-up energy.

Luca stared at him intently. "Are you okay? You seem anxious."

"Just very...primed."

"How do you usually handle the restlessness?" Luca asked.

Tanner rolled his head to stretch his neck. When he was part of the pack, he went to clubs with other wolf males after a hearty feeding and then quietly sniffed out a gay or bisexual human to help rid him of the excess energy. These days, he pulled up free porn on his phone and hoped his hand was up to the task. Or go for a long run like he'd been doing the night he'd come upon Luca in the forest. He didn't have the disposable income for the local gay club's cover charge yet. Tanner wasn't about to share any of that information with his new boss so he remained silent. Luca grabbed his chin and turned his face so they were looking at each other.

"You'll answer my questions one day soon, my sweet boy."

Gold bled and swirled hypnotically in Luca's brown eyes. Tanner had been told humans were pulled into a trance by the motion and dragon shifters frequently used it to convince people they didn't actually exist should one of them accidently be seen in dragon form. Ancient stories told of dragons using their eyes to lure humans into a false sense of safety in order to eat them, but Tanner had never found any proof. He did, however, find the colorful motion of Luca's eyes to be beautiful and couldn't stop staring. Luca's gaze dropped to Tanner's mouth, causing Tanner to wonder if he was about to be kissed. Without thought, Tanner grabbed his dick through the thin fabric of his shorts and squeezed. He'd never wanted to be kissed so badly in his life and was surprised this dragon, his boss, would be the one to elicit such a strong reaction. Luca snapped his eyes shut and jumped off the bed, breaking all contact.

"Your hours are eight to five with an hour for lunch. I'll see you in the morning."

Luca left the room with such speed Tanner was left dazed. He was certain he hadn't misread the vibes rolling off the man, but dragons were difficult creatures to read sometimes. Maybe what he thought was sexual desire was something else entirely. Tanner rolled off the bed to the floor and knocked out a couple hundred pushups before rolling to his back and doing the same with sit-ups. He stood and jogged in place for several minutes before stripping. He pulled back the covers of the bed and slid beneath the cold sheets, determined to get a good night's sleep so when he showed up for his first official full day of work he'd be well rested.

Tanner's plan failed miserably.

He woke the next morning to heavy rain, wailing sirens that pained his sensitive ears, and an exhaustion no amount of crappy hotel coffee would cure. He hadn't slept well, his adrenaline buzz keeping him from falling asleep, and when sleep finally did happen, he'd dreamt of claiming Luca. Tanner needed to get laid immediately if a dragon shifter was beginning to look like good mating material. That was the prevalent thought when he walked into work and saw the handsome long-haired paranormal he'd seen briefly the day before.

The man leaned casually against the doorframe of his office and smiled at Tanner as he approached. His intense light-blue eyes looked even more inhuman close up. Tanner still didn't know what type of paranormal the man was, but he was very attractive and appeared to be a much better choice for no-strings-attached sex than his boss. He let his gaze slide leisurely over the man's entire body, admiring every inch of his massive, muscular form and leaving no doubt as to his attraction. The paranormal smiled broadly and held out a hand in greeting. Tanner took it and felt odd little bolts of electricity dance across his palm.

"Deacon Linvale."

"Tanner Mc—"

"I know who you are, Alpha," Deacon interrupted.

"How?" Tanner asked but was kept from receiving an answer when Luca came down the hall and addressed him.

"I have a meeting in ten minutes, Tanner. I need seven copies of this presentation and a pot of coffee in the conference room."

Luca gave him a stack of papers and a firm glare, meant to remind Tanner who the boss was. Tanner took the papers and headed down the hall to his desk. He dropped off his coat and then went to the conference room to get the coffee started. While it brewed, he went across the hall to the copier. Mindless tasks like this gave his thoughts time to wander, and inevitably, he got lost in the mystery surrounding Deacon Linvale. He claimed to know who Tanner was and had called him Alpha, which suggested he spoke truth. And then there was the enigma of what exactly Deacon was. Tanner cursed his father's decision to keep him sheltered when he was growing up. There were dozens of paranormal races in the world, and Tanner couldn't identify half of them. Now that he was on his own his ignorance was a dangerous thing.

"Forget him, pup. He's not for you."

Tanner startled, feeling the involuntary need to shift tickle across his skin, but he was able to clamp down on it and remain in human form. He shot daggers at Luca, who should've known better than to sneak up on him. At the same time, Tanner really should have been paying attention to his surroundings. A distracted wolf was a dead wolf, as his father had been fond of saying. He hated that his father had been right. The dragon could have killed him easily in that moment.

"What is he?" Tanner asked, turning back to pull the copies off the machine.

Luca gave a humorless laugh. "It doesn't matter, stay away. He has questionable associations."

"So do I," Tanner said.

He stared Luca in the eye as he passed to enter the conference room. From the gold bleeding into the dragon's pupils, Tanner's meaning was fully understood. Luca's attempt to control him, tell him what he could and could not do in his personal life, made Tanner's inner Alpha bristle. There was no exchange of words, but Tanner felt the dragon's stare as he finished setting up the conference room, making sure pens, notebooks, cups, sugar, and creamer were stocked and ready. Tanner wasn't required to be present during the meeting, so once his tasks were completed and the businessmen took their seats, he closed the meeting room door and went in search of Deacon. He wasn't sure if he was pursuing the man because he was determined to learn what the man was, because he felt the need to dispel Luca's belief Tanner belonged to him, or because Tanner was desperate for physical contact.

*

Tanner scanned the dance floor of Elysium, a club catering to the paranormal LGBTQ+ community, located in the sublevel of a nondescript building in the heart of the city that offered retail on the lower levels and high-end lofts on the upper levels. He was searching the sea of flesh for Deacon the same way he searched a herd of deer for dinner. He'd been growing more anxious and desperate with each hour that passed. Tanner was going to have sex tonight, with someone, anyone.

Moving gracefully through the crush of dancing bodies, soaking in the pressing heat and the scent of sweat and pheromones all around him, he hunted. It soothed the man but did nothing for the wolf pacing circles in his head. He'd come to Elysium a year ago when he first admitted to himself that he was attracted to men and had been blown away by how free the patrons were with their sexuality. Despite his father's claims that a gay wolf shifter was unnatural, Tanner had identified at least two other wolf shifters on his first visit. He'd already scented at least four as he pushed his way across the dance floor, searching for Deacon. He planned to accidentally bump into the man, request a dance, and then move in for the kill.

Dealing with an ever-increasingly dominant dragon had Tanner itching in an unfamiliar way. The uneasy, anxious feeling grew to the point he wanted to claw at the bugs skittering beneath his skin. Tanner recognized what was happening. He'd been separated from his pack for over a month, the psychic connection to them strained by distance, weakened through inactivity. He was starting to lose his shit.

The day before, he'd passed by the break room and overheard Deacon talking on the phone, making plans to meet at Elysium. Tanner's intention to speak to the man and garner an invite to the club had once again been interrupted by Luca and another tedious task, as he had done for the past two weeks, but Luca's attempts to keep them apart only worked in the office.

Tanner caught sight of Deacon sitting at the bar, alone, drinking a beer. Deacon turned his head to the dance floor and their gazes locked. Tanner took a few steps toward his prize when strong fingers wrapped around his arm and pulled him back. He spun around and crashed into a muscular chest and looked up into dark eyes swirling with gold. Luca did not look happy, but he pulled Tanner against him gently, arms wrapped around his back, and then began moving their bodies to the beat of the music. When Tanner relaxed into Luca's arms, because the physical contact settled his nerves, Luca calmed as well; his eyes returning to their chocolate hue and the fangs Tanner had caught a glimpse of, retracting. Luca leaned in and brushed his lips across Tanner's jaw, nuzzling up to his ear.

"Why are you here?" Luca asked, his warm breath ghosting across Tanner's sweat-damp skin, making him shiver.

Half a dozen lies rocketed through Tanner's mind, but after everything Luca had done for him in the past month, he found he was unwilling to voice any of them. The dragon shifter had paid his hotel room bill for three full months, in advance. Luca had accompanied Tanner on all of his hunts, watching his back, keeping him safe, and he'd made certain Tanner had fresh meat on the nights he was too tired to hunt for himself. Luca had even increased his pay so he could afford a new wardrobe for the office. The man had become more than a boss; he'd taken on the role of protector and provider. For that alone, Tanner owed him the truth.

"I'm lonely. I was planning on hitting Deacon up for a one-night stand," Tanner answered.

He knew Luca's enhanced hearing allowed him to catch the words. Luca's arms tightened around his body, and he buried his face in the crook of Tanner's neck. Tanner felt the press of lips on his skin.

"No, my sweet boy," Luca breathed, as he moved his head back to look at Tanner. "You deserve better, and I know you want more."

"What I want is to meet my mate, but who knows when, or if, that will ever happen? I don't want to be alone right now and...god, I want to be fucked. It's been months since I've been with anyone. Wolves weren't meant to be alone like this," Tanner told him, his desperation bleeding into his words.

Wolves were pack animals, very rarely alone and when they were, it wasn't for long. They needed and craved constant companionship. Tanner was beginning to feel the pain from being disowned by his pack. He was desperate to feel connected and loved again, even the temporary connection and false love that came with casual sex. Luca would never understand because dragons were typically loners.

"I lost the pack bond," Tanner said, fighting back panicked tears.

The bond between a wolf pack was strong, even stronger between family members. He had continued to feel that bond until two days ago, when it snapped like an overstretched cord. He felt very much alone and lost. The connection had been present since his birth when he'd bonded first with his mother, then his father, and eventually the rest of the pack. Tanner didn't know how to function properly without it. He hadn't thought it possible to completely lose the bond until he woke in the middle of the night, feeling the hollow emptiness left behind. The loss had literally jolted him awake.

"I'm sorry. I know that scares and hurts you, but it doesn't matter. You have a new one to replace it."

Tanner scoffed and glanced at Luca. "I would know if I had a new one. I can feel them, you know, and I don't feel one."

"You do. It just feels different than the one with your pack because it's not with another wolf."

Luca kept one arm locked around Tanner's waist as he stroked the back of Tanner's head with the other. The sensation was relaxing and Tanner leaned farther into Luca's embrace, gripping Luca's hips.

"If a bond exists, I need to find it, Luca. I feel like I'm going crazy without it."

"Too many people here. Too many distractions. You need to be alone in a quiet place to sense it because it's still new and weak. But I promise you, sweet boy, it's there. Come with me and let me show you?"

Tanner's desperation exploded. He was becoming so crazed without a connection he would do anything to get it back. He had no idea how a dragon knew about wolf telepathy, but he needed it so badly. He pushed the curiosity aside and nodded. Tanner stared into Luca's eyes and swallowed hard at his smile. Damn, the dragon was gorgeous, and he had fast become Tanner's rock in the shitstorm he called life. Luca moved his hands over Tanner's shoulders and down his arms where he entwined their fingers. Without another word, Luca led Tanner out of the club.

Chapter Eight

DEACON

Deacon knew the moment the Alpha's gaze was on him. Even in a crowded club full of paranormal beings, his stare carried a weight and power unlike any other Deacon had sensed. The connection he had to his mate, Ross, allowed them to sense emotions in the other, and he'd known the exact moment Ross and Tanner had crossed paths from the awe-tinged fear mixed with longing Ross had experienced. His mate, and the other wolves Deacon had taken in, needed a true Alpha to bond with. They were falling apart psychologically, and Ross was ahead of them all. Deacon's beautiful mate was suffering from homicidal and suicidal ideation almost daily now, and Deacon was desperate to save him.

Turning on the barstool to face the crowd, his gaze immediately found Tanner among the dancing masses. He held the Alpha's stare, until Luca intervened, pulling him back onto the dance floor. His dragon boss wasn't part of the plan. Deacon closed his eyes against the despair and frustration threatening to pull him under. He refused to give in, though, because Ross and the others were lost without him, and he'd never allow that. He'd made certain Tanner had overheard his phone call with Ross the day before, as they planned on meeting at Elysium, instinctually knowing Tanner was in need of others like himself.

"A shoot and a miss," said a voice behind him.

Deacon glanced at the young bartender as he took Deacon's empty beer bottle and replaced it with a fresh one. Deacon smiled and took a swallow of the cold brew as he passed a twenty across the bar.

"No shot taken really. Besides, my interest in him isn't sexual in any way," Deacon said. The bartender shrugged as he took the cash.

"Good thing the dragon got to him first, then, because that wolf was on the prowl for sex."

The bartender flipped his long brown hair over his shoulder and moved on to the next customer and Deacon grunted. He didn't believe that for a second. Tanner was probably confusing the anxious, itchy sensation that heralded the beginning of blood lust as sexual tension, but Luca would clear it up.

Deacon wasn't a wolf, or a dragon, but after nearly a year in close proximity to his four wolf shifters, he'd learned what was needed for their survival and their sanity. Ean, Ross, Vance, and Theran were all wolves who'd been separated from their packs for one reason or another. They had become a pack unto themselves, what other wolves derogatorily referred to as a wild dog pack, and Deacon knew Tanner was going to need a new pack soon. The answer seemed simple.

Ross and the others were in desperate need of an Alpha, a role which Deacon had attempted to fill, but Tanner was a true Alpha and could offer the pack the leadership and telepathic connection Deacon hadn't been able to provide. The four wolves emerged from the sea of bodies to surround him. He opened his arms and Ross stepped into his embrace.

"We saw him leave with Luca," Theran said.

Theran was the biggest of the wolves, trained by his previous pack to one day become an enforcer. Vance stood beside him, staring at Deacon with hopeful eyes. He was the youngest and smallest; an Omega naturally born to be the caretaker.

"Did you see him? Get to talk to him at all?" Ean, the pack Beta asked. He was brilliant when it came to strategy. Deacon had learned the hard way never to play chess with the guy. He was always thinking two steps ahead of everyone else.

"No. Luca caught him before he got to me."

All three wolves sighed and Ross nipped at Deacon's jaw in displeasure.

"Don't give up, yet." Deacon told them. "Luca is an unexpected complication, but he can be dealt with. I'll seek out Tanner on Monday and make him aware of the situation. I will fight for you until the end."

Ean, Theran, and Vance each nodded and then disappeared back into the dancing crowd. Ross pressed his warm lips to the sensitive skin beneath Deacon's ear in a soft kiss, where the mating bite had been placed, sending shivers through his body. Ross lifted his head to look Deacon in the eye. He tightened his arms around his mate in what he hoped was an encouraging gesture. Deacon had known, from the beginning, he and Ross were destined mates, and he loved the wolf with all his heart.

"Do you know why you'll fight to the end?" Ross asked.

"Because I love you."

Ross shook his head and leaned closer, running his fingers through Deacon's long hair. "Because I'll take you with me."

"Ross—"

"I'll kill myself one day," he said, matter-of-factly.

Deacon hugged his mate tighter against his chest and kissed along his jawline to his neck, pushing every loving, accepting, happy emotion he could muster through their telepathic link. It grew harder to lift Ross from the depths of the depression pulling him down with every passing day.

"But the thought of you with anyone else, loving another after I'm gone... It makes me angry." Ross scraped his fangs across Deacon's carotid, making his heart race, before Ross kissed the shell of his ear. "I'll take you with me. Mates forever," he whispered.

Deacon stared over his mate's shoulder at the dance floor where dozens of people danced, laughed, and flirted while the love of his life held him, kissed him, and whispered sweet nothings in his ear a mere heartbeat after threatening murder/suicide. Fear pricked at him, though not for his own life. There was no doubt in his mind one day Ross would attack him and attempt to take his life, but Deacon was a powerful Elemental. He was capable of defending himself. He desperately wanted to save Ross, to bring him back from the edge, but he was terrified the fight would result in his mate's death. He never wanted harm to come to Ross, especially by his own hand, and that meant he needed to get Tanner into the pack. Now.

Chapter Nine

TANNER

Tanner didn't ask where they were going, as Luca maneuvered his Mercedes onto the road. Instead, he focused on trying to locate the psychic connection Luca said he was forming. If it was real, and not another of Luca's attempts to keep him away from Deacon, he wasn't able to find it.

"I can't find a bond. Were you just bullshitting me to get me out of the club? Are you jealous I was going after Deacon and decided to lie to get me away?" Tanner accused.

"Jealous, yes, but I never lie to those I care about. You are forming a new bond," Luca answered. He reached over and covered Tanner's hand where it rested on his thigh. Tanner looked down at their hands and then let his eyes travel up Luca's muscular arm to his chiseled jawline as Luca spoke. "You're trying too hard and looking in the wrong place. You'll need to relax and let the connection reveal itself to you."

Tanner stared a moment longer at the slight dusting of a beard gracing Luca's cheeks before shifting his gaze out the front windshield, but he didn't see the passing street signs or the change from business to residential. His thoughts were focused inward.

"Have you had sex with Deacon?" Luca asked.

The question caught Tanner off guard enough that his answer was instant and without thought. "No, but I planned to."

"Why? Am I not what you want?"

Luca stopped the car at a red light as Tanner struggled with how to answer that question. He stared at the dragon with his mouth open, ready to speak if words ever formed. When no answer was forthcoming, Luca glared at him. Tanner swallowed hard and blinked several times before once again staring out the front windshield. Luca squeezed his fingers.

"Answer me," he said softly, though the demand was no less evident. "Am I not what you want?"

"You are, but…"

"But?" Luca pressed.

"Deacon is available."

"As am I."

"I feel an odd…tug? Pull? Something, when I'm around him," Tanner said.

Luca released his fingers and moved his hand away. Tanner fought an internal battle over whether to reach for Luca's hand to regain the physical connection again or not. Luca's skin had been warm and comforting. Without his touch, the emptiness Tanner's pack bond had left him with was more pronounced. He gave in when the desire to be touched became too much. Tanner snapped his arm out and rested his palm on Luca's hard thigh, and then he closed his eyes to focus on seeing with his fingers.

With his mind's eye, he watched fabric stretch tight over muscled thigh when Luca moved his foot from one pedal to the other as he drove. Tanner felt the movement of strong muscles beneath his fingertips, and his imagination had Luca naked and ready, leaning over Tanner's body. Tanner's cock immediately responded, and he opened his eyes to kill the fantasy. He found they were parked outside a large, beautifully landscaped house, and Luca's swirling gold gaze was on him.

"Deacon is available to just about everyone. As I understand it, he has at least four men he sees regularly. He's not the mate you're looking for," Luca said.

"I know. My mother always told me I would know my mate when I saw her. She didn't know I was gay at the time, of course, but I'm sure her words are still true. I'll know him when I see him," Tanner said. Then more softly added, "I hope."

"I believe you will see him when you are ready to see him, and he will not be what you expected."

Luca lifted Tanner's wrist to his lips, and Tanner held his breath as Luca's fangs elongated to scrape across sensitive flesh. Luca didn't cut the skin or sink his teeth into the artery pulsing beneath the sharp tips, and Tanner let out a breathy sigh as tingles raced up his arm. God, if Luca did that to his cock, Tanner would explode. Luca's golden-hued eyes brightened for the briefest second before they returned to their normal brown, his fangs retracted, and he released his hold on Tanner.

"Go inside, my sweet boy. Find a bedroom—it doesn't matter which one. Lie on the bed and close your eyes. In the comfort and quiet, with no distractions, you will be able to feel the bond you so desperately want."

Tanner got out of the car and walked up to the house. He stopped at the front door and looked back at Luca, leaning against the hood of his Mercedes. Luca motioned for him to enter, so Tanner reached for the doorknob to find the door already unlocked. Not surprising. Anyone stupid enough to enter a dragon's home uninvited was begging to become dinner. They'd not even be alive long enough to realize their mistake.

Casting one last glance over his shoulder at Luca, still relaxing against the car, Tanner walked into the house. Several lights were on, suggesting Luca had no concern whatsoever about the electric bill. Tanner stood in the foyer and looked around. Beyond the tiled entry was an expansive open-concept floorplan with high ceilings where the living room bled seamlessly into the dining room and kitchen. At the back of the house were French doors leading outside. The place was huge, as befitted a dragon, and for the first time since coming upon Luca in the woods a month ago, he wondered what the shifter looked like in dragon form. To his right was a grand staircase leading to the second floor. Tanner's gaze traveled up the steps before his feet followed, moving on pure instinct.

At the top of the stairs was a hallway with three doors on each side. Tanner stopped outside each of the open bedroom doors, but none seemed right to him; too small, too frilly, too white. Fuck, he needed to stop being so picky. One room had a large table and a sofa in the center of it with every other available space overrun with books of all kinds.

At the far end of the hallway, at the fifth door he came to, he pushed all judgment to the back of his mind and entered the room. The bed was illuminated by the light in the hallway, and he made his way over to it. Climbing on top of the blankets, he settled onto his back. This room felt comfortable, warm, and familiar. He closed his eyes as Luca had instructed and slowed his breathing.

He relaxed until he hovered on the brink of transition. The house was completely silent, but he knew the instant Luca entered the front door downstairs. He didn't hear it. He saw it. He watched as Luca's gaze moved to the stairs and he smiled, and Tanner instinctually knew the man's happiness came from the fact Tanner was in his room, lying on his bed. Tanner inhaled sharply and bolted upright in the bed, eyes flying open. Seconds later, Luca's body darkened the doorway.

"I've bonded to you," Tanner whispered.

Shock and horror swept through him. Tanner had thought it impossible for a wolf to create a psychic link with a dragon given they were different species, and he was terrified he had done it unknowingly. He had no idea what it might mean for the paranormal world, what it meant for him.

"Yes," Luca confirmed, his deep voice soothing Tanner's tumultuous emotions. "It started the moment you fed me, or rather, the moment you chose to put your life at risk to save mine. I felt the connection immediately. That's why I hired you. I have to keep you close so I can ensure your safety and provide for you."

"Do you think...? Is this why my pack severed their bond with me? Because they sensed my bond with you, with a dragon?"

"They didn't sever the connection, my sweet boy. You did."

Luca entered the room and walked to the side of the bed. Tanner examined the slow, precise movements with curiosity. Luca acted as though he expected Tanner to attack him.

"You have vivid dreams of me, pup. This psychic link is new to you so you've not tried to strengthen it, haven't even noticed it, but I have felt it from the beginning. When you sleep and your guard is down, I can connect to you and experience everything. It was during one of those dreams two nights ago you severed the bond to your father's pack. You told me I was all you needed. Do you remember?" Luca asked, gently placing one knee on the mattress and leaning ever so slightly closer.

Tanner nodded, remembering quite well the dream Luca was referring to. In the dream, he had come upon a clearing in the woods where a large onyx dragon with hypnotic golden eyes sat. The dragon extended massive wings, flexed them once, creating a breeze that carried a familiar scent, before folding them along its sides and lying in the grass. Inexplicably unafraid, Tanner had approached the dragon and extended a hand to run his palm over surprisingly smooth scales. He expected them to be rough, but instead found them to be almost silky to the touch, and so amazingly beautiful.

The dragon pulled away from Tanner's touch, and the air grew heavy as the gorgeous beast shifted back into human form. At the sight of Luca standing in front of him, naked, and having shown his dragon form, Tanner was overcome with desire. He'd launched himself into Luca's arms, claiming the man's mouth with a hot, deep kiss. The dream had indeed been vivid, right down to the battle for dominance and Tanner gaining the upper hand, pressing Luca's chest against a broad tree trunk. He had taken Luca from behind, erupting inside him and sinking his fangs into the dragon's neck, marking him, claiming him. Still encased by his lover in the most intimate way, Tanner had whispered against Luca's sweaty skin that they were mated; Luca was all he ever needed.

Tanner had snapped awake, the emptiness from the missing pack bond making him feel lost and afraid, an ember floating on the wind farther away from the flames that created it. Tanner was pulled from the memory by movement. He looked into Luca's eyes as Luca joined him on the bed, and words spoken earlier about Tanner finding his mate came back to him. *You'll see him when you are ready to see him.* Well, Tanner was damned certain he was seeing him now.

Chapter Ten

LUCA

Without warning, Tanner jumped him and Luca had his arms full of hot, aroused male. Never in his life had he imagined one day he would take a wolf shifter as a mate. And until his handsome pup's dream, he had assumed Tanner would always be submissive to him. But, every day, Luca noticed the scale would even up a little more. He didn't believe Tanner would ever be stronger than him, but Tanner was quickly becoming Luca's equal, and he found that more erotic and satisfying than he'd expected.

He lifted Tanner into his arms, knee-walked farther onto the bed and lowered their bodies to the mattress, Tanner hot and hard beneath him. The wolf wrapped his legs around Luca's waist and carded his fingers through Luca's hair, holding him captive as he devoured Luca's mouth in a kiss that touched his soul. Tanner's forest scent filled Luca's nose and his earthy flavor burst across Luca's tongue as they once again battled for dominance, this time in reality.

Luca loved how Tanner was fighting for the upper hand, taking what he wanted, despite being physically pinned beneath Luca. The Alpha was surging forward, making himself known. Luca rotated his hips, grinding his erection against Tanner's impressive bulge, to show the Alpha just how much Luca was enjoying the display of power, how strongly Luca wanted to be claimed. Tanner's response was a deep, animalistic groan that had Luca fighting not to come in his pants, and he pulled from the kiss. Tanner narrowed his eyes, bit Luca's lower lip, and sucked on it to show his displeasure. Luca fisted Tanner's silky dark hair and tugged.

"I want you naked, sweet pup," Luca said.

The lust that flashed in Tanner's eyes made Luca's fangs elongate. Before he was aware of what he was doing, Luca used his grip on Tanner's hair to pull his head to the side, leaned down, and scraped his fangs along the tender skin overlaying Tanner's throbbing jugular. Tanner's breathing hitched, his hands fisted in Luca's shirt, and he squeezed his legs tightly around Luca's hips.

"God, yes," Tanner growled.

Luca withdrew his fangs and gathered his wits enough to disengage from Tanner's hold, though it took a lot of effort. Part of it was his own reluctance to leave Tanner's embrace, but the other part was Tanner's refusal to let go. He'd yet to shift into dragon form in front of Tanner, and the need to change bubbled just below his skin, but his bed was not the place. Only the open floorplan downstairs with its vaulted ceilings allowed for the dragon's size.

Luca had to use every ounce of his dragon strength to move away from his gorgeous young wolf because Tanner fought the separation, and that pleased Luca to no end. Luca pushed off the bed, keeping his eyes on his man, sensing the Alpha was preparing an attack. Tanner rolled to his hands and knees, watching Luca with narrowed, sparkling blue eyes. The wolf was very close to the surface right now, just like his dragon, and shifting into animal form wasn't conducive to sexual intimacy.

"Sex isn't needed to create or strengthen a bond, my sweet boy, you know that. We merely need to provide for each other, protect and trust one another."

Luca slid his suit coat off his shoulders, letting it drop to the floor, and then pulled his tie free, dropping it to the floor beside his coat. Tanner licked his lips and prowled across the bed to the edge. Luca groaned and took a step closer as he unbuttoned his shirt, loving his Alpha's fanged, predatory smile. Luca let his shirt fall as he moved within Tanner's reach. Tanner lifted to his knees and pulled Luca in for another kiss, looping strong arms around Luca's neck.

Luca allowed Tanner to have his way with the kiss, choosing to focus his attention on getting the wolf naked. He'd waited weeks for Tanner to see him, to want him, and while this moment might be borne of Tanner's fear and desperation, Luca wasn't going to waste it. He grabbed the hem of Tanner's T-shirt and lifted. Hot, smooth skin brushed his fingertips, and he was momentarily distracted by the feel of Tanner's bare flesh, contrasted with the cold metal of his nipple piercings.

Luca pressed his palms to Tanner's back and slid them over his shoulder blades. When his hands reached the back of Tanner's neck, he broke the kiss to pull the T-shirt over Tanner's head. Tanner released his hold only long enough for Luca to yank the shirt free before he was pressing his bare chest against Luca's larger body. Being skin to skin with Tanner, teeth biting along the base of his neck and those sexy damn nipple rings digging into his flesh, set Luca on fire. The dragon roared in his head. He once again fisted Tanner's hair and pulled his wicked mouth off him. Tanner's sharpened nails bit into the skin of his shoulders.

"Naked. Now, pup," Luca growled. "I want to see you, feel you. All of you."

Chapter Eleven

TANNER

Tanner shuddered as Luca released the fist in his hair to caress his cheek and jaw lovingly. He took Tanner's head in both hands, kissed him, and sucked his tongue into his mouth, but kept their bodies separated. Tanner slid his palms over Luca's lightly furred chest and mourned the loss of Luca's heat. He stared into Luca's swirling gold-brown eyes as he opened his jeans and pushed them down his hips. In anticipation of sex with Deacon, Tanner had forgone underwear, and he was grateful for that decision.

He was moments away from fucking the man he truly wanted. Tanner now admitted to himself he'd wanted the dragon from the moment he found him trapped in the woods. Luca had haunted his dreams almost every night since then, turning Tanner into an inferno of hot lust and clawing need. Tanner was well aware sex wasn't required for a bond of any kind, even one with Luca, but he wanted more than just the psychic connection. He wanted to make his dream a reality and make love to Luca.

He wanted to claim his mate.

Luca's swirling-gold gaze took Tanner in, head to toe, and sent anticipatory shivers through his body. Tanner's cock was thick and throbbing, standing erect and leaking, ready. Luca licked his lips, nostrils flaring, and the idea of Luca taking him into his mouth made him weak in the knees, but he wanted to taste Luca first. Tanner shoved his jeans off the bed to the floor. On hands and knees, he hooked the waistband of Luca's dress slacks and pulled him closer.

He grinned up at the dragon wickedly before nuzzling the massive bulge nestled between thick thighs. Tanner opened his mouth and bit Luca's cock through the soft fabric, careful to keep his fangs withdrawn. He didn't want to cause pain or draw blood; he wanted the dragon to burn alive with him. Luca caressed his head and pressed his hips forward gently, showing Tanner how much he liked the contact.

Tanner sat back on his heels as he moved his lips up Luca's body to kiss his abdomen and chest while he worked to open Luca's belt and trousers. He pushed the expensive, custom-made fabric down Luca's legs before wrapping long fingers with sharp claws around the dragon's thick length. He circled one of Luca's nipples with his tongue before sucking it into his mouth and casually pumped his fist along the rigid shaft, making both of them groan.

"Fuck," Luca growled as he pulled Tanner's lips off his nipple. Tanner swiped at the taut bud with his tongue one more time and then smiled.

"We will," he promised as his dragon's eyes narrowed.

Tanner lowered his body until he was eye level with Luca's cock. He teased the tip with his teeth and flicked his tongue at the pearl of liquid clinging to the slit, as he gently worked his hand up and down the shaft. He continued to stroke as he cupped Luca's balls and took the entirety of Luca's hardened length into his mouth. He inhaled the dragon's rich, smoky scent that reminded him of the bonfires his old pack gathered around during the full moon.

He buried his nose in thick pubic hair, suppressing his gag reflex, and then slowly pulled back, dragging his tongue roughly along the prominent vein on the underside of the shaft. Tanner extended his index finger and lightly brushed over Luca's pucker as he licked and sucked, reveling in Luca's intense flavor on his tongue. Tanner's wolf wanted more. He wouldn't stop until he pulled every drop of Luca's essence down his throat. Luca widened his stance to give Tanner better access, growling in approval, as Tanner inserted the tip of his finger.

"Tanner, pup," Luca gasped. Tanner gave a hard pull on his dick and Luca's entire body shivered. "Yes, Alpha, just like that."

Tanner's wolf puffed up at Luca's acknowledgment he was the Alpha. He released Luca's cock with a soft pop, slicked two fingers in his mouth, and then carefully introduced them into Luca's ass as he began to work Luca to a fever pitch. Tanner tucked his knees farther under his body, distributing his weight more comfortably so he could play with Luca's balls while thrusting his fingers into Luca's ass and sucking him. Luca scraped his nails over Tanner's back and shoulders with one hand while he fisted Tanner's hair with the other.

Precum dripped from Tanner's cock onto his thigh in excitement as he urged Luca to the breaking point. He was so close, balancing on the edge, so Tanner increased the suction and tempo of his mouth on Luca's cock. He worked a third finger into Luca's hole, the tight ring of muscle clenching around the digits. Luca's breathing became erratic, his thighs trembled, and his cock throbbed in Tanner's mouth. Tanner pushed his fingers deeper and crooked them, pressing that magic spot as he took the entirety of Luca's length into his mouth, holding it there, roughly tonguing the underside of the thick cock.

"Fuck, Tanner," Luca gasped and then roared in orgasm, filling Tanner's mouth.

Tanner swallowed the salty liquid greedily, coaxing every last drop from Luca until the dragon reached his tolerance and gently pushed him away. Tanner licked his lips, loving the smoky aftertaste of his mate as he eased his fingers from Luca. He wiped his hand clean with his shirt, still clinging to the edge of the bed, and then carelessly tossed it to the floor. Luca lifted Tanner and pressed their bodies together as he climbed onto the mattress with shaky legs. Luca eased down on Tanner, holding his head with both hands as he kissed him, sucking Tanner's tongue into his mouth. Tanner bucked his hips, pressing his still-hard cock into Luca's pelvis and spreading his wetness over Luca's stomach.

"How do you want me, my sweet boy?" Luca whispered against feverish, damp skin as he licked and kissed his way over Tanner's neck and jaw.

Tanner rubbed his hands down Luca's back, over the round globes of his ass, dipped his fingers into the crease and pulled his cheeks apart. He pumped his hips to rub against Luca's pelvis once more before answering.

"On your back. I want to look into your eyes when I take you," Tanner answered.

Luca wrapped his arms around Tanner and rolled so Tanner was draped across his chest. Tanner closed his eyes and smiled. "Damn, you feel good underneath me."

"You felt good beneath me too," Luca said. He smiled and ran a hand through Tanner's hair. "You're beautiful, and so fucking perfect."

Tanner planted his palms against Luca's muscular chest and pushed up to straddle his hips. He rubbed over defined muscles and spread his fingers through silky chest hair. Tanner was pleasantly surprised Luca was willing to bottom for him and took in the sight of his dragon naked, ready, and waiting.

"Lube is in the top drawer," Luca said, never looking away from Tanner. He sat up and pulled Tanner into a tight embrace, sucking an earlobe between his lips. "God, I can't wait to feel you inside me, pup." Luca's whispered words caressed Tanner's hot skin, making him shiver and his cock pulse between their bodies in excitement.

"Get comfortable, dragon," Tanner whispered back and pushed off Luca's lap.

Chapter Twelve

LUCA

Luca released his grip but only because he knew Tanner wasn't going far. He lay back and stretched his arms over his head in an attempt to relieve some of the stiffness from his orgasm earlier. The snick of the lube being opened had him rolling his head to the side in time to watch Tanner pour a copious amount into his palm and carefully work the gel over his long, thick cock as he dropped the tube onto the bedside table. Luca's gaze was riveted to his lover's glistening dick as he moved gracefully across the bed. Luca spread his legs and bent his knees, giving Tanner access to his ass. Tanner settled between Luca's knees and used the excess lube in his palm to slick Luca's entrance before he inserted two well-lubricated fingers. It had been a long time since Luca allowed anyone to fuck him. He knew he was tight. He reflexively clenched down around Tanner's long digits.

"How long has it been?" Tanner asked softly as he gently twisted his hand, rotating his fingers inside Luca's clenching channel. It had been easier to relax when his dick was being sucked, but he didn't have the distraction of an impending orgasm anymore, and he was intensely aware of the burn.

"Years," Luca answered with a strained chuckle. That was an understatement.

"How many years?"

Luca thought about it. He hadn't bottomed for a man since before he'd moved to the city.

"Thirty-seven years, eight months," he answered on a groan because Tanner had crooked his fingers and hit that special spot again. Tanner introduced a third finger, stretching and relaxing the ring of muscle so Luca could take his girth without pain. He leaned over Luca's body and brushed Luca's mouth with the barest of kisses.

"Thank you," Tanner whispered.

Luca gripped the back of Tanner's neck and pulled him down into a hard, dominating kiss that stole their breath. They broke apart on a gasp as Tanner pulled his fingers free and lined up his cock for entry. He kissed Luca's chest, neck, jaw, and then his lips as he slowly and carefully entered Luca's body. Luca hissed and adjusted on the bed as he struggled to let Tanner in. Tanner smiled, showing fang, when he finally got the angle right and slid home. He grabbed Luca's thigh and squeezed as he bit down on the cord of muscle at Luca's neck.

"Fuck, you feel good, Luca. Hot and tight," Tanner breathed against his lover's skin as he slowly withdrew and then pumped his hips forward, burying himself deep inside his dragon's body. "And mine," he growled.

Luca locked his arms around Tanner's back, holding him securely as Luca was stretched and filled by his young, handsome wolf. He lifted his legs, resting his feet on the back of Tanner's strong thighs, and pure pleasure blasted through him as Tanner slammed into him. Pleasant tingles raced down his spine and into his limbs. Luca closed his eyes and fought the urge to sink his fangs into Tanner's neck as Tanner pumped into him with increasing speed and force.

"Open your eyes. Let me see," Tanner demanded on a particularly hard thrust. Luca looked his mate in the eye, knowing Tanner saw gold bleeding into the brown like oil in water. "I love it when your eyes do that."

Tanner's eyes sparked with lust and he drove his hips into Luca harder and faster. Luca's fangs elongated, on a shout, despite his efforts to keep them sheathed. To sink his teeth into Tanner's jugular while Tanner fucked his ass would send Luca into the stratosphere of bliss, but not right now. Not during their first time together. Eventually, he'd claim the wolf as his mate, but he wanted to wait until their bond was stronger and more familiar. Maybe after they'd shared each other's bodies a few more times, he would claim the pup as his own. Tanner's fangs distended farther, and Luca growled low in his throat.

"Do it, pup," Luca rumbled. "Bite me."

Tanner's eyes flared, his cock thickened and throbbed, and Luca knew the Alpha was close to orgasm. He grabbed Tanner's ass and pulled him harder into him, helping Tanner bury himself deeper, using only the slightest bit of his dragon strength to help Tanner achieve orgasm. Luca didn't need to come again. He didn't need to sink his fangs into his lover. His only need at the moment was for Tanner to release inside him.

Tanner roared as his cock convulsed inside Luca's body, and he sank his teeth into Luca's shoulder.

"That's it, my sweet boy," Luca whispered as Tanner strained and shuddered in his arms.

Luca kissed Tanner's ear as Tanner retracted his fangs and licked the small puncture wounds on Luca's shoulder. Luca was disappointed Tanner had missed the mark and sank his fangs into muscle instead of a blood source, but the bruises would show the world he'd been claimed. Just not yet mated. A mating wasn't something he could force, so he contented himself with the physical connection they had shared, instead. He lowered his feet to the bed, making sure to keep his knees bent to cradle Tanner's body and rubbed the quivering muscles of Tanner's back as his body relaxed from his orgasm. Luca rolled to his side, laying Tanner on the bed beside him, and grimaced at the unusual soreness. Tanner rubbed a hand over his hip in a lazy circle.

"Are you okay?"

"I'm fine, sweet boy."

"You made a face. Did I hurt you?"

Luca smiled broadly. "No. I'm sore because it's been so long."

"Thirty-seven years and eight months," Tanner said around a yawn. "Broke that streak like an Alpha," he mumbled.

Luca shook his head and chuckled. "Yes, you did," he whispered.

He'd forgotten how uncomfortable it was to bottom after orgasm, rather than during peak arousal. He was sore, tired, and thirsty, but he refused to move from his mate's side. This was the first time he'd shared his bed with another being. It had always been the other person's bed, or a hotel bed, never *his* bed. Tanner's body relaxed in Luca's arms, his face smoothing out, and Luca lay there for what seemed like hours, watching his wolf sleep.

Chapter Thirteen

DEACON

Deacon entered the break room and gently closed the door behind him. While it seemed Tanner's recent mood swings had smoothed out a bit, he was still without a pack and edgy. He was coiled up tight and the other wolves sensed it. Deacon wondered how much of Tanner's anxiety had to do with Luca. Dragon shifters were notoriously difficult to deal with because they were accustomed to being in charge and getting what they wanted. Being a very large beast that breathed fire and had hypnotic eyes tended to make things easier in that regard.

Ean, who was currently acting as pack Beta, had warned Deacon earlier, after being informed of Deacon's plan to talk to the Alpha, to not sneak up on him or make sudden moves. Tanner was more likely to succumb to fight rather than flight with anything he perceived as threatening at this stage. Dealing with wolf shifters was a unique experience, especially those without a pack. There was no structure, no discipline, and no peer pressure to keep the wolf in line. Ean was the oldest member of Deacon's pack, and he had insisted Tanner was unlike any other lone wolf and was therefore unpredictable. So, Deacon heeded the Beta's warning and decided to err on the side of caution.

Tanner's head tilted to the side slightly, alerting Deacon to the fact the Alpha was cognizant of his presence. Tanner had chosen a high-end charcoal-gray suit and tie that highlighted his athletic build. Deacon understood the dragon's obsession with the wolf shifter; Tanner was a gorgeous young man. Tanner finished pouring his coffee and replaced the half-filled pot on the burner. He stirred in sugar, looking completely unconcerned he was no longer alone in the room, but Deacon knew better.

"What are you?" Tanner asked without turning. "I've been trying to figure you out for almost two months now, ever since my first day here, but I can't." Tanner inhaled deeply. "You smell like a thunderstorm."

When Tanner finally turned to face him, Deacon was once again struck by those amazing bright-blue eyes. Surrounded by all the dark hair and framed by thick black lashes, the color was stunning. Deacon slid his hands into his pockets and held Tanner's gaze.

"I thought wolves were able to identify all paranormal beings by their scent," Deacon challenged.

Tanner shrugged and lifted his mug to his lips. "Maybe, given time, I'll be able to. Will you tell me?"

"I'm an Elemental," Deacon answered.

He moved to stand beside Tanner and leaned his back against the counter. He deliberately kept his stance casual and as nonthreatening as possible. Despite Tanner's friendly tone, his muscles were tense and his eyes watchful, mind and body alert and ready for anything. Tanner cocked his head to the side, inhaled again, and then straightened with a nod.

"I've never met an Elemental before, obviously, since I wasn't able to identify you." Tanner's gaze took Deacon in, studying him one inch at a time, slow and deliberate. "How old are you?"

Deacon smiled and looked askance at Tanner. "Aw, you aren't very good at being subtle, are you? You, of all people, should understand age and power are not necessarily linked."

"What do you mean?" Tanner asked, his eyebrows knitting. The kid was genuinely confused. Deacon rolled on the counter so he was leaning on one hip facing the wolf.

"Luca is over a century old, but he's no more powerful than any other dragon. You're young, but you carry extreme power. You just don't know it yet. It radiates off you and announces you to every paranormal in the vicinity as an Alpha to be reckoned with. Me? I'm only fifty-two, young for my kind, but I'm one of the most powerful Elementals out there."

Deacon lifted an arm and cupped his hand to form a bowl. Small electrical bolts zipped between his fingers and danced across his palm. Tanner reached out to touch one, only to jump at the shock as he rubbed his fingers together.

"Cool," he said softly, smiling at Deacon. Damn. Tanner was handsome to begin with; factor in that smile, and his beauty was devastating. Deacon closed his hand into a fist and swallowed thickly.

"You should see me outside where I can really let loose. I'm a sight to behold," Deacon told him.

"Conceited much?" Tanner asked, still smiling as he drank his coffee.

"No. Confident," Deacon corrected.

He stepped away from Tanner and walked toward the door, trying to look casual. Something was different with the wolf, but he didn't know exactly what, and it made him nervous. When he turned back toward the Alpha and inhaled, the answer practically slapped him in the face, it was so obvious. How he'd missed it when he'd first entered the room, he didn't know.

"Your scent is changing. You smell less like fresh grass and more like a brush fire."

Tanner grinned wickedly. "I like that analogy. I've always thought Luca smelled like a bonfire."

Deacon looked at Tanner's throat for any sign he and Luca had mated, but the wolf's skin was smooth and unblemished. Their scents were mingling, though, so they were bonded, at the very least. But not yet mated. Still, every paranormal in the vicinity would pick up on the mixed scent of wolf and dragon and give wide berth. Deacon was already questioning the safety and repercussions of a strong Alpha wolf mating with a dragon.

After a moment's thought, he dismissed the concerns. He, himself, was a powerful Elemental, mated to an insane wolf shifter, and was about to ask a powerful true Alpha and the Alpha's future dragon mate to take over his little wild dog pack. There was nothing about this situation that was safe, or sane, and any paranormal with a brain would avoid such a potentially volatile mix.

Desperation evidently made him a fool.

Deacon sensed Ross drawing closer and knew the moment he and the rest of the pack were on the other side of the door. Tanner picked up on them as well, apparently, because he stiffened, his gaze jerking to the closed door. Tanner's nostrils flared as he inhaled the other wolf shifters' scents. His brow creased and he canted his head to the side. Deacon had witnessed the same action with his wolves when they were processing smells and trying to identify the cause.

"It's my pack," Deacon said. "Do you want to meet them?"

"Elementals don't have packs," Tanner said without looking away from the closed door.

Tanner's attention would remain on the closed door until he decided those on the other side were no threat. Deacon felt the combined anxiety of his pack and the Alpha across the room from him and decided action was needed. Deacon hoped his presence prevented the bloodshed that sometimes accompanied the meeting of lone wolves, especially when it was one against many. Plus, Deacon was never entirely sure what Ross was going to do. His mate was becoming increasingly erratic and unstable.

The entire pack hoped Tanner chose to join them, to take over Deacon's position as their Alpha, but that had been before Tanner bonded with a dragon. Luca threw an uncomfortable amount of uncertainty into the situation. Because of it, Tanner might never accept another wolf pack; may never need to. Deacon moved to the door and opened it as Tanner set his mug on the nearby table. Ross was the first to enter, followed by Vance and then Theran. Ean came in last. Risking an escalation, because Tanner might feel trapped and threatened, Deacon closed the door for privacy.

Tanner earned another degree of Deacon's respect when he didn't react to the tension a room full of wolf shifters created. Tanner looked the wolf shifters over, much the same way he'd studied Deacon a few minutes before, and then held eye contact with each of them until, one by one, they lowered their heads in submission. Though Deacon wasn't a wolf, when Tanner looked at him, he lowered his head in submission as well, though he kept his gaze locked with the Alpha's. Until Tanner accepted leadership of the pack, Deacon was still in charge. Tanner reached for his coffee and lifted it to his lips while the pack waited in deferential, but apprehensive, silence.

"How does an Elemental become the leader of a wolf pack?" Tanner asked calmly.

The tension in the room eased substantially when it became clear Tanner was at ease with the pack, had accepted their submission. They lifted their heads and the shifters relaxed their postures. Even Tanner's demeanor changed, becoming friendly and conversational. He hadn't yet agreed to lead them; he would first mark Deacon when he ascended to pack Alpha, but he had at least decided against aggression, acknowledging the pack meant him no harm. Deacon and the other wolves looked at Ean, deferring to the elder Beta wolf to answer Tanner's question.

"We needed an Alpha, someone more powerful than simply each other to bond to. We were coming apart. Deacon was the most powerful paranormal we'd met, and Ross was able to offer something Deacon was missing as well." Ean looked at Deacon and smiled before returning his attention to Tanner. "He's done well leading us, keeping us together, but he's not a wolf shifter. The bond to him is different. Now that you're here..." Ean left the rest unsaid.

Everyone in the room knew Deacon had never truly filled the void. Only a true Alpha like Tanner had the ability to actually cement the bond they needed. Tanner studied Ean closely, then moved to Deacon. He inhaled deeply, then shifted his gaze to Ross. Deacon smiled at the Alpha's ability to pick out the wolf he was bonded to so quickly. Tanner opened his mouth to say something, but the atmosphere changed, thickening, becoming menacing. Deacon and the wolves stiffened in alarm, prepared to fight. Tanner lifted a hand, signaling for them all to remain where they were.

"He's just being protective," Tanner said.

Seconds later, Luca burst through the door. Luca's eyes found Tanner instantly, and once he realized Tanner was calm and safe, the intense heat and danger rolling off him diminished. It didn't completely disappear, though, so Deacon and his pack didn't stand down. Luca might be their boss and fully aware of what each of them was, but he was a dragon shifter in close proximity to his mate and therefore a threat to the pack. Deacon placed himself between the dragon and his wolves, ready to protect them with his life, like every other respectable pack alpha. Tanner smiled and nodded when Deacon's gaze slid from Luca to him.

"Tanner," Luca growled as he moved to stand beside him.

Luca placed his hand on Tanner's lower back as they stared into each other's eyes. After a moment, Luca shook his head and turned his attention to Deacon and the wolves. If there had been any lingering doubt the dragon and Alpha were bonded, it was now long gone. The two had shared a conversation without speaking a single word aloud. The dragon closed his eyes and growled low in his throat. Deacon felt the pack's hackles rise at the sound; Ross actually snarled. Deacon lifted his arms out to the sides to keep them from making a move.

"Fine," Luca huffed, actually producing a small puff of smoke. Deacon had never seen a dragon do that in human form before. It was unnerving.

Luca cupped Tanner's face in his hands and kissed him. Tanner opened to Luca as he deepened the kiss. When Luca finally pulled away, both men were visibly affected. Luca made eye contact with each pack member, ending with Deacon, as he left the break room, slamming the door closed behind him. Whatever conversation had transpired between the Alpha and his lover, clearly the dragon had lost and was quite unhappy about it. Tanner watched the dragon's retreat until the door closed, and then he returned his attention to Deacon.

"You're the Alpha," Tanner said as he placed his now empty mug on the counter and moved to stand in front of Deacon. Deacon nodded with a smile, hoping he wasn't misinterpreting Tanner's body language.

"And you're willing to step down?"

Deacon again nodded. Ross pressed his slightly smaller body against his back and Deacon reached behind him, wrapping his arm around Ross's waist, holding his mate tightly to him. His lover's violent jealousy flared with the Alpha's close proximity. Tanner's gaze darted to Ross then back to Deacon and Deacon swallowed hard. Ross was teetering on the edge of insanity, and if Tanner turned away from the pack because of it, Deacon would lose the man he loved, his mate.

"I'm not sure how to do this," Tanner said, his voice soft and low. "How are you all connected?"

"Ross is my mate," Deacon answered. "The four of them were already bonded when I met them. I'm not a true Alpha, though, because I can only communicate with Ross, but he can communicate with all the others. I think it has something to do with wolves bonding to each other versus other paranormals."

Tanner nodded. "So, other than the mating, no blood was exchanged?"

"No."

"My dad merged two packs once, and all it took was one bite to the Alpha to establish the psychic bond to the remainder of the pack, but like you said, they were all wolves. I don't know what will happen if I bite you, or if it will even work."

"Only one way to find out," Deacon said.

He pulled his hair to the side and tilted his head, offering his neck to Tanner. He wasn't sure if it was his fear or the collective fear of his pack that had his pulse thundering in his ears, but he could do this, *would* do this, for them. As the current Alpha, his submission to Tanner spoke for the pack as a whole, but Tanner gave each of them another chance to make a choice. Deacon didn't have to see them to know they all lowered their heads in submission once again. Without another moment's hesitation, Tanner's fangs elongated and he bit into the base of Deacon's neck, taking a small amount of the Elemental's blood onto his tongue.

And then the room exploded.

Chapter Fourteen

LUCA

Luca growled low in his chest as he stomped around his office in agitated circles. Every so often, he huffed out a smoky breath and fought the urge to shift. God help him, he loved the stubborn wolf pup, but he'd be damned if he sat back and watched Tanner bond with Deacon and his shifty pack of wolves. He didn't trust any of them. Deacon was far more dangerous than he let on, and his good looks and charming nature helped divert attention away from his paranormal ability. Luca had picked up on the Elemental's immense power the first time they'd met two decades earlier. And he didn't even want to think about the uncontrolled crazy wafting off the wolf shifters. They were a whole different kind of dangerous, but he'd failed at making his lover see it.

He stopped in front of the floor-to-ceiling windows overlooking the city when his skin began to scale and his fingers sprouted talons. Luca needed to get a grip on himself, and he needed to do it now. Tanner had promised to come to his office and discuss Luca's concerns once he'd listened to what Deacon and the other wolves had to say. Nothing worth hearing, Luca was certain, but Tanner had been insistent. Because of the equalization of their status, Luca found he was unable to sway Tanner's resolve. Luca wasn't sure what made him angrier—the fact Tanner was making a mistake, or the fact he could do nothing about it.

Once the urge to shift was under control, Luca stared out over the cityscape. The sun glinted off glass and metal, making the city shimmer and shine. The mountains rising majestically beyond the towering steel buildings were capped in white reminding him spring had only just begun. Luca smiled at the beauty of civilization tucked up so closely to wilderness. The proximity of one to the other was the main reason Luca had settled here. A place where he and other shifters were able to be themselves without fear of discovery, and being a short thirty-minute flight east of horde lands was too good to pass up. He had deliberately chosen to build at the edge of the city closest to the mountains, where thick trees crept up to the back of residential areas and a fresh meal was a brisk hike or short drive away.

Luca doubled over as a pained scream ripped through his head and an explosive blast shook the building. His legs gave out and he collapsed to the floor on his back, trying to catch his breath. Something had happened to Tanner, and Luca needed to get to him. He rolled to his knees and unsteadily got to his feet. Despite the explosion, there was no smoke or fire outside his office. Broken glass from vases, interior windows, and pictures from the walls littered the floor and desktops. As he made his way down the hall to the reception area, he noticed the door to the break room had been blown off its hinges, the interior wall bowing out into the hall with a massive crack through the center.

People were evacuating as the alarms blared overhead, and a strong wind was blowing through the halls, making it difficult for Luca to get to the break room quickly. He stepped through the mangled doorframe and stopped, taking in the destruction. An eight-foot-tall tornado whirled in the center of the room. Tiny fires burned in places they shouldn't have been able to burn, like along the rim of the glass coffee pot and inside a plastic bottle of water. Five of the six men who had occupied the room were injured, but all were alive. Deacon was unscathed except for a small bruise on his neck, and that pissed off Luca to no end. He'd known the Elemental was dangerous, and this just proved it. Rage to an extreme he had never experienced before blasted through Luca as he narrowed his eyes on the man responsible for Tanner lying unconscious on the floor, bleeding.

"It's not me, dragon," Deacon said as he helped the wolf nearest him away from the vortex and leaned him against the wall. The other three were able to move themselves, and they circled the injured shifter defensively. They were all his employees. He'd interviewed and hired each of them, but he didn't remember a single name, and right now, he didn't care. Deacon began to move toward Tanner, but Luca roared, stopping him.

"He's channeling my power, and he doesn't know what to do with it. Let me help him," Deacon said.

Enhanced hearing allowed Luca to hear the sirens of approaching emergency vehicles. The sound was enough for him to put his animosity toward the Elemental aside for now. Luca had no idea what the hell had happened and certainly didn't want to try explaining such odd occurrences and destruction to the human authorities. He nodded to Deacon who rushed to Tanner's side and began whispering to him. Luca realized Tanner wasn't unconscious as he'd originally expected when his beautiful wolf opened his eyes. Those bright blue orbs swirled with Elemental power, confusing the hell out of Luca. After several futile attempts to talk Tanner down from whatever Elemental high he was on, Deacon looked up at Luca and then over at his wolves.

"Get out of here, boys. Go to the palace and I'll meet you there as soon as I can."

The three uninjured shifters lifted the fourth and hurried out of the room, joining the last few evacuees. Deacon adjusted his position so he was squatting, rather than kneeling, and punched Tanner in the jaw, rendering him unconscious. Ignoring the fact the fires and tornado put themselves out instantly, and not caring what his increased size would do to the already destroyed room, Luca shifted into dragon form and went for the man who dared hurt his mate.

Deacon had apparently anticipated his reaction, because he jumped to his feet and immediately erected an ice shield around himself before Luca had even finished shifting. Luca rammed the block of ice with his body, sending it flying against the wall, making another massive hole. He stepped over Tanner and scooped his body up with his front talons. As firefighters made their way onto the floor from the stairwells, Luca cradled Tanner to his chest and leapt out of the hole the blast had created in the side of the building, and flew toward the mountains.

He would kill Deacon later.

*

Luca lay on the massive floor mattress in his childhood room with Tanner tucked tightly against his scaled chest, his tail wrapped protectively around Tanner's small body. He'd flown them over the mountains to his horde's commune on the western slope, trying to put as much distance between them and the wild dog pack as possible until he could figure out what had happened. The instinct to protect his mate had him seeking out the one place where he'd always felt the safest—home.

Luca gently nuzzled Tanner's hair, aware of how fragile he was in this moment. The heat from his large dragon form made Tanner overly warm, a light sheen of perspiration making his skin glisten, but Luca refused to move away or shift. It had been interesting carrying his unconscious and bleeding wolf shifter into his family home amidst whispers and conjectures about what he'd planned to do with "it."

Luca had accepted the beautiful pup into his life without a second thought, and it grated against his already frayed emotions that the horde, his own blood relatives, had a problem with Tanner being anything other than a dragon. So, Luca locked them in his room and had yet to venture out. As soon as Tanner woke, he would take him hunting and allow the shift to accelerate the healing process, but until then, Luca was content to hold him and protect him like the cherished mate he was.

Concerns over Tanner's sudden inability to heal played over and over in Luca's head. He carefully slid a talon over the bruise on Tanner's jaw where Deacon had punched him. It had gone from red and swollen to a dark purple instead of disappearing the way it should have. The multiple cuts on Tanner's face and arms from the explosion had stopped bleeding but were still present, which was also wrong. So many things had happened in the past few hours Luca didn't understand, not the least of which was how Tanner had channeled Deacon's power in the first place.

That was something that should have been impossible, and Luca would never have believed it if he hadn't seen it with his own eyes. Tanner stirred, fighting toward consciousness, and Luca shifted back to human to press a calming kiss onto Tanner's temple. The anxiety and fear his mate suffered clawed at his head through the bond, and after so many hours of nothing, the strength of Tanner's emotions made Luca wince in pain.

"Shh, my sweet boy, you're safe. I have you," Luca whispered as he held Tanner tightly and nuzzled into his neck and hair.

Tanner's body relaxed once again as he settled back into sleep. Luca fluffed the pillows and mattress surrounding Tanner and then pulled the blankets over him so he wouldn't get cold. He'd undressed Tanner to inspect his body for potential wounds, and without Luca's dragon form keeping him overwarm, his temperature would drop. Luca didn't want to leave him. He didn't like the idea of Tanner potentially waking up alone in a strange place. But now, while Tanner was sleeping and the majority of the horde were outside the house, was the best time for Luca to pay a visit to the thousands-year-old library his horde kept in the vaults beneath the compound. There were a few books he vaguely remembered from his childhood that had mentioned interspecies mates. Given the way the horde had reacted upon seeing Tanner in his arms, he'd be making the visit to the library on his own.

After another kiss to Tanner's sweaty brow, Luca maneuvered off the massive floor mattress. He dressed hurriedly, opened the door enough to peek into the hall, and upon finding it empty, rushed across the wide expanse of granite and down the back stairs. As he descended the stone staircase, the temperature dropped significantly, signifying the shift from above ground to below ground, the walls gradually changing from stone to concrete and then to impacted dirt. In the vault, intermittent concrete columns and stone outer walls supported the massive structure above. Row upon row of floor-to-ceiling shelving filled the space. The farther back one walked, the older the shelving and the books they held became. Luca headed straight to the far end of the room.

The books he wanted were ancient by human standards. He rounded the corner of the shelving unit he wanted and came to a rather sudden stop. Either that or run down the other dragon shifter standing in the aisle. The dragon's ink-black gaze held Luca still and quiet, the same as it did when he was a hatchling and got caught climbing the stacks in search of old books deliberately kept out of reach.

"Been a long time, Luca."

Luca swallowed and nodded once. "It has. How are you, Matthias?"

Matthias's black hair and trimmed beard were now shot through with white. Ancient runic tattoos covered nearly every inch of his muscular chest, defined arms, and over the backs of his hands telling the story of a life Matthias never shared. Decades spent beneath the compound in the dusty darkness of the vault did nothing to weaken the dragon's strength or dim the man's intelligence. He was gorgeous despite his age and dangerous despite his chosen profession.

"A sight better than you, considering I've not yet lost my senses," Matthias answered.

Luca knew what the old dragon shifter was referring to, and he had to bite back his urge to defend Tanner. A few deep breaths later, he'd gained enough control to speak.

"He's my mate."

Matthias seemed to deflate a bit with that information, his eyes softening a bit. "Is he?" he murmured. He straightened his stance and locked a dark stare onto Luca. "I once believed my mate was a Phoenix, but time revealed her to be nothing more than young love. Lust for a beautiful woman who was forbidden and mysterious."

"Tanner is more than that."

"I couldn't be convinced otherwise either. Youthful folly."

Luca's temper began to simmer. He didn't like being questioned, doubted, especially about something as certain to him as who his mate was. "We share a bond," he snapped. "We can speak telepathically. Wolf shifters can only do that with their packs, but Tanner can do it with me. We're mates."

Matthias lifted his chin, eyes narrowed in warning.

"Why are you down here while he is up there, alone, at the mercy of whatever dragon finds him?"

"The place is practically empty right now, and I need information," Luca said.

"What kind of information?" Matthias asked, glancing at the shelves on either side of them.

The tomes lining these shelves were beyond old, but Luca suspected the answers to his questions were among them.

"Remember the summer of 1927? I was an antisocial hatchling and preferred hanging out down here, reading and learning from you, rather than out causing mischief with the other boys."

Matthias dipped his head in acknowledgement though he was probably remembering several such days from Luca's youth, not only those from 1927. Luca had practically lived in the vault until he was about fifteen when one of the girls had followed him down. She'd pinned him to the table and kissed him, and the hormones had kicked in.

"I came down one afternoon, but you weren't here, so I grabbed a book on my own. It was dark red or brown. I'm not really sure which, but it was heavy," Luca said, trying to get all the details of the book he wanted correct so Matthias recognized what he was looking for. "It had an emblem of some kind on the cover, made of metal or something...Do you know the book I'm talking about?"

"No."

"Really? You took it away from me, and I felt like I'd been caught reading something illicit, except I wasn't. It talked about a male dragon who mated with a female wolf—"

"Nothing of the kind exists," Matthias interrupted.

Luca narrowed his eyes. "Well, I sure as shit didn't make it up."

"Perhaps not, but you were, what, eight years of age? You probably have no true recollection of what you were reading, assuming you even understood half the words."

"Come on, Matthias. You can't tell me I'm the first dragon to mate with a wolf. I won't believe it."

Matthias shrugged and kept his steely gaze on Luca. Even now, as a one-hundred-year-old dragon rather than an eight-year-old hatchling idolizing the man, Luca believed Matthias hadn't always been a librarian. This dragon had once been in a position of authority. The shifter exuded power and knowledge Luca hoped to achieve one day. Understanding he would get nowhere with Matthias, Luca resigned himself to finding another way to get the information he needed.

"I hope you know it doesn't matter," Luca said.

"I don't understand…"

"Whatever it is you're hiding down here. Whatever it is you don't want me to know. It doesn't matter. I *will* claim Tanner as my mate."

"If you do, he will never be safe," Matthias said.

"I won't let anyone hurt him. I will do whatever it takes to protect him."

Matthias's demeanor softened a bit as he gave a humorless laugh. "It's not the boy that will need protecting."

A loud roar reverberated through the walls, shaking dust from the old tomes above Luca's head. He recognized the sound as his mother, even if he'd not sensed her presence enter the house upstairs. Both he and Matthias shifted their gazes upward momentarily.

"You should get back to your *mate*…before your mother discovers his presence. I can guarantee she already knows you are here. She is likely already hearing the gossip of what you brought with you onto horde lands."

Luca's nervous gaze bounced around the books on the shelves beside him. His need for the information contained inside them flared to life, but so did the undeniable truth he had to get to Tanner before his mother did. Frustrated anger had him clenching his fists at his sides and biting back the roar clawing at his throat.

"Matthias…" Luca said through clenched teeth. "I need to know."

"Go. I will send you a few books I think can help you with the situation you find yourself in, but only the ones I know won't be missed."

Luca relaxed slightly. "Thank you."

He turned on his heel and ran back to the stairs. He took them two at a time despite the fact he felt his mother momentarily moving in the opposite direction. Something else was taking her attention, and Luca planned to use that to his advantage. Tanner was still asleep, hurt and vulnerable, and he needed Luca at his side when the horde's matriarch decided to pay him a visit.

Luca entered his bedroom to see a Tanner-sized lump beneath the blanket. Amidst all the fabric from the blankets and overstuffed bedding, he didn't actually *see* Tanner, but he knew he was there, right where Luca had left him. Luca climbed across the mattress and pulled the blanket off Tanner's head. Tanner blinked his eyes open haltingly, taking in the unfamiliar room.

"Where are we?" he asked.

"My horde's commune. This is the house I grew up in, the family home, though I doubt we'll stay long. Once you're healed, I'll take you back home. My only thought in bringing you here was to keep you safe."

Tanner turned in his arms to face him and stared intently into his eyes. "But you don't think I'm safe here."

"No," Luca sighed, simultaneously loving and hating the bond that allowed Tanner to read him so easily.

"You don't hide your thoughts and emotions very well when you're upset," Tanner said as he dragged his fingertips across Luca's forehead. He kissed Luca's chin and then lowered his head back to the pillow and closed his eyes. "I need to get back to my pack, anyway."

"Your pack?" Luca asked.

At what point during the day did he step into an alternate universe where Tanner took on an Elemental's power and then decided to return to the pack that disowned him? Not to mention Luca's own family displaying a prejudice he'd never known they had. Luca's perfect, controlled, and rather mundane life had been upended and nothing made sense anymore. For the first time in decades, he had no idea what to do, or what to expect, or even how to feel. The only thing that hadn't changed was Tanner was his mate and he would do whatever it took to protect him.

"I don't know what happened, Luca. What are you protecting me from?"

"I wish I knew," Luca answered. "Deacon said you were channeling his powers, and while I don't know how that's possible, I do know you blew a massive hole in my building. You were quite destructive until Deacon knocked you out." An action the Elemental would pay for the moment Luca saw him again.

Luca tightened his arms around his mate's body when Tanner stiffened and pressed closer, hiding his face in Luca's neck. The distress his wolf pup was feeling bled through the bond, piling on top of his own uncertainties, made worse by his conversation with Matthias. The old librarian knew more than he was letting on. Matthias's memory was a damn impenetrable vault of its own.

A moment later, Tanner pushed away from him. Luca's confusion was replaced with understanding as he caught his mother's scent. By the time her knock sounded on the bedroom door, Tanner had rolled across the mattress and shifted into wolf form, ready to fight if necessary. Luca smiled in amusement at his wolf's behavior. Tanner growled and pinned his ears back, calling Luca all kinds of creative names through their bond. Luca fought back the laughter as he walked across the room to open the door.

"Mother," Luca said in greeting.

He opened the door wide, thankful she was in human form. She wore a long, flowing dress and her hair hung down her back in soft waves. She smiled warmly at him, despite the animosity he felt coming from her, before her gaze took in the wolf across the room. Her smile immediately disappeared as she gazed at Tanner and entered the room.

"Tanner, this is my mother, Sadie Duray, matriarch of the horde. Mother, this is my mate, Tanner McBane, Alpha," Luca said firmly, watching her for any threatening actions. The tension in the air was unmistakable.

"I doubt it, son. He's a wolf shifter. Your mate will be a dragon like you; preferably one who can have hatchlings to carry on the matriarchy," she said. Tanner growled at her words. Luca understood Tanner's reaction perfectly; he wanted to growl at her dismissive behavior too. Ignoring their combined anger at her words, Sadie added, "This little...animal...is a short-term distraction you'll soon grow tired of."

Luca swallowed everything he wanted to say because it made no difference. When Sadie Duray made up her mind about something, there was rarely anything that could be said or done to change it. A hard and true fact he'd learned at a young age. Speaking to Tanner through the bond, Luca asked him to step out onto the balcony because they were leaving. He watched with amusement as surprise and indignation spread across his mother's face as Tanner turned his back on her and walked away. Luca's heart swelled at Tanner's trust and faith Luca would protect him, even against his own flesh and blood.

"What is he doing?" Sadie asked.

"I asked him to go onto the balcony." The glare his mother pinned on him was blistering, filled with anger and disbelief. "Thank you for allowing us to rest here for a bit, but we both need to eat, and it's clear to me we're not welcome here."

She grabbed his forearm when he started for the balcony where Tanner waited, watching Sadie through the opened glass door with distrust.

"You are always welcome here. And the wolf can stay as long as you keep close watch over him. Those creatures are deceitful and unpredictable, not to mention prone to insanity. And that one," she said, tilting her head toward Tanner, "is close to the edge. Dangerous."

"Mother—"

"There's something wrong with him, Luca. You'd see it, too, if you looked at him as an impartial observer, as I am. Instead, you look at him with eyes tainted by lust, following your libido instead of your brain. I will not lose you because you followed him blindly into an ambush."

Luca did know something was wrong with Tanner, and he would find out exactly what in due time, even without Matthias's help. His mother's concerns came too late anyway. He and Tanner were already bonded, on their way to being mated, but something inside told him to keep silent. Luca nodded and joined Tanner on the balcony. As he drew closer to his wolf shifter, he realized his decision not to argue with his mother was, in large part, due to Tanner exerting his will through their bond. Luca informed Tanner of what he was feeling and Tanner whined softly. Luca heard the apology in his mind and expressed his acceptance. The bond was new and both of them were still learning how they affected each other through it. Missteps were going to happen.

Once out on the balcony and a good distance from Tanner, Luca shifted — the first time he'd done so when Tanner was awake to witness the change. Even in wolf form, Tanner's awe at Luca's dragon was clear.

You're beautiful, Tanner told him.

Luca lowered to his stomach, making himself as small as possible. *So are you, my sweet boy. Run or ride?*

Chapter Fifteen

TANNER

Unconcerned with the inevitable state of undress, Tanner shifted to human form. He had to touch, so he reached out his hand to run his fingertips over Luca's onyx scales. He expected them to feel rough and hard, but instead, his skin was met with warm silk. When he pressed on the scale, though, it was as hard as stone. Tanner had never imagined he would be this close to a dragon, and he'd certainly never expected to learn firsthand what they felt like. Fascinating. Luca was a gorgeous dragon of deep black that seemed to swallow the sunlight, except for his eyes, which were gold. Luca's rumbled *careful* whispered through his mind as Tanner slid a palm along razor sharp horns. Luca's talons and spiked tail looked equally as lethal.

Luca's mother, Sadie, stepped onto the balcony. She remained in human form, which was good because the space was really only large enough for one dragon. Balcony was probably the wrong word for the slab of concrete they stood on. It was more of a platform or launch pad with no railings; nothing to keep Tanner from falling to his death if he were pushed. The heat from Luca's body seeped into Tanner's skin, warming him despite the cool mountain breeze blowing across his bare skin.

He didn't know how far into the mountains they were, but the smell of snow tinged the air and piles of the white stuff still lingered in nooks and crannies where the sun's rays never reached. Sadie exuded power, so Tanner kept his attention on her as she walked to the edge of the overhang and looked out over the rolling hills surrounding her home. Luca was watchful and wary, notably keeping his large body between Tanner and the edge, but didn't overtly act as though his mother was a threat, so Tanner followed his lead.

"I can't get a solid read on you, wolf," Sadie said, still looking out at the landscape. "You've obviously bonded with my son, which I don't approve of, but it seems I have no say in the matter. Luca has always been headstrong and independent. Nothing like his rookery brothers and sisters, whom the horde has had no trouble with.”

Sadie turned to face them with a stern expression, and Luca lifted his head higher, moving a little closer to Tanner. There was caution and annoyance, but not alarm.

“As the matriarch of this horde, I want both of you to listen and think very hard on what I say.”

Luca dipped his snout in understanding, and Tanner reached up to rub his hand over Luca’s face, once again admiring the dragon’s lethal beauty. He could easily spend years exploring and admiring his massive body.

“Dragons mating with wolves will not be tolerated, and as you are intent upon attempting it, you’ll be made an example. If you continue down this path, you will no longer have a place here. Word will spread to other hordes. I’ll see to it, and there will be nowhere you can go that you will not be condemned for your choice.”

Sadie’s eyes did the same swirling gold thing Luca’s did when he was emotional, and Tanner canted his head to the side. There was the distinct possibility what Sadie said as horde matriarch and what Sadie felt as a mother might be very different, but at the moment, he didn’t care. Repairing family ties would be up to Luca if he chose to do so in the future. As for the present, Tanner felt Luca’s decision form through the bond and smiled up at his mate. His dragon wasn’t outwardly showing any of the pain, sadness, or betrayal he experienced at his mother’s declaration, but Tanner knew those feelings intimately. He also knew exactly how to get past them. Tanner stepped around Luca’s wing, running his fingers over the silken scales, and climbed on Luca’s back, settling himself between the wings.

“Your speech reminds me of my father’s when he disowned me. His was because I was gay, rather than an interspecies mating, but I’m sure he’d be as medieval as you, if he knew. Kicking me out of the McBane pack was the best thing my father ever did for me, and I’m absolutely certain kicking Luca out of the horde will be just as beneficial. For us, not you.”

Tanner worked his fingertips under the edge of a scale above each wing for grip, pressed his feet into the dragon’s body, and spoke to Luca through the bond. *I’m ready to go, I think.* He looked down at his precarious hold and wondered if it would actually be enough to keep him on Luca's back. It sure didn't feel secure. The scales didn't lift away from Luca's body so Tanner was holding by his fingertips. He extended his claws and hoped like hell the sharp tips dug deep enough into the underside of the scales to keep him on Luca's back rather than plunging hundreds of feet to his death.

Lie flat and hold on, pup.

Tanner did as Luca instructed a moment before Luca stepped off the edge of the balcony and spread his wings. Tanner's stomach lurched into his throat as they freefell and he bit back a very un-Alpha-wolf scream. The big body beneath him shook with a deep rumble as Luca laughed, the dragon's amusement warming their bond. The urge to vomit grew in intensity as Tanner watched the ground grow nearer with incredible speed.

I felt the same way my first time. Have faith in the wings.

How old were you?

Three.

Much later than Tanner thought wise, Luca leveled out, flapped his wings to slow their descent and reached all four legs out toward the ground. They landed much more softly than Tanner had expected, but he wasn't impressed by the feat while his stomach was churning. He slid off Luca's back, and the moment his feet hit solid ground, he hunched over and puked.

That had been a terrifying rush.

Never again, he swore.

He was a wolf. His paws belonged on the ground. The dragon walked to a squat building that reminded Tanner of an outhouse made of stone, and Luca's wing brushed over his back in what felt like a caress. A few feet from the building Luca shifted and then entered. A cold breeze blew across Tanner's naked skin, making him shiver so he shifted, his thick coat of fur immediately providing comfortable warmth. While he waited for Luca, Tanner sniffed the air, trying to ascertain where in the mountains they were. Nothing smelled familiar. Even Luca's bonfire scent was blocked by the stone building.

Luca exited the building carrying two dead foxes. He tossed them on the ground, and Tanner's stomach growled. He hadn't noticed how hungry he was until now. He nosed the dead animals to find they were frozen solid and he looked up at Luca for explanation.

"It's an ice house. We stock wild game here for the winter. We can't kill all our livestock off and with the appetites some dragons possess, that will happen easily and quickly if we aren't careful. I know you prefer your meat raw, but you'll have to suffer it cooked. We can't stay on horde lands long enough for this to thaw, and you need to eat. You've shifted twice, but your wounds still haven't healed completely."

Luca carded his fingers through the fur on top of Tanner's head, then backed away and shifted again. He lowered his massive bulk to the ground, opened his mouth, and sent a stream of fire blazing over the dead game. Tanner shook his head as the acrid scent of cooked meat tickled his nostrils. Not the most appetizing smell, but Luca was right, he needed to eat. They each ate a fox, with much internal grumbling from Tanner because cooked meat simply didn't taste good to him.

When he'd eaten as much as his queasy stomach allowed, he backed away from the remains. Without warning, Luca snatched him up in a claw, held him against his massive chest, and took flight. Tanner let out a startled yip but resigned himself to the fact that wherever they were going, it would be with Luca in dragon form flying them. After several minutes of disorientation and fear, and the cooked fox threatening to make a return appearance, Tanner calmed. Luca held him securely, and he began to enjoy the bird's-eye view of the world passing below him.

After a while, the sights and smells became familiar, and he knew they were back home. At the edge of the forest Tanner hunted in, Luca landed with a soft thud and placed him on the ground. Thick foliage crunched beneath his paws as he took a few unsteady steps, trying to get his balance back and once again fight to keep the contents of his stomach where they belonged.

Cooked meat followed by dragon flight was a bad combination. Luca shifted to human and pulled a duffel bag from under a nearby bush. Tanner walked over and shoved his nose into the bag as soon as Luca pulled the zipper open, sniffing the fabric contents and inhaling Luca's smoky scent. Luca gently pushed his snout aside to pull out a pair of jeans. As he dressed, he spoke.

"Same plan as always, pup. We walk out of here as man and dog, except instead of the hotel, we'll go to the office to get my car, and then I'll drive us home."

Tanner pushed his acceptance of the plan through the bond, and Luca nodded as he pulled a T-shirt on. Tanner mourned the loss of Luca's dragon form followed by the covering up of all that hot, delicious human skin, but it was necessary. Once they were inside Luca's house, though, Tanner intended to refamiliarize himself with his mate's amazing body. Maybe he'd be able to convince Luca to shift downstairs and allow Tanner to explore the dragon half more thoroughly. Luca slipped his feet into sandals, and they began the two-mile walk to the office.

As they drew closer to the building, Tanner saw how much damage his pack bonding created. Channeling Deacon's power, if what Luca said was true, hadn't been something he ever expected. Deacon must not have known there was a possibility either, or he would have warned Tanner. He may have decided to bond with the pack one member at a time, given how few of them there were, and avoided biting Deacon altogether, if they'd known the repercussions. Luca slowed his pace and pulled a long strip of cord from his pocket. When he stopped and knelt to wrap the cord around Tanner's neck in noose fashion, Tanner identified it as a dog's leash. He growled as Luca secured the D-ring over the strap, causing Luca to sigh.

"I don't need you getting impounded because you're not leashed. There are cops everywhere, and you're all I have left."

Luca grabbed Tanner's snout and kissed him between the eyes, Tanner still baring his teeth in discontent. He wasn't all Luca had left. Tanner was Alpha to a pack now, and the members of that pack would be willing to allow Luca entry. They were a nontraditional pack and a dragon as Alpha mate wouldn't be frowned upon. Luca didn't know about any of that yet, and Tanner wondered what reaction he'd have to the news. He walked down the sidewalk beside Luca, the smoky scent of his man mingling with the additional smells of the city. There were so many at once. Tanner was overwhelmed sometimes, and he was still trying to learn how to deal with the onslaught of stimuli since moving into the hotel.

As they approached the building, Tanner was surprised by the amount of police activity still going on. A bomb-sniffing Labrador was leading her handler around the perimeter, nose to the ground, plowing through debris and trash. Her ears perked up and the fur on her back spiked as she turned her head toward Tanner, sensing a predator. A massive concrete blockade kept vehicles from entering and exiting the underground parking garage, so the plan to recover Luca's Mercedes was out of the question. Using the new telepathic link with the pack, he reached out to the other wolves. The connection was weak and strange, but it was there.

I need help. Any of you available?

Yes, Deacon answered.

What do you need? Ean asked.

We're outside the office and need a ride.

I'll be there in fifteen, Theran responded.

Luca continued down the street as though he was simply out walking his dog, giving a cursory nod to the officer near the barricade as they passed.

"Gorgeous Malamute," the officer said, and Tanner suppressed a growl.

"He is beautiful, isn't he?" Luca replied with a broad smile.

Tanner nipped the hand holding the leash and let his irritation ripple through the link to Luca. He was a wolf shifter, an Alpha, and it was degrading to be led around like this. Luca laughed and then slid his palm over Tanner's ears in a sweet caress. At the corner, Tanner stopped walking, grabbing the leash with his mouth and tugging Luca to a stop. While he understood the necessity of the damn thing, he wasn't keen on being choked by it. Luca stopped and looked down at Tanner as he sat to wait.

"What are you doing?"

Theran is picking us up.

Luca dipped his chin and narrowed his eyes. "Theran," he repeated in a low rumble that sent chills of arousal dancing across Tanner's skin.

As though speaking the man's name conjured him, Theran pulled up to the curb in front of them. He reached across the cab of the SUV and opened the door. Tanner jumped onto the seat and then over the middle console into the back. Theran stared at him as Luca settled into the passenger seat with a huff, and slammed the door.

"Is that a leash?" Theran asked. Tanner ignored the grin forming on Theran's lips and looked out the window while Theran pulled back into the late evening traffic. Tanner turned back to the front when he heard Theran chuckle. "You put a leash on the pack Alpha?" Theran asked, glancing at Luca. "That's...well, either very brave or very stupid."

Luca glared at Theran. "I'm a dragon."

"Right." Theran glanced back at Tanner and laughed. "Stupid it is."

You became Alpha to the wild dog pack, didn't you? Luca asked Tanner through the bond, glancing back between the seats. Tanner knew this conversation would happen eventually, and though he was uncertain of Luca's reaction, he knew now was a good time.

Yes. I needed them as much as they needed me. I was going crazy. I summoned the pack because we needed a ride. I also need Deacon to tell me what happened when I bit him. Unless you can tell me?

I already told you what I know. You blew shit to pieces when you channeled Deacon's powers. Luca turned in the seat to glare at Tanner. *You bit Deacon? You bonded to him?*

Tanner stared back. Luca had come to the correct conclusion about the bonding, so no response was needed in that regard, but Tanner needed to know if that's why he'd been able to channel the Elemental's powers. Luca said every curse word Tanner knew, and some he didn't, as he turned back to the front. Tanner experienced Luca's anger as though it were his own, but he didn't really understand why his becoming Alpha to a pack was such a problem for Luca. Or perhaps the bonding to Deacon had raised Luca's ire. Luca had exhibited a jealous animosity toward Deacon from the beginning.

The remainder of the drive to Luca's house was spent in tense silence. Tanner elicited the occasional laugh from Theran as he bounced and rolled in the back seat attempting to paw the leash off. It would have been so much easier to shift back to human and remove it, but something about being naked with a dog leash around his neck in front of another wolf shifter, especially one of his own pack members, was beyond embarrassing. That was an image Tanner was absolutely certain he'd never hear the end of.

After a few minutes, he snarled and yipped at Luca in frustration. He pushed himself over the center console between the men. Luca slid the leash off over Tanner's head before kissing the side of his snout. Luca buried his face in the fur of Tanner's neck and held his head until Theran parked the SUV in Luca's driveway. Theran got out of the vehicle and joined the others, who were waiting for them at the front door. Luca growled against Tanner's neck and gripped the fur.

"There is a pack of wolves on my front lawn, isn't there? I can fucking smell them," Luca mumbled.

Tanner licked the bare skin of Luca's forearm, his smoky dragon flavor coating his tongue, and he suddenly wanted to lick other parts of

Luca—but that would have to wait until later. He had unfinished business with the pack bond that needed attending. Without another word, Luca exited the vehicle and waited until Tanner jumped out before slamming the door and stomping into his house. Tanner asked the pack to wait a moment and then followed Luca inside. He shifted in the foyer and followed the scent of his man down the main-floor hallway to the in-home office.

He felt his mate's emotions morphing from one to the next in a rolling mass of confusion that only grew stronger the closer Tanner got. Luca's defenses must be down if Tanner was able to read him so easily. Usually, the dragon was better at masking his feelings. Tanner felt guilty he was the reason his man was so upset. Now that he'd accepted Deacon's offer and created the bond, he knew he had made the right decision to become their Alpha. The pack was dangerously close to losing its cohesiveness. It was only a matter of time before Ross went completely insane and attacked one of the other wolves, or Deacon, his own mate.

Deacon's love and fear for his mate had been thick in the air of the break room and had gone a long way toward Tanner's decision to take on the responsibility of being pack Alpha. Now, he needed to make his own mate understand. Tanner knew Luca was aware of him even though he never turned toward the door. Tanner took several steps toward Luca before the dragon spun around and slammed Tanner's back against the nearest wall. Tanner stared into swirling gold eyes as Luca bracketed him with strong arms and kissed the breath out of him. When the kiss ended, they were both gasping for air.

"What were you thinking?" Luca asked, his words laced with concern. "You're still a pup. Why did you take on a wild dog pack, especially one so close to the edge?"

"Because, they're good men who have been pushed to the brink by their circumstances, just like me. They didn't choose to be lone wolves any more than I did," Tanner answered.

"You don't know that," Luca argued. "You don't know *them*."

Tanner slipped his fingers into the waistband of Luca's pants and tugged his mate's body flush against him. The need to soothe his dragon's concerns was strong and undeniable, but the only way he knew how to do that was physical contact and sending calm vibes through the link as he let his hands and body convey his emotions. Luca relaxed against him, his eyes returning to their dark-brown hue as he gazed into Tanner's blue eyes.

"Damn, you are a seriously powerful wolf," Luca whispered, his lips brushing across Tanner's mouth.

Tanner smiled and kissed Luca gently, slipping his tongue inside when Luca opened for him. Tanner had felt his powers as Alpha strengthen after he'd had sex with Luca even though they had yet to officially claim each other as mates. Now that he had a pack of five others, one of which was an extremely powerful Elemental, he sensed the additional power coursing through his body, and everything came easier to him, except for healing. He wasn't sure why his injuries from the pack bonding were taking so long to heal, but that was a discussion he'd have with Deacon later.

Tanner knew the pack benefited from the pack bond as well. He and the others were able to communicate across great distances telepathically, but he alone had a connection with Luca. He was certain the pack would benefit from the connection to a dragon, and he wanted Luca to be a part of his pack more than anything. Unfortunately, given the amount of discontent coming from Luca, Tanner didn't think that was going to happen anytime soon. He still had to try. Tanner pulled out of their kiss to look into Luca's eyes and gauge his mate's response.

"Will you join the pack?" Tanner asked.

Luca pushed off the wall, moving out of Tanner's reach and turning his back. The action itself was telling. "No, Tanner, I won't. It's done something to you I don't like. I can feel the power shift."

Luca walked to the window and stared out into the inky darkness. Tanner closed his eyes against the stabbing pain and disappointment of Luca denying the pack. Luca was his mate. He needed the dragon within the fold, but he would save the argument for another time. Right now, he had a pack to see to so he pushed the hurt aside—a hurt Luca also experienced if his sudden rigid posture was anything to go by. Tanner was shocked at how intense the pain was. He was barely able to draw breath through the crushing weight.

"I'm taking the pack on a hunt. I'll see you in the morning," Tanner said.

"You're too young to lead a pack," Luca said without turning to look at him.

"I'm twenty-two years old," Tanner told him.

"Exactly," Luca snapped and finally faced him. "You're still a pup with a lot of years ahead of you. You shouldn't be playing Alpha to a pack of wild dogs."

The many unpleasant events of the day mixed in with all the emotions rolling through Tanner's gut made him nauseous. A good part of the sensation was his lack of decent food, and he was mentally exhausted. Tanner took a deep breath and slowly let it go.

"I'm hungry and so are they. I'm taking them hunting."

It took every ounce of his newfound power to turn away from his mate and leave the office to join his pack outside, but he managed it. This wasn't how their mating was supposed to be.

Chapter Sixteen

LUCA

Tanner's pain and something akin to disappointment ripped through Luca's body. He braced himself on the desk with one hand and clamped the other over his chest because it felt like his heart was being torn free. He'd never felt anything so intense. Not even his mother's rejection had hurt like this. Unquestionably, he'd denied his mate something necessary, though he wasn't quite sure what. Luca only knew he had to make it right.

The sensation had started when he told Tanner he wouldn't join the pack. If it really was as simple as becoming a member of the pack, then he would do it, because causing this level of distress in his wolf pup was unacceptable. He still believed Tanner was too young for the responsibility of pack Alpha, but he also knew it was too late.

Luca's incredible sense of loss when Tanner walked away was replaced with determination as he left the comfort of his home once again. Theran's SUV and the red sedan parked in front of the house earlier were both gone. Luca headed for the woods at the edge of town where Tanner liked to hunt. The very same woods where his amazingly beautiful wolf had found him locked in a steel beartrap.

Luca was several minutes behind the pack, but he located Theran's SUV parked at one of the trailheads, so that's the direction he walked. About half a mile in, he spotted Deacon leaning against a massive tree trunk, pouring water from one hand to the other, staring out into the trees. His initial rage at the man for hurting his pup came back full force. Hands balled into fists, he huffed out a smoke-filled breath. The water in one of Deacon's palms cascaded into the other where it pooled as though it were being contained by glass, until Deacon dropped his hands, and the water splashed to the ground.

"They have a bear cornered down near the stream," Deacon said, voice calm, but the Elemental's demeanor told Luca he was prepared for an attack.

"You hit him," Luca growled.

Deacon nodded and turned to face him. "To stop the destruction."

Luca had a strange pulling sensation beneath his skin that made him shudder as a strong wind blasted around them, and then died off as quickly as it started.

"What the hell are you doing?"

"Not me." Deacon tilted his head in the direction of the stream. "Tanner pulls on my power every so often. He's testing the pack bond, strengthening it, so we can become cohesive. The wolves need to learn, feel each other out, and figure out their roles. Tanner is a true Alpha and he knows what's needed, but the others have been without one for so long they need to reacquaint themselves to pack dynamics. Who's the leader, who's the enforcer, who's the strategist...you get the idea. I can guess who will end up doing what, though."

"Except this is no ordinary wolf-shifter pack, is it?" Luca said. Deacon didn't respond, only stared back at Luca, waiting. "What's your role? Where do you fit in?"

"I don't know. I think because I was acting Alpha when Tanner took over, I've become the Beta, but that's how it works in a traditional wolf-shifter pack, and ours is certainly not traditional, as you pointed out, so..." Deacon shrugged.

Seconds later, Luca felt the swell of pride Tanner had in his wolves as though it were his own and reached out with a gentle psychic stroke to let his pup know he was present. He didn't want to do anything to break Tanner's concentration, especially while he was taking the lead in bringing down a bear. Deacon shook his head. His face twisted in disgust and he looked a little sick.

"Ugh. Ross just got a mouthful of bloody bear fur. I love the mating bond as far as the telepathy goes, but the whole tasting what he tastes and smelling what he smells is a bit much sometimes."

"I don't have that kind of bond. I have the telepathy, and I can sense Tanner's emotions, but that's it."

"Interesting," Deacon said, darting a glance at Luca's neck. "Perhaps because you haven't completed the mating. Or maybe because I'm Elemental. You'll have to tell me."

A swell of excitement had Luca straightening and looking in the direction of the stream. Deacon grinned and whispered "Good job, boys," before smiling at Luca. "Want to watch our mates take down their prey?"

"Absolutely."

Luca followed Deacon deeper into the forest. They moved briskly, but quietly, so as not to disturb the hunt. He saw a flash of white fur and then heard a long, low growl as they drew closer to the stream. The wolves had injured the bear, but it was still putting up a fight, despite being surrounded by ferocious predators, swiping a massive paw at the gray wolf in front of him.

Luca squatted behind a thick bush, Deacon peeked around a tree, and together they watched Tanner creep up behind the bear. It still amazed Luca how stealthy the wolf was. He made no noise at all when he decided he didn't want to be heard. All five wolves moved at once, Tanner landing on the animal's back, and the other four each sinking their teeth into soft flesh. Deacon covered his mouth as he gagged, and Luca had to laugh at the poor Elemental. Being a dragon shifter, the flavor of fresh blood and raw meat was quite appetizing to him.

Once the bear was dead, Luca rose to his feet and joined Tanner at the bear's side. He smiled and caressed Tanner behind the ear when the pup looked up at him with those beautiful blue eyes, so filled with pride and happiness, though the earlier pain still simmered underneath it all. Tanner backed a few steps away and sat, allowing the pack to pull what meat they wanted from the carcass. Three of the wolves took their meat closer to the water and settled down to eat. The white wolf, whom Luca now realized was Ross, pranced with his tail held high toward Deacon. The man still looked a little sick, but he smiled at his mate and sat on the ground beside Ross while he ate.

Tanner walked over to the bear carcass and put a paw on the torn flesh of the rump. Luca smiled when Tanner asked if he was hungry, and then shook his head. He was amazed and proud at how seamlessly Tanner had taken on the role of Alpha, seeing to the needs of his pack before his own. Being a leader was Tanner's destiny. Luca fell more in love with Tanner each day. He was shocked how easily the pup had stolen what little heart Luca had, but he didn't think the wolf pup was ready to hear the words, I love you, so Luca decided to show him instead.

Luca smiled at how little of the bear was left when the wolves were finished eating. His own Alpha pup had quite an appetite. Tanner's nose and chest were covered in blood, so Luca reached out to rub Tanner's head, but the wolf pulled away. Tanner shook his head and took off at a dead run into the stream. Tanner never wanted to be touched while he was dirty from a meal. Luca laughed out loud as Tanner splashed and rolled in the cold water. Two of the wolves, one gray and one tawny, jumped into the river as well and the three started playing, burning off the adrenaline-infused energy. Several minutes later, Tanner left the water soaked through, but clean.

Luca held out his hand in silent invitation. Tanner did a full body shake, sending water droplets flying in every direction, and then sat in front of Luca. Luca crossed his legs and pulled Tanner closer by his scruff, scratching behind his ears and down his neck to his sides. Tanner stood and tucked his cold, wet nose beneath Luca's chin. Luca closed his eyes and tugged Tanner into his arms where he petted, rubbed, and caressed Tanner's cold, drenched fur, not caring he too was getting wet.

Tanner pulled away, indulging in another full body shake before tentatively moving closer. Luca was confused by the sudden timidity. They held each other's eyes for a moment, dark brown to bright blue, before Tanner jumped forward, shifting to his human form as he went, and crushed Luca's lips in a kiss. Luca caught Tanner's naked body against him and held tight, his hands sliding across Tanner's smooth skin. Luca opened his mouth to Tanner's insistent tongue and sucked. His fangs elongated and his dick hardened. Luca was so tempted to mate his boy right now and finalize the bonding here in the forest that was like a second home to his beautiful wolf.

The rest of the pack forgotten, Luca listened to the symphony that was Tanner, his heart beats quick and hard, his breathing short and shallow. It was all a hum that stirred Luca on the most primal level. It had been decades since another being had made him feel this way. For that alone, Luca was determined to never let Tanner go. Tanner pushed Luca to his back and blanketed Luca with his body, the wolf's heat and vitality surrounding him. The need to breathe had Tanner pulling away, but Luca tightened his grip around Tanner's waist and smiled when he saw Tanner's canines were also distended. Tanner's arousal pressed into Luca's pelvis, causing Luca to roll his hips against the hard shaft to increase the pressure.

"You're so beautiful," Luca said against Tanner's mouth.

"So are you," Tanner replied and brushed his lips softly over Luca's jaw. "Mate," he whispered.

"Yes," Luca whispered back with a smile.

Tanner leaned down for another kiss, but just before their lips connected, his head whipped up, and he pushed off Luca so fast it took Luca a moment to realize the wolf had moved. Tanner had shifted back to wolf form swiftly, flattened his ears, and bared his teeth with a menacing growl. He lowered his body, preparing for an attack from an enemy Luca had been unaware of until this moment. Using his dragon abilities, he rolled to his side and lifted to his feet in less than a second, his fangs out and ready to kill.

An older man stepped through the trees, followed closely by four wolves. He looked to be in his fifties or sixties, and one sniff told Luca all five new arrivals were wolf shifters. Tanner moved in front of him in a protective gesture Luca both loved and hated. He was a dragon shifter; he didn't need protection. The older man looked at Luca with a sneer before leveling his disapproving gaze on Tanner.

"What the hell do you think you're doing, boy?" the man asked loudly.

Tanner growled and snapped his jaws. Luca kept his eyes on the four wolves, prepared for any one of them to launch an attack. If any of these animals attempted to come near Tanner, Luca was going to rip them apart. Their scent was similar enough to Tanner's Luca was certain they were related. At the very least, they were old pack. The way the shifters deferred to the older man, he was clearly the Alpha and Luca was convinced he was meeting Tanner's father.

He heard a rustling of leaves behind him. Luca's instinct to turn around to see who was coming up from behind them was negated by Tanner's bond to him—it was Tanner's pack. Deacon stepped up beside Luca. They shared a quick glance, before returning their attention to the possible threat of the McBane pack Alpha. Energy crackled around the Elemental, causing the hairs on Luca's arms and neck to rise. Ross, Ean, Theran, and Vance flanked Tanner on each side, all in wolf form, prepared to fight beside their Alpha. Luca didn't know which wolf was who, but that was something he would learn down the road.

Tanner reached out to Luca through their bond. Tanner refused to change back to human in the presence of his father's pack, but he had things to say. Under the current circumstances, Luca needed to speak for him. Without pulling back on any of his dragon abilities, Luca moved to stand closer to Tanner's flank. The wolves adjusted their positions and Deacon moved to the side, where it was safer for him to call upon the elements, without harming his own pack, but still have a clear pathway to the enemy.

What is your father's name? Luca asked. Tanner answered and pushed a question of his own to Luca.

"The Alpha asks what business is it of yours what he's doing, Ethan?" Luca repeated for Tanner, using the man's first name as a sign of indifference to his equal status as Alpha.

Ethan McBane's head snapped from his son to Luca in shock. An angry red flush spread across the man's face. "What have you done?" Ethan asked scarcely above a whisper. Luca didn't respond because Tanner didn't. Ethan's eyes bounced between his son and Luca.

"This is my pack. What do you want?"

Luca heard his own voice, he felt his mouth and tongue form words, but he had no conscious control over what those words were. He glanced down at Tanner. The boy had grown stronger since his disownment from the McBane pack. The creation of the bond between Tanner and Luca had kick-started the transformation, but the addition of Deacon and the others had only strengthened Tanner's abilities. Luca had no idea this level of mind control was something a wolf shifter could achieve. Cool, yet slightly terrifying. He had known the moment he'd met Tanner the wolf would be powerful. It was the primary reason Luca had kept the pup close and fostered every connection possible. Now, those connections were bearing fruit. Luca smiled at the older McBane, showing plenty of fang.

"You've cut ties with your family, bonded with wild dogs, and taken a male dragon for a lover," Ethan spat.

"Mate," Luca and Tanner growled together.

Silence descended. The one word echoed through the clearing and pulled all eyes to Tanner and Luca. The response had only been spoken through Luca's mouth, but both Luca's and Tanner's voices came out. Tanner was literally speaking through Luca.

"Jinx," Luca whispered with a smile, glancing down at his wolf mate.

The joke was meant to lighten Tanner's mood and ease the anxiety the pack was feeling. Tanner relaxed marginally and pulled the telepathy back a bit.

Sorry, Tanner offered.

It's all good. Scared the ass.

The wind picked up, and the scent of rain became pronounced, reminding Luca that Deacon was standing to the side, likely behind the storm building in the sky above them. Luca turned back to the McBane pack and their very pale-faced Alpha. Ethan stared hard at his son after darting a rapid glance in Deacon's direction.

"You disowned me, turned your backs on me, and left me on my own. I have a real pack now where each member will die for any of the others. We have trust. We have friendship and love. And because we've not limited ourselves to the preconceived rules about who a pack should consist of, we have power," Tanner said through Luca.

"Your *pack* is an abomination," Ethan spat out. A lot of anger and a tinge of fear colored the statement. "Everything about it goes against nature. It must be disbanded, and if you resist, it will be destroyed."

The threat was not received kindly by any of the members in Tanner's pack. Luca had yet to become a member, mostly due to his own misgivings, but he now knew he would definitely mate Tanner and officially join the pack because it was necessary. Forming a pack and creating the bond was the only thing keeping Tanner sane and healthy. In the face of his own mother's proclamations, and the McBane Alpha's threats, Luca's additional power was most definitely required. He *would* protect what was his.

Luca felt the first drops of rain hit his head and shoulders. From the corner of his eyes he watched Deacon wave his hand over his head in a large circle. The clouds opened and a downpour ensued, except the only ones getting wet were the McBane wolves. If Ethan needed any further proof of the power his son's pack wielded, he was seeing it now as he and his wolves were soaked to the skin while Tanner and his pack stood in a patch of dry ground as though standing beneath a massive invisible umbrella. Or perhaps the show of power would have the opposite effect and strengthen the Alpha's resolve to disband them. Deacon pursed his lips and blew, and the McBanes were hit with a strong gust of wind, pelted by horizontal rain. Luca knew the moment Tanner pulled some of Deacon's power and when the Alpha growled, thunder rolled overhead.

The McBane wolves inched back, but Ethan stood his ground. Luca recognized Tanner's stubbornness in the older man. It was what he didn't see that Luca was fascinated with. Luca admired Tanner's stubbornness sometimes, and his unwillingness to back down when his beliefs were being challenged, but he loved Tanner's inner strength, his boldness, his kindness, his empathy, and his refusal to be anything other than honest with himself and everyone else he came into contact with. Tanner had respect and honor. All of which the elder McBane seemed to be lacking.

Without another word, the McBane pack turned to leave, Ethan casting one last glare over his shoulder at his son. Deacon pulled back on the downpour as the enemy pack retreated. Luca knew Tanner was powerful, that the pack wielded incredible strength due to his dragon and the Elemental, but the fear and hate they generated among the other paranormals was unexpected. His mother had threatened them with exile, and now Tanner's father was threatening outright death. Luca wasn't sure why their pack warranted such animosity, but he planned on investigating further once they returned to the house.

As far as dragon shifters, Elementals, and wolf shifters went, Luca, Deacon, and Tanner were powerful, but there were others of their species who were even stronger, so it must be their combined power that was putting dragons and wolves on edge. Elementals were a bit rare in the cities, but Luca expected if their pack came across another, the reaction toward their unity would be the same—fear and intolerance. He once again cursed Matthias and his secrets. If the old librarian had been more helpful, Luca might have already had the answers the pack needed. Instead, they were left floundering.

Everyone remained tense, prepared, until Tanner calmed. The other wolves turned to their Alpha for instruction. Luca didn't know any wolf packs intimately, but he figured Tanner's pack, though small, was already something to be reckoned with. He wondered if it was due to him and Deacon, or if the five wolves had bonded so rapidly on their own. From what Luca witnessed, each of them knew what to do if attacked.

We need to move. Now. Somewhere we have tactical advantage. Tanner said to the entire pack, Luca presumed.

"My house," Luca offered, though he'd never allowed anyone other than Tanner inside, but this was his mate's pack, so he would sacrifice his solitude for their safety.

No. You're in the city. Too many people. Somewhere else.

Deacon walked up to Ross and rubbed his ears while the wolf leaned against his thigh. "We'll take you to the palace," he said.

Luca wasn't sure what words passed between the pack members but Tanner suddenly ran toward the trailhead where Theran's SUV was parked. The wolves took off after him, leaving Deacon and Luca to bring up the rear.

"There's no hurry. They all left their clothes in the back of the truck. We have time to catch up while they get dressed."

"What is this palace you mentioned?" Luca asked.

"Nothing even remotely close to an actual palace," Deacon answered with a cheeky smile. "It's actually an abandoned cabin a few miles up the mountain. There's a small clearing around it so whoever attacks has to come into the open to do it. Best of all, there's no one else around for miles and no roads in."

Luca cast Deacon a questioning look.

"Vance stumbled across it during a hunt, and we claimed it as ours. We go there on the weekends or for vacations so the wolves can chill, play, hunt...whatever they want. They've always felt safer there. Probably because of Ross..."

Deacon's voice trailed off, making Luca wonder what wasn't being said. He'd always thought the wild dog pack was close to losing it, but perhaps only Ross was dancing with insanity. Luca hadn't wanted to look too closely into the paranormal men working for him; the very men Tanner had decided to take responsibility for. He hoped like hell the bond to Deacon and Tanner kept Ross from becoming so blood thirsty he went after his own. Luca would defend Tanner to the death, even against his own pack.

"How homicidal is he?" Luca asked in a lowered voice. They were approaching the wolf shifters, who were now dressed and waiting in front of the SUV. Ross was spinning in a circle with his arms out for reasons known only to him, making Theran laugh as he flipped the truck keys around one finger.

"The blood lust is there," Deacon answered in the same low voice. "But he hasn't attacked anyone...yet." Deacon stopped, grabbing Luca's arm to hold him back, keeping a good distance between them and the wolves. "If there's a battle the way Tanner thinks there'll be... I'm concerned once Ross gets a taste of blood and violence, I won't be strong enough to pull him back."

"He goes after Tanner you won't have to worry about pulling him back. I'll kill him."

Deacon looked resigned but pained by his response, though he said nothing as they resumed their trek to the SUV.

Chapter Seventeen

TANNER

The cabin, otherwise known as the palace, and the surrounding area were exactly as Deacon had promised. Isolated and defensible. Located a few miles from the main road in a small clearing ringed by forest, the back of the cabin was flanked by a few hundred feet of trees and a sheer wall of rock. Tanner and the wolves had stripped and shifted to run the distance to the cabin, while Deacon packed their clothing into a large duffel they kept in the back of the SUV. They had parked in an out-of-the-way camping area, where a vehicle left vacant for days wouldn't raise concern. Luca shifted into dragon form so he could fly Deacon and a second duffel of supplies to the cabin rather than hike in on foot. The sooner the pack was ready for Ethan McBane and his wolves, the better.

Tanner had an uncomfortable feeling his father was going to be coming for them soon and in larger numbers. Tanner had no doubt his father intended for him to cower, give into his demands without question simply because they were father and son. That was Tanner's behavior in the past when he'd had ultimate faith in his father. Things were different now. He was an Alpha in his own right, with a dragon mate and a pack of his own to lead—albeit a small, unconventional pack.

That was another thing causing an anxious flutter beneath Tanner's skin—Luca had come to the hunt. He stood among them as they faced off against Tanner's father. Tanner felt Luca's acceptance of the pack through the bond, and was overjoyed his dragon had changed his mind and decided to become a pack member. After the successful hunt, Tanner literally pounced on Luca in front of everyone. He was so intent on claiming his mate, he didn't notice his father's presence or his old pack mates until they were practically on top of them. First priority was to complete the mating with Luca so his focus remained on protecting his new family and not being so easily distracted by the sexy dragon.

The five wolves stopped at the edge of the forest where about fifty feet of clearing lay between the tree line and the cabin and scrutinized the area for activity. Soft light filtered through the slats of the board-covered windows, but otherwise, everything was quiet. Too quiet. There were no crickets. No critters of the night moving about. No leaves rustling. Not even the slightest breeze. It seemed like the entire outside world had ceased to exist.

He sensed Deacon inside the cabin, but getting to the structure unseen was the issue. Luca's proximity tickled his psyche, but pinpointing exactly where the dragon was proved impossible. He pushed the question, *where are you?* through the bond. It wasn't a question he would have to ask once they were mated; he would just know.

Rock face. I can see you, Luca told him. *You're clear.*

At the same time, Ross communicated with him. *Deacon's inside,* he said before launching into the clearing at a run.

The others tensed at the sudden movement, worrying Ross had done something dangerous, but Tanner gave the okay, and they all followed. Deacon opened the door in time for Ross to bound inside and skid across the wood flooring. Tanner stepped into the cabin more slowly, followed by the other wolves. They all shifted, Ean and Theran moving to the duffel bag in front of the couch to pull everyone's clothing out. Ross went straight to Deacon's arms, where Vance confronted him.

"You've got to stop being reckless. What if that other wolf pack had been waiting? Or human hunters had been around? We'd be caught in a situation we're not prepared for."

Ross narrowed his eyes but didn't move from Deacon's embrace. "Tanner and Deacon are here."

"I'm not invincible," Tanner told him.

Deacon ran a hand through Ross's hair, down to his chin, where he turned Ross's face up to his. "Neither am I. Please, be more careful."

"It's okay," Ross whispered seductively as he kissed Deacon's jaw. "We'll die together."

The smile Ross gave following the comment made Tanner a little uneasy, and Deacon's expression showed the same wariness. Not quite sure what to do with his Beta's mate, Tanner turned his attention to the tasks at hand—defense against his father's pack and the mating with Luca. He looked around the small, dilapidated cabin.

There was a main room where a couch, armchair, and a table with two chairs were located. One cabinet along the wall with a stove, sink, and refrigerator identified it as the kitchen, though technically it was all the same room. Two doors off the main room led to bedrooms. Tanner noted there was no bathroom, but considering they were all "animals," aside from Deacon, it was hardly a problem. There was one door leading outside and only two windows within sight; one at the front of the main room and one at the back above the kitchen sink.

A ground-shuddering thump, rattling the cabin's meager furnishings, heralded Luca's arrival mere seconds before the man stepped through the door, smelling of smoke and gloriously naked. Tanner's body responded immediately and with nothing to hide his rising cock from view, his excitement was evident to everyone else too. Luca's body reacted similarly as his heated gaze drifted over Tanner's erection and then slowly returned to his eyes.

Not now, sweet boy.

Tanner nodded his understanding because there were more important things to deal with this moment than taking his dragon shifter to bed. Ignoring his and Luca's obvious arousal and hoping the others did the same, Tanner addressed the pack.

"I like the perimeter around the cabin, but the lack of windows works against us. We'll have to set up patrols outside, which isn't ideal, but necessary. The rock face at the back might also present a problem if it allows them an elevated advantage." He looked to Luca for confirmation.

Luca shook his head. "No. I have wings, so I can make use of it as a lookout, but anything that can't fly will find it hard to scale. It's steeper and less stable than it looks."

"Good. The rock wall is to the south and my father's pack is north of here so that's the direction they'll come from. They'll begin to circle when they hit the tree line around the clearing. Their strategy will be to come from as many sides as possible. They *might* assume if they can't get up those rocks, we can't either, so they'll put some warriors in the trees right at the base which would be in our favor if we have Luca up there."

"Except he's a big-ass dragon," Ean said from the armchair. "Pretty sure if he can see them, they can see him."

"But that might be a good thing for us. If they see him up there, they might have second thoughts about attacking us at all," Theran added with a shrug. He'd taken a seat on the arm of the ratty sofa.

Ross was nuzzling into Deacon's neck, seemingly unaware of the conversation going on around him. Deacon had his fingers threaded into Ross's hair, massaging the back of Ross's head, but his attention was focused on the discussion. Tanner was happy to see his Beta could keep a straight head, even while his mate was playing. Vance sat in a chair at the table, feet propped up on the second chair and arms crossed over his chest. Considering there might be a showdown with another pack soon, everyone was awfully relaxed.

"Is anyone at all concerned about being attacked?" Tanner asked, though he didn't feel exceptionally anxious over the prospect himself. He wasn't sure why.

"Not particularly," Theran answered.

"We have Deacon and Luca," Ean said, as though that explained it all. Having a dragon and an Elemental did give them the advantage when it came to ability, but they were horribly outnumbered. The human saying "strength in numbers" had some truth to it.

"And we have you," Deacon added. "You can channel my power. It's like me being in two places at once."

"Except I don't know how I did it," Tanner admitted.

"But you've done it twice now. You'll do it again, I have no doubt," Luca said as he wrapped strong arms around Tanner's body. Tanner stiffened everywhere, and his thoughts derailed for a moment. The mating pull was so damn distracting.

"How quickly do you think your father can gather his pack?" Theran asked, trying not to stare at Tanner's arousal.

Forcing his mind back on the issue, Tanner answered. "Morning, I think. He has to gather everyone and then track us. Won't be easy because we drove most of the way, but he can track Luca's smoky scent. It's very distinctive. And obviously he can pick my scent out of a crowd."

"It's interesting he was able to track you at all, given how your scent is changing because of Luca. I noticed it immediately," Deacon pointed out, joined by a chorus of agreements from the wolves. Tanner didn't have an answer for that, but he now wondered the same thing.

"I have no idea how he found me, but if he did it once, he can do it again. We need to be prepared."

"Let me take care of the defense preparations while you and Luca go into one of the rooms and take care of *that*," Deacon said as he indicated Tanner's hard-on with a dip of his head. "You'll be stronger once you're fully mated, and you know it."

Tanner did know; it was true of all wolf shifters. They became physically stronger and more resilient once they were mated, but he wasn't sure what would happen. He'd been unprepared when he'd bitten Deacon. He refused to be stupid again, especially now that he had a pack of his own. Ross pulled his face away from Deacon's neck with a laugh and everyone turned to look at him.

"Everyone needs to fuck," he said before burying his face in Deacon's neck again. "Let's all fuck."

He wrapped a leg around Deacon's thigh and bumped his hips forward. Deacon palmed his bare ass in an attempt to stop the movement which earned him a fanged bite on the shoulder and sharp claws slicing into his back. Deacon hissed in pain. In what must have been practiced intervention, Vance, Theran, and Ean all jumped into action. Ean pulled a bottle of liquid from the cabinet and measured out a shot, while Theran and Vance pulled Ross's fangs from Deacon's flesh. All three worked together to lower Ross to his back on the floor, Deacon's weight holding most of his body down. Vance pulled Ross's arms over his head and held them immobile while Theran held his head still for Ean to pour the liquid into his mouth.

"It's okay, baby. I'm right here. I won't leave you. Just let the medicine work," Deacon whispered as Ross slipped into unconsciousness, his body going limp. "Everything's going to be okay."

"This happens a lot, I assume?" Tanner asked as the others returned to their seats, leaving Deacon on the floor with his unconscious mate. He was bleeding from the bite and slashes to his back, but no one seemed concerned about it, so Tanner let it go.

"We have bottles of sedative stashed anywhere we spend a lot of time because we never know when we'll need to knock him out," Ean said as he returned the bottle to the cabinet. "Don't worry, though. The effects are short-term, but last long enough we can get him or anyone else to safety. He'll be awake in about thirty minutes.

"These outbursts are becoming more frequent. He's erratic, reckless, harder to control," Deacon said as he pushed to a seated position on the floor. Tanner noticed Deacon never stopped touching his mate, even as he stared hard into Tanner's eyes. "I pray it's reversible."

Tanner simply nodded in agreement because he really had no idea. Unfortunately, he had never heard of a wolf shifter recovering from blood lust. In his father's pack, once the condition set in, the shifter affected was exiled. Even then, blood lust was a rare condition for a wolf shifter within a pack to suffer from, but was rampant among those without one. Tanner was acutely aware of everything he *didn't* know, and the weight of responsibility he'd taken on by assuming the role of Alpha had him sagging into Luca's arms. Luca held him effortlessly; the dragon's strength hiding Tanner's weakness from the others.

"Theran, Vance, and I will take first watch," Ean offered as he rose to his feet and began undressing.

Vance and Theran did the same, placing their folded clothes back into the duffel. As they filed past on their way outside, Theran taking the lead, Vance addressed Tanner.

"Complete the mating, Alpha. We need all the strength and power we can get," he said and then joined Theran outside the cabin.

Tanner nodded at Vance's back before turning to Ean. "Deacon will stay with Ross, but Luca and I will take over patrol in a few hours."

Ean nodded his agreement with Tanner's plan as he exited the cabin and shifted.

Can you stand on your own? Luca asked him.

Tanner glanced over his shoulder to offer a soft smile. *Yes.*

Luca released him only long enough to take Tanner's hand and lead him into the bedroom. Deacon scooped Ross into his arms and moved to the couch where he lay back, tucking his unconscious mate between his big body and the sofa back. Even in his drugged state, Ross curled into Deacon's warmth, seeking out the physical connection only his mate was able to provide. Tanner swallowed his initial reaction to the vulnerable position Deacon placed himself in as Luca closed the bedroom door. He had to remind himself he wasn't dealing with just wolf shifters anymore. Deacon was a powerful Elemental; as long as he was awake and aware, he wasn't truly vulnerable.

"Something's bothering you," Luca said, drawing Tanner's attention away from the rickety wooden door he'd been staring at, as if it held the answers to all his fears. Luca sat on the edge of the bed, naked and aroused, but doing nothing more than holding Tanner's hand. Tanner stepped closer to rake the fingers of his free hand through Luca's hair.

"You're so handsome," he whispered.

Luca smiled, but it didn't reach his eyes. "What's wrong, my sweet boy?"

Tanner sighed, pulled his hands free, and then sat beside Luca, making sure no part of their bodies touched. He needed physical distance if he was going to admit his shortcomings to the man he loved.

"It occurs to me the extent to which my father kept me sheltered and uneducated. I thought it was because he was overprotective, but now I believe it was deliberate."

Luca scoffed. "I can guarantee it was deliberate."

Tanner looked at him questioningly.

"Your father is an Alpha, but he's average. You are anything but, and he had to have known that as you got older, so he made a preemptive strike to keep you from challenging him. He knew he didn't stand a chance if you ever learned how powerful you were, so his answer was to oppress and imprison."

"But he kicked me out of the pack. Why would he do that if his intent was to keep me from becoming...whatever it is I'm becoming?"

"That's the beauty of short-sighted, egotistical, Alpha assholes. Look at me, pup," Luca said as he cupped Tanner's chin and turned his face. "He never expected you to survive."

Tanner winced as the old, nearly forgotten pain of his father rejecting him blossomed in his chest. Hearing his father might have wanted him dead caused his eyes to burn, and one lone tear found a path down his cheek. Luca wiped it away with his thumb.

"His mistake"—Luca whispered as he kissed Tanner below one eye—"will ultimately be"—he said before kissing below the other eye—"his downfall."

"How? I'm stupid and naïve. Too young to lead a pack, like you said. I don't have a fucking clue what I'm doing," Tanner said.

Luca pressed his warm lips to Tanner's neck, right where the mating mark would be once Luca claimed him. After the simple, chaste kiss, Luca wrapped his strong arms around Tanner's waist and hefted him farther onto the bed where he covered Tanner with his large body, instantly surrounding him with heat and the smoky scent he loved. His flagging erection sprang back to life as Luca sensually rocked between his legs, adding more fuel to the mating fire.

"Not anymore. You have several deep wells of knowledge to dip into at any given moment."

"What?"

Tanner was trying to follow Luca's words, but thinking clearly was damned near impossible when the dragon shifter's cock was sliding alongside his own at such an infuriatingly slow pace. He palmed Luca's ass, digging his fingers into the muscular globes as they contracted on an upward glide.

"Six, to be exact," Luca said, breathlessly, proving to Tanner he, too, was affected.

"Six, what?" Tanner asked, then moaned loudly as Luca took both their cocks in one hand and began stroking.

Tanner bucked his hips and squeezed Luca's ass. He needed more pressure on his cock, more sensation on his skin, more Luca inside him. He dipped a finger into the crevice of Luca's ass, putting firm pressure against his taint. Luca growled, the vibration of the deep rumble dancing pleasantly across Tanner's sensitized flesh. Abruptly, Luca released their cocks and pushed off Tanner, leaving him cold, rock hard, and irritated. Tanner released a growl of his own, but it quickly turned into a contented groan when Luca grabbed him behind the knees, pushing them to his chest, folding Tanner until his butt was up in the air, giving Luca full access to his entrance.

"Hold them," Luca said, and Tanner's hands replaced Luca's behind his knees. Luca stroked his palms over the back of Tanner's thighs as he released a hot puff of smoke over Tanner's scrotum. Tanner gasped and jerked at the unexpected, yet delicious sensation of hot air followed instantly by the cool wetness of Luca's tongue as he licked over the pucker. Tanner watched from between his legs as gold bled into Luca's eyes in that hypnotic swirl he loved, overwhelmed by so many sensations and feelings, as his mate licked, prodded, prepared him. He wanted to run his fingers through Luca's damp hair, but that would mean releasing one of his knees, and he didn't want Luca to stop.

All too soon, but not soon enough, Luca lifted, slicked two fingers in his mouth, and pushed them into Tanner's hole. They went in easily enough, the burn barely noticeable as Tanner released his legs and pushed his heels into the bed on either side of Luca, pumping his hips up and down in a desperate search for deeper penetration.

Luca bent over Tanner as he held his hand still, allowing Tanner to ride his fingers, and whispered, "We don't have lube."

Tanner grabbed the back of Luca's head, holding him steady as he glared into the dragon's swirling gold gaze. The fire in his blood was out of control, burning too hot for them to stop now. God, he hoped Deacon had thought to stash more than just sedatives in the cabin.

Lube. He pushed the single word to Deacon because he was incapable of much more. Thankfully, his Beta understood and came back with an answer right away. *Dresser.*

"In there," Tanner told Luca as he pointed to the dresser along the wall to the left.

Attaining the item required them to separate, but it was a necessary evil. Luca pulled his fingers free, and with a speed Tanner truly appreciated, he located and retrieved the tube, slicked up, and repositioned himself between Tanner's legs. Tanner lifted his knees along Luca's sides when the tip of Luca's cock pressing against his entrance, his eyes almost completely gold. Luca pumped his hips forward, forcing the crown of his cock past the tight ring of muscle, making Tanner gasp in shock and then groan in pleasure.

The dragon braced himself with elbows planted beside Tanner's head, surrounding him completely, and began moving, sliding deeper into Tanner's welcoming body with each thrust. Tanner raked his nails over the straining muscles of Luca's back and shoulders, occasionally digging them into Luca's contracting butt cheeks as he pumped harder, deeper, faster.

Luca lowered himself onto Tanner, trapping Tanner's weeping cock between them, each thrust pushing Tanner closer to orgasm, as Luca moved a hand to cup Tanner's ass. Every time he drove into Tanner, he pulled Tanner's butt upward, helping him take more of his length, delivering the burning stretch and fullness only Luca's body provided. Such exquisite pain.

"Oh, fuck," Luca bit out when Tanner clenched down on his shaft.

Apparently, that was all Luca needed to drive him closer to the edge, his thrusts then becoming punishing in their speed and strength, but Tanner didn't care. He met his dragon thrust for thrust, dancing them both along the razor edge of orgasm.

"I would fuck you forever if I could," Luca rumbled against Tanner's mouth. "Stay buried deep inside you so you never forget who you belong to."

Tanner accepted Luca's kiss, matching him with equal fervor. "I won't forget," Tanner whispered when the kiss broke. He growled out the word "mate" as he crested, streaking their stomachs with ribbons of pearly liquid. Luca's movements became erratic and he stiffened.

"Tanner...pup..."

As Luca emptied into him, Tanner came to an understanding. He was right where he was supposed to be. And with the sharp, euphoric pain of Luca's fangs sinking into his neck, claiming him, mating him, the world around him became perfectly clear. It all made sense. The knowledge, the power—everything he needed in order to defeat his father was right here—and always had been.

Chapter Eighteen

LUCA

Luca retracted his fangs, kissed the mating mark, and collapsed on top of Tanner. The juice of Tanner's release, mixed with their combined sweat, was slick between their bodies. His body hummed with a mating not yet complete, an uncomfortable itch beneath his skin that, if left unfulfilled, might well drive him mad. Tanner hooked his legs over the back of Luca's thighs, slid an arm around his waist, and fisted Luca's hair, pulling his head to the side so he had unobstructed access to Luca's neck. Without further warning, Tanner bit, sucked, and completed the mating bond. The itch beneath Luca's skin became a burn that steadily worsened with terrifying speed.

He pushed away from Tanner, falling off the foot of the bed to curl into a ball on the floor as he fought an involuntary shift. If he allowed the dragon free now, he'd destroy the cabin. A pained scream filled his ears followed immediately by a high-pitched howl. Smoke filled the room, becoming thicker with each passing second, but nothing made sense to Luca. His scream joined the howl as his body begin to shift despite his efforts to remain human. Luca had never had to fight against the change before, and he felt as if he were being ripped in two. The bedroom door slammed into the wall as Deacon burst through.

"Shit!" Deacon said as he ran farther into the room, giving Luca a wide berth as he struggled on the floor, trying to keep the shift under control. "Hold on, hold on."

Deacon grabbed the edge of the bedspread, folding it haphazardly on the bed. Luca was distantly aware there was smoke billowing from the mattress. He was concerned he'd somehow set it on fire and experienced a small twinge of fear because he'd left his mate in the middle of the bed. Deacon lifted the bundled blanket over his shoulder and rushed from the room, before yelling over his shoulder, "Your mate is out of harm's way, dragon, let it go."

Realizing the bundle Deacon carried out was Tanner, Luca stopped fighting. He was already losing the battle anyway. The fire in his veins was too strong, too painful for him to hold at bay any longer. The fact another man was touching his boy—his mate—added fuel to the inferno. Once he let go, the shift became painless. His tail punched a hole through the wall at the head of the bed, his head and body exploded into the main living area, while his wings went through the roof. Fully shifted, Luca's head cleared, and he sighed at the situation he found himself in.

There were two ways out of what remained of the cabin. Simply stand up and destroy what was left, or he shift back to human and walk out the front door. He attempted option two, but the shift didn't come. Not only was his shifting to dragon involuntary; apparently transitioning back would be too. The silence was broken by howling wolves and a pissed-off Elemental who shouted at him.

"What did you do to him, dragon?"

Luca stood up. Lately, Deacon had made him angry one time too many, in regard to Tanner, so he decided destroying the cabin was fair. He stretched his wings and looked down on Deacon and the wolves. His anger died the moment his eyes fell on his mate, lying motionless in wolf form on the blanket. The acrid scent of singed fur reached his nose as grief, fear, and the powerful need to protect washed over him. Luca sent a short blast of flame toward the pack that dissipated before it reached them, but it had the desired effect of making them back away from Tanner.

He moved into the grass, lay on his stomach, and wrapped his massive dragon body around his wolf pup, sheltering him from above with a sloped wing. Luca bumped Tanner's head with his nose, huffing out a breath and sending ash fluttering into the air. Beneath the soot, Tanner's fur was normal, as though nothing unusual had happened. Pain, sharp and cold, stabbed at his head in tiny pricks. Luca swung his head around to see Deacon creating ice pellets in his hands and launching them at him. He growled in annoyance.

"Tanner was burning when I got into the room," Deacon said, voice hard. He opened his hand and blew, sending a shower of much larger ice pellets into Luca's face. Luca shook his head at the sting. A minor pinprick to his tough hide, but still irritating. "You lost control, dragon. Set your own mate on fire."

Luca roared at him in denial as Deacon rolled a ball of ice between his hands, making it bigger with each pass of his fingers. It wouldn't take long before the icy object was large enough to actually cause pain when Deacon threw it at him. Luca pulled his wing back, allowing the pack to see Tanner was fine, at least physically. He wasn't burned, but he was still unconscious. That concerned Luca more than the weapon of solid ice Deacon was creating. He pressed his large nose against Tanner's cheek and opened his mind to the new mating bond now thrumming through his veins.

Open your eyes, sweet boy.

He poked and prodded at his mate's mind until he felt Tanner clawing toward consciousness, using the connection to Luca as a guide. Luca heard the soft call Tanner sent out to the other wolves, and they all responded by lowering their guard, stepping closer to their Alpha. Deacon was a member of the pack; he had to have heard Tanner's call, but the Elemental chose to ignore it, still rolling the ever-growing ball of ice in his hands and glaring at Luca. Luca growled and hunched over Tanner protectively. When the ball of ice hit his scales, it would disintegrate into sharp little icicles that might injure Tanner, and he wouldn't allow that to happen.

"Step away, dragon."

The ice ball was nearly the size of a watermelon as Deacon casually circled him. Luca wanted to check his mate's health but didn't want to turn away from the Elemental. He decided if the ice ball was thrown his way, he'd blast it with fire before it made contact and caused damage. A foreign howl pierced the quiet night and was quickly joined by too many others to count, the eerie sound echoing off the rock wall. The McBane pack had found them in a far-too-short time, and they were caught out in the open, unprepared. Deacon's hands flashed orange and the ice ball melted, splashing the ground at his feet.

Ross squealed in delight, drawing everyone's attention. He did a back flip and in midair, shifted into his wolf form, landing on all four paws. Apparently, the sedative he'd been given earlier had no lasting effect whatsoever on his energy. Ross's excitement over the coming violence buzzed through the pack bond setting them all on edge. Deacon immediately changed directions to stand beside Ross. The others had already been in wolf form and spread out in front of Luca, his massive dragon form protecting their flanks. A brush of fur against his wing pulled Luca's attention to his mate. Tanner stood in wolf form and shook the soot from his fur. Luca stared at him with a mixture of shock and fear.

The mating between dragon and wolf had a side effect he'd never imagined. Tanner's wolf had morphed to twice his original size, the fur now solid black, and his eyes burned crimson red. The visual was demonic. He now understood Deacon's love of Ross in the face of the wolf's insanity, because despite the changes Tanner had just undergone and the immense power flowing through his pup's veins, Luca still loved him and would die to protect him.

From the edge of the tree line, dozens of wolves stalked into the clearing. Tanner stepped from beneath Luca's wing and sniffed the air. He yipped once, softly, causing Deacon and the four wolves to glance back at him. The enemy pack was momentarily forgotten as they took in the sight of their Alpha's new form. Proving he was still Tanner, still the leader they'd bonded to, Tanner spoke through the bond calmly.

Ean, Vance, Ross, and Theran stand as close to Luca's legs as possible. His wings will offer cover. Engage only if they get through. Deacon, take up position at Luca's flank, protect the rear. Luca will protect the front. I doubt they'll get close enough to do harm, but be prepared just in case.

Without argument, they all moved into the positions Tanner ordered, the pack well-being taking precedence over any personal acrimony between members.

Engage only if they get through, what? Ean asked.

Tanner's answer was simple. *Us.*

More howls, yips, and vicious snarls filled the air as the McBane pack closed in on them from all sides. They were still thirty to forty feet away, moving extremely slowly, probably hoping their numbers alone would douse the wild dog pack's will to fight. Understanding the McBane pack mentality, knowing exactly how his father operated, allowed Tanner to remain calm, the relaxed emotion bleeding through the pack bond to settle all of them.

I think they're close enough, Tanner said. *Deacon, tornados, please. Five or six small ones will do.*

Luca felt Deacon's smile and watched as six whirling tornados spun up from the ground, lifting dirt, grass, and debris from the destroyed cabin, into the air. Once they reached the height of a three-story building, Deacon began moving them in a broad circle between them and the McBanes. The wind whipped around viciously as the cyclones moved, but the force of it seemed to be directed outward, away from them. The enemy howls were drowned out by the deafening sounds of destruction. Tanner turned his back on the massive forces of nature whirling around them and looked up at Luca with blazing eyes.

Set them on fire.

The command was simple, but Luca knew it to be impossible. Dirt and air didn't burn. The debris from the cabin would light but would burn out quickly once the fuel was consumed. He told Tanner as much.

Remember the break room? Deacon pushed in. *Fire's burning on top of water, in thin air? He can make it happen.*

Luca did remember the odd sight of flames existing where they shouldn't. He'd not given it much thought at the time, and he didn't have the time to analyze it now. He lifted his body, spread his wings, and sent a blast of fire toward the nearest tornado. In completely unnatural fire behavior, the flame hit the cyclone of wind, dirt, and debris, and then shot out around them like lightning to ignite the remaining tornados. Their little pack was now surrounded by a deadly ring of wind, smoke, and fire.

A blast of hatred lanced through the pack's psychic link. It shocked them all to the point Ross was halfway to the circle of swirling fire before anyone realized he'd moved. Tanner issued a thunderous command of *STOP* the exact instant Deacon screamed Ross's name. The white wolf shot back the thought of *Death will be mine* as he ran into the thick smoke and disappeared from sight. Deacon doubled over in a pain Luca and the others only experienced for a second. Tanner had blocked the link, denying them access to Ross's suffering as he ran through fire and flying debris, but nothing sheltered Deacon from the agony. A mating bond was too strong to divert. Luca had issues with the Elemental, but he never wished to inflict this sort of torture on him.

As Deacon slumped to the ground, Luca adjusted his stance, moving his large body over the prone Elemental to offer protection. The other wolves howled brokenly, but moved with him, keeping their group together. The only one who didn't follow was Tanner. He remained where he was, staring at the spot through which Ross had disappeared. Luca wasn't at all surprised the wind and fire remained active despite Deacon's collapse. Tanner was pulling the Elemental's powers, as well as Luca's, through the bond. Luca felt it. He imagined they all did. It was an uncomfortable sensation, like ants skittering over flesh.

Two McBane wolves found a way through the ring of swirling wind and fire into their protected circle. Ean, Theran, and Vance snapped and snarled as they ran to meet the invaders head-on. Right now, Tanner's pack had the advantage, but if more wolves like these two and Ross decided to risk it, they would find themselves outnumbered rather quickly.

Without looking back, and without his power wavering the slightest bit, Tanner spoke to them. *Stay here and stay together. I'll be back.* Tanner took off at a run, heading for the exact spot where Ross had disappeared. This time, however, as Tanner reached the edge of tornadic fire, the path ahead of him cleared. For the brief moment it took Tanner to cross the line, Luca saw the trees on the other side bending beneath the onslaught of wind, as rocks tumbled down the cliff face at the far end of the clearing.

A group of enemy wolves took advantage of the opening and charged through. Luca adjusted his position over Deacon, lowered his chest, and sent a stream of flame over the attacking wolves. Broken barks and howls of pain filled the air as Luca and his pack inflicted debilitating, but survivable, injury.

Chapter Nineteen

TANNER

As he exited the clearing, the calm from inside the circle of destruction was replaced by the chaos he'd incited outside it. He knew some of his father's pack would make it past the fire-tornados, some already had, but he trusted his pack was capable of defending themselves, even with Deacon out of commission. Luca was a force to be reckoned with on his own. The dragon was huge.

Many of the McBane wolves hunkered down within the relative safety of the tree line. If Tanner chose, he could easily expand the tornados into an ever-widening circular path to chase those who remained away, but his desire was to scare, not destroy. He only needed to protect his mate and his pack. Unlike Ross, Tanner only killed when absolutely necessary.

Stopping at the edge of the forest, Tanner lifted his nose and sniffed. He'd cut off Ross's connection to the rest of the pack, but he and Deacon continued to feel everything Ross felt until the wolf shifter died. The mating bond the wolf and Elemental shared guaranteed Deacon would suffer horribly until Ross's pain ended. The crazy wolf was badly injured, but if Tanner could find him in the next few minutes, Ross might survive. The wounds he sensed weren't life threatening themselves, but the blood loss was dangerous.

Tanner used his Alpha bond to track Ross to a spot where forest, river, and cliff met. Three McBane enforcers, massive wolves tasked as pack guards, had the injured wolf backed against the rocks, all three of them snarling and snapping their jaws aggressively. One of them was his oldest friend, Tyler, and he mourned the loss of their bond. To the depths of his soul, he believed if he could talk to Tyler then his friend might understand Tanner's pack wanted nothing more than to be left alone. Tyler was a pack enforcer following his Alpha's edicts, so shifting to speak was out of the question.

Despite the many burns, lacerations, and the piece of wood that had been driven through his front leg, rendering it virtually useless, Ross was fighting mad and ready to die. Beneath the layers of pain, fatigue, and raging hatred, Tanner felt Ross's deep love for Deacon and the fierce need to protect his mate. The emotions were familiar to Tanner on a cellular level, especially now with his own mate to love and protect.

Pulling more power from Luca, Tanner growled as his muscles bulged and expanded. The enforcers looked at him in horror as Tanner stomped the ground, making it shake, and a puff of smoke blasted from his nostrils. He didn't know what he looked like, but he must have been terrifying because all three wolves, even Tyler who knew him, had grown up with him, hunkered down, whimpering and shaking. The stench of fear and urine permeated the air before they took off running, disappearing deep into the trees. Once the threat was removed, Ross shifted back to his human form and smiled weakly. He lifted his arm, stared at the piece of wood impaling it only an inch below the elbow, and then lost consciousness, crumpling to the ground.

Deacon's pain subsided as the bond between mates was given a respite. Ross was injured badly, and he would likely have scars and a weak arm for the rest of his life, but he was alive. And Tanner had every intention of finding a way to bring him back from the cloud of insanity he was lost in. Tanner's fight response eased, and his size returned to normal, though he remained in wolf form. Luca's mind nudged against the block Tanner had erected to protect the others from Ross's pain. With Ross unconscious, he allowed the block to drop.

We're airborne. Your father's pack is retreating.

You're flying? With Deacon and three wolves?

I'm a dragon, Luca answered.

Tanner heard and felt the answer through his bond to three terrified wolves, which strengthened his original stance that a wolf's paws should never leave the ground. The roar of tornadic wind in the distance died out as Tanner released Deacon's power, leaving only the sounds of the forest, distant voices as his father's pack left, and Tanner's heavy breathing.

Find us where the creek meets the cliff, he told Luca as he moved to stand over Ross. He would maintain a stance of protection over Ross until Deacon and the rest of the pack arrived; only then would he shift back to human. The forest grew eerily silent as he waited for the others.

Not a bird, squirrel, or even the wind, disturbed the leaves or the brush. The soft trickle of water from the creek and Ross's occasional small movements were all Tanner heard. He blamed the unnatural silence on the mayhem he'd created. The fire-tornados had been deafening so now the quiet was more noticeable. His muscles were growing tired from the constant vigil he kept, still primed for a fight should the McBane pack return before Luca found them.

The snap of a twig caused Ross to stir, with a groan, and Tanner instantly snarling as his hackles rose. His father stepped through the trees on the other side of the river, in human form and seemingly alone, but Tanner didn't trust him. His father hadn't remained Alpha for forty years by being careless. There were others in wolf form hidden among the trees and foliage of the forest.

"When we tracked you here, we had no idea what you were capable of. Now, we know. This is your last chance to come to your senses, boy. To see the right way of things. Disband your abomination of a pack or it *will* be destroyed. Creatures like you cannot be allowed to live."

Each word his father spoke sent a dagger through his heart. Tanner had seen this version of his father before when he faced his enemies during Tanner's childhood. However, Tanner never imagined his father would turn on him. He was hurt enough when the pack disowned him for being gay. But his own father calling him a creature, referring to his pack as an abomination, and threatening to kill him caused a soul-deep pain and confusion. Tanner's stance weakened and he shifted. A dangerous move when facing an enemy, but the little boy inside him who'd always looked up to his father, mimicking everything he did, and was once proud to be Ethan McBane's son, needed to understand.

"Why?" Tanner asked. "Why such vile hatred? We've done nothing to you or anyone else."

"It's bad enough you chose to be gay—"

"It wasn't a choice."

"But this is a whole new level of shame I will not tolerate. I will not allow my son to become a Chevalier," his father yelled.

His voice echoed off the cliff, loud in the silence of the forest. Turning his back in dismissal, his father walked back into the forest. Tanner's hurt, confusion, and intense need to understand had him calling out to his father.

"What's a Chevalier?" As his father retreated, other wolves appeared from the underbrush to follow their Alpha. None looked back at him. Tanner tensed, ready for anything. "We're not evil. We deserve to be loved and to live in peace," he shouted.

Whatever a Chevalier was, was obviously not good. Or at the very least, his father perceived it to be bad. Tanner heard soft footfalls behind him and instantly relaxed, breathing out a sigh of relief. He felt his pack drawing near, Luca's smoky scent and Deacon's stormy emotions reaching him before the men themselves. Tanner turned toward his mate, utterly defeated despite the confrontation ending in their favor without having to kill anyone, and accepted the clothing Luca offered. The shirt and pants were dirty and ripped, Luca having pulled them from the rubble of the cabin, but the remaining fabric still gave his vulnerable human skin some protection against the elements.

"You got here faster than I expected," Tanner told Luca as he pulled the T-shirt over his head.

"Deacon knew exactly where he was," Luca said, nodding toward Ross where he lay on the ground. "As for me and you, we have a strong mating bond, too, pup. I knew where you were, who you were with." Luca glanced in the direction Tanner's father had gone. "I can feel everything you feel. Tell me you're okay."

"I'm really not," Tanner told him. "But I will be." The words came out strong, though he wasn't entirely sure they were true. He might never be okay again. Pushing his own grief aside, he focused on the needs of his pack. They needed food, shelter, and medical attention. Tanner looked down at Ross's burned and bloody body, and took comfort from the steady rise and fall of his chest.

Deacon kissed his mate gently, eyes glassy with unshed tears, and then he surveyed the injuries Ross had suffered. His fingers wrapped around the wood impaling Ross's arm, and he looked up at Tanner with a pained expression. Tanner experienced Deacon's agony, fear, and the horrible sense of failure at protecting his mate, as if they were his own emotions. Luca stood at a distance, surveying the surrounding forest. Theran and Vance, still in wolf form, moved closer to Ross and Deacon, pressing their noses to one or the other of them in pack solidarity. Ean lowered to his knees on the fallen leaves beside Deacon and placed a hand on Deacon's shoulder, the other on Ross's knee. Tanner eased between Theran and Vance, affectionately pulling their ears as he knelt beside Ross, opposite Deacon.

"He'll survive and heal," Tanner told them. "It will take all of us, together, but we can help ease his pain and get him through this." Tanner made eye contact with each of his pack members before looking up to catch the swirling golden-brown gaze of his mate. "I need you to pull the wood from his arm," Tanner told Luca, who nodded and knelt beside Ross's injured arm, getting into position.

To Deacon, Tanner said, "Place one hand over the entrance wound and the other over the exit wound and use fire to cauterize them once the wood is removed. The rest of you push as much serenity at me as you can. I'll feed it into Ross to help dull the pain." It had the added benefit of dulling Deacon's suffering as well, given he felt everything his mate did—including the cauterization of the wounds by his own hands.

Placing one hand on Ross's forehead, the other over his heart, Tanner nodded to Luca and Deacon. Tanner channeled every feeling of love, happiness, and tranquility from the pack into Ross. The lines of pain creasing both Ross's and Deacon's faces smoothed out, their bodies relaxing, despite the immense pain created when Luca quickly, but efficiently, pulled the wood from Ross's arm. Deacon pressed his palms to the open wound and sighed in relief when the searing pain morphed into pleasant tingles.

Once the job was done, Deacon lay on the ground and pulled his mate into his arms, careful of his other smaller lacerations and burns. Deacon spooned behind and wrapped around his wolf mate protectively. The sense of peace Tanner was feeding them lulled them both into a deep sleep that would help them heal, at least from the psychological trauma of recent events. Ross's physical injuries would take longer to heal. Theran and Vance curled up against Deacon's back and knees, offering their support and comfort. Ean sagged where he sat. The rush of fear and adrenaline was now leaving their bodies, leaving them all drained of energy. Tanner wasn't immune to the adrenaline crash, and he was also fatigued from the high level of exertion it took to maintain the level of power he'd channeled, even for the short time he'd done it.

Tanner crawled a few feet away and leaned heavily against the nearest tree. He was physically, mentally, and emotionally exhausted. He fought the fatigue trying to pull him under but knew on a deeper level unconsciousness was inevitable. He felt Luca's presence, smelled that bonfire scent, even before the dragon's strong arms wrapped around him. Luca pulled Tanner across his lap and Tanner tucked his face against Luca's chest.

"You overdid it, my sweet boy. Pushed your power too hard, too far."

"For you," Tanner mumbled, snuggling into Luca's warmth. Luca kissed the top of his head, nuzzling into Tanner's hair, as his embrace tightened. For the first time in months, since being disowned, Tanner felt safe, accepted, and loved. A smile tugged at his lips as he relaxed in his mate's arms and allowed sleep to claim him.

Chapter Twenty

LUCA

"I found Chevalier," Tanner said.

Luca closed the book he was reading on dragon history and looked at his mate across the table. They sat in Luca's expansive library, researching everything available to learn more about wolf shifters, dragon shifters, and Elementals, specifically looking for any information on previous interspecies matings such as theirs. Matthias had come through on his promise to send Luca books that might offer some help, though he still felt the older dragon was holding back vital information. Some of the tomes were extremely old while others were fairly recent, having been written within Luca's lifetime.

The books had yet to give up their secrets, but Luca refused to believe he and Tanner were the first dragon/wolf pair in the history of the world, or that Deacon and Ross were the first of their kind. It seemed impossible; and damn it, Luca remembered reading about it as a boy. Tanner had been intently focused on his father's last words to him. He was determined to find out what a Chevalier was; to that end, he'd apparently been successful. Whatever Tanner had just read must have been upsetting, though, because he was pale and he worried at his bottom lip with his teeth.

"What is it, pup?"

"Not a what. A who," Tanner corrected softly. "The Chevaliers were a mated wolf/dragon couple in France. They were powerful in their own right because of the same mating bond we have, and they didn't shy away from using those powers. Their children then mated with various other paranormals and became...monstrous. The whole family was evil. The things they did, Luca." Tanner's horror over what he'd read bled through the bond to Luca.

"Tanner—"

"They hunted humans," Tanner interrupted. "They'd capture them and torture them for sport, and then when they grew tired of them, they ate them. They terrorized and destroyed entire villages. Their abilities corrupted them, and they wielded those powers in the most horrific ways—"

"Tanner," Luca growled, interrupting the tirade Tanner was getting into. The pup was already close to panic. "The offspring of a dragon/wolf couple did horrible things," he pointed out. "Hybrids with a genetic makeup we don't need to worry about because we're both male. Unless there's something about wolf shifters you haven't told me."

Luca's attempt at injecting some levity into the situation was met with an indulgent smile from Tanner. "No. I can't have puppies any more than you can lay eggs."

"About that..." Luca scratched his head and peeked up at Tanner through his lashes.

"Oh my god! You can have babies?"

Tanner's stricken expression made Luca burst into laughter. He couldn't have stopped it if he'd tried.

"I was kidding, my sweet boy."

"Damn," Tanner breathed. He relaxed substantially, which had been Luca's aim. "Listen, I'm not worried about kids. I'm worried about me. I mated you, but yours isn't the only power I have access to. I have four other wolves, one of which is suffering blood lust, and I have a strong bond with his Elemental mate. From what I've read, the Chevalier children weren't evil because they were dragon/wolf hybrids. They became evil once they mated and other paranormal powers were added to the mix. It took an entire dragon horde, a coven of vampires, and a storm of Elementals, along with a perfectly placed attack at the top of a cliff to kill them. They were *that* powerful." Tanner fisted his hair and tugged. "Fuck, Luca, what if my dad is right? What if they're *all* right? Maybe it's not hatred, fear, and intolerance we're facing, but a simple fact we can't see because our love makes us blind. What if I really am dangerous and don't know it?"

The panic feeding through the bond made Luca a bit nauseous. Tanner was completely freaking out over this. Luca rose from his chair and circled the table to pull Tanner out of his seat and into his arms. He kissed the top of Tanner's head before nuzzling into his hair. As far as Luca was concerned, there was no comparison between the Chevalier family and his mate, though their story sounded eerily familiar. He glanced at the edge of the book peeking out from beneath the yellowed pages. Reddish-brown. Maybe Matthias really had come through for him.

Luca smiled slightly and sighed. He was more likely to be evil than Tanner, given his initial thoughts of power and control when he'd first met Tanner. His pup was powerful, no denying it, but that power was tempered by compassion, humility, and honor. The very traits that had pushed Tanner to become Alpha to a wild dog pack were the same ones that prevented him from using his powers against others maliciously.

"There are far too many variables to make the connection between them and you. Their home life, genetics unique to hybrids, circumstances, environment, outside forces, not to mention the sanity and personalities of their individual mates. We know nothing about any of that. There's no reason to expect you'd be anything like them. We are dealing with fear and prejudice, sweet boy, just as we've always known."

Tanner relaxed into Luca's embrace. He finally released the grip he had on his hair and wrapped his arms around Luca's waist, pressing his face into Luca's neck.

"Besides, did you look at the dates?" Luca asked, remembering how long ago the events they were discussing had occurred.

"The dates?" Tanner parroted.

"The Chevalier family was wiped out over four hundred years ago. They're nothing more than a historical event, like the Spanish Inquisition or Salem Witch Trials."

"Lovely analogy," Tanner quipped.

Luca suppressed the shiver Tanner's lips created as they pressed against the mating bite. He cleared his throat and focused on the conversation. There'd be plenty of time to lose himself in Tanner's touch later.

"My point is just because it happened once, doesn't mean it will happen again."

"Except it's a known fact history repeats itself. Witch trials, lynch mobs, terrorist attacks. There's always a religious war of some kind going on, it seems," Tanner argued. Luca sighed. "But I get what you're saying."

Luca adjusted Tanner in his arms to look into Tanner's eyes without releasing his hold. "Don't let self-doubt and uncertainty take hold. Don't let your father and his hatred in. You're doing a great job with your pack. You're an amazing Alpha."

"He's my father, Luca. He taught me everything I know about how to be a good Alpha. He'll always be inside my head, whether I like it or not. I just... I wanted to understand where he was coming from, and now I do." Tanner extricated himself from Luca's hold and closed the book he'd been reading. The oxidized silver emblem Luca remembered graced the cover. "I only understand as far as the Chevaliers are concerned, though. I don't think I'll ever understand his stance on my sexuality."

Luca's gaze tracked Tanner as he moved to stand before the sliding glass doors that opened to a balcony overlooking the backyard. Tanner was tense and scared, and Luca had no idea how to make him feel better. Perhaps only time would ease Tanner's concerns. Luca approached his mate from behind, slid his arms around his waist, and pulled Tanner against his chest.

The memory of standing in front of the wall of windows in his office with Tanner, gazing out the window at the cityscape, played through Luca's mind. They'd just met, but even then, Luca had known Tanner was something special. Never had he imagined they'd find themselves here, in this particular situation, surrounded by these particular people. Deacon relaxed in a lounge chair on the patio below, watching his mate and Vance play with each other in wolf form. Theran and Ean were out of sight, but Luca sensed them out there.

"You're not like them," Luca murmured into Tanner's ear. "Your pack, *our* pack, is not dangerous. I have complete faith in your ability to control this power you have."

The words *You have to say that because you're my mate* whispered through his mind. Luca spun Tanner in his arms and kissed him.

You know I'm not just saying it. You feel the truth.

Yes, I do.

Tanner threaded his fingers through Luca's hair, kissing back with equal intensity. Luca lifted him off the floor, and Tanner hooked his legs around Luca's waist. In a matter of seconds, Luca had them across the hall in their bedroom where he lowered Tanner to his back on the mattress. He truly loved their ability to speak to each other telepathically. It allowed him to whisper sweet nothings to his lover while never taking his lips off him. They broke their kisses and stopped touching long enough to pull their shirts off over their heads. Determined to show Tanner he was loved, Luca took his time. He kissed every inch of skin, made love to him slowly, and made certain when they crested the peak, they did so together.

Chapter Twenty-One

DEACON

Ross ran around the backyard, chasing Vance like an excited puppy. Deacon felt the twinge of pain every so often, when Ross put too much weight on his front leg or landed at an odd angle, but the pain was temporary and didn't stop the wolf's activity. Ross simply adjusted his weight distribution and moved on. Deacon hadn't managed to identify exactly what he was feeling, but something inside Ross had changed. Oftentimes, he'd succeed in pushing the sensation aside, but at night, in the dark and silence when Ross was tucked safely against him, Deacon allowed the hope living in the depths of his soul to surface. It was the desperate hope Ross's insanity might be dissipating.

Ean and Theran sat at the small metal table right outside the patio doors playing a game of chess. Deacon wasn't sure how pack members with a bond were able to play a game of strategy with each other, but the two managed. They were settling into their roles as enforcers nicely, while Vance happily continued his Omega role as pack caretaker. Deacon currently held the role of Beta, but it didn't feel right. He was a powerful Elemental unaccustomed to being subservient. If any of the other wolves showed an inclination to challenge him, he'd be happy to step down.

He leaned back on the lounge chair at the edge of the patio, where he enjoyed the shade from the house while still watching his wolf mate play. He winced a bit when Vance tackled Ross to the ground, the two wolves wresting and nipping at each other. Small pains shot through his body, referred pain from Ross's injuries, but he remained seated. This playtime was important for Ross, the mock fighting and hunting helped strengthen his muscles and taught him how to survive despite his altered physical ability.

At the soft hiss of the patio doors sliding open, he turned to see Luca exiting the house. Despite their original animosity, he and the dragon had found common ground and were comfortable with their positions as mates within a pack of wolves. Luca watched Ean make a move on the chessboard, and then glanced out at the two wolves tussling in the yard. With a slight shake of his head, he walked over to where Deacon sat and claimed the matching lounge chair beside him.

"Tanner asleep?" Deacon asked. The entire pack had heard their Alpha and his mate making love about an hour before.

"Yes, thankfully."

Their Alpha had been pulling long hours over the past few weeks. The first two days after the confrontation with the McBane pack, Tanner had done nothing but sleep. His body had shut down after the exertion required to channel both Deacon's and Luca's powers the way he had. Upon waking, however, he'd been driven to find a reason for the racism and hatred his pack was facing from wolves and dragons alike. Deacon had to admit, he didn't understand it, either. If the species weren't meant to intermingle, then why was his mate a wolf shifter? Why was Tanner's mate a dragon shifter?

Tanner spent hours reading through history books from Luca's immense library and whatever else had been delivered from Luca's old friend. He was learning everything he could about the different paranormal creatures inhabiting their world, their cultures and beliefs, and most importantly, their special abilities.

"That boy has become voracious for knowledge," Luca said.

"Well, forewarned is forearmed, and all that," Deacon told him.

"Yes," Luca agreed with a sigh. "Sad, but true. I hate having to defend my love for him against my own kind, against my own damn family."

Deacon hadn't yet had to face that problem, but he experienced the betrayal Luca and Tanner felt through the bond, diminished as the emotion was. Everyone felt Tanner's tense presence seconds before he stepped through the patio doors, all eyes turning to him. He wore only rumpled sleep pants, his brow creased and nostrils flaring as he scented the air. Vance and Ross stopped playing; Ean and Theran stood and flanked their Alpha. Picking up on the slight change in the air, Luca and Deacon rose to their feet. Ross trotted over to stand in front of Deacon, the stance he took one of defense.

"We have company," Tanner announced as a blur of motion whipped across the grass between Vance and the rest of the pack.

Watching one of their pack being separated from the rest resulted in growls and raised tension. Uncaring of the clothes being torn and ruined,

Ean and Theran shifted, snarling as they stalked to the edge of the patio, the three shifted wolves more than prepared to attack whoever, or whatever, was threatening their friend. The blur of motion stopped to reveal a pale-skinned man with ice-blue eyes and white hair that hung to mid-back. The man looked vaguely familiar to Deacon. Perhaps someone they'd run into at Elysium. The club was always packed with paranormals of varying kinds.

Vance crouched, not in defense as Deacon expected, but in shock. The entire pack felt his surprise as it rippled through the bond. The man stared down at the tawny wolf, fangs in full view. Tanner stepped off the patio into the grass, drawing the paranormal's attention to the rest of the pack. High cheekbones and angular features suggested the man had Native American roots. Deacon spread his fingers, summoning the element of lightning to the palms of his hands, ready to strike and defend at a moment's notice.

"What do you want, vampire?" Tanner asked.

The vampire gracefully turned his gaze back to Vance, who whined and took a small step back.

"My name is Sakima, and I want *him.*"

Vance began to shake and realization dawned on the entire pack at once, even before Vance gave voice to the truth.

Alpha. He's my mate.

Deacon was aware Tanner and Luca hadn't known they were mates on sight, but he and Ross had. Now, it appeared Vance and the vampire did. As Sakima squatted down to Vance's level, his eyes never once straying from the wolf, Deacon wondered what added benefit and trouble would come with the vampire's addition to the pack. Without a doubt, things were about to become far more interesting—and dangerous.

Hearts of Blood

Chapter One

SAKIMA

Sakima glanced around the yard at the wolf shifters, both in human and wolf form, before settling his gaze on the one he'd come for—his destined companion. He had waited hundreds of years for this creature to arrive. The beautiful golden-brown wolf whined and took a small step back, crouched in wariness, tail tucked.

"What do you want, vampire?" the Alpha asked.

"My name is Sakima Hawke, and I want him," Sakima answered as he took in the tawny wolf.

The wolf began to shake, making Sakima's skin itch. This creature was his destined companion; he should never be fearful of him. Sakima squatted so he was eye level with his wolf, his gaze never straying from him, in an attempt to show through action he was not a threat. He'd known the moment the tawny-haired man had brushed against him at Elysium they were meant to be together, but the place had been packed that night and the wolf shifter had quickly melted away into the throng. Sakima had searched the club, attempting to pick the man out from the crowd, but the wolf shifter had turned out to be quite elusive. He'd lost the wolf's scent for weeks before finding it again quite suddenly moments ago while on his way home.

It was an act of the fates Sakima had decided on a leisurely stroll rather than traveling home at hyperspeed after visiting one of his oldest friends: a human donor who was declining in health. Excitement he'd not felt in decades thrummed through his veins at the sight of the wolf now crouched before him. The sharp tang of fear wafting from him increased Sakima's discomfort. Perhaps the wolf wasn't aware of what they were to each other yet, though it was more likely he was simply uneducated about vampires. Sakima was well aware of the fear his kind generated. Too many rumors, myths, and misunderstandings circulated about vampires.

Many believed they were the walking dead, that anyone they fed from would become a vampire as well, but that was all fallacy. Sakima was no more dead than anyone else present, though he knew he appeared to be with his pale skin, long white hair, and ice-blue eyes. He could love, mate, and feed from his partner without changing the beautiful creature. Sakima would take great care in helping his destined understand he was no more of a threat than the Elemental, dragon, or Alpha he kept company with, each of whom had their own myths and rumors.

Desire to touch the gorgeous animal before him had Sakima extending a hand. He did so with extreme caution, so as not to frighten the wolf further, but was unsuccessful. The wolf curled into himself, becoming as small as his bulk would allow, crouching lower to the ground on shaky legs, ears flattened to his skull. Sakima lowered his hand to the grass but otherwise remained still. Instilling trust with a shifter while they were in animal form being ruled a great deal by their animal instincts was difficult. This would be far easier if the young man would shift back to human, though Sakima understood why he wouldn't do so at this moment. When the man shifted, he would be naked, which the shifter may view as a vulnerability in his human form.

"You must know I won't hurt you," Sakima said softly. "We are destined companions."

The wolf whined and turned to the pack leader. If Sakima understood wolf shifters well, there was a bond between his wolf and the Alpha that allowed them to speak telepathically. He'd never been jealous of such a thing before, but he didn't like his fated companion being able to communicate telepathically with anyone other than him. Unfortunately, the telepathic bond was an inevitable part of being in a wolf pack. And if he wanted to claim this wolf shifter, he would have to accept the pack as a whole because there would be no removing his companion from them. Not safely. Sakima rose to his feet, his heart sinking a bit when his wolf scurried away to hide within the house. He gave no reaction outwardly, but he gave a mental sigh as he turned to face the Alpha.

"My apologies," the Alpha said. "I asked him to go inside for a moment. He's a bit overwhelmed."

"Frightened, you mean," Sakima corrected.

The Alpha wasn't concerned with semantics. "We've all been through quite a lot recently, and this is a bit of a surprise. I'm sure you understand...Sakima? May I call you that?"

Sakima inclined his head in acceptance. "And you would be?"

"Tanner McBane. I'm the Alpha, and Vance is a member of my pack."

Vance. A unique name for a uniquely beautiful wolf. Sakima scanned the "pack," his gaze drifting from a gray wolf to a gray-and-brown wolf to a dragon to a white wolf with wild eyes to an Elemental, finally coming to rest once again on the Alpha.

"Quite the unconventional pack, if I may say."

"Yes, I know."

"Word has spread through the paranormal ranks of a pack of outcasts who have gained more power than is considered safe or wise. I feel I should be concerned for the welfare of my destined companion being bonded to such a pack."

The statement was met with several growls and a strong wind that only affected Sakima, whipping his long hair in every direction. Sakima smiled. Vance was clearly cared for and protected. Tanner glanced at the dragon on his left.

"Have you ever heard of a wolf mating a vampire? Chevaliers aside."

"No," the dragon answered. "But I'd never before heard of a wolf mating an Elemental either. Or a dragon."

The expression that passed between dragon and Alpha was not missed by Sakima. The name Chevalier shook him, but he pushed the memory aside—a centuries-old mistake best left to the dust of time.

"So, the rumors are true," Sakima said.

"What rumors?" the Elemental asked.

"Of same-sex, interspecies matings taking place openly. I had hoped, given what I now know of my own destined companion, but had remained skeptical," Sakima answered.

By way of introduction, Tanner said, "The dragon shifter is Luca. He's my mate. The Elemental is Deacon and his mate is the white wolf, Ross. The gray wolf is Ean, and the grayish brown wolf is Theran. If you truly plan to claim Vance as your mate, you, too, will be an openly mated interspecies couple. You need to be comfortable with that if you're going to become part of the pack."

Sakima showed plenty of fang when he spoke. "Oh, I have every intention of claiming my fated mate, *Alpha*, but I said nothing of joining your pack."

Movement at the patio doors drew Sakima's attention. Vance in human form was as handsome as his wolf was beautiful; golden-brown hair and the lithe, toned physique all wolf shifters possessed. Those hazel eyes showed fear and hesitation, but also recognition, making Sakima believe Vance knew they were destined companions. Vance simply wasn't accepting it, yet.

"You would risk his safety and sanity by taking him from his pack, severing his pack bond? What kind of mate would do such a thing?" Deacon asked through clenched teeth.

Sakima was surprised by the vehemence and animosity coming from the Elemental. He'd made the simple suggestion that claiming his wolf did not necessarily equate to him joining the pack. Nothing more. Though perhaps removing his destined companion was something to consider, given the volatile nature the pack exuded.

"I won't leave my pack," Vance said softly.

His voice was melodic to Sakima's ears. Despite the fear and uncertainty, Vance's words didn't waver. They were strong and decisive, despite the fact the wolf was still hiding behind the pack. Vance had donned a pair of shorts and a tank top, leaving his toned arms, legs, and feet bared to Sakima's perusal, and he soaked in the sight.

"I know what I'm about to suggest will be difficult for you," Tanner said. "But I think you should leave. Perhaps stay away for a few days to give Vance time to acclimate to the idea of having a vampire for a mate."

"Not as difficult as you might think," Sakima said.

He'd been living a solitary life for nearly forty years, and he planned to use the time apart from Vance to prepare for the wolf to join him. He moved with vampiric speed past the pack to stand before Vance. While he was willing to leave for a short time, he wouldn't allow his companion to put the pack between them. When he stopped, he stood face-to-face with his beautiful man. Vance yelped and jumped back, but Sakima caught him with an arm around his waist, aborting any attempt at escape. Heat immediately seeped through the cloth of his shirt, warming his skin.

"Until next time, pet."

Sakima placed a chaste kiss on Vance's lips so as not to cut him with his fangs. Not yet. He would draw blood from Vance only after they became lovers, and Vance demonstrated his willingness. As quickly as he had appeared before Vance, he disappeared, leaving the outcast pack and his destined mate behind. It was a temporary situation, after all. Now that he knew where his wolf companion was, he felt far more relaxed and willing to let things progress at a pace comfortable for Vance.

*

He continued in hyperspeed until he reached the loft above Elysium he called home. While the wolf would be most comfortable near trees and wildlife, Sakima could live anywhere. There were no rules truly governing what, or who, he could feed from and life of some kind could be found everywhere. In all reality, wolves and dragons could eat humans, but there was something about shifters being partly human that made most of them shy away from the idea. Sakima could well understand. He'd been desperate once, long ago, and fed off one of his own kind. While his hunger had been sated, the act had felt...wrong.

Sakima stopped at his front door, pulled out his keys, and entered his loft. The heartbeats of three employees downstairs thumped softly against his eardrums. Though quiet for now, soon the club would open, and he would be hit with hundreds of heartbeats, thundering music, and the scent of paranormals from every species. Taking a deep breath, he reveled in the scent of his wolf still lingering on his clothes. Such a brief moment of contact, but the combined smells of wolf and man would be forever burned in Sakima's memory.

One particular heartbeat drew closer, so he lingered in the entryway. A knock sounded on the shiny wood surface a moment later, and he opened the door to find his head bartender, Colby, standing on the other side. Sakima's nostrils flared as he once again attempted to identify Colby's species. He knew he was paranormal, but the boy had a myriad of scents clinging to him, and those scents changed almost daily. It was intriguing and annoying.

"Are you well?" Sakima asked.

No one bothered him at home due to an unspoken rule that he not be approached unless he was in his office, or on the main floor of the club working. Otherwise, you might be feasted upon. The rumor was wholly untrue, but Sakima valued his privacy enough to allow the assumption to stand. He momentarily wondered why the young bartender never appeared to be afraid of him, and how Colby always seemed to know where to find him.

"I'm quite fine, thank you," Colby said.

Colby's face remained expressionless, as was typical when he wasn't tending bar. Behind the mahogany, the boy was a flirt, a tease, the unobtainable dream. With his long brown hair and sparkling eyes, he earned abundant tips from first-timers and regulars alike. Away from the bar, he was as unapproachable as Sakima. The only thing that did not change was Colby's dry, sarcastic humor. His manner allowed him to deliver insults disguised as playful ribbing that left the recipient unaware of the fact Colby truly found them repulsive. Sakima spent hours at the end of the bar enjoying the show as the boy hurled his daggers with a flirtatious smile on his face. Sakima cocked his head to the side.

"I'm restocking the bar and it appears we've sold out of vanilla vodka," Colby told him.

Sakima did inventory on a weekly basis, and because of this rigid schedule, Elysium rarely sold out of anything. In fact, it had been years since the last occurrence.

"How is that possible?" he asked.

"Well," Colby said. "It's a bar and we sell drinks. All night. And some of those drinks require vanilla vodka...that we've sold out of."

Sakima couldn't decide if he wanted to slap the boy or smile at him. Colby was often entertaining and infuriating simultaneously. Rather than decide, Sakima kept a straight face as he turned away from the bartender and walked into his home office. He kept quite a bit of cash inside the bottom drawer of his desk. He pulled out a few one-hundred-dollar bills and then returned to Colby, who still stood outside the door. Colby's eyes raked over Sakima when he held the money to him. He wrinkled his nose.

"You smell like dog," he said.

Sakima ignored the comment. Vance was not a dog; he was a wolf shifter. There was a paranormal world of difference.

"Go to Hallahan's and buy as much vanilla vodka as the money will allow. I want the receipt and the change."

Colby rolled his eyes. "Like I'm stupid," he mumbled as he headed back down the stairs to the building's exit. Sakima tracked the progress of the bartender's heartbeat until the steady thump melded into the hundreds of other heartbeats out on the street.

Chapter Two

VANCE

Damn, he was dizzy. The vampire had popped up in front of him, grabbed him, kissed him, and disappeared again all before the rest of the pack had managed to turn around at his yelp of surprise. And why had Sakima called him pet? He was the vampire's mate, not his pet. He may resemble a dog in some aspects, but that didn't mean he was one. Vance was terrified and intrigued at the same time and completely lost. He was still reeling from the situation he'd found himself in with his new pack.

Deacon had always been a part of them, slotting easily into their meager group, but the dragon was something else entirely. He was an entity none of them had expected. Now they were faced with Vance's mate being something other than wolf, and he wondered if they were all drawn together by fate because they were all destined to be with someone outside their own kind. Thinking such thoughts was heavy and made his brain hurt.

Vance pressed his fingers to his lips. He could still feel the vampire's featherlight kiss. His body still thrummed from the too-brief touch of mouths, the heat that had engulfed him when Sakima's arm wrapped around his waist, and the knowledge that he could have the feeling forever if he were brave enough to make the claim. Unfortunately, Vance wasn't brave. He never had been.

"You're okay," Tanner said. "Just take a minute and breathe."

The other wolves shifted to human and then surrounded him, offering him comfort. The entire pack knew what he was feeling because the shock of the past several minutes had rendered him incapable of stemming the flow of his emotions through the bond. They had felt everything he had. He closed the connection sluggishly, but completely.

"I'm sorry," Vance murmured. "I just didn't expect...*him*."

Brain fried, he wasn't able to think of an adequate word to describe everything his mate was. Sakima was only an inch or two taller than

Vance's own five feet eleven. He was lean and strong, owing largely to his vampire nature. Vance had felt the controlled power in Sakima's hold but could only fantasize about what the man's body looked like beneath the jeans and loose-fitting, long-sleeved T-shirt. He wondered if the vampire's pale skin would be marred in any way or perfectly smooth. He wondered how all that long white hair would feel trailing over his back, or what it would feel like when the vampire sank his fangs into his neck and claimed him.

Vance shuddered at the highly sexualized images forming in his mind. He didn't particularly care for the idea of becoming a vampire. He wasn't even sure how that worked with him being a wolf shifter. His kind were already prone to blood lust. Ross and countless others before him were solid proof. He had no idea what a wolf shifter-turned-vampire might be capable of, but his imagination was supplying plenty of horrific ideas. It was too much to take in. Vance whirled and briskly walked to the front of the house. He pulled the tank top over his head, tossing the shirt onto the sofa as he passed. At the door, he removed his shorts.

"Where are you going?" Theran asked, following Vance into the living room. His natural-born concern for his pack was why he'd been the obvious choice for pack enforcer.

"Given everything that's happening, it might not be smart to run around out there alone right now," Deacon called from the dining area.

The house had been designed and built by Luca so the cavernous open floor plan could accommodate his dragon form. It also offered ample space for the entire pack to congregate and voice their opinions. Vance shifted prematurely, unable to keep his wolf in check any longer, and pawed at the front door when he got to it. He knew their situation was dangerous, but he needed to run. Ross clapped his hands and practically skipped to the front door, pulling it open with his good arm and grinning. The wolf was healing from the physical wounds he'd sustained in battle, but his psyche was still way off-kilter. Vance yipped his thanks to his friend but was gently pushed aside by Tanner. The Alpha was bigger than him; everyone was bigger than him, even in wolf form, and Tanner preceded Vance out the front door. On the front porch, Tanner stopped and regarded him.

I've been where you are. You need to run, to think. I had Luca to watch my back, and now I'll watch yours. Run where you wish. I'll follow.

Vance sidled up beside Tanner and licked the side of his snout in a show of affection.

Thank you, Alpha.

Trusting Tanner to keep up and knowing the pack bond would keep them connected, Vance took off down the driveway, rounded the corner at the bottom of the street, and made a beeline for the forest a couple of miles down the road. His mind cleared as his paws pounded the pavement and the wind ruffled his fur. The sun was still high and the sky pure blue, but humans saw what they wanted to see, mistaking them for stray dogs rather than wolves, and left them alone. As they entered the cover of trees, Vance let his wolf fully take over.

He jumped over rocks, dodged around trees, and tried to bite pesky insects from the air as he ran. At one point, he decided to mess with his Alpha by running tight circles around him and nipping at his tail. Tanner snarled and yipped when Vance caught his tail wrong. In playful retaliation, Tanner bit Vance's legs and ears, but otherwise didn't engage. Both wolves understood there was no vicious intent behind the attacks.

About a hundred feet ahead was the creek where they'd caught the bear during their first pack hunt. It seemed like ages ago Vance had felt the pressure in his chest ease and the fog in his mind lift as the pack bond solidified. They all owed Tanner a huge debt for taking on their little ragtag group; especially given how Ross had already fallen prey to the blood lust, and how close Vance, Theran, and Ean had been to succumbing to the same. Wolf shifters were pack animals, and they needed the bond that existed within the pack to stay healthy and sane. Vance lapped at the cold, clear water before sprawling out on the rocks nearby. Tanner lay in the grass a few feet away.

Were you scared? Vance asked, knowing Tanner would understand the larger underlying question. He'd never considered finding his mate would be so frightening, and he needed to know if he was the only one.

Yes, Tanner answered. *I didn't know what it would mean for me to mate with a dragon. I didn't know what it would mean to become Alpha to a wild dog pack suffering blood lust, or what it would mean to bond to an Elemental.*

But you did it anyway.

Yes. And now I'm faced with potentially being bonded to a vampire. I don't know what that will mean for you, or me and the pack, and I'm terrified.

Will you try to stop me if I choose to mate with him? Vance asked. He wasn't sure what he would do if the Alpha turned his back on him now, but he had to know.

Never. Tanner snorted, rose to his feet, and walked to the creek for a drink. *That would be hypocritical, and I refuse to become my father.* After lapping at the water, Tanner scaled the rocks to lay beside Vance. Tanner began licking the ear closest to him as he continued to speak through the bond. *My father disowned me for being gay. Why were you without a pack?*

Vance sighed, leaning into Tanner's ministrations on his ear and taking comfort from the connection. He hated thinking about his family. The memories were painful. *My father was Beta. He was never affectionate toward me. More like he put up with me. He and my mother weren't true mates, and I don't think they actually loved each other. I've always felt like it may have been a forced pairing because as soon as his true mate came along, he kicked us out without a second thought.* Vance lowered his head to the rock between his paws, and Tanner rested his snout across the back of Vance's neck. *We were taken in by a neighboring pack. I left a year ago after my mom died. A buffalo kicked her in the head during a hunt.*

Were you Omega in your other packs too? Tanner asked.

Yes. Part of why my father hated me so much, I think. I wasn't as dominant as him. I wasn't as ambitious as he thought I should be. I accepted my status even if I wasn't happy in it at first. Why? Is it important?

No, Tanner answered, lifting his head and sniffing the air. *It just occurred to me I never asked about any of you. I'll do better.*

The bond will help. We wish your dragon would allow us to get to know him better. We're still afraid of him a little, Vance admitted.

Give Luca time. Pack life and the bond is natural for us, but completely unnatural for our mates. I think you'll find Sakima will struggle with it too.

An internal shiver coursed through Vance's body at the vampire's name. The man's arrival had completely thrown him at a time he'd only begun getting his feet back under him. Now that Vance had taken time to calm down and get his thoughts in order, he was able to control what fed through the bond to the others. He didn't particularly want everyone to know what he was thinking at every moment. It was bad enough the entire pack was treated to Ross's uncensored thoughts from time to time when Deacon was caught off guard. The Elemental had an amazing gift for cutting Ross's thoughts off from the rest of the pack.

The last thing Vance wanted was for his Alpha to know the deeper emotions he was struggling with at the moment. Tanner had asked Sakima to stay away for a few days, and Vance hated the idea. He hadn't objected because he didn't quite understand why he was bothered by the separation. The vampire scared him, mostly because he didn't know much about them, but the idea of being apart from Sakima for an extended length of time didn't sit well.

After half an hour of listening to the gurgling creek and soaking in the sun that squeaked through the canopy to dapple the rocks in warmth, Vance followed Tanner up the path to the parking area where Theran waited in the SUV. They shifted in the back seat and dressed in the extra clothing they stored in all the vehicles. Vance glanced at Tanner when Theran turned right out of the lot instead of left.

"Theran?" Tanner asked softly. "What is Luca doing? He's blocked the bond."

Half a mile up the road, Theran eased the SUV to the side of the road, stopping behind Deacon's red sedan. Ross and Ean waved at them from their perch on the trunk. Deacon leaned against the hood of the car, arms crossed.

"Nice of you to join us," Deacon said when they all exited the SUV.

Vance and Theran joined Ross and Ean at the back of the car while Tanner approached Deacon. Tanner's posture was stiff, but not the tiniest hint of what he was feeling bled into the bond. The Alpha had quickly become an expert at shutting the telepathy off whenever he chose. Vance had never known another Alpha who could do that so completely. But then, he'd never met another Alpha who could manage any of the things Tanner was capable of doing. While the Alpha and Beta spoke to each other in hushed tones, Vance turned his attention to Ean. Ean was the eldest of the wolf shifters, the highest-ranking Gamma, and the one who'd kept them together, even after Deacon mated Ross and accepted the position of temporary Alpha.

"What's happening?" Vance asked.

"Cops came to the house to arrest the dragon," Ross blurted out.

Ean shook his head. "Shush," he told Ross, who stuck his tongue out in response. Ean sighed and returned his attention to Vance. "Two cops knocked on the door, said they needed to speak to Luca about the damage to his building and asked why he hadn't been heard from in the days since. They asked who we were, and Luca told them we were employees concerned about their jobs."

"Which I will admit is not completely untrue," Theran added.

They all nodded their heads in agreement.

"Deacon told the cops we were all about to leave anyway and herded us out the door. He said Luca will let Tanner know when it's safe to go back," Ean finished.

"Were they human?" Vance asked.

Ean and Theran both nodded.

Ross put his hands by his face and wiggled his fingers. "The dragon is going to hypnotize them with his swirly eyes and eat them," he said.

"No, he won't," Ean stated.

Ross dropped his hands and sighed. "I'm hungry now."

"Why'd you ask if they were human?" Theran asked Vance.

Vance glanced at his friend and then watched Deacon and Tanner talking a few feet in front of the car. He'd been feeling off center since the moment Tanner had bitten Deacon, and that discomfort only intensified when Luca and Tanner mated. All while dealing with the attack by Tanner's familial pack. Only an hour ago he'd been introduced to his mate, his *vampire* mate, and now human cops were appearing at the front door.

"Am I the only one uncomfortable with the amount of attention our pack is drawing?" he asked.

"No," Theran answered.

"I'm hungry," Ross said again.

"Later," Ean told Ross and then to Vance said, "We're all uncomfortable. A lot has happened that isn't normal. But don't worry. Tanner is powerful, and Deacon and Luca have been alive for a long time. The four of us will be fine."

Vance narrowed his eyes at his older friend. "Seriously? We're going to be fine?" He felt his emotions spiraling upward, felt a bit manic and panicked, and he couldn't stop the anxiety from making his voice loud and shrill. "We've been bonded to an Elemental for a year. Our new Alpha is mated to a dragon and he can use both Elemental and dragon powers like they were his own. He blew a hole through the side of an office building for fuck's sake. Made it thunder and created tornados. My mate is a goddamned vampire, and I'm terrified of what that means for me. Not to mention Ross is completely insane."

"And hungry," Ross added. "Please don't forget that."

Vance fisted his hair in frustration. "Oh my god! We are so far from fine; it's not even funny."

As quickly as his tirade started, it ended. An overwhelming sense of calm flooded his body and relaxed his muscles. Vance dropped his hands to his sides and offered a weak smile to Tanner. He knew the calm was being pushed at him by the Alpha through the pack bond. While he was grateful for the assistance, it didn't ease the turmoil in his mind or the ache in his chest the thought of Sakima brought on.

"We can head back now," Tanner told them. "Luca convinced the police the building was damaged by a self-contained natural gas explosion, whatever the hell that is." Tanner shrugged.

"Doesn't matter. It got the human authorities off our back," Deacon said as he looped an arm around Ross's back.

Ross leaned in and nipped at Deacon's jaw. "I'm hungry," he growled.

"There's fresh rabbit at the house for you," Deacon said.

He cupped the back of Ross's head and kissed him. Ross wrapped his arms and legs around Deacon, who lifted him effortlessly off the trunk of the car. Deacon carried him to the front passenger door where he pressed Ross's back against the warm metal. Knowing Ross's last comment about being hungry could mean either for food or for Deacon, the three remaining wolves looked at Tanner.

"We'll ride with you," Ean said.

Chapter Three

LUCA

The silence in the library was a welcome relief to all the noise that came with opening his home to a pack of wolf shifters. The privacy he'd once cherished had been completely overrun by his love for one stubborn, powerful, and handsome man. Luca had never considered this possibility when Tanner first arrived at his office for an interview, or even when he took his mate to bed the first time. It wasn't until he'd brought Tanner back from the horde compound to learn Tanner had bonded Deacon and the other wolves that it truly hit him what mating Tanner meant. The mating itself was not something he regretted, but he deeply mourned the loss of silence and solitude.

Luca still struggled with Deacon's presence. They were connected now, thanks to the pack bond, and had come to a tenuous ceasefire, but that didn't mean they liked each other. They tolerated each other, at best. If what Vance claimed was true and Sakima was his mate, Luca might end up with a damn vampire in the house soon too.

Luca had initially thought it was a cool side effect when Tanner could speak through him, but he was concerned that Tanner could channel and control not only Deacon's elemental power, but Luca's dragon power as well. What would happen to the boy if he started channeling vampire power or, god forbid, all of them at once. One body could only contain so much, a mind could only control so much before both simply gave out. That fear was what had Luca in the library the moment the police officers left, combing through the books Matthias had provided, searching for answers to Tanner's ability. So far, he'd failed at finding any other paranormal outside the Chevalier family who exhibited that sort of talent, and the information regarding the family itself was minimal. Just enough detail existed to instill fear and disgust, but not enough to actually be of use.

"Pleasure or pain?"

The soft, familiar voice of a longtime friend had Luca lifting his gaze from the tome he'd barely cracked open toward the door of the library. The question harkened back a century to Luca's childhood when the librarian would find him sequestered among musty books and ask if he was reading because he wanted to—pleasure—or because he was being forced to—pain. He smiled broadly as Matthias entered the room and closed the door behind him.

"Pain, I'm afraid," Luca answered, rising to his feet.

"My condolences."

Luca wrapped Matthias in a hug. A strong slap to Luca's back had him gasping for breath. Matthias was centuries old but still damn strong. When they parted, Luca smiled down at his old friend. Matthias's white-streaked black hair had grown out a bit since they'd last met, and the dragon's neatly trimmed beard, which tended more toward salt than pepper, and had grown thicker. The increasing amount of white was the only outward sign of Matthias's advanced age one could see. Otherwise, he had the physique of an athletic man in his forties.

"I didn't feel or smell you coming," Luca stated, only slightly concerned by the fact.

"Herbal dampener. I used it to sneak from the compound. It will wear off soon enough."

"I see. What brings you here? And why did you have to *sneak* to do it?"

"You have a unique problem. I knew when you came in search of answers for your wolf mate something wasn't normal. Since your departure and the edicts your mother has instituted, I have learned exactly how unusual your situation is," Matthias answered. "I've spent practically every moment since you left combing through the archives. I've brought some scrolls with me, though I'm not sure how much help they'll prove to be."

"Edicts? Dare I ask?"

Matthias shrugged as though Luca's mother's antics didn't concern him, so Luca let the topic drop for now. He had more pressing matters to deal with than his mother being unhappy with him choosing Tanner over the horde. Tanner's father was definitely more of a threat to them at the moment. Unless she planned on combining forces with Ethan McBane, Luca could easily ignore her issues.

"I appreciate anything and everything. I doubt this will be as easy as opening one book and getting all the answers. It's going to be tiny shards of information scattered everywhere like puzzle pieces we have to collect and assemble," Luca said.

Matthias gazed into Luca's eyes with such intensity Luca fought the urge to squirm. He could practically feel the unpleasantness of Matthias's thoughts.

"What?" Luca asked, wary of the answer.

"I wonder what you will do if the knowledge you gain suggests your mate should die," Matthias answered.

Luca was instantly on alert. Their pack had plenty of enemies, some they knew and some he was certain they'd yet to encounter, but he had never suspected Matthias would be one of them. He narrowed his eyes and felt his dragon bleed into them.

Matthias tilted his head to the side, unconcerned by Luca's reaction, and whispered, "I see."

Before Luca could ask the elder dragon what he meant, a knock sounded on the door. Luca opened himself to the pack bond, something he'd quickly learned how to shut down in order to keep his private thoughts private, and recognized Ean on the other side. He'd been completely unaware the pack had returned. Luca was dangerously distracted. He pushed his acceptance of the interruption through the bond and Ean opened the door. He scanned the room upon entering until he found Luca.

"I'm sorry, but Tanner sent—"

Ean stopped midsentence as his gaze took in the dragon beside Luca. The wolf shifter's eyes swept over the older dragon slowly. Luca could feel the surprise emanating from Ean before the wolf snapped the bond closed, effectively shutting himself off from the rest of the pack. Given the way Matthias and the wolf shifter stared at each other, Luca felt compelled to introduce the two men.

"Ean, this is an old friend of mine from the horde, Matthias." Luca turned his gaze to Matthias. "This is Ean. He's the eldest wolf in the pack. He helped Deacon keep them together until Tanner became Alpha."

Luca wasn't exactly sure what had him adding that last part, but it had felt important to let Matthias know Ean's contribution to the pack. Neither shifter spoke. Matthias dipped his head in acknowledgment of the introduction, and Ean averted his gaze back to Luca. He swallowed thickly before making another attempt to speak.

"Um...Tanner wants... I don't know...um..." Ean was clearly searching his thoughts for the message he was supposed to pass on, but the words escaped him as evidenced by his creased features. He shook his head slightly.

"It's fine, Ean. I'll ask him what he needs later," Luca assured him. He was baffled Tanner would send Ean to him with a message rather than communicate through the mate bond, but he'd ask his mate later.

"Yeah, yeah."

Ean's gaze darted from Luca to Matthias and then to the floor before he spun around and hurried from the room. Once the door clicked closed, Luca glanced at Matthias. The dragon was doing a fabulous imitation of a statue, appearing to be lost in thought. Ean's interruption had lasted less than a minute, but Luca was certain something more significant had happened. He wasn't exactly sure, but the moment tasted similar to Vance's first meeting with Sakima—the flavor of mate recognition.

"Something wrong, Matthias?"

The older dragon shook his head. "Nothing of importance." Matthias faced the table covered in books and scrolls of every size and vintage. "Shall we?"

"Yes, of course."

Luca allowed the change of focus. At the moment, his need to understand what was happening with Tanner overrode his suspicions Matthias might possibly be Ean's mate. They worked in companionable silence, same as they had decades ago when Luca would sequester himself in the horde library, his thirst for knowledge continually fueled by Matthias and his books. Luca closed the tome he'd opened when his old friend had first arrived. After three hours of combing over 822 pages full of horde history, diagrams, portraits, and family trees, he had no more information about the Chevalier than he had when he'd started.

"I don't get it," he said.

Matthias lifted his gaze from the scroll he'd been studying. He didn't ask what Luca was talking about; he simply stared back in silence.

"If the Chevalier family was such a horrible, dangerous abomination, then why is there *nothing* written about them beyond the few paragraphs Tanner found? You'd think something like that would be front and center. Hey, look how bad this was. Don't allow this to happen again. But no. Nothing."

Matthias released the edges of the scroll, allowing the old paper to curl into itself, and reclined in his chair. He sighed heavily as he regarded Luca.

"Chevalier. A name I hoped to never hear again."

Luca wasn't surprised Matthias knew about the family, but he was extremely curious *how* he knew about them. Given his age, it was entirely possible Matthias had actually known the family firsthand. He would've been a young dragon then.

"What do you know of them?"

"They are dead, the bloodline eradicated, and therefore no longer of importance," Matthias answered, a hard edge to his voice.

Luca shook his head. They were of importance if their story offered insight into Tanner's unique ability. They were important enough for Ethan McBane to fear his son was becoming one of them. Luca scrubbed his hands over his face. His eyes were tired and gritty.

"Tanner can channel my power, Matthias. And Deacon's." Luca watched the surprise spread across Matthias's face.

"That's not possible," the dragon murmured.

"It is, and if what the Chevalier family was, how they became what they were, can help me understand what's going on with my mate, then I'll exhume their memory from whatever deep, dark hole it's been buried in. I don't care what I have to do or who I piss off in the process either."

"Careful, fledgling. You're dealing with things you don't understand."

"I'm not a child anymore, and maybe I don't understand. Not yet. But mark my words, *I will*." The last emitted from Luca's throat with a growl.

Chapter Four

VANCE

The house reeked of human fear when the pack returned. Vance wrinkled his nose at the acrid scent as he entered the house behind the others. He preferred the woodsy scent of other wolves, or the stormy scent Deacon carried. Hell, he even preferred the charred scent that radiated from Luca to that of a human sweating bullets in the face of intimidation. The human cops may not have known Luca was a dragon, but they'd known they were in the presence of something bigger than them, more powerful, even if they couldn't quite identify why they felt that way.

"Damn. What did he do? Scare the piss out of them, literally?" Theran asked.

If any of them had been hungry, the scent might have been appetizing. Like any food, not all meat smelled good to every wolf. Theran crossed the room to the French double doors at the back and opened them. Tanner opened the windows at the front of the house. The resulting cross breeze of fresh air was a welcome relief. Tanner sent Ean upstairs to fetch Luca from the library and then pulled out his phone to send a text. It was likely a message to Deacon, whom they'd left on the side of the road with Ross.

On autopilot, Vance began picking up stray cups and collecting dishes from the earlier meal. He felt bad he'd neglected his duties, favoring a little playtime with Ross, but he also knew the Alpha and other pack members would ignore the slip, given all that happened. He rinsed the dishes and loaded them into the dishwasher. Once he pushed the start button on the Auto cycle, he grabbed a dish rag and began wiping every flat surface within reach. Kitchen tasks complete, he then gathered all the dirty laundry.

As Vance moved through the motions of loading the washer, his mind wandered to Sakima. The vampire hadn't left his thoughts since appearing in the yard. His unexpected mate was now an all-consuming obsession. Thank god the pack wasn't relying on Vance to help coordinate a pincer movement on encroaching wolves or to negotiate a peace treaty between rival packs. For the first time in his twenty-two years, Vance was grateful for his Omega status. His distraction wouldn't kill anyone. At worst, he'd have to rerun the clothes wash cycle because he forgot to put the laundry detergent in.

Vance returned from the basement washroom to find Tanner, Ean, and Theran sitting at the long dining room table. The stench of human had been blown away on the wind. He crossed the expansive room and took the empty chair beside Ean, who appeared to be as distracted as Vance felt. There was a faraway cast to his eyes and he didn't blink much. He caught Vance staring at him and gave a small smile.

Ean leaned close and whispered, "We'll talk later."

One of the things Ean, Ross, and Theran had learned about Vance when they'd formed their wild dog pack was that he resembled a bank vault. He was the keeper of confidences and secrets, and he would only release them if granted permission by the person who'd put the information there. The wolves could tell him anything, and their words would go absolutely nowhere else. Confidentiality wasn't a service Vance had set out to offer; it was simply his personality, but he loved that they all trusted him with things they'd never share with anyone else. He suspected things would change as each wolf found their mate and had someone much closer to rely on, but until then, he'd be an open ear and a closed mouth.

Heavy footsteps sounded on the stairs, and all of them turned to see who was coming down. Vance tilted his head to the side. One set of footfalls definitely belonged to Luca; his campfire scent preceded him into the room. The other steps were a mystery. The lower-ranking wolves watched their Alpha as he rose to his feet. Luca had to have felt the increasing tension in the pack because, when he rounded the bottom of the stairs, he lifted his hands in a placating manner.

"Easy boys. He's a friend."

Luca stopped a few feet away from the table. The other man, who scented lightly of dragon, boldly stood beside him, not the least concerned he was in a room full of wolf shifters. Vance supposed their meager pack didn't appear intimidating to a being as high on the paranormal chain as a dragon. Luca had never shown fear either, only dislike and malcontent. Ean became extremely uncomfortable and began bouncing his leg. Vance wasn't the only one who noticed the older wolf's agitation; he drew the attention of both dragons, as well.

"Tanner," Luca said, almost pleading.

The Alpha took a deep breath, and as he exhaled, he pushed calm through the pack bond. It made Vance feel better immediately, but didn't do much for Ean, who was still clearly upset by the strange dragon's presence. He took his friend's hand under the table and squeezed, letting Ean feel his support and caring. Ean stared at the tabletop, but he squeezed Vance's hand in return.

"Now that everyone is calm, or at least calmer," Luca said, glancing quickly at Ean before giving his full attention to Tanner. "This is Matthias Caillamar. He's been the horde scholar for centuries, and a good friend. He's here to help."

A few moments of silence followed while Luca and Tanner had one of their mate-bond conversations. Ean shifted in his seat so he was facing Vance more than the table, his grip on Vance's hand tightening slightly. Vance glanced at his friend and then Matthias, who was also watching Ean closely. There was no malice in the dragon's eyes; he was simply observing. Luca's voice drew everyone's eyes to him. He extended his hand to Tanner, who stepped around the table to link their fingers together.

"This is Tanner, my mate, and Pack Alpha."

The dragon finally turned his gaze away from Ean. Tanner and Matthias nodded to each other in acknowledgment of the introduction. Tanner took over introducing the rest of the pack, indicating each of them as he said their name.

"This is Vance, Ean, and Theran. The two coming in the door behind you are Deacon and his mate, Ross."

Ross bounded to the table and sat, completely unfazed by the stranger in the house. Deacon scrutinized Matthias but joined the others at the table after a quick introduction by Luca. The dragons also took seats at the table, and the pack began discussing their next move. Luca had already reached out to his contractor about getting the office building repaired, and Deacon expressed his eagerness to return to work.

The entire pack held jobs at Luca's marketing firm, and they wanted to get back to work. Their bank accounts required it. Even if the pack decided they would all live under Luca's roof, they still had car payments, cell phone bills, and were frequently in need of new clothing, thanks to the necessity of shifting while dressed.

Vance's job was the simplest and lowest paid. He worked in the mailroom, sorting and delivering letters and packages throughout the company, but he missed the work. He enjoyed getting to walk around the entire building, rather than being stuck in a cubicle like the others. Deacon had an office because he was an advertising agent, but he was still stationary. Vance needed to move and serve, and his job fulfilled both requirements.

For several blessed hours, Vance was free from thoughts and worries over Sakima. Briefly, as he got ready for bed in the guest room he shared with Ean, he wondered what Sakima did for a living. What would the vampire think of Vance's chosen profession? Ean came into the room freshly showered, wearing sleep pants and toweling his short ash-brown hair. Vance waited until Ean had shut the door before speaking.

"Are you okay?"

Ean tossed the towel on the foot of the bed and then joined Vance on the mattress. The other wolf's discomfort was still visible in the lines of his face, but he'd kept the bond closed so no one really knew what was going on with him. Ean fiddled with the blanket as he spoke.

"When you first saw the vampire... What's his name?"

"Sakima," Vance answered, watching his friend closely.

"Yeah. When you first saw Sakima, did it feel like a gut punch? Like all the air left your lungs, and you couldn't breathe?"

"No. It was more like an earthquake. I felt like the ground literally tilted beneath my feet, and I got vertigo. But I don't think it's the same for everyone. I heard Tanner say it was like a light turned on in the room, and he could finally see Luca for what he was. Deacon said Ross was like a tsunami washing over him, and I don't think it was because he's crazy and crashes into everybody that way. Why?"

Ean lifted his gaze from the blanket to the bedroom door. He bit his lower lip and creased his forehead.

"Ean?" Vance touched his friend's shoulder and felt the muscle tense. "Do you think you found your—"

"Matthias," Ean interrupted. He exhaled loudly. "Matthias is my mate, but he...I..." Ean gave up trying to speak and shook his head.

Vance well understood Ean's position. Until Ross had taken an Elemental for a mate, the idea their mates would be anything other than wolf had never occurred to any of them. Mixed-species matings weren't something previously known, at least not in their secluded little world.

They'd not even known paranormals intermingled with one another at all until Deacon took them to the nightclub, Elysium, for the first time.

The four of them had huddled around the bar and watched in amazement as paranormals they'd never known existed danced and flirted all around them. Their eyes had been opened to the world, and they were still trying to navigate their way through it. Even Tanner, who was far newer to this than they were, was making a better adjustment than the other wolf shifters. He had taken Luca as a mate without a second thought, or so it appeared to the rest of the pack. Vance was definitely having doubts about Sakima. And Ean was clearly at odds with Matthias being his mate.

"I'm terrified what will happen if I let Sakima give me the mating bite," Vance admitted quietly.

"He can't turn you," Ean said. "At least that's what Deacon told us while you were out running with Tanner. He says you're either born vampire, or not. Just like us biting a human can't turn them into werewolves, despite their idiotic stories to the contrary."

"But Tanner bit Deacon and created tornados. And when he bit Luca, he became massive and breathed fire. What if Sakima *can* turn me? What if when he bites me, I become some kind of zombie wolf who feeds off humans? Or, what if—"

"Stop!" Ean barked. He didn't raise his voice, but the demand was clear, and Vance snapped his mouth closed. Ean often had the predisposition of a Beta wolf, rather than his current station of Gamma. "You'll go crazy if you go down the 'what if' road, so just don't. The one thing you need to keep in the front of your mind at all times is that Sakima is your mate. He's going to be extremely protective of you, even from himself. He won't hurt you."

"Okay," Vance murmured. He wasn't sure he believed Ean's words. He wasn't sure Ean believed them, but he wanted to. So much.

"Get to know him." Ean lay back on the bed and pulled the blanket over his legs. He patted the bed beside him, and Vance settled next to him. "You'll see I'm telling you the truth."

Chapter Five

SAKIMA

The deep rumble of the Dodge Viper's engine died as Sakima turned off the ignition and removed the key. He'd chosen to drive the car for multiple reasons; first, he wanted to make a good impression on his destined companion. Second, he knew even in wolf form, Vance wouldn't be able to keep up with his vampire speed, but would no doubt leave Sakima in the dust at normal speed. The car would allow them to get where they were going together. Sakima had been instantly drawn to the shiny black sports car with its sleek lines and 645 horsepower. Not as fast as his vampiric speed, but certainly faster than his companion's four legs. He hoped Vance found the car as impressive and sexy as he did.

Sakima exited the car and had barely stepped onto the sidewalk before the front door of the house opened and Vance stepped out onto the porch. The wolf shifter's beauty hit Sakima in the chest as he once again got a good look at him. Vance's tawny hair was in disarray, the midday sun making the strands appear more blond than brown, and his mouth hung open as he took in the Viper. Sakima beckoned him to the street. Several of Vance's pack members filed out the door behind him, but they remained on the porch as Vance walked across the grass on bare feet to join Sakima. His well-worn jeans clung to his hips and thighs, and the loose T-shirt did nothing to stem Sakima's desire for the wolf. His fangs dropped as the scent of his companion wafted to him on the breeze.

"Hello, pet."

Sakima offered his hand, and Vance accepted with a soft smile. His thumb brushed over the vein on the back of Vance's hand. He salivated and remembered the main reason he'd come for Vance. He needed to feed, and he hoped his companion was hungry as well.

"Have you hunted recently?" Sakima asked.

"Myself? No, but Luca and Matthias brought home two cows the night before last. Don't ask me where they got them. Tanner says we don't want to know anyway."

Sakima glanced at the door to the house. Apparently, every occupant was interested in his conversation with Vance. Or maybe it was the car they were interested in. Either way, Sakima had had enough of being watched.

"Come with me," he said and opened the passenger door. "I need to feed, and then I will take you hunting."

Vance smiled broadly at him. He waved over his shoulder at the pack and then eased himself into the car. Sakima grinned back, elated to see the wariness and uncertainty that tainted their first meeting was nonexistent. While Sakima had struggled to stay away, the past few days of separation had been beneficial in the end. His companion was well on his way to acceptance. Without looking back at the house, not caring if his unexpected theft of Vance was frowned upon or not, Sakima rounded the car and settled behind the wheel. The vehicle came to life with a growl, and he tapped the gas pedal, revving the engine and delighting in the sound of Vance's excitement.

"Wow. Got some serious power, but I've got to point something out."

Sakima arched a brow when Vance peeked up from where he was smoothing his palm over the raised center console.

"Red leather?"

It was cliché for a vampire to have red leather interior, Sakima knew, but those were the design elements the car had come with. He slid the gear shift into drive, gave Vance a full-fanged, predatory smile, and pulled away from the curb to the sound of squealing tires and startled male. He took the corner at the end of the street faster than he should so he could show off and was rewarded when Vance grabbed the doorframe with one hand and Sakima's forearm with the other.

"Shit, okay. If wolves were meant to go this fast, we'd have been given... I don't even know. Wings? Six legs? Fuck, slow down."

Sakima chuckled when Vance slammed his bare foot onto the floorboard as though it were the brake pedal, but he eased his foot off the gas. As he shifted gears, he felt the sharp pinch of nails against his arm. A quick glance showed Vance's claws had come out, though they'd not yet punctured cleanly through the material of his shirt.

"Easy, my pet, unless you're ready for other sharp things to come out to play," Sakima teased.

He wasn't the least bit concerned with Vance cutting him, but he wasn't keen on having to replace an expensive dress shirt. Though if replacing his clothing was because Vance had been hasty in the removal of all barriers with the end result of the wolf shifter naked and sated beneath him, Sakima would happily incur the cost. He had to stifle the sigh of regret when Vance quickly pulled his hand away.

"Sorry," Vance muttered. "Um, where are we going?"

"Paying a visit to my human donor. I need to feed."

"*Human* donor?"

"Yes. Some humans, through simple bad luck, become aware of paranormals. Typically, they will find a way to make themselves believe they didn't actually see what they think they saw. Others remain silent out of fear. Every once in a while, a brave one will seek us out. Justina was one of the brave. She has prolonged her life by allowing me to feed from her, but she is losing the battle. The healing properties of a vampire's bite can only do so much."

"Is she just old, or does being a donor eventually kill them?"

"She's ill."

"What happens when she dies? Do you find another donor?"

Sakima glanced at his companion, the truth weighing heavy on his tongue, but he wasn't ready to tell Vance he'd be the bulk of Sakima's nutrition once they were mated. He figured that kind of information fell into the too-much-too-soon category, so he went with the safe, but still true answer.

"Yes."

"Does it have to be a human?"

"No, but they tend to be the most willing thanks to prevalent misconceptions."

"Eternal life?"

Sakima nodded.

Vance fell silent as Sakima turned down a nicely maintained neighborhood street. The houses were small, yards were green, and the residents blissfully unaware paranormals of any kind existed. Sakima parked in the driveway of a blue ranch-style house with white trim, beginning to peel. He got out of the vehicle and pocketed the keys. Vance eased himself from the car more slowly and wrinkled his nose. Sakima knew what his wolf was smelling. Death had a distinct odor, and Justina's was particularly pungent.

"What is she sick with? Smells like rotting flesh."

"Final stages of pancreatic cancer," Sakima answered.

They approached the house at a leisurely pace. Normally, he would just enter the house, but this time he stopped at the front door and sighed heavily.

"Are you okay?" Vance asked softly.

"This will be the last feeding. I intend to draw the life from her, what remains of it. I cannot offer eternal life, but I can give eternal peace. I won't pass judgment if you are unwilling or unable to stay at my side."

Vance glanced at the door, uncertainty etched on his face, and then back to Sakima. "This is part of who you are, and I need to see it. I don't want to be uncomfortable around you. That's not how mates are supposed to feel when they're together."

Tension Sakima was barely aware of suffering released from his neck and shoulders at Vance's declaration. It might still prove jarring for the wolf shifter to see a vampire feed off a human until death, but at least he was willing to make the attempt. Justina knew this was feeding day and, as was tradition, had left the door unlocked for him. Sakima entered the house with Vance close behind and walked into the bedroom. Justina lay on the bed, looking for all the world to be dead already since she was so gaunt and pale. She smiled at Sakima and then frowned when Vance stepped into the room behind him. She glanced at Sakima questioningly.

"My destined companion, Vance," he answered.

"You finally found him," Justina rasped out.

"I did," Sakima whispered.

"He's younger than I expected, but he's quite the looker..."

Justina's words trailed off into a bone-rattling cough. Another new problem. She'd not been suffering a cough during his last visit only a few days before. Her body was gradually shutting down. The smell of death was thick on her breath.

"Yes, he is," Sakima whispered.

Even if he hadn't decided to take her life with this feeding, she would not survive the week. Without hesitation, he let his fangs drop fully, leaned over Justina's body and sank his teeth into her jugular. The healing properties of his saliva revitalized her blood as he drank, though it did nothing for her body. No amount of supernatural power he possessed could save her. As he pulled the blood from her, he felt invigorated and energized; a feeling that would hold for several days before the need to feed struck again.

Sakima felt her last inhalation as her chest rose to brush against his, the final exhale tickling across his ear. When her heart had given the final beat, he pulled his fangs from her neck and straightened. After a moment, Sakima rose to his feet and realized he was alone in the room. As was typical of wolves, Vance had left the room without a sound. The fact the shifter was barefoot helped. Sakima arranged Justina in the bed to appear as though she died in her sleep and then went searching for Vance. Sakima found his companion sitting on the front porch, legs outstretched, toes flexing in grass that needed to be mowed. Sakima squatted behind Vance and ran his fingers through the silky strands of his hair.

"Too much?" Sakima murmured.

"Yeah," Vance admitted. "Couldn't take the smell anymore." He turned his head to glance at Sakima over his shoulder. "Does human death always smell so terrible?"

"No. At least not to me," Sakima answered, aware some things would smell stronger to a wolf shifter. "Certain diseases can be quite odoriferous."

"I couldn't eat meat that smelled like that. Did the blood taste as bad as it smelled?"

Sakima smiled at the innocence of the question. "No. The properties of vampire saliva change the flavor of diseased blood to something more palatable."

Vance looked up and down the quiet street, deep in thought, while Sakima enjoyed the feel of his companion's hair slipping over his fingers. After a moment, Vance turned to gaze up at Sakima again.

"What will you do with her now?"

"Leave her where she is for her family to find. Her daughter visits once a week on Saturdays."

"Won't finding her mom dead be...distressing?"

"Her death is not unexpected, my pet."

"I know. It's just... I remember finding my mom..."

Vance's voice trailed off, and his eyes became distant, pained. Sakima wanted to ask what had happened to his mother, who was obviously dead given Vance's reaction, but he didn't want to pry. He trusted as they got to know each other, Vance would open up voluntarily. He leaned forward to bury his nose in the hair above Vance's ear, his lips brushing the shell.

"Let's get you fed, pet," he whispered. He smiled when Vance shuddered.

Chapter Six

VANCE

Sakima rose to his feet and offered him a hand, which Vance accepted without thought. All his reservations about having a vampire for a mate had disappeared over the few days they'd been apart. The pull toward his mate was enough to dispel all his concerns. As long as he could be near Sakima, he was safe and comforted. Finding his mate and having a pack bond once again, now that Tanner was Alpha, filled all the holes left in Vance's soul after his mother's unexpected death. He was finally whole. And once the pack returned to work on Monday, things would be back to normal. Sakima turned the ignition and Vance smiled at the sound of the deep rumble of the engine. Shiny black exterior, powerful supercharged engine, and red leather interior, the Viper was a sweet-ass car.

"Where to, my pet? Your usual hunting grounds or somewhere of my choosing?"

Vance gave the question a moment of thought as Sakima pulled out of the driveway. "Do you know a place I might find fox? I haven't had fox since I moved to the city."

And the animal was small enough Vance could hunt it alone without threat of injury. Usually, the pack would hunt together for prey big enough to feed them all, but they each had their favorite small prey. Ross was partial to rabbit, which could be found anywhere. Ean and Theran preferred beaver, also a hard animal to find in the city. Tanner was lucky because his favorite meal, deer, could still be found in the forest they'd claimed as their hunting grounds.

Even in the clearing, where the old cabin had once stood, Vance was unable to find fox. Another favorite was sheep, but farmers tended to get all snooty when their sheep were found slaughtered in the field. His mind wandered to the cows Matthias and Luca had brought home. No doubt there was a rancher somewhere going crazy over his missing livestock. Sakima's voice brought him back to the present.

"The only place I know that has fox is the zoo, and I can't very well take you there to hunt."

Vance chuckled. "No."

"There's a secluded campground about an hour west. I've been told there are elk in the area. I know the larger ones are dangerous to a lone wolf, but I can help cull a small one from the herd for you."

"Okay, but a really small one. One I can eat by myself and not leave too much waste. I hate wasting good meat."

"Scavengers will thank you," Sakima said.

He took the on-ramp to the freeway and gunned the engine. They shot off toward the mountains at a speed Vance found alarming, but Sakima handled the vehicle with such expertise Vance eventually relaxed into the seat. Ten minutes into the trip, Sakima moved his hand from the gear shift and offered it to Vance. Just as twice before, Vance took the offered hand in his. Sakima laced their fingers and rested his arm on the center console.

For several minutes, Vance was enthralled by the differences in their skin tone. He'd never considered himself tan by any means, but next to Sakima's pale skin, Vance's was a stark tanned shade. He studied the shapes of their hands and arms, the way their fingers intertwined comfortably, and smiled at how natural it all felt to him. Forty-seven minutes later, Sakima released his hold on Vance to downshift, pulling the car off the freeway onto a two-lane road and then turned onto a narrow gravel path that led to an old, forgotten campground. Despite how close it sat to the freeway, it was secluded in the trees, and the only sound was the chirping of birds and the occasional rustling of leaves in the breeze.

Vance stood beside the Viper, which Sakima had parked next to a picnic table and rock-rimmed firepit. Sakima slid onto the bench and rested his arms on the worn, weather-beaten wood tabletop. Vance sniffed the air as he walked to the other side of the picnic table. There were definitely elk in the woods, as well as a bear he would be sure to stay clear of, and the typical rabbits and squirrels, both of which would make an acceptable snack if he couldn't find a small enough elk to feast on. Vance turned to face Sakima, pulled his shirt over his head, and then tossed it onto the tabletop.

"I thought you said you'd help me," Vance pointed out. Sakima didn't look like he was going to help at all, given how settled he appeared to be.

"I'll not hinder the hunt. When you've found your meal, howl. I will find you and help you take it down."

Holding his mate's icy-blue gaze, Vance opened his jeans and pushed them down his legs.

"Commando. Good to know," Sakima observed.

Vance smiled coyly, lower lip caught between his teeth, before he spun on his heel and leaped into the air. When he landed, he was on four paws. He shook his fur out, woofed once at Sakima, and then took off at a run, following his nose toward dinner. Half a mile into the trees, Vance stopped in his tracks, ears twitching, mouth salivating. Fox. Determined to have his treat, he began sniffing out his prey. Enjoying his time in the woods and momentarily forgetting about the troubles his pack was facing, Vance toyed with the red fox, chasing it from one hiding spot to another, until his hunger got the best of him. Once he caught and swiftly killed the animal, he picked up the carcass by the neck and pranced back to the campsite.

Sakima still sat at the picnic table in the same position Vance had left him. He would have thought the vampire was hibernating if it wasn't for the deliberate blink of his eyes. Vance tossed his head side to side, whipping the fox around, proudly showing off the kill to his mate. Sakima smiled. Vance dropped the fox on the ground at his feet, put a front paw on it, and woofed at Sakima. It was only right for him to offer his more dominant mate first bite. Sakima rose from the bench and joined Vance on the ground. Vance sat and nosed the carcass closer to his mate. Sakima lifted a hand and caressed one of Vance's ears.

"I've already fed, my pet, remember? Thank you for the offer, but please, eat."

Vance pawed the fox back toward him, lowered to his stomach, and began to eat. If seeing a wolf tear into a carcass close-up bothered Sakima, he didn't show it. Additional proof that true mates accepted each other as they were, understanding the other's natural way of being, without judgment. Ross had found it with Deacon, who accepted the fact he wasn't entirely sane. Luca loved Tanner despite his fearsome abilities. Vance could only hope Ean found it with Matthias, and that Theran would one day meet his mate, as well. It felt good to have a pack, and a home. But it was amazing to have a mate, even if they hadn't actually claimed each other yet.

Once he'd finished eating, Vance sniffed the air, searching for water. When he didn't find any, he glanced at Sakima and whined. He'd have to shift back to human for the ride back, and his snout was covered in blood. Vance licked his paw and began cleaning himself as best he could without water. The need to be clean was a human thing all the wolf shifters suffered from. They couldn't very well walk around with blood on their chins among humans. Vance glanced up at the soft caress between his ears. Sakima smiled. This time with full fangs. He cupped Vance's head with his hands and gazed into his eyes.

"Shift, pet," he murmured.

Vance sat up and shifted. In his human form, he was squatting with his hands to the ground between his feet, his face still held within Sakima's palms.

"Beautiful," Sakima murmured. He leaned forward and licked a spot of blood Vance had missed from his chin. "And delicious," the vampire growled.

Sakima laved his tongue across Vance's lips, cleaning them of whatever fox blood was left. Vance, completely entranced by his mate's actions, opened his mouth. Sakima understood his wordless request and took Vance's mouth in a kiss, dipping his tongue in for a taste. Sakima repeated the action multiple times, ending each lick of Vance's skin with a kiss, until Vance was completely clean of blood. Licking the snout clean was something Vance had seen other wolf shifter mates do for each other while in wolf form. He never imagined he'd experience such a thing, especially not in human form...with a vampire. Logically, it made sense to him, but the moment still sent his emotions haywire.

One second, he was squatting in front of Sakima. The next, he was flat on his back with the vampire on top of him. Sakima kissed across his jaw and down to his neck, thrusting his clothed cock against Vance's bare shaft. The soft cotton of the slacks glided smoothly between their bodies, but Sakima's weight offered the perfect friction to the underside of Vance's hardened cock. He rolled his head to the side to offer his mate access to his neck, silently begging for the bite that would make them one.

Instead of giving Vance what he wanted, Sakima lifted onto one elbow, reached between their bodies, and wrapped strong fingers around Vance's dick. The vampire worked the flesh with centuries-old skill, bringing Vance to the edge of orgasm faster than he'd ever experienced before. Beyond articulate speech, Vance grabbed the vampire's biceps, lifted his hips from the ground and came with a howl, shooting thin white stripes across his stomach and chest.

The rush of blood in Vance's ears dulled his hearing, and he panted, trying to catch his breath. He hadn't realized he'd closed his eyes until they snapped open in surprise at the cool wetness of Sakima's tongue on his navel. He glanced down in time to see Sakima follow the trail of semen up his stomach to his chest, taking the fluid onto his tongue. The vampire's eyes had gone almost completely white. They held each other's gazes as Sakima swallowed and then licked his lips.

"Delicious," he whispered.

Vance's tongue felt heavy in his mouth. He wanted to tell Sakima how good it felt to be cleaned in such a way. He wanted to tell him how much he loved being touched, that he'd enjoyed the orgasm. He wanted to tell his mate so many things, but when his tongue finally formed words, he blurted out, "Why didn't you bite me?"

Sakima canted his head to the side before getting to his feet. He reached out and assisted a limp-muscled Vance from the ground.

"I'm sorry. That's not what I meant to say," Vance said, feeling the heat of embarrassment warm his cheeks.

"And yet, you said what you meant."

Rather than risk saying anything else he'd regret, Vance averted his gaze to the horizon. The sun was starting its descent into evening. They'd been out all afternoon.

"Get dressed, my pet. It's time I took you home to your pack."

Vance bit his tongue to keep from asking why he couldn't go home with Sakima. They were mates, after all, and hadn't claimed each other properly yet. No one would frown on them for it, but he kept the question to himself. He'd been needy enough for one day.

Chapter Seven

LUCA

Luca relaxed in the overstuffed chair he'd tucked into the corner of the library. He sipped at his glass of Balvenie and blew smoke rings into the air as thoughts tumbled through his mind. Matthias was stretched out on the couch nearby, napping. They'd spent most of the night before and all day combing over scrolls, though Luca had the distinct impression he was searching for information with more intent than his friend. Matthias was likely humoring him, rather than actually assisting, and Luca wasn't sure how to handle the situation. If there was even a situation at all, because he wasn't entirely certain of Matthias's intentions. The older dragon-shifter was distracted and disinterested. Luca felt the gentle push of his mate in his head and smiled.

Relaxed body but troubled thoughts, Tanner said. Luca closed his eyes and let his mate fully into his mind.

It will all work out, my sweet boy.

I don't want to upset you...

But?

An envelope arrived sometime last night. It was tucked into the doorframe. No names or addresses, but it smells like dragon.

Luca's brow furrowed and he rolled his head toward Matthias. A house with two dragons, an elemental, and four wolves, and still another paranormal was able to get close enough to slip a letter into the doorjamb? It seemed impossible, but then he remembered how Matthias had gotten all the way to the library before Luca was aware of him. Luca rose to his feet as Tanner quietly entered the library with the envelope in hand. Luca slid his fingers through his mate's dark hair and took a moment to stare into his beautiful blue eyes. He leaned in close, resting their foreheads together, and sighed.

"To think, all of this is happening because I fell in love with you," Luca whispered.

Tanner slid his arms around Luca's waist. "No. This is happening because other people think they have the right to tell us who we can love."

"This is happening because you have powers you shouldn't have," Matthias said.

Luca glanced over his shoulder to find the older dragon now sitting on the sofa, staring intently at them. Matthias's nostrils flared a mere second before a howl reverberated through the house and the pack bond flared to life. Matthias quirked his head in confusion as Tanner tossed the envelope at him before turning on his heel and running out of the room. Luca walked to the windows overlooking the backyard.

"Who is it?" Matthias asked. "Smells like dog."

Matthias's voice was calm and steady, completely unaware of the storm rolling through Luca's head. All the wolves had shifted, ready for the fight that would occur should the powder keg they were standing on be ignited. Luca tensed as three wolves that were not part of his pack stalked into the backyard.

"Rabid dog. It's Tanner's father."

Luca shook his head, hands on hips, as he watched the three wolves pacing along the back fence. He wasn't quite certain what they were doing. Three wolves were no match for one dragon, let alone two. Matthias joined him at the window and casually handed over the envelope.

"I believe the Elemental's mate is the rabid dog. Tanner's father is perhaps just an idiot," he said.

Luca grunted in response. He couldn't really argue his friend's assessment of Ross, or Tanner's father. "Who sent the letter?"

"Your mother."

"And?"

"You've been renounced," Matthias answered with the same level of emotion he'd have stated the weather was warm.

Oddly, the fact his mother had cut all ties with him and would deny Luca was her son, deny his existence even, fell flat. Luca didn't know if it was because he'd not been a part of the horde for so many decades that he didn't feel the loss, or because he now had more "family" than he knew what to do with. Being a member of a pack was vastly different than being a member of a horde, but Tanner and the wolves felt more like home than the mountain compound ever had.

Luca observed the wolves below and half listened to the conversation Tanner was having with his father. Ethan McBane truly hated that his son could speak through others, rather than be forced to shift like every other paranormal shifter. Tanner was doing it on purpose, of course. A not-so-subtle intimidation tactic and a reminder that Tanner was the more powerful Alpha. The roar of an engine echoed through the neighborhood before abruptly cutting off. Luca smiled as, through Tanner's eyes, he watched Vance and Sakima exit the Viper, right behind Ethan and two of his wolves. The dynamic had shifted once again in Tanner's favor, and Ethan became visibly nervous. The man was constantly underestimating his son and the rest of the wild dog pack. It was a miracle the Alpha hadn't been challenged, given how inept he appeared to be.

Matthias grunted. "Vampire."

Luca glanced at him.

"I may not be a part of your odd little pack or it's rather invasive bond, but I can still smell," he said, tapping a nostril.

The calm, relaxed stance Matthias usually affected suddenly became tense and angry. Luca followed the older dragon's gaze into the yard in time to see a gray-brown wolf step off the porch into the grass, facing off with the three wolves pacing the fence line. Ean snarled and growled, bunching his shoulders in preparation for an attack.

"What is he doing?" Matthias growled.

"Now that Vance and Sakima are present, Tanner is dividing his resources. Theran is back there too, but you can't see him from here. He's on the porch."

Matthias growled again as he turned to leave the room. Curious about his friend's sudden interest in the situation, Luca followed. At the bottom of the stairs, Luca decided to table his curiosity in favor of layering on a little more intimidation to his mate's cause. As Matthias joined Theran and Ean in the back, Luca stepped out front to stand beside Tanner.

"Nice of you to finally join us, dragon," Deacon mumbled from Tanner's other side.

Luca ignored the comment as he glanced around at the neighboring houses. Those who were visible to the neighbors were in human form, including Ethan's pack members, and Vance, standing near the curb with Sakima, who wasn't showing fang. Ross and Tanner stood near Deacon and Luca, giving the illusion they were pet dogs. The back of the house was shielded for the most part by trees and foliage. Convinced this little showdown wouldn't escalate within sight of humans, Luca crossed his arms over his chest and waited as Tanner withdrew from Deacon's mind to push into Luca's.

"Do you think these creatures will help you?" Ethan asked, gesturing around wildly. "When I came here, I thought only to speak with you, Alpha to Alpha, father to son. Instead, you take to threats?"

"You want to talk Alpha to Alpha, you come alone," Tanner responded through Luca. "You made the threat when you surrounded the house with my pack inside," Luca added himself.

Ethan wouldn't know which of them was speaking, but Tanner and the rest of the pack knew. For the first time, Luca had voiced aloud he was part of the pack, part of their family, rather than just the Alpha mate.

Sakima moved quickly. One moment he was standing beside Vance. The next, he was directly behind Ethan, fangs bared, making it very clear whose side the vampire was taking in this little pissing contest. The entire McBane pack jumped in surprise. Luca, Deacon, and Vance laughed out loud, adding insult to the confrontation, though the speed with which he'd moved had also taken them by surprise.

"Fine," Ethan bit out; however, with Sakima so close to him, he remained very still. Luca supposed it was possible until that moment the McBane pack hadn't identified Sakima as a vampire. Idiots, as Matthias had pointed out. "If you want to continue to act like a spoiled pup, then you will be brought to heel like one."

A collective growl went up as the entirety of Tanner's pack bristled at the threat to their Alpha, and Luca barely contained the shift pulsing beneath his skin. Ignoring them all, Alpha McBane turned on his heel and crossed the street to a dark-blue sedan idling at the curb. Once they were all inside, the car pulled away. A second vehicle parked farther down the street pulled a U-turn, stopped at the house next door, and the three wolves from the backyard bounded over to it. Another pack member got out to open the car door for them. As the shifter closed the door, he glanced back at Tanner.

Tyler. Tanner's recognition of a man he used to call friend, followed by sadness at the loss of their friendship, slipped through Luca's psyche. The two wolf shifters had once considered themselves brothers. Luca glanced at his mate. For Tanner's part, there was still brotherly love mixed in with the newer feelings of betrayal and grief. Tyler ducked his head and returned to the front passenger seat. As the door of the SUV closed, and the vehicle pulled away from the curb, Tanner stepped into the yard. He emitted a few broken yips as the SUV slowed at the stop sign before disappearing around the corner.

Tanner shook out his fur and then returned to the porch. The pack entered the house from both sides and met in what Luca referred to as the great room. It was the only room in the house large enough for his dragon. When he'd remodeled the house three decades ago, he'd chosen an open-concept floor plan for the main living area where the living room, dining room, and kitchen flowed seamlessly into one another. Seeing the pack now circled within, Luca wondered if somewhere in the back of his mind he'd known what his future held and that was the real reason he'd designed the room this way, because not once in the past thirty years had he shifted to his dragon form while inside.

The wolves who had shifted returned to their human forms and donned their discarded pants before rejoining the circle. Tension wafted from Vance, who stood to Luca's left, and he took a small step closer to Sakima. Luca followed the new couples' gazes across the gathering to Matthias who stood with his arms crossed and a scowl on his face. The dragon wasn't looking at Vance or Sakima, though; his attention was solidly fixed on Ean. Luca wasn't the only one to notice, either. Tanner broke the increasingly tense silence.

"Thank you, Matthias," he said.

"For what?" the dragon asked without turning from Ean.

"Coming to our aid."

Matthias blinked slowly as he slid his gaze to Tanner. "They were outnumbered," he accused.

"I had it handled," Ean snapped.

"We're a small pack. We're always outnumbered, but we're stronger than most," Tanner added.

"I don't need some huffing, puffing, centuries-old dragon to come to my rescue," Ean bit out.

"Careful, little boy. I'm not a dragon you want to piss off," Matthias growled.

Luca felt Ean's tension and annoyance ratchet up before he was able to cut off the bleed into the bond. Tanner glanced at him before quickly defusing the situation.

"The wolves are agitated and hungry. We need to go hunting," Tanner announced.

"Yes. Matthias and I should get back to the research."

Matthias grunted in response.

"I'll be in the car," Ean stated as he headed out the front door. Theran and Ross followed him. Vance was speaking to Sakima in soft tones.

"The hunt goes better if we're all together," Vance said.

"I must be leaving anyway, my pet." Sakima took Vance's hand and they walked outside together.

Deacon nodded once at Tanner as he passed him on the way outside. The Elemental had been unusually quiet, but Luca knew Tanner would be hearing plenty during the drive to their hunting grounds in the forest. Having once been acting Alpha to the wolves, Deacon often gave advice about their health and well-being. With Vance about to be mated to a vampire and Ean clearly at odds with Matthias, Deacon would have plenty to say. Matthias quietly disappeared up the stairs, leaving Luca and Tanner alone in the great room.

"That was fun," Luca said sarcastically.

Tanner smiled and then groaned. "We need to talk."

"Yes, sweet pup, but later. Go see to your wolves."

Tanner smiled at him beautifully, blue eyes sparkling, before heading out the front door.

"Don't call me pup, dragon," he called over his shoulder.

Chapter Eight

SAKIMA

Coven headquarters was every bit what Sakima remembered, despite the full decade that had passed since he last set foot inside the opulent high-rise. Plush area rugs dotted the hardwood flooring of the penthouse, where seating areas were strategically placed in front of the floor-to-ceiling windows offering an incredible view of the mountains to the west. The waning evening sunlight filtered in, warming the room.

Contrary to the tremendous number of human stories out there about vampires, they did not spend their days in coffins filled with dirt, hidden in dark basements of stone. He often wondered where the rumor about sunlight killing vampires had started, but his curiosity was never strong enough for him to investigate.

The Coven leader, Arden Cowell, summoned Sakima shortly after he'd dropped Vance at home with his pack. Leaving his destined companion in such a charged environment had been horribly uncomfortable, but Vance insisted everything was fine, and the wolf certainly knew his pack's dynamics better than Sakima. Still, Sakima returned home with the firm belief his beautiful wolf had no idea what the definition of "fine" was. He vowed to correct that as soon as possible. Vance deserved to know what protected, loved, and cherished truly meant.

Sakima stopped in front of one large window to gaze out at the scenery. The camping area he'd taken Vance to wasn't visible from this vantage point, but the pack's hunting grounds were. He took in the sight of the city where it melded gently into the forest dotting the foothills, the trees growing thicker and taller as they moved up the side of the mountain only to thin out once again as they reached the higher elevations. There were at least two other packs in addition to Vance's that moved among those trees. The McBane pack was the largest, eclipsing the Salter pack to the south by several dozen. Then there was Vance's pack of seven. Small. Powerful. Feared.

As the sun dipped behind the mountains, painting the sky in pink and orange, Sakima gazed out over the hunting grounds again. He witnessed only a portion of Vance's wolf nature earlier that afternoon. The remembered taste of blood and semen thick on his tongue made him salivate. It was so easy to imagine the tawny-colored wolf running alongside his pack mates, breaking off to circle their prey, cutting off any avenue of escape and helping take it down. They were hunting for the entire pack, so the prey would be large and therefore dangerous. Even as he worried over his companion's safety, he longed to see Vance in action, to watch his wolf shifter interact with others of his kind on such a basic, primal level.

"Fantastic view, is it not?" Arden asked as he joined Sakima at the window.

"Beautiful," Sakima answered, though he was speaking more to his vision of Vance than the actual view of the mountain sunset.

"Such beauty can make us forget the troubles we face."

"Can it?" Sakima asked. He wasn't so sure.

"Elysium is doing well? I hear your club has become *the* gathering place for paranormal interspecies mingling."

Sakima glanced at Arden. "It has become a rather successful venture," Sakima confirmed, uncertain exactly where the older vampire was going with this conversation, having hit on three different topics in rapid succession, but his thoughts momentarily stopped on the club.

Elysium had barely broken even in the early days of its existence. It wasn't until Sakima had advertised the club as exclusive for LGBT paranormals that it had truly become profitable. He hadn't expected Elysium to become as successful as it was, but he was quite happy with the outcome. Though there was plenty of opposition to the club's "delinquent" clientele. In that respect, paranormals were no different than humans.

As the sun disappeared completely and the sky darkened, the interior lights came on automatically.

"A blood moon is expected in the next several months," Arden said.

Sakima furrowed his brow at yet another subject change. He knew the Coven leader was working toward saying something where all of this would make sense, but Sakima wished the old vampire would get to the point.

"Some species are more powerful beneath a full moon. Even more so, a full moon eclipsed." Arden faced Sakima directly. "Wolf shifters, for example, feel the pull rather strongly. Their animal nature rising closer to the surface. It happens to be the genesis of human stories regarding werewolves being changed against their will on the full moon."

"I know," Sakima said.

It was one of the few fables about paranormals with a precisely known starting point. A fairly young wolf shifter, who had very little control over herself, shifted unexpectedly in front of her human lover during a blood moon. She was old enough, however, to realize her mistake and attacked her lover in an attempt to kill him. She failed, but the shifter community protected her, spreading their own rumors and muddying the issue. The situation happened thousands of years ago, but the stories still ran strong through human culture, as did those about dragons and vampires.

"It's somewhat disturbing to consider what a wolf shifter already made powerful by his bonds would be capable of during such an event as the blood moon. It is not of immediate concern, obviously, as the blood moon is still several months away, but it would be remiss of us to ignore such a situation."

Whisperings and rumors of Tanner and his pack had clearly reached Arden's ears in much the same way it had Sakima's. He'd been shocked to find his destined companion among the very pack fueling such rumors. Now that he knew, he found he was fiercely protective of them; not so much for the pack's sake as for Vance's. The survival of the wild dog pack was directly correlated to the survival of his companion. Not yet ready to inform Arden of his direct connection to the wolf shifter in question, Sakima merely tilted his head in acknowledgment.

"As this individual is known to be gay and has been seen within your establishment, I am recruiting your assistance in learning as much about him as possible. Facts only, please. Fiction, rumor, and grandiose statements serve no purpose. Use Elysium to set up a network of information gathering. Have your staff covertly ask questions over the coming weeks. If the information coming to us is proven untruthful, we will move on."

Sakima watched Arden's face closely as he asked the only question that mattered to him. "If the information proves to be true?"

Arden stared out the window as he contemplated Sakima's question.

"So far, what we've heard suggests he is a Chevalier, which, if true, is quite concerning and would need to be dealt with harshly. That whole distasteful event was bad enough when it took place four hundred years ago. Imagine the chaos and destruction that would ensue if such a thing happened in this day and age. Humans are far more industrious now than they used to be."

Unpleasant memories of fire, screams, and death from that day centuries ago played through Sakima's mind in horrifying detail. He didn't want them, so he forcefully pushed them aside. The entire situation he now found himself in left a bad taste in his mouth. If he asked his employees to start spying for the Coven, he and Vance would have to be far more careful than he'd originally planned. Elysium was a second home to Sakima, and he hoped to be able to share that with his destined companion. Until such a time as he could convince the Coven Tanner was not a Chevalier, whether that actually proved to be true or not, he would need to keep his wolf companion secret. He also needed to decide what he would do if Tanner *did* prove to be Chevalier.

"So I'm clear, what exactly do you mean by 'harshly'?" Sakima asked.

"The Chevalier and all associated with him would be eradicated," Arden stated. He turned without another word and left the room. Clearly, the Coven leader had said his piece and was done with Sakima.

"Understood," he whispered to the empty room.

Sakima had suspected, but hearing the words sent ice through his veins. Tanner being proven a Chevalier would not only mean Tanner's death, but the death of Sakima and his destined companion. For the first time in centuries, Sakima felt fear.

Chapter Nine

SAKIMA

Sakima luxuriated beneath the spray of the shower much longer than he'd planned, but he'd had a hard night. The club was packed beyond the usual, but the staff handled the crush with ease. Only Sakima suffered from the long work hours as his mind continued to replay his conversation with the coven leader mixed with flashes of ugly memories. He hadn't noticed the passing of time until morning dawned. The elder vampire's promise of eradication deeply unsettled him, but the rising sun brought with it a new day and renewed hope that he'd find a way to protect his companion's pack. Exhausted from thinking about Arden's threats and his own memories of death, he stood beneath the hot spray, longing for the water to wash his mind as clean as his body.

The water eventually turned cold, so Sakima shut the tap off and reached for a towel. The dull steady thump of a heartbeat finally pushed beyond his distraction. Someone was inside his apartment—uninvited. Angry that he was so lost in his head, he hadn't noticed someone entering his home mixed alluringly with intrigue over how they'd managed such a feat. Stealthy. Brave. And ultimately stupid.

He wrapped the towel around his waist and, smoothing his long white hair away from his face to hang down his back, he stepped from the cold tile floor to the plush beige carpeting of his bedroom. Even if the man himself were not sitting on the bed directly in front of Sakima, he would have recognized his mate's scent, undiluted as it was outside the steamy bathroom. Vance's essence filled the room, and Sakima inhaled, leisurely releasing his breath before addressing his unexpected visitor.

"Good morning."

"Don't you know it is unwise to enter a vampire's lair without notice, my pet?"

Vance blinked rapidly before forcing his gaze upward from the towel at Sakima's waist to his face. His pretty eyes showed concern, but no fear. He canted his head to the side in a uniquely lupine fashion.

"Why?" Vance asked.

The question was asked with such innocence Sakima was taken by surprise. The answer was so obvious. Clearly, his wolf was in need of a lesson on how to protect himself from the dangers of the world. Given the pack in which Vance was a member, Sakima thought his destined companion should be better educated. A smile spread across Vance's face, crinkling the corners of his eyes.

"Look at your face," Vance said. "I'm not dense, Sakima. I know not to intrude on vampires, in general, but...it's you. We're mates. I suppose it didn't occur to me I would be overstepping, or that I should be afraid of you."

"You should never be afraid of me," Sakima rushed to assure him. Fear was the last thing he wanted Vance to feel. "I like that you are comfortable coming to me without provocation."

Vance's gaze moved from Sakima's face over his still-damp chest, stopping once again at the towel circling his waist. A beautiful flush of color spread across Vance's cheeks. "I felt pretty provoked."

"Did you?" Sakima asked as he stepped closer to the bed.

He stopped when Vance's knees brushed his shins, skin separated only by the thin fabric of Vance's trousers. Sakima's desire for his wolf shifter spread through his body, tenting the towel slightly and dropping his fangs. Vance swallowed roughly, drawing Sakima's gaze to his throat. He gripped Vance's brownish-blond hair and pulled his head back, exposing the delicious artery pulsing in his neck, and watched in fascination as Vance's eyes darkened with lust.

Not an ounce of fear showed in his expression, despite having fangs so near his life's blood. Sakima bared them just to see what reaction he would get. Vance's gaze darted to them, but he otherwise remained still. Vance licked his lips and then sucked the bottom one into his mouth. When he released his hold, Sakima lowered his head and gently grazed the tip of his fangs across Vance's lower lip. He wanted Vance to feel the sharpness, but he didn't want to break skin. Vance sucked in a breath and shuddered.

"What are you thinking?" Sakima asked.

Vance's cheeks went impossibly redder as their gazes collided.

"Tell me, pet."

"I was wondering..." Vance swallowed. "Um, what those fangs would feel like when...you..."

"Yes?"

"Suck me. I mean my dick, not me...exactly...um."

Vance's face screwed up as he stammered. Sakima smiled at his companion's entertaining befuddled state.

"How my fangs feel depends upon my intent. If my goal is to feed, it stings and then burns. If my intent is to injure, there will be a great deal of pain. In the case of pleasuring you, it will feel amazing. You have no idea how erotic it is to have something sharp and dangerous sliding over such a sensitive area. Let me show you."

He pressed their mouths together in a heated kiss. Their first kiss had been quick and chaste. Their second had been driven by a blood frenzy. This kiss held the promise of more to come, of everything that would pass between them. Vance parted his lips and Sakima pounced on the offer, sliding his tongue inside for a taste. He didn't need to take control of the kiss or the wolf. Vance handed the power over to him without thought or reservation. When Vance left Sakima's loft, should the vampire decide to allow such a thing given the danger they were in, any scrap of doubt existing in the wolf's mind about who he belonged to would be wiped out.

Vance lifted his hands to Sakima's hips where his fingers dug into the skin above the towel. He wasn't as strong as Sakima, but he wasn't weak. Sakima ran his fingers through Vance's disheveled hair as he devoured his mouth. He sucked on Vance's tongue, loving the flavor of his beautiful wolf. Sakima skillfully dragged his fangs across the surface of Vance's tongue. Centuries of practice in the bedroom ensured his lover wouldn't be harmed. The reward was a sexy groan and a sharp tug at his hips.

Sakima allowed Vance to pull him between his spread thighs. Due to the difference in height with Vance sitting on the bed, the closer proximity forced Sakima to break the kiss. Vance stared up at him with lust-blown eyes as he opened the towel and let it drop to the floor. Sakima had been erect from the moment he'd scented his companion, and the kiss only strengthened his desire. His cock was hard and curved toward his navel.

"I've been thinking about this since you took me hunting."

The wolf wasn't in any rush. He slid his hands up Sakima's hips to his ribs and then over his chest, intent to touch every dip and curve. Vance's fingers sent tiny shivers over Sakima's skin as they danced over his nipples and stomach. He planted one hand on Sakima's lower back above the swell of his ass, and wrapped the other around his cock, the heat from the wolf shifter's palms branding him.

"Thinking of what, exactly?" Sakima asked as pleasure washed over him from Vance's slow strokes and tentative touches. Being with his destined companion was more effective in drowning out Sakima's concerns than anything else he may have thought of. Some of the rumors spreading through the vampire coven could be dangerous to his wolf, but Sakima would see to that later. Right now, the handsome man would receive his undivided attention.

"Answer, pet."

"You, me, sex, mating, bonding, all of it."

Sakima smiled as he smoothed his palms over Vance's hair, down his neck to his shoulders, drawing in ragged breaths as the beautiful wolf shifter worked his cock with timid fingers.

Chapter Ten

VANCE

Vance stroked the vampire carefully at first, unsure how much pressure would be too much. His thoughts unwillingly jumped to the last man he'd had sex with and the pain he'd caused with his supernatural strength. The man was human, but Vance had forgotten that while they were giving each other blow jobs. His orgasm barreled through him, and he'd squeezed the cock in his hand a little too hard with a little too much claw. Vance still heard the human's screams of pain, smelled the metallic scent of blood. He didn't want to repeat the experience. Until now, the memory kept him from becoming intimate with anyone.

As though reading his thoughts, Sakima threaded his fingers through Vance's hair, gripped tightly, and then pulled Vance's head back until their gazes locked.

"I'm a vampire. I won't break." Sakima placed his hand over Vance's at the base of his cock and squeezed. He bared his fangs on a groan as he demonstrated exactly how hard he liked to be touched. Sakima pulled Vance's hand to the tip, working a bead of fluid out from the slit.

"Yes," the vampire hissed when Vance flicked his tongue out to collect the drop.

One taste and all of Vance's worries about causing pain disappeared. He took the vampire's cock into his mouth, desperate for more of his mate's flavor. Sakima released Vance's hand in favor of touching his head, neck, shoulders, anywhere he could reach without pulling his cock free of Vance's mouth. He swallowed Sakima to the root and then slowly pulled up, dragging his tongue along the thick vein as he went. At the tip, he hollowed his cheeks and sucked. A rumbling groan indicated he was doing it right; Sakima was enjoying the blowjob as much as Vance.

"That's it, pet," Sakima praised, roughly threading his fingers through Vance's hair. "Good wolf. Take me inside you."

Vance soaked in the words. He'd never been a bold, brave wolf, instead preferring to let others take the lead. He was much better being the one to take orders. He got great satisfaction from seeing a project completed, another individual's needs seen to, and he reveled in the approval he received for doing it. As a teenager, he'd thought the predisposition to submit was a weakness. As an adult, he understood and accepted his place in a pack, understood that every pack needed an Omega like him.

There was a reason there was only one Alpha couple, one or two Beta couples, with the remainder of the pack consisting of Gammas and one, maybe two Omegas like Vance. While Tanner and Luca and Matthias investigated who and what the Chevalier were, and the rest of the pack worked on defense strategies and fighting techniques, Vance made sure there was fresh food in the house, the clothes were washed or replaced when damaged, and the house was kept tidy.

Sakima cupped his jaw and lifted, the action resulting in his dick slipping free of Vance's lips. "You're thinking too much," he said. "And I doubt it's about pleasuring me."

Vance didn't respond. He simply stared into his mate's eyes, hoping Sakima would recognize his submission without him having to give voice to what he needed. Sakima held his gaze for a moment before releasing him and stepping back.

"Clothes off, pet."

Vance stood and pulled his shirt over his head. He barely noticed the coolness of the room anymore, but his nipples pebbled. His hands went to his fly and he popped the button free. When Sakima's eyes slid shut, Vance froze with the zipper halfway down.

"Did I do something wrong?" Vance asked softly.

When Sakima opened his eyes, the irises had gone completely white. Only a thin blue edging announced where they separated from the cornea. The change was cool and freaky, and Vance was once again entranced by the change.

"You're an Omega."

"Is that a problem?" Vance asked, barely above a whisper as dread that Sakima would reject him over his status in the pack filled him. He was the lowest-ranking wolf, but he had worth.

Sakima gave a fanged smile. "I think, as things progress between us over the next few hours, you will find you are quite suitable to me. Lie back," he demanded with a soft shove to Vance's chest.

Vance fell to his back on the mattress and watched as his lover crawled over his body to straddle his chest, pinning Vance's biceps beneath his shins. The vampire stroked his cock a couple of times while gazing into Vance's eyes.

"I'm going to feed you."

Sakima planted a hand on the mattress above Vance's head and then gently slid his cock into Vance's mouth. He took the entire length, relaxing his jaw as Sakima slid in, then sucking and rubbing his tongue along the underside as Sakima pulled out in an attempt to make the blow job as good as he could manage from the position Sakima had him locked in. He flattened his tongue and laved the underside of Sakima's dick. On each withdrawal, he tightened his lips and sucked at the tip. After a few minutes, Sakima pulled away and shuffled back over Vance's body to sit astride his hips. Vance's cock slid comfortably between the globes of Sakima's ass.

"As gentle and reserved as you started, I thought perhaps you were inexperienced. Your oral skills suggest otherwise."

"I'm reserved because I've hurt past lovers," Vance admitted. "I'm not a virgin, if that's what you mean."

"It's odd, but I find I am both pleased and annoyed I'm not your first."

Sakima furrowed his brow, and Vance chuffed out a laugh. The vampire narrowed his eyes and bared his fangs, but it did nothing to dispel Vance's mirth. A sense of rightness bloomed in his chest because he was finally where he belonged—naked beneath Sakima, surrounded by his scent and overpowered by his strength.

"Don't move," Sakima said. "And don't try to keep track of me."

"Keep track—"

Air whooshed out of Vance's lungs as the vampire's weight shifted and then was gone, leaving Vance lying naked on the bed. He shivered in the breeze wafting around the room in Sakima's wake. His mate was a blur of motion Vance couldn't truly locate. He saw vague humanoid shapes in his peripheral vision, but by the time he turned his head in that direction, the man creating them had moved elsewhere in the room. Vance closed his eyes and reached up to grab the corner of the comforter because he was getting cold without his mate's body heat. As his fingers closed around the edge of the blanket, a hand grabbed hold of his forearm in a gentle, but damned strong grip, locking Vance's arm in place. He glanced up as Sakima began wrapping a length of silk cord around his wrist.

"What are you doing?" Vance asked.

Vance rolled to his side and shifted his body upward on the bed as far as his pinned arm would allow. Sakima's long white hair flowed over his shoulder. Vance reached with his free hand and wrapped the strands loosely around his fingers, amazed at the softness. Sakima leaned down to brush a soft kiss across Vance's lips as he pulled Vance's hand from his hair. Vance followed Sakima's actions as the vampire brought his wrists together and bound them, securing them to one post of the headboard, and Vance remembered he'd asked a question.

"What are you doing?" he asked again.

"Tying you down," Sakima answered.

Vance grabbed the rope and tugged. It was well secured, but it was still rope. "I can slice through this with my claws."

"You can, but you won't."

"Why?"

Sakima knelt beside the bed so he was eye level with Vance. He canted his head to the side and brushed his thumb across Vance's lips.

"While wolf shifters and vampires are fairly equally matched, claws can still cut, and strength can still injure. You've already shown me how fearful you are of hurting me, so I've removed the possibility." Sakima rose to his full height and palmed his rigid shaft. "Seeing you tied up and at my mercy has the added advantage of making me desperate to claim you."

Vance shivered again when Sakima dragged his fingertips lightly over his arm to his shoulder and then over his ribcage. He squirmed when those fingers got a little too close to a ticklish spot. Sakima smiled, leaned down, and took the sensitive chunk of skin into his mouth. Vance yelped, caught in a mixture of desire and discomfort. Having Sakima's teeth on him shot his lust through the roof, even if it was the most ticklish spot on his body. It would be so easy for the vampire to sink his fangs into the flesh.

In another mind-blowing blur, Sakima had Vance facedown on the mattress, his body draped over Vance's back, and his full weight pressing on him, holding him captive. Sakima licked the shell of his ear before nipping the lobe. Vance pulled on the rope keeping his arms stretched above his head, testing the strength of the binding, and finding comfort when it held fast. He released a contented sigh as Sakima slotted his cock in the crack of his ass. Sakima slid a palm over Vance's shoulder and arm, leaving pebbled skin in his wake, until he could wrap his fingers around the rope at Vance's wrist.

"You needed this, didn't you, pet?" Sakima whispered, nuzzling into the hair at Vance's temple. Vance nodded. "Your Omega nature presses you to submit to other's desires, whatever they may be. You have a compulsion to please everyone, to take care of those around you, and a deep-seated desire to be dominated that has gone unanswered until now, but don't worry, love. I will see to your needs. I *own* you."

Every word Sakima spoke was truth. Vance couldn't and wouldn't deny it, but that final statement lit him up from the inside out. Three words, whispered into his ear, carried the impact of a punch to his gut. The knot constantly coiled tightly in his chest eased its grip a bit, his body relaxing beneath his mate.

"Fuck," he sighed.

Sakima moved over Vance's body, alternating between licks, kisses, and bites to his back as he dragged his nails over Vance's skin. The combination of differing sensations had Vance squirming on the mattress, pulling at the ropes around his wrists, and trying desperately to get friction on his dick, but Sakima easily held him still. He squeezed Vance's butt cheeks in a quick massage before bringing an open-palmed slap down onto one and then the other. Vance gasped at the sharp, unexpected sting, but then groaned, driving his hips into the mattress as warmth spread through his body. He tugged against the rope when Sakima pulled his cheeks apart and every muscle in him quivered when Sakima dragged his tongue over Vance's pucker at a maddeningly slow pace.

Chapter Eleven

SAKIMA

The flavor of his wolf spread across his taste buds. One swipe of his tongue wasn't enough—a million might not be enough. He was addicted instantly. Sakima lapped at Vance repeatedly, feeling Vance's hole clench and relax against the intrusion of his tongue on every inward stab until Vance was an incoherent mass of writhing male beneath him. Sakima was lost in the sensations until his wolf shifter yanked on the bindings.

Vance's actions didn't feel like an attempt at escape, but rather an attempt at momentary relief as his body moved up the bed away from Sakima's ministrations. Or perhaps, as would be suggested by the guttural groan Vance emitted with the movement, he was attempting to put friction and pressure on his cock. Sakima couldn't have that: Vance searching out his own pleasure.

Sakima moved down the bed only far enough to grip Vance's ankles and flip him onto his back. Vance whimpered in distress, his cock red and leaking precum as it strained against his stomach. Sakima spread his legs and lowered between them over Vance's body to take his mouth in a dominating kiss. His wolf opened for him immediately, allowing him to take what he wanted. Sakima carefully scraped his fangs across Vance's lower lip and received another adorable, needy whine.

"Trust me to give you what you need," Sakima whispered against Vance's lips before giving into the temptation of another kiss.

When Vance planted his heels into the mattress and bucked his hips upward, searching for contact, Sakima broke the kiss. One hand on a hip held Vance still as Sakima peppered kisses across his chest and stomach on his way to Vance's neglected cock. Grabbing the base with his free hand, Sakima took his companion's beautifully aroused dick into his mouth. He worked the head between the roof of his mouth and tongue while simultaneously swallowing around the flared tip. Wolves were strong, but still not nearly as strong as vampires. Despite Vance's pleasure-driven attempts to thrust his hips upward, Sakima easily held him in place, making him more desperate and crazed. Sakima wondered what it would take to make his sweet, young wolf howl.

Pulling off Vance's shaft with a pop, Sakima released his grip at the base and sucked two fingers into his mouth. Once he felt they were sufficiently wet, he circled them at Vance's entrance. Vance instantly bent his legs, spreading them as far as Sakima's hold on him allowed. Sakima slid his hand from Vance's hip to his sternum. Tight heat enveloped Sakima's fingers as his wolf drove himself onto them with a gasp.

"Yes, more," Vance panted. He tugged at his wrist ties as he undulated his body on the mattress.

Sakima carefully worked a third finger into his companion's grasping heat. Vance tensed at the additional penetration, but his sweet, needy little sounds increased, so Sakima continued to stretch and open his lover. Rotating his hand palm up, he crooked his fingers in search of the bundle of nerves that would rocket his wolf to the point of no return.

"No, Sakima." Vance lifted his head to look Sakima in the eye when Sakima froze, fingers buried inside his lover's ass. "Don't want to come like this. Please?"

Sakima laved his tongue along the thick vein of Vance's cock as he pulled his fingers free. Lifting Vance's legs, he moved closer until his thighs were snug against Vance's butt cheeks. He reached behind him for the bottle of lube he'd thrown on the bed during his preparations and quickly coated his shaft. He rubbed the excess across Vance's pucker before placing the flared head of his cock against it. Sakima grabbed Vance's hips as he slowly pushed inside his companion's body. His breath hitched as the ring of muscle finally gave and his dick was surrounded by Vance's smooth heat.

"Fuck, pet, you feel amazing," Sakima whispered. "So hot and tight, and mine."

Vance yanked on his restraints as he lifted and lowered his pelvis, working Sakima deeper into his body. Content to let his companion take him in at his own pace, Sakima scraped his fangs over the smooth skin of Vance's shoulder, collarbone, and chest leaving thin scratches that healed almost immediately. Unable to take more of the exquisite torture of his lover impaling himself on his cock, Sakima lifted one of Vance's legs over his shoulder and slammed in to the root. He leaned over Vance so he could kiss his wolf while ramming his cock hard and deep inside his lover's welcoming body. Vance gasped into the kiss as Sakima fucked him into the mattress. He wrapped his free leg around Sakima's hip, holding him close in the only way he could with his wrists bound to the bedpost above his head.

"Yes. Right there...Sakima..." Vance gasped out.

Vance's movements became erratic, signaling his impending orgasm. Judging by the tightness around Sakima's cock, his beautiful wolf's release was going to be explosive. Sakima lifted off far enough to see Vance's canines had dropped, eyes wild and glassy, and his claws were lengthening. He grabbed Vance's cock with one hand and began pumping the shaft to the rhythm of his thrusts. Vance's entire body went taut seconds before his orgasm blasted through him with a roar, shooting ribbons of semen across his lithe body. He dissolved into a mass of quivering, sweaty flesh as Sakima powered into him, chasing his own release. He bared his fangs as the first tingles of orgasm raced down his spine.

"Going to come inside you, my pet," he panted as his balls drew up.

"I want to bite—"

"Not now," Sakima interrupted. As much as he wanted to claim and be claimed, this wasn't the time.

Vance squeezed around him and Sakima erupted. He fisted Vance's hair and nipped at his jaw and neck as he convulsed inside him, marking his destined companion from the inside even as he fought the urge to mark him on the outside. There were so many things they needed to discuss and decisions to make, before he would feel comfortable claiming his wolf and bonding to him.

Sharp nails trailed over his shoulder blades and lower back before his butt cheeks were squeezed in strong hands, tugging him closer, deeper. Sakima didn't know when Vance had sliced through the cording around his wrists, but he made a mental note to invest in a set of chains for future encounters with him. Rope had been good enough for his previous sexual conquests, but clearly his wolf companion required more.

Sakima rocked into Vance's body, watching his love recover beneath him. He scratched lightly behind Vance's ears with his fingertips until the wolf shifter's strength gave out and he dropped his limbs to the bed with a lazy smile. Sakima carefully freed himself of his lover's body and rolled to his back. Fatigue pulled at his consciousness, and he fought to stay awake. He needed to see to Vance's comfort before he would give in to his body's need for sleep. While Sakima searched for the strength to rise from the bed, Vance had already leaped into motion. He used a tissue from the box on the nightstand to clean Sakima's body and then folded the comforter over him.

"I'm not ready to retire, yet." The words didn't come out with the strength Sakima had intended.

"You're beyond ready," Vance said with a gentle chuckle.

Sakima couldn't truly argue the point. He hadn't slept in well over twenty-four hours. With his wolf shifter's scent clinging to his skin and the contented relaxation from his orgasm, he was teetering on the edge of sleep. A few minutes later, Vance returned to the bed and curled against Sakima's side. His skin was cool, even to Sakima's sense of temperature, and he was certain he felt Vance shiver, though the wolf made no complaint.

"Let's get under the blankets properly, pet. You're chilled."

Moments later, they were both warm beneath the covers, Sakima spooned behind his young companion. He buried his face in the hair at the back of Vance's head and fell asleep breathing in his lover's scent, content his wolf was safe from all the dangers of the world—for the time being. Sakima needed to have a discussion with Vance's Alpha soon. Tanner needed to know the new threat his pack faced. Sakima drifted off to sleep with the decision to summon the Alpha the next day.

*

Sakima's gaze moved through the kitchen, noting all the empty cabinets, the never-before-used stove, and the refrigerator that wasn't even plugged in. As a vampire, he had no use for this room, but with a wolf shifter in the house, the need for a kitchen became apparent. Vance's human form needed fruits and vegetables, while his wolf form received the nutrients needed from the fresh meat the pack hunted.

With modern technology, groceries and dinnerware could be delivered, but the only computer Sakima owned was downstairs in the office. He heard at least two heartbeats in Elysium which meant, if he went there now, he'd be confronted by employees, and he wasn't ready to burst the bubble of contentment having Vance in his bed had created.

"What are you staring at?" Vance asked and Sakima turned to face him.

Vance's hair stuck up in disarray. He had an indentation across his cheek from where the fold of the sheet had pressed against his skin while he slept. He'd pulled his jeans on but hadn't fastened them, so Sakima was treated to an enticing view of neatly trimmed pubic hair. He'd never seen anyone as sexy as his gorgeous young companion sleepy-eyed and fresh from bed.

"A newly identified need," Sakima answered.

Clearly not completely awake, his wolf glanced around the kitchen in confusion. "Are you hungry?"

"No. Are you?"

"Not at the moment. Would you like me to make coffee or tea? Do you want some water? Can you even drink that stuff?"

"Yes, I can, but I don't *need* to."

"Okay, well..." Vance's gaze darted around the pristine loft Sakima called home.

Sakima smiled as Vance's Omega nature surged forward, struggling to find some way to serve his mate. "Come sit with me."

Sakima walked into the living room with Vance on his heels and lowered himself into the plush oversized chair. He could have chosen the sofa, but he liked the forced proximity the chair would provide. He patted the small spot of cushion between his thigh and the arm of the chair, beckoning his wolf companion to join him.

"I'm small, but I don't think I'm going to fit here," Vance said, trying to squeeze his butt into the tiny space.

"Allow me."

Sakima adjusted Vance so his legs draped comfortably over Sakima's lap, feet dangling off the armrest, and then pulled Vance into his side where he could comfortably wrap an arm around his lithe body.

"Yes. I like this," Sakima murmured, tracing the pinkened imprint on Vance's cheek with a fingertip. A drowsy smile was Vance's only response. "Are you comfortable, my pet?"

"All you're missing is goldfish," Vance told him.

"Goldfish?"

Vance smiled sadly and tucked his face against Sakima's neck. "I was scared a lot as a kid, still suffer from crippling terror sometimes. I don't like the dark or loud noises, never have, and my dad was always mean about it. Said no son of his was going to be a chickenshit puppy afraid of his own shadow."

Vance took several deep breaths while Sakima waited to see if the goldfish comment would be explained.

"My mom comforted me like this. She'd hold me in her lap and rub my ears. Once I was calm, she'd give me those crackers shaped like goldfish. My reward for being brave, she said, but I'm not brave. I hid behind a rock during the buffalo hunt because I was afraid of how big they were. If I'd been brave, I'd have been there to protect her when the damn thing charged. But I wasn't. It kicked her in the head and she died and I wasn't there. After the hunt, some pack members noticed she was missing, and we started searching. I found her. My punishment for being the chickenshit puppy my dad hated."

Vance's words came out in a hushed tone, but they were steady and calm, despite their gut-wrenching nature.

"How long ago?" Sakima wondered out loud.

"Year and a half, maybe? I was a few weeks shy of twenty, I think," Vance answered. "That's why I ran away and joined the wild dog pack. Because it was the worst thing I've ever done and the wild dogs didn't know about it, still don't. They have no idea they have a coward hiding among them. So, now you know who you got stuck with as a mate."

Sakima sighed and squeezed Vance against his chest. He could easily point out all the reasons the wolf shifter was the exact opposite of a coward, but he didn't think Vance would acknowledge any of them. Not yet.

"Would you care to hear about the worst thing I have done, so you know who *you* got stuck with as a mate?" Sakima asked, and Vance nodded against his shoulder. "I killed a child, barely six years of age. She was of mixed parentage and had no idea she'd been marked for death. Even if she had, she would not have understood why. She had yet to harm anyone, but her innocence didn't matter. She was killed simply because of whom she'd been born to. I drained her blood and left her body among the burning remnants of her family home on the command of my Coven leader."

Vance pulled his face from Sakima's neck and canted his head to the side. "How long ago?"

"Four hundred years, give or take a decade, and I have spent the centuries since trying to forget." Sakima cupped Vance's chin and brushed a light kiss over his lips. "You see, my pet, we have both suffered horrors we had no real control over. Now we have each other and we will face the dangers beyond our control together."

Chapter Twelve

SAKIMA

Two days after Sakima and Vance shared their darkest moments with each other, Sakima led Tanner across the empty expanse of Elysium's dance floor to the back hallway. Setting up the meeting during the day, when the club was closed, was the only way Sakima could ensure the encounter wouldn't be reported back to Arden. Over the past several nights, the club had shown an increase in vampire patrons. The Alpha remained silent until the door of Sakima's office was closed. In the confined space of the room, Sakima could feel the power pulsing through the wolf shifter's veins with every heartbeat.

The hum was easily missed when Tanner was among his pack and blended in with those who rightfully wielded the abilities, but when he was alone, his power was quite noticeable. The danger this young man presented as he stood now was enough to give Sakima pause, especially after his conversation with Arden a few days prior. Adding his own vampiric speed and strength to the abilities already swirling within Tanner would be foolish. Sakima would need to be very careful in his mating to Vance.

"You requested my presence," Tanner said. "Why?"

"Your power combined with your ignorance is dangerous, and we need to rectify that."

"I'm not as naïve as you think." The words were spoken calmly, conversationally. Tanner didn't appear insulted or defensive, which was unusual for Alpha wolves in Sakima's experience. "I am aware there are things I don't know, or understand, but I'm learning. Luca and Deacon are helping."

Sakima huffed as he took a seat behind his desk. The fact the Alpha wolf was at least aware of his limitations and already taking steps to improve them would make this conversation much easier.

"Do you know your place in the hierarchy of the paranormal world?" Sakima asked.

Tanner sat in the chair opposite him. "I'm Alpha to a wolf pack...that also has a dragon and an Elemental in it." Tanner stared directly into Sakima's eyes. "And a vampire."

"All true," Sakima acknowledged, though he believed Tanner's inclusion of him in the pack was still premature. "But you misunderstood the question and that misunderstanding is exactly why I asked you here today. Paranormal power is all well and good in a fight, but knowledge is the power that will keep you from having to fight in the first place. Right now, you are lacking the knowledge to keep your pack, and my companion, safe. I won't have you march your pack into a fight that may kill Vance simply because you didn't know you were outnumbered and underpowered."

Sakima felt his emotions bleed into his words. His concern for Vance's safety would be damn clear to anyone. Tanner grinned at the vehemence, but then sobered and nodded.

"Teach me," he said.

Sakima let out a satisfied sigh and relaxed into his chair. Tanner might be ignorant of certain things, but he wasn't a stupid young man.

"When I refer to the hierarchy of the paranormal world, I'm talking about every paranormal species inhabiting the planet and where each falls along the spectrum of power. Think of it as a building made of blocks you can't pass between, with the least powerful beings comprising the blocks at the bottom and the most powerful at the top."

Tanner nodded. "Okay. Start at the bottom and work your way up. First would be humans?"

"Humans don't fall on the spectrum. They're not paranormal," Sakima corrected. "First would be humanoid paranormals, like a succubus or vampire, but each of us in our own separate block."

"Really," Tanner said, surprised.

"Yes. Knowing where you fall on the spectrum means knowing your strengths, and your weaknesses. Vampires don't have a whole lot of magic in them. We have strength and speed, nothing more. The next few levels are the shifters. Which creature they shift into determines the level they fall on. Those without claws or wings fall the on the bottom. Those with claws, but without wings are next up. Those with claws and wings above them. Each of them contained within their own block. Understand?"

"I think so, yes."

"The next few levels, stopping one level below the peak, are those whose power can be extended beyond their bodies."

"Elementals," Tanner supplied, showing he truly was paying attention, thinking, and learning.

"Precisely."

"Who's in the penthouse?"

"Those who are able to not only extend their powers beyond their bodies but also take power from others. Believe me when I tell you sorcerers are the last beings you want to find yourself on the wrong side of."

Sakima watched Tanner assimilate this new information, reformatting the world he knew to include what he'd learned. As he waited, Sakima's mind wandered once again to the distant past that plagued him. The memory of standing in stunned horror as a sorcerer performed the severance on a wolf shifter, pulling all the magical energy that made her what she was from her body. The human half of her hadn't survived. The wolf half had run into the nearby woods. It was the last anyone had seen of Mariana Chevalier, though it was whispered her wolf had been killed by her dragon mate's horde who were unaware a sorcerer had successfully removed her shifter ability. The similarities of Stephan and Mariana's mating to that of Luca and Tanner were disturbing.

"So where inside this paranormal 'building' would someone like me be found?" Tanner asked, pulling Sakima from his troubled memories. "You know, the paranormals who can shift and channel other paranormal power?"

Sakima tilted his head to the side. "Someone like you should not exist. No one should be able to step outside their block and scale the building to a higher level of power. That's why you are met with such fear, why the entire paranormal world is on edge, and why you are considered to be so dangerous. It's not because you mated with a dragon or bonded to an Elemental. It's because when you did, you also took on their abilities, and that should *never* happen."

"But it has happened. The Chevalier family existed. I exist. How do you explain that?" Tanner asked, leaning over the desk and staring into Sakima's eyes.

"You're distressed by this," Sakima noted.

He had expected Tanner to have some level of arrogance toward his unusual ability, to display some belief they made him better than other paranormals, as it had in Stephan and Mariana's firstborn, Gaetan. Instead, this Alpha was displaying fear and uncertainty.

"Distressed." Tanner huffed as he stood and began pacing the small office. "Yeah, I guess you could say I'm distressed. Truth be told, I'm scared. It's not like I've been doing this my whole life or even went looking for it. All I wanted was a mate and a pack, to love who I wanted, and to be accepted. That's still all I want."

Tanner sat in the chair across from Sakima, deflated, vulnerable, and too young to be carrying such a burden. Appearances were certainly deceiving. Tanner was more than capable, even at such a young age, to handle everything being thrown at him. Hundreds of years observing people, and judging them, made Sakima far more certain of Tanner than the wolf himself was. He thought back once more to Mariana Chevalier and the way the paranormal world used to be before her family became evil, before it became necessary to destroy them.

"For thousands of years, the paranormal world coexisted and did not condemn such things as interspecies matings," Sakima muttered.

"But the Chevalier family changed that?"

Sakima held Tanner's gaze as he considered the question. "I'm not sure."

Exactly what and when things had changed was nebulous in his mind. No single moment in time stood out as the precipitating event. He couldn't even pinpoint when things had turned ugly with the Chevalier. The only memory that stood out was the destruction of the entire family, which was ultimately the massacre of three generations.

"I suppose it doesn't really matter," Tanner said. "I've only met two people who have a problem with me, and I wouldn't say either of them was focused on the interspecies part. It's more the fact Luca and I are both males, despite my father spouting his BS about me being a Chevalier. As if that were even possible." Tanner huffed again. "How can I be a member of the Chevalier family if my parents aren't?"

"I imagine you are more of a genetic anomaly that makes one *think* Chevalier rather than you actually *being* Chevalier, but all that aside, who else besides you father has spoken against your mating?" Sakima asked, grateful for the opportunity to change the topic of conversation and extremely interested in how many other paranormal species were concerned about Vance's pack.

"Luca's mother. She's the matriarch of the horde, and I think she wanted grandkids. She wasn't too pleased when she learned Luca had mated another male. Plus, she thought I was close to unhinged." Tanner shrugged.

Sakima sighed. "Increase your number to three."

"Three? My father, Luca's mother, and...?"

"Arden, the leader of my Coven."

"Why would he, or she, care who I mated?"

"He, and it's not who you mated he cares about. Or even your mating being interspecies and same sex. It's the ever-increasing number of rumors that you are indeed another Chevalier he's concerned with."

"Rumors no doubt started by my father. The name didn't even pop up until after he yelled it at me."

"Possibly," Sakima agreed. "But be warned and be careful. Arden's attention has been caught. Keep your pack close and quiet. Do nothing to warrant more suspicion or concern. He has asked me to start a spy network within Elysium to gather information on you, and I don't know who, other than me, he may have approached, but I can tell you there are more vampires coming into the club recently."

"Great. Now I have vampires to worry about." Tanner sighed and rose to his feet. At the door, he stopped and glanced back over his shoulder at Sakima. "For the record, my pack has done nothing to warrant all of this attention. We just want to be left alone to live out our lives with our mates and be happy. It's my father who's causing all the trouble."

Sakima dipped his head in acknowledgment. "As self-centered as it may sound, Vance's safety is my only concern. I will deal with Arden and the Coven. I expect you and your mate to deal with your parents. If my destined companion is injured, or god forbid killed, you will have far larger concerns because I will bring the entire paranormal world down on you."

Inexplicably, the Alpha wolf smiled broadly before leaving Sakima alone with his troubled thoughts. If the sanity of his wolf shifter wasn't a concern, Sakima would uproot in a heartbeat and take Vance as far away from this situation as possible. He and Vance spent a good portion of the past three nights in each other's arms, making love, kissing, and talking. Sakima now knew how important the pack dynamic was for all the wolf shifters involved, though as he understood it, things hadn't happened quickly enough for Deacon's mate, Ross. He wouldn't allow the same thing to occur with Vance.

Glancing at the clock on the wall, he smiled at the time. Tanner had agreed to leave work early in order to meet with Sakima, but the rest of the wolves would just now be getting off. Vance had told him more than once how nice it was to return to his day job, as dull as mail sorting sounded to Sakima. His beautiful wolf did like to feel useful. As he exited his office and made his way out of the club up to his loft, Sakima wondered what it would take to get Vance working at Elysium once all the spying nonsense was over. What sort of job could he offer that would appeal to the wolf?

It usually took Vance fifteen or so minutes to travel from Luca's office building to Elysium. They had plans for dinner, to spend another night talking and getting to know each other. Sakima was eager to discuss so many things with Vance—a job change, their living situation, their formal mating. He'd bought a fresh duck, rice, and some vegetables from the Asian market down the street for Vance. His kitchen was gradually being filled with necessities, and the refrigerator was now plugged in and being used, but he still had no use for the room.

He'd fed from the young female cashier behind the counter. Her blood hadn't tasted the way he'd wanted, but it had served its purpose. Sakima knew that because he was already bonding to his wolf, only Vance's blood would have the delicious flavor he craved. There was one solid knock on the door in warning before Vance let himself into Sakima's loft. Vance gave him a sultry look that hardened Sakima's cock and promised to make the rest of the night quite enjoyable.

Chapter Thirteen

VANCE

There was something different about human bars Vance couldn't quite identify, but he was absolutely certain he hated them. For what felt like the hundredth time, he reminded himself he was doing this for Sakima, but as a particularly stinky female brushed past him, he almost decided to let his mate hunt for himself. The odor of perfume mixed with sweat and pheromones was so overwhelming to his heightened senses, he didn't think he'd be able to stay here long enough to find Sakima a willing food source.

"Can't your mate find his own food?" Ean asked as he brushed shoulders with Vance.

Vance nodded and then shrugged. "I'm the Omega."

No further explanation was needed; Ean understood. In the traditional packs, an Omega like Vance was responsible for helping feed and care for the pups, as well as the expectant mothers. In the pack that had adopted Vance and his mother, that had been Vance's favorite job. He would help the pregnant females manage their other children and get household chores done when their bellies got too big, or they were simply too exhausted. He'd felt useful and necessary. Service was his way of contributing to the pack. Seeing to his own mate in the same way came naturally.

"Is there a specific reason he has to feed on humans?" Ean asked as they pushed their way past undulating bodies on their way to the bar.

A man who looked good, but smelled awful, gave Ean an assessing once over as he vacated his spot at the bar. Ean's nose twitched, but he raked his gaze over the man's retreating form appreciatively before taking the man's spot and returning his attention to Vance. Vance raised his eyebrows at his friend.

"Not in a million years," Ean answered his unspoken question. "Couldn't stand the smell. How does your vampire get close enough to them to feed?"

"Vampires don't have the sense of smell we do is all I can figure. His last human was dying of cancer and smelled horrific, but Sakima was able to feed off her like it was nothing. You've never been with a human before?"

Ean shook his head. "No. I was terrified of them when I was younger. My parents loved to tell me horror stories about wolf shifters who got caught by humans. Their way of protecting me, I guess. I'm older and wiser now, but…" He glanced around the crowded room and wrinkled his nose. "I have no interest. Have you been with a human?"

"Only twice. Neither time ended well."

A female who appeared too young to be tending bar came over and asked what they wanted to drink. They both ordered beers and watched as the scantily clad woman filled glasses from the tap. Her dark brown hair fell to her hips with bright pink stripes that reflected the rapidly changing colors of the strobe lights. Vance and Ean had been having their conversation at a normal volume, and they winced when they had to yell for her to hear them over the loud thumping music. Damned human hearing. The noise of the club was giving Vance a slight headache, thanks to his heightened hearing. Maybe if humans listened to their music at normal decibels, they wouldn't all be deaf.

This was going to be a short trip. He hoped he could find someone deep into the occult quickly so they could get the hell out of this place. The nightclub was too loud, too crowded, and too stinky for Vance's tastes. Ean's as well, judging by the constant wrinkle of his nose. Vance leaned back against the bar so he could scan the overly crowded dance floor. Ean sidled closer as he glanced around as well.

"Do you think they all taste the same?" Vance asked.

"I don't know," Ean answered with a shudder.

Moving his gaze from one human to another, Vance realized he had no idea what criteria vampires used to discern who would be an appropriate meal versus who wouldn't. As a wolf shifter on the hunt, he would go for the bigger, meatier options. It wasn't meat Sakima fed on though. It was blood. If Sakima had allowed a proper mating when they'd first had sex two weeks ago, or any of the times since, Vance could ask him through the mating bond what he preferred, but since he'd been denied the bite, he would have to guess and Sakima could suffer if Vance made the wrong choice.

"So, once you find someone you think is suitable, how do you go about getting them to your mate? Do they just follow you, or do we have to knock them out and kidnap them?" Ean asked before drinking practically his entire beer in one gulp.

Vance stared at his pack mate. When Ean's gaze locked onto his, he answered, "I have no fucking clue."

"Seriously?"

"I hadn't thought that far ahead."

Ean heaved a sigh and placed his empty glass on the bar. "No. As an Omega you wouldn't think of such things, but I'm a born Beta and I should have remembered that. Planning and strategy are my thing, not yours." Ean surveyed their surroundings, suddenly deep in thought. "Give me a few minutes to put a plan together."

Vance smiled and nodded, grateful he'd thought to bring his pack mate along. Thinking about finding his mate a meal and the actual reality of doing so were two completely different beasts, but he had absolute faith Ean would figure out a solution. He'd been a great Beta to Deacon and would continue to be a valuable member to Tanner's pack whether or not he became official Beta to the Pack Alpha. That role was currently held by Deacon, but all the wolves wondered if he would choose to remain Pack Beta or if he'd step down. Now that they had a proper Alpha, Deacon had become more focused on Ross and his mental state than pack affairs. Vance could understand. Right now, he wasn't overly concerned with pack affairs either. Only seeing to it that his mate had what he needed.

"Well now, aren't the two of you a pair of delicious little morsels," came a deep purr from Vance's left.

He jumped to the side, his shoulder bumping into Ean's chest. Ean put a protective arm around Vance and turned them so his body was between Vance and their uninvited guest. The woman's eyes were a stark pale blue and the tips of fangs could be seen between her dark-red lips revealing she was a vampire. Long black hair and heavily coal-lined eyes gave her a distinct Goth look. Apparently, Vance and Ean weren't the only paranormals prowling the human club for blood.

"Don't be shy, you darling little wolf. I just want to play a little," she said, gaze raking over Vance's body head to toe.

"He's mated," Ean said, drawing the vampire vixen's attention.

"Not the sharing type?" she asked. She danced her fingers from Ean's stomach to his chest where he grabbed her hand and pulled it away.

"Not to me. He's mated to a vampire named Sakima Hawke."

She once again slid her gaze over Vance, head to toe, though the playful flirting was now gone from her eyes, to be replaced by cold assessment. Either she knew of Sakima or was trying to figure out how a wolf shifter had ended up mated to a vampire. Eventually she shrugged and turned her attentions to Ean.

"Shame," she pouted, then gave Ean a sultry smile. "What about you, big boy? Are you spoken for?"

Unashamed, she stepped right up to Ean and plastered her breasts to his chest, taking a quick nip at his chin. She was a good head shorter than them, but she was a vampire. Equally strong, not to mention much faster than the two of them. Vance hoped Ean played this situation well, or things could turn ugly quick, and there were too many humans around for that. Ean's discomfort increased with the question and he swallowed thickly.

"No," he croaked and then cleared his throat. Vance wondered how much it hurt his friend to say that one word while knowing Matthias was his mate. "I'm not taken, but I'm afraid, as beautiful as you are, you're simply not my type. I'm gay."

The vampire smiled up at him wickedly before laughing. She stepped back and once again danced her fingers over Ean's chest. "And if I told you I had what you wanted?" She grabbed Ean's hand and pushed his palm to her crotch. Vance watched Ean as he tried to school his features while also attempting to politely remove his hand from the vampire's grasp.

"If it was just the dick I was attracted to, I'd say yes." Ean draped an arm over her shoulders and turned her to face the dancing crowd. He pointed and leaned down to speak directly into her ear conspiratorially. Vance's enhanced hearing picked up every word. "That's what I'm interested in. Older, muscled, tatted, great ass."

Vance couldn't help but notice all the traits Ean listed belonged to one ancient, overprotective dragon currently residing in their pack house. He watched in fascination as Ean redirected the vampire's attention away from them in a way that didn't offend her, something he would have never been able to do. He wasn't suave or worldly. Once the woman found another suitable male to accost, she headed out to the dance floor.

The man she decided to pursue closely resembled Vance and Ean, but oddly Vance knew the vampire's attention was still on him. He continued to scan the room for potential marks, but his gaze kept coming back to the female vampire. Every time, he caught her staring at him before she would casually look away. He was getting very nervous, given everything else going on with his pack. Giving into his paranoia and forgetting the search for his mate's next donor, Vance turned to Ean.

"Let's get out of here. I can't take any more."

"Good idea," Ean said, pushing closer to Vance. "I think we've drawn the wrong kind of attention."

While Ean pushed Vance toward the exit, he noticed the vampire female and two additional males, who had joined her, were following them. The three skirted the crowd on the dance floor in such a way that Vance and Ean were never out of sight. Vance was nervous enough on his own, but feeling Ean's concern bleed through the bond made him all the more eager to get out of the club. This night was not going according to Vance's plan. Granted, he hadn't exactly planned the visit well, but a fight with three vampires had certainly never entered his mind. They had just passed through the club doors to the street outside when the three vampires caught up to them.

"Leaving so soon?" the female vampire asked. "I was so looking forward to a dance or maybe a blow job."

Ean pushed Vance behind him again. "I already told you, beautiful," Ean said sweetly, a smile on his face that belied the anxiety Vance could feel through the bond. "You're not my type, and he's mated."

The vampire showed her fangs when she smiled at Ean. "The Omega will be taken care of later, but you, my lovely, are exactly what I want. And I always get what I want."

Before Vance could blink, the two male vampires had Ean on his knees, arms behind his back. What were they thinking? They were out on the street, right in front of the doors to the club where anyone could see. Ean let out a pained *woof*, the air knocked from his lungs. As fast as the vampires had moved, Vance wasn't certain Ean hadn't actually been punched. The pack bond snapped open as both Ean and Vance howled in anger and fear, reaching out to the pack for help.

On our way, Tanner told them.

The entire pack would be coming to their rescue, but they were all shifters, except for Deacon. Ean was being attacked with a speed their wolf pack couldn't match. Vance took advantage of the fact all three vampires were focused on his pack mate to slip into the tight alley between the club and the restaurant next door. He stripped his clothing as quickly as possible and shifted. Without a second's hesitation, he launched from his hiding spot and attacked the vampire closest to him. Clamping his jaws around the man's arm and snapping his head side to side, he forced the vampire to release his hold on Ean. Ean took immediate advantage of his newly freed arm and swung a fist at the vampire still holding him.

The vampire took the hit, looking more pissed than injured. Apparently, the punch didn't phase him at all. Ean, on the other hand, likely broke his hand as his friend's pain could be felt through the bond. Forgoing another punch and further injury, Ean threw his entire body toward his attacker. The vampire stepped to the side with incredible speed, and Ean missed the mark. He sprawled across the pavement with a grunt followed by an infuriated growl.

Vance dug his teeth in deeper as his vampire pulled his arm free. The action caused the man to lose a good-sized chunk of skin to Vance's grip. Vance snapped and growled as the two male vampires disappeared in a blur only to reappear behind the female. Her eyes had gone white, reminding him of Sakima's pale gaze. Except Sakima's eyes burned with passion and fire, rather than this woman's ice-cold hatred. It occurred to Vance there was more to this confrontation than Ean's rejection alone. He would have more time to think about it later. Right now, he and Ean had their hands full defending themselves.

One moment Vance was standing between the vampires and Ean, protecting his pack mate as Ean pushed himself to his feet. The next, Vance was flattened to the hard concrete with the female vampire on top of him, fangs sinking past the fur and ripping open the skin and muscle of his side. He yelped in pain as he struggled to free himself from the vicelike grip. Pain unlike any he'd ever felt before blasted through his body. Ean cradled his broken hand to his stomach, face twisted in rage as he kicked the woman's shoulder, jarring her and sending a bolt of agonizing pain slicing through Vance's side. He felt like he was being cut in half. While he appreciated Ean's attempts to dislodge the bitch's bite, he truly hoped he wouldn't try again.

Vance's vision went blurry, black spots dancing in front of his eyes, as his strength and life bled away. The fight drained out of him leaving him weak, heavy, and numb, as he struggled to stay conscious, his instinct telling him death would come with unconsciousness. He had no idea how much time had passed when he felt the pack bond once again flare to life with the arrival of his Alpha and Beta.

A ball of flame erupted a foot in front of Ean that sent the male vampires flying backward. The flames were immediately followed by an eight-foot tall, self-contained tornado that blew over Vance and the vampire, coming to a stop directly behind the female. She tore her fangs through Vance's side, leaving behind a gaping wound, and had just turned around in surprise when the swirling dirt and wind coalesced into a massive black wolf with flashing red eyes, acrid smoke puffing from flared nostrils as the beast snarled and snapped at the vampire.

On the most basic level, Vance knew this devil wolf was his Alpha, but his higher brain functions couldn't make sense of what he was seeing. The roar Tanner released would definitely draw attention. *Humans*, Vance warned weakly while a flurry of activity he couldn't track took place around him. Dark spots filled his vision and he emitted a pathetic whine as Deacon lifted him off the ground. The Beta draped him over his shoulder in a fireman's carry. Now that he was safe, Vance allowed the pain to drag him into oblivion, trusting his pack mates would keep him alive.

Chapter Fourteen

SAKIMA

Sakima moved swiftly, grateful for every bit of his vampire speed. He felt Vance's pain, the agony slicing through his companion's body with every breath. They'd not yet officially mated, but he felt his love's fear, anger, and the spike in adrenaline that could only accompany a fight-or-flight response. The tenuous bond allowing him to feel his companion's emotions wasn't important. All he wanted to know right this second was why Vance was in such excruciating pain. Sakima had left his wolf's side only a few hours before.

After years of owning Elysium, experience had shown him how quickly things in the paranormal world could change. He'd had his share of problems erupt within the club's confines. Paranormals were unpredictable, especially around other species they'd never encountered or simply didn't understand. Unfortunately for Vance, he belonged to a powerful, interspecies pack that had drawn very negative attention and made the pain he was currently in far more disturbing to Sakima.

Burning pain isolated to his left side had Sakima gripping his ribs as he slowed to a stop at the pack house front door. Careful not to rip the door off its hinges in his haste, he stepped into the towering foyer. Voices carried down the stairs amid the sound of racing hearts and the scent of blood. He stood at the landing confused.

There was no hint of threat in the house. No unusual scents or sounds, and no damage to the house whatsoever, making Vance's howl of pain all the stranger. Worry and fear for the sweet Omega propelled Sakima up the staircase as quickly as possible. A frigid numbing sensation encompassed his chest and abdomen as he entered the large bathroom off the hall.

"What has happened?" Sakima bellowed to be heard above Vance's pained howl.

The sight that greeted him horrified him, and he knelt on the floor at Vance's side. Vance was in wolf form. A pool of blood had spread beneath his body, a large gash across his left ribs gaped open beneath a thin sheen of ice coming from Deacon's hands where the Elemental held them above Vance's injury. Eventually, Vance's howls and cries became whimpers of relief. The ice patch had the dual effect of stopping the bleeding and numbing the pain. Sakima nodded to the Elemental in appreciation. He scanned what would normally be a sizeable bathroom but was much smaller with so many large males crammed inside. He noted Ean was favoring one arm and Deacon's shirt was covered in blood, though the Elemental didn't appear to be injured himself. In fact, the majority of the pack was unharmed.

Avoiding the injured area, Sakima brushed a hand over Vance's bloodied, dirty fur and gently slid his other hand under Vance's head. He hunched over his companion's body and gently kissed his temple, rubbing his cheek across Vance's ear. Vance turned his head enough to lick at Sakima's shoulder before lowering back to the floor in exhaustion. Sakima buried his face in the fur of Vance's neck before brushing his lips over the wolf's ear.

"Please, my pet," he whispered. "Let me bite you."

"No!" said Luca and Deacon together.

Sakima shifted his head to give the two paranormals a scathing glare. Perhaps feeling the dangerous rise in tension, Tanner inserted himself between them. He knelt on the other side of Vance and held Sakima's gaze.

"Forgive them. They have reason to be apprehensive, given everything we've experienced with regard to bites," Tanner said.

Sakima showed his displeasure at the interference with a show of fangs. Tanner wasn't concerned by the overt threat. His heart rate didn't elevate; his pupils didn't dilate in fear. He was an Alpha wolf who put his pack first, with little thought to his own safety. An admirable trait Sakima could respect, when it wasn't keeping him from offering aid to his mate. Sakima nuzzled into his companion's neck fur.

"We don't know what will happen if you bite him," Tanner said calmly.

Sakima ignored him.

"The vampire enzymes will help you heal faster," he murmured into Vance's ear.

It was Vance's choice whether or not to accept Sakima's bite. No one else had that right. If Vance declined, Sakima would respect the decision and nurse him back to health the human way. None of the other pack members knew how many times Vance had begged for Sakima's bite over the past weeks, and he hoped Vance would accept his help. Sakima opened the hand on the floor where he cradled Vance's head. His fingers extended right in front of Vance's snout. Until they shared the mating bite Sakima had to rely on non-telepathic communication. In this moment, he was irritated the entire pack would be part of their private conversation.

"Let me help you. Accept my bite. It won't be the mating bite you long for, but it will jumpstart your natural healing. Nudge for no. Lick for yes."

Vance pressed his cold nose against the tips of Sakima's fingers and remained there long enough to make Sakima believe he might refuse before his tongue lapped out across his palm.

"Thank you," he whispered.

Sakima brushed the fur covering Vance's shoulder muscle upward to reveal a thin line of skin beneath. The less hair he ended up getting in his mouth, the better, though he would suffer a great deal more for the well-being of his destined companion. He dropped his fangs as he wrapped an arm around Vance's head to keep those sharp teeth turned away.

"This is a bad idea," Deacon said.

"Tanner?" Luca asked.

Sakima held the Alpha's gaze as long as possible, conveying without words that this would happen no matter what he said, before lowering his head to the bared strip of skin and sinking his teeth in. During a feeding, the first release of enzymes would numb the donor to the discomfort that would follow when the vampire began pulling blood, and then help to replenish the donor's cells and close the wounds upon completion.

There was no interest in pulling blood from Vance. Not until they officially mated. Sakima's interest lay solely with the numbing and healing properties of the bite. Vance yipped and pawed at the floor weakly until the initial pain from the breakage of skin eased and the vampiric enzymes took effect. As a wolf shifter, Vance's body had already begun the healing process, but this would boost the speed and efficiency by helping his bone marrow produce new red blood cells to replace what had been lost. When the urge to suck gripped him, Sakima withdrew his fangs from Vance's neck.

Tanner's gaze lifted from Sakima's mouth to his eyes. "No blood," he noted.

"I was not feeding, only giving aid."

Tanner nodded, staring down at Vance who now rested comfortably, and then turned to glance over his shoulder at Luca. A silent conversation ensued, of which Sakima cared little. He lowered himself to the hard, tiled floor, spooning against Vance's back, and lazily rubbed his wolf's chest and shoulders as he rested and healed. The constant gentle stroking let Vance know he was still present.

Vance let out a small, pained whine. Placing a palm to the wolf's chest, Sakima pulled him closer to his body and kissed the tip of his ear. "Easy, my pet. Your wounds are healing, but slower than you're used to. Rest."

Vance's thick coat of fur obscured many of the smaller wounds, but the large gash in his side was knitting together, albeit slowly. The pace suggested deeper and more severe damage than was apparent on the surface. Half an hour later, Sakima's hip and shoulder ached from lying on the tile floor of the bathroom. The scent of old blood was making him gag. Vance's breathing wasn't as labored as it had been so Sakima levered himself from the floor. Vance lifted his head unsteadily but Sakima placed a hand on him to keep him down. Clearly the wolf still had no energy. Sliding one arm under Vance's neck and the other beneath his pelvis, Sakima cradled Vance's sizeable bulk to his chest and lifted him.

The way Vance sagged in his arms would have been concerning to Sakima if they'd not made eye contact seconds before. He carried the beautiful, yet still bloodied, wolf into the nearest bedroom and lowered him gently onto the large bed. When he pulled his arms from beneath Vance's body, he was pleased to find them free of new blood. Vance was healing, but it still bothered Sakima how long it was taking. The wolf shifter must have been at death's door for his condition to be so prolonged.

The moment Vance was able to withstand the effects, they would be exchanging the mating bite. Another event like this where Sakima was unable to converse with his companion would not be tolerated. He eased onto the bed behind Vance and spooned him. One deep inhalation had him gripping the fur of Vance's neck as he all but growled in his lover's ear.

"Why does this bed smell of you and another wolf?"

Vance was instantly agitated, yipping and whining brokenly, attempting to answer Sakima's accusation while still shifted. Sakima had no doubt if Vance were able, he would shift back to human form. Sakima felt guilty for putting his mate in such a spot, but he'd been overwhelmed with jealousy and possessiveness like he'd never felt. The words had come out of his mouth without much thought.

"Quiet, my pet. We can discuss it later when you've healed. I apologize for upsetting you."

Vance settled a bit, though he continued to *woof* quietly as Sakima stroked the fur on his head and neck.

"He's not cheating on you."

Surprised he'd not heard anyone else enter the room, Sakima snapped his head toward the door to find Ean standing there, hand iced and bandaged. The scent wafting to Sakima was the same one he'd caught a whiff of on the bedding.

"We share the room," Ean added, matter-of-factly. "And the bed, obviously. The house is big, but not big enough for the entire pack. We all share rooms."

Sakima dipped his head in acknowledgment, as Ean turned around and left the room, pulling the door closed behind him. As the latch clicked into place, understanding of Ean's sudden appearance crashed over Sakima. He felt instantly better and cuddled close to his young wolf shifter. Vance's earlier yipping and whining had been a call to his pack mate for help. Ean had spoken Vance's words at a time when Vance could not. While there was no replacement for being able to speak to Vance himself through the mating bond, it was enough for now. Sakima pressed a kiss to Vance's face, below his eye, and held it for long minutes as he breathed in his scent.

"Thank you, love," he whispered into the fur. Vance pressed his snout into Sakima's hand, licked at his fingers, and then rubbed his head along Sakima's elbow and forearm.

Chapter Fifteen

VANCE

Vance jolted awake. He'd been having a nightmare, in which he was being drained of life by a seductive female vampire. He yelped in pain as freshly knitted wounds sent sharp knives slicing through his body and reminding him that he had indeed been ripped open by a vampire. His body seized until the intense discomfort subsided, and then he relaxed back onto the mattress. The bedroom door opened and Sakima entered, carrying pills in one hand and a glass of water in the other.

Vance glanced out the window, trying to gauge how much time had passed. The attack occurred late in the evening, and the sun had been down for hours, but it was daylight now, meaning he'd at least slept through the night. He remembered his mate coming to him, helping him, curling around him protectively as Vance fell asleep in his arms. His mate's scent surrounded him, infused every cell of his body. The scenario would be perfect if he'd not been severely injured, but it was what Vance needed at the moment.

Without a doubt, his accelerated healing had been given a solid push by Sakima's bite. The vampire had missed the mark when he sank his teeth in, preventing the act from being the mating bite Vance wanted so much, and he wondered if that was intentional. Sakima eased onto the mattress, his hip brushing lightly against Vance's thigh, and held the pills out to him.

Vance shook his head. "I'm okay."

"Your scream of pain suggests otherwise," Sakima countered, holding himself unnaturally still.

Vance wasn't certain the noise he'd made upon waking could be categorized as a scream, exactly. He grinned at Sakima.

"I just moved wrong." He scooted closer to his mate as Sakima's eyes bled from pale, ice-blue to white. Vance ran his open palm along Sakima's stomach, admiring his mate's strength and power. "Thank you for helping me."

"Of course—"

"How did you know?"

Sakima sighed through the interruption. He lifted the hand holding the pills. "Take the medication and I will answer your question."

Vance held Sakima's sharp gaze but was unable to keep the happiness and contentment he felt in his mate's presence from his face. Sakima had to see the adoration because Vance couldn't hide it. He shrugged with one shoulder.

"I could just ask Ean or Tanner," Vance suggested.

"They won't have the answer. I assure you, they were as surprised by my appearance as you."

Unwilling to break the physical connection he had to his mate, Vance moved as close to Sakima as he could, the sheet wrapped around his lower body inhibiting extensive movement, before accepting the pills and the water. He dropped all four anti-inflammatories onto his tongue and swallowed them with the water before placing the empty glass on the side table. Sakima opened his arms and Vance happily eased himself into the vampire's embrace. Sakima's clothing rubbed against the exposed skin of Vance's chest and stomach. Only the thin sheet covered Vance's nakedness.

"I felt your pain," Sakima said as he hugged Vance to his chest, carefully easing him into a lounging position across his lap. Vance loved the feeling of being cradled to his mate's body. He felt safe.

"How is that possible? We haven't mated yet."

"No, but we have bonded. Sex is not required for a wolf shifter to create a bond. Trust and friendship, even simple platonic love, is enough for a bond to develop," Sakima told him.

"It feels weird that you know more about it than me. Have you bonded to a lot of wolf shifters in your lifetime?" Vance asked.

"I've dated several wolves, but you're the only one I've actually experienced a bond with."

Vance rubbed his hands along the length of Sakima's back while he thought about that. He hadn't been aware he was creating a bond already. He hadn't even thought about the possibility, but he liked it. If he and Sakima had already created a bond strong enough for emotions and physical ailments to be felt, what would their telepathy be like when they finally shared the mating bite? The idea was exciting and terrifying at the same time making his heart rate kick up. Sakima cupped his cheek and gazed into his eyes.

"What's wrong?" He brushed his fingers down Vance's neck and over his jugular where his pulse was thrumming. "Your eyes are on fire," Sakima whispered, as he slid his thumb over Vance's cheek.

Vance pushed out of Sakima's embrace, careful not to pull on freshly healed wounds. He yanked the sheet from his body and climbed onto Sakima's lap, straddling his thighs. He put their foreheads together and threaded his fingers through Sakima's long hair.

"Mate with me. Now. Please," he begged.

His cock was painfully hard between them, his blood pulsing through his veins. He felt like he was about to explode right there in Sakima's arms. They came together in a hungry crush of mouths, tongues, and fangs. Vance felt his wolf at the surface, elongating his canines and nails. His wolf danced below the surface at what was to come. Sakima palmed his ass and stood, turned them around, and gently laid Vance on his back.

Vance clung to his mate with arms and legs, biting at Sakima's lips, sucking on his tongue in an attempt to get more of his mate inside him. When Sakima tried to stand, leaving Vance on the mattress, Vance whined and gripped tighter, claws threatening to tear his mate's clothing from his body if he even so much as tried to break their connection. Sakima pressed their bodies closer together even as he pulled out of the kiss. Vance refused to let him go too far.

"I will not claim you fully dressed, my pet. Nor will I claim you with a frenzied fuck. You're injured, and even if you weren't, this is not a time to rush. You deserve to be loved, cherished, and I intend to show you just how much you are."

Vance stared into Sakima's eyes, as the vampire straightened within the clasp of his legs, but didn't attempt to move away. He'd never been cherished, or loved, before. He had no idea what to expect, but he knew he wanted to experience it all with Sakima. Awe and fascination gripped him as he watched his mate, *his vampire mate,* pull his shirt over his head and toss it behind him.

Only the white could be seen in the eyes staring back at him, and his long white hair flowed over strong shoulders to brush across defined pecs and taut nipples, while deft fingers worked the soft fabric of dress pants over powerful thighs. Vance's mouth went dry. He licked his kiss-swollen lips and swallowed convulsively. He struggled to wrap his mind around the fact this man was his forever, or at least until one of them died, but he refused to think such dark thoughts right now. He was about to be mated—claimed.

His cock throbbed, bouncing against his navel in anticipation. His balls tightened and he clenched his ass. It felt like the first time; like he was losing his virginity all over again. The look Sakima gave him made him feel like he really was a virgin, a sacrifice to the evil vampire lord for the sake of the other villagers' safety. Vance chuckled at the overly romanticized image of being tied naked to the sacrificial stake at the edge of town while he awaited his fate. Sakima stroked a thumb across Vance's smile.

"If you only knew what it does to me to see this beautiful smile directed at me," Sakima murmured.

"I will soon," Vance whispered back. He flicked his tongue against the pad of Sakima's thumb and then sucked the digit into his mouth.

Sakima leaned over and kissed him while simultaneously maneuvering him more toward the center of the bed. He was extremely gentle, careful not to jar Vance too much. Vance assumed his mate was being cautious because his wounds were still visible in the form of dark-red raised slashes across his ribcage and side. But Vance barely felt them, his mind too focused on the sensations Sakima was creating to be concerned with the dull ache radiating from his side.

Sakima broke their kiss with an annoyed groan. "No supplies," he bit out.

Vance ran his hands across his lover's chest and laughed. "This is a pack of gay men. I swear there's got to be lube in every drawer of this house."

The announcement made Sakima tilt his head. "Somehow, that pleases me, even as it drives spikes of jealousy through my heart." He lifted off Vance and reached toward the side table behind him. He pulled the drawer open and rummaged through the contents.

"I don't love them the way I love you," Vance told him, eager to ease his mate's discomfort.

"This, I know," Sakima said. He turned back toward Vance wiggling a half-full tube of slick.

"Then why the jealousy?" Vance asked as he watched Sakima coat his fingers with lube.

"My brain is far more intelligent than my heart. True destined companions are rare, and my primal instincts demand I keep you hidden and secure even though my higher brain functions tell me I can't. Wolf shifters don't make for the best kept men."

"I like the idea of being your kept man."

"You may like the idea, but the reality would kill you. Wolves require community, pack, and a great deal of space to run. You would not survive being cut off from the world."

"No, you're right about that."

All further conversation was forgotten when Sakima circled Vance's pucker with a slick finger before slipping past the tight ring of muscle.

"Oh, damn," Vance gasped in pleasure and undulated his hips, trying to get the deeper penetration he craved.

The smile Sakima gifted him promised all sorts of wicked things, but on Sakima's schedule. "Easy, my pet, you'll get what you want... eventually."

A second finger slipped in alongside the first. Vance was going insane with the slow pace Sakima was keeping. When he attempted to roll his hips downward, his wounds pulled painfully, and he stopped. Sakima didn't have to restrain him to control him this time; Vance's own body was doing it for him.

He wanted to cry in frustration, but Sakima apparently knew what he needed. The vampire wrapped his hand around Vance's straining cock and began a controlled squeeze-release-stroke pattern while simultaneously working his fingers in and out of Vance's pucker. The movements were meant to prepare Vance rather than get him off, and the rhythm was pushing the limits of Vance's control. Sakima released Vance's dick and pulled his fingers free, much to Vance's disappointment. The actions may not have been taking him to orgasm, but they felt amazing, and he didn't want them to end. Sakima bent and kissed him. Vance groaned around Sakima's tongue, wordlessly begging for the cock he could feel bumping against his hole.

"Stop teasing and fuck me," Vance mumbled against Sakima's lips.

Sakima kept Vance's mouth busy with his lips and tongue while he maneuvered their bodies where he wanted them. With a deliberately controlled push, Sakima impaled Vance with his cock. The slow entry allowed Vance to feel every inch of his mate's impressive shaft as the flared head lit up every nerve ending it rubbed over. Tingles of pleasure tickled into his lower back and thighs. He pulled his legs up Sakima's body to press his feet into the swell of Sakima's ass. He tipped his head back, breaking the kiss and exposing his neck to his mate, the move second nature after so many nights spent together. Sharp fangs slid across sensitized skin, but didn't sink in. Sakima slid his tongue along Vance's collarbone, along the length of his jugular, to the lobe of his ear. A nip of teeth made him shiver.

"Never put yourself in harm's way again," Sakima whispered into Vance's ear. "I'm not ready to lose you."

Sakima increased the speed and power of his thrusts as Vance nodded in agreement, scraping sharpened nails across Sakima's spine. The glide of Sakima's muscled abdomen over Vance's cock rocketed him toward completion. When Sakima nailed his prostate, he screamed.

"Fuck, Sakima, I can't—"

Vance's canines dropped in anticipation and he arched his back as much as his wounds allowed as his orgasm crashed over him. Sticky fluid erupted between their bodies. In the most dominant move of his life, Vance fisted Sakima's long hair, yanked his head to the side, and sank his canines into his vampire's neck.

Warmth blossomed in his brain as he felt Sakima's telepathic presence nudging against his. He withdrew the bite and licked over the minor wound to help close it. He let his hand slide through Sakima's long locks as his lover rose over him. Sakima gripped his hips, lifted his pelvis a little, and pounded into him in a mad chase after his own release. It didn't take long before Sakima roared through his orgasm. Vance smiled with the knowledge his mate had marked him on the inside and was only seconds away from marking him on the outside.

One final thrust and Vance offered his mate unobstructed access to his jugular by canting his head to the side. Sakima shoved in to the root and then bent over Vance, fangs on full display. The sharp pain of those fangs sinking into his skin was immediately replaced by a hot, pleasurable pull and the amazing sensation of their mating bond snapping into place.

Finally, thought Vance, intentionally keeping the new link to his mate open.

A long wait for me, as well, my pet, Sakima said, the words a pleasant buzz in Vance's mind. It was the best kind of connection that went far deeper than the pack bond he was accustomed to.

I love having you inside me, Vance told his mate while running his palms over every inch of exposed flesh he could reach. He was surrounded by his mate's physical presence, cock still buried deep inside him, and his telepathic essence soaking into his psyche. It was the most incredible feeling he'd ever experienced. Vance wanted the moment to last forever, and so did his mate. The sense of contentment bled through the bond, letting Vance know this was right for Sakima too.

Sakima gathered Vance into his arms and rolled them to their sides. Once they were settled, legs and arms comfortably intertwined, Sakima grasped Vance's chin and then stared into his eyes.

"Now," he said, his tone all business. "You will tell me how you came to be injured, and I will know if you lie to me."

"I would never lie to you," Vance told him softly. "Mating bond or not, I hope you know that."

Vance allowed every ounce of truth to flow through the bond so Sakima would feel his sincerity. Sakima didn't respond as he stroked Vance's back soothingly.

"Not outright, no. Deceit goes against an Omega's nature, especially with their mate, but I believe a…softening of the truth, if you will…would not be beyond you."

Vance averted his gaze from Sakima's pale eyes to his chest. He felt guilty because that's exactly what he'd planned to do. Glaze over the truth a bit to keep Sakima from losing his shit. He placed his palm over Sakima's heart, taking solace in the strong, steady beat.

"Like you said, I'm Omega. It's my instinct to take care of my pack, of those I hold dear. I do it every day. Outside of the pack hunt, I make sure there's food for everyone and clean clothes. I see to the basic needs they would otherwise overlook." Vance took a minute to breathe and get his thoughts in order. Sakima seemed confused so Vance clearly wasn't making sense though the explanation was so clear to him. At a loss, he shrugged with one shoulder. "I needed to feed you," he said with a sigh.

"Feed me?" Sakima asked.

"Your donor died. I was looking for a replacement," Vance explained.

The hardness of Sakima's eyes softened as understanding dawned. He caressed Vance's hair. "Sweet and appreciated, but I can find my own meals. And…" he added, pointedly. "That does not explain your injuries."

Vance pushed the memory of the confrontation to the back of his mind. He'd never felt that level of fear and helplessness, and he didn't want to relive it. He pressed in closer to Sakima's body, soaking in his mate's heat, and tucked his face into the crook of Sakima's neck. He lovingly stroked his fingertips over the mating bite he'd placed there, awed by the fact this man, this vampire, was his.

"Vance, my pet," Sakima pressed gently. "I saw a flash of that memory, felt a sliver of your fear, before you shut it down. Let me see it all."

Surprised by the statement, Vance pulled back to stare at his mate. "You can see my memories?"

"If you let me."

"Is that a vampire thing? Does it go both ways?"

"It is, and I don't know," Sakima answered with a smile. "Being mated to a wolf shifter is new territory for me." He caressed Vance's cheek. "Let me see."

Vance closed his eyes. He didn't want to remember, and he didn't want Sakima to see how weak, afraid, and ineffectual he'd been. He hated feeling useless. His side ached with the remnants of his failure.

"You have already survived, my pet. The memory cannot hurt you."

Curled into Sakima's embrace, Vance shuddered. Sakima yanked the bedspread over their naked bodies. Cocooned in warmth and his mate's scent, Vance relaxed. He could do this. Replaying the memory would certainly be easier than trying to relay it in words. Sakima pressed their foreheads together.

"I've got you," he whispered.

Wrapped in strength, warmth, and safety, Vance allowed the memory to flow through his mind. He tried to keep the sequence of events in order, but his mind jumped around from one moment to another, playing out non-chronologically as memories often do. Sakima held him tightly through it all, muscles taut, breath coming fast. A trace of his anger bled through to Vance. He hated that his mate was witnessing his failure and that said failure was resulting in anger. He wanted Sakima to be proud to call him mate, not be angry because he couldn't hold his own in a fight. Vance fought back tears of shame and defeat.

I am proud of you, Sakima told him.

Vance scoffed. Obviously, he needed more practice with blocking his mate bond. It was stronger than the pack bond and not as easily controlled.

You're angry with me, Vance said.

Not you. I'm angry Onmarie, Steffan, and Micai thought they could put their hands on what is mine.

They wanted Ean, Vance said.

No. Ean stood between them and you. He protected you. They were removing that obstruction. And I will remove Onmarie's head for what she did to you.

*She wanted Ean, and he rejected her. She bit me when I attacked...*Vance said. That was his interpretation of the events, but apparently Sakima came away with something else. Something far more sinister.

You were her end goal.

At the sound of a knock on the door, Sakima told them to enter, effectively cutting off any further questions. Vance had always had trouble understanding the evil in the world and typically thought the best of everyone. Hearing that this female vampire had actually wanted to hurt him didn't sit well. He couldn't remember doing anything to warrant such violence. But then, everyone seemed to be gunning for his pack. The bedroom door opened, and Ross stuck his head in. A huge grin spread across his face.

"Yay! More family," he squealed as he ran into the room and jumped onto the bed.

Like a puppy seeking attention, he crawled over Vance and wiggled his way between them. Sakima released Vance and rolled away in time to save his valuables from being crushed by an overexcited, full-grown wolf shifter. Ross ignored the vampire's outward grumbling, choosing to snuggle against Vance.

I'm going to shower. Get rid of him quickly, and you can join me.

Vance watched as Sakima's perfectly muscled, naked ass disappeared across the hall to the bathroom. Ross's pointy finger poking him in the chest drew Vance's attention.

"Vance. Vance. Vance."

"Ross."

"Congratulations. He's not as big as my Deacon, but he takes care of you, so I like him."

Vance grabbed Ross's annoying finger and pulled it away from his body. He was sore enough. "Thank you. Is there a reason you came in here?" He asked as he sat up and tossed the blanket off. He'd been invited for a shower with Sakima, and he had every intention of joining him.

"Tanner's daddy made threats, and Tanner called a pack meeting so we can kill him and rule the pack."

Vance stopped and glanced over his shoulder at Ross. Tanner's father had been making threats for a while, and he did believe a meeting had been called, but he seriously doubted it was to discuss killing Alpha McBane and taking over his pack. Ross often made fantastical leaps in his logic. Ross smiled at him.

"You look happy."

Vance returned the smile. "I am happy. Tell Tanner we'll be there in a few minutes."

He stood and headed across the hall to join Sakima. Ross bounced across the bed on his knees until he reached the edge, and then he hopped off the mattress and ran from the room. He'd barely gotten to the top of the stairs before he started yelling.

"Sakima and Vance are fucking in the shower. They're gonna be a minute."

The announcement was followed by a lot of thumping as Ross tromped down the stairs. He could hear several groans and unintelligible comments from the main room. He stepped into the steam-filled bathroom, closed the door, and thumped his head against the frame.

"He makes everything so embarrassing and awkward."

Sakima chuckled. "Come in and get clean, pet. We've mated and the rest of your pack will understand."

Vance grunted and then joined Sakima under the spray. They washed quickly, sharing only a few kisses between rinses. They dried and returned to the bedroom to dress. Sakima was on a mission given the deliberate, concentrated way he was moving. When he caught Vance staring, Vance tilted his head to the side and allowed the question to form in his head so Sakima could see it.

"I have a nightclub to open. Now that you are significantly better than when I arrived twenty-eight hours ago, I must get back to it."

"Twenty-eight hours?"

Vance had wondered how much time had passed, but he hadn't expected it to be quite so long. He really shouldn't have been surprised given the severity of his wounds. No wolf shifter healed *that* fast.

"Yes, and I had to leave my bartender, Colby, in charge while I was away. I'm terrified of what I'll find upon my return. He may have painted the entire bar area in pink glitter just to annoy me or erect stripper poles on the dance floor to run a wet boxer briefs competition."

Vance chuffed out a laugh. "Seriously?"

"Unfortunately, yes. He's great at mixing drinks and bringing in cash, but he's a mischievous little shit."

Sakima led the way out of the bedroom and down the hall. At the bottom of the stairs, he kissed Vance goodbye. While Vance understood the need for Sakima's return to the club, he didn't appreciate being left alone to face the pack after Ross's embarrassing announcement. He refused to complain outwardly, but he let Sakima feel his reluctance and discontent with the situation.

"Go see to your pack, Omega mine," Sakima called out with a laugh and then blew a kiss over the roof of the Viper before climbing behind the wheel. Vance felt his mate's amusement even as the car disappeared from sight. Vance closed the front door and the bond so he could focus. Tanner only called meetings when there was something important to discuss.

Chapter Sixteen

LUCA

Luca sat beside Tanner at the long dining table. As had become the norm since becoming a pack, they all congregated there for the meeting. While they waited for Vance and Sakima to join them, they shared stories about their days.

"I just don't understand why he has to be such an asshole about everything," Ean complained about his department supervisor. Matthias made a deep-throated noise that sounded suspiciously like a growl, and Ean glared at him. "I have it handled," he growled back.

"I can handle it, as well," Luca said. "I *do* own the company in case you've all forgotten."

"The janitor was sad he didn't get to see the full moon last month so I gave him one," Ross tossed in.

"You gave the janitor the moon?" Deacon asked his mate.

"He did," Theran said with a roll of his eyes. "Dropped his pants right there in the hall and wiggled his bare lily-white ass."

"Jesus, you are an HR nightmare," Luca said.

"Ross, not Jesus," Ross corrected as he bounced his chair a few inches closer to Deacon. Droll, boring, and normal were not things this pack ever needed to worry about, but these moments allowed them all to feel like coworkers enjoying a casual conversation rather than a pack of shifters facing the threat of annihilation.

Still unhappy with the distance between them, Ross climbed onto Deacon's lap, buzzing with energy. Matthias sat at the far end of the table in brooding silence, staring intently at each of them in turn. Luca couldn't help but notice how often the older dragon's attention returned to Ean, where his gaze always lingered a bit longer. Ean completely ignored the glances cast his way. Across the open expanse of the living room, Luca watched Sakima kiss Vance goodbye and leave. The Viper's engine roared to life, gunned, and then gradually dissipated into silence.

Vance took a deep breath, rolled his shoulders, and then joined them at the table with pink cheeks. He chose the nearest chair and eased himself into it. Luca smiled. Leave it to the Omega to be embarrassed about finding and claiming his mate. Ross leapt off Deacon's lap and sat in the chair beside Vance. Grinning like a maniacal child, he scraped the chair along the hardwood floor, moving closer to his pack mate.

"Vance. Vance. Vance," Ross repeated excitedly until Vance finally looked at him. "What's it like being bitten by a vampire? Did he drink your blood? Are you going to turn into a zombie wolf now? Because that would be cool, and nothing could kill you, and when you shift your fur would fall off, and you could run so fast no—"

Vance clapped a hand over Ross's mouth. "Oh my god, stop," he said with a laugh.

His cheeks were still pink, but his body was relaxed and his smile soft as he took his pack mate's curiosity in stride. The young Omega's happiness was written all over his features and his joy bled into the pack bond. Luca was pleased to see the wolf shifter who gave so much and put everyone else first had found his other half. Vance might have thought his actions and caretaking went unnoticed, but every single member of the pack knew how valuable the sweet-tempered wolf was. Now it was Vance's turn to be taken care of.

"The vampire better treat you right," Luca warned. He didn't think fate would get a pairing wrong, but who really knew?

Vance glanced up at Luca's words and held his firm gaze. They exchanged smiles before Vance dipped his head in his usual shy, submissive way. Vance's newfound joy was in stark contrast to the emotional turmoil Luca's own mate was currently suffering. He'd felt the change before Tanner could regain control over the mate bond. He didn't like being cut off when his mate clearly needed him, but Tanner refused to answer questions or let him in. Instead, the Alpha wolf called a pack meeting and sent Ross to inform the others. The crazy wolf took great glee in running around the house telling everyone.

"Why not announce it through the bond?" Luca had asked once Ross tore out of the room.

Tanner smiled and shook his head, before shrugging. "We all need to feel useful, and he enjoys it."

Despite the stress he was obviously under, Tanner still put his pack mates first. Luca's heart swelled once again with his love for the beautiful pup.

"I think he's getting better," Tanner murmured.

"Wounds eventually heal," Luca said, thinking back to the injuries Ross suffered during Ethan McBane's initial attack several weeks prior.

"I was referring to the blood lust."

"You seem surprised by that. Isn't that normal once a lone wolf finds a pack?" Luca asked. Tanner had slipped into the beginning stages of blood lust before Luca had bonded to him, but he was fine now. It stood to reason Ross would do the same.

Tanner sighed. "I don't know. Maybe. We're taught it's irreversible and it only gets worse until we eventually kill ourselves, but now... I'm not so sure anymore. One more thing I thought I knew, but don't. The list is getting really long."

Luca had spent long minutes trying to convince Tanner that he was still new to the role of Pack Alpha and he couldn't be expected to know everything, but Tanner was stubborn and refused to accept that. Eventually, Luca fell silent and hoped his presence was enough to keep Tanner grounded.

Tanner shifted in his seat at the head of the table, cell phone clutched tightly in his hand. He was agitated, but also content to watch and wait as the pack members teased one another and showered Vance with attention, peppering him with questions about his new mate. Luca focused all his attention on his own mate. The wolf pup might believe he was screwing everything up, but it was moments like these he showed how a true Pack Alpha should behave. When Tanner's troubled gaze connected with Luca's, he gave a subtle dip of his head and an encouraging smile. Once the side conversations abated, Deacon spoke.

"So, what's going on?" he asked.

Luca watched as Tanner took measured breaths, using the time to gather his thoughts and composure.

"My father is holding my oldest and closest friend captive. Tyler managed to get hold of a cell phone and called me. We were disconnected pretty quickly but not before he could tell me he was in the basement of the main pack house chained to a pipe. I called this meeting to discuss options for rescue."

"I don't believe a word of that, Alpha," Ean said.

The anxiety among the pack ratcheted up with every word. The silence following Tanner's explanation and Ean's subsequent doubt was long and absolute.

"We could send the zombie wolf in to get him," Ross suggested seriously, breaking the silence. The remark was followed by several groans, Matthias's short bark of laughter, and the solid thump of Vance's forehead hitting the table.

"I really don't like this," Ean said at the exact moment Deacon stated, "This feels wrong." The wolf shifter and Elemental shared a glance and then refocused on their Alpha. Luca felt Tanner's anger build, but not a scrap of anger was evident when he spoke.

"He's a friend in trouble—"

"It's a situation we don't know enough about," Ean interjected.

Tanner's gaze slid from Deacon to Ean. The Beta wolf didn't back down from Tanner's concentrated stare. Luca's respect for the wolf shifter rose another few degrees. He felt as though the hierarchy of the pack were shifting right before his eyes. Luca leaned back in his seat, crossed his arms, and settled in to watch the exchange of power. Above all, he wanted to see Deacon's reaction to being so subtly challenged.

"I'm sorry I interrupted you, Alpha. I understand where you're coming from. If it were one of them being held captive"—indicating the other wolves at the table with a jerk of his head— "I would feel the same way. But we have to consider this is just another one of your father's attacks. None of your former friends stood up for you when he kicked you out of the pack. None of them has made any attempt to contact you since. Why now?"

Luca stared at Tanner as he took in Ean's words. To his credit, Tanner at least gave them some thought before arguing.

"If I would give my life to protect all of you, wolves I've been with less than six months, wolves I'm still getting to know, imagine what I would do for a wolf I've known my entire life. We were pups together. I don't know why he waited until now to contact me. Maybe when he found himself in trouble, I was the only one he could think of to turn to. I don't know, but I need to help him."

Tanner and Ean focused on each other, forgetting the entire pack sat at the table listening.

"I *know* you would go to the ends of the earth for us, for anyone you care about. That's what makes you a great Alpha. I'm simply saying the timing is off, and I suggest he reached out to you because your father told him to."

"You don't know Tyler..."

"Which means I can be more objective than you. If your father kicked you out of the pack, his own son, why wouldn't he kick out anyone else who didn't agree with him? What's the point of chaining Tyler in the pack house where any number of other pack members could free him? And, by the way, why didn't they? You can't be his only friend. How did Tyler get a phone? And when he did get a phone, why didn't he call someone already on pack lands with open access to where he's being held? I have to say it was rather convenient the call was cut off before any *real* information could be exchanged. I'm looking at this entire situation as a wolf on the outside, and all I'm seeing is a trap. A trap to get you, me, and as many others in our pack into enemy territory so we can be eliminated, and I can't let that happen."

Long moments of silence passed before Theran spoke. "Are you challenging the Alpha?" he stage-whispered to Ean.

Ean's gaze never left Tanner's as he shook his head. Tanner's thoughts and emotions bumped and bounced against the mate bond hard enough for Luca to notice, but not so much he could pinpoint exactly what his wolf pup was thinking or feeling.

"He's doing what any good Beta would do. Keeping his Alpha grounded." Tanner reached out and clapped Ean on the shoulder. "And I appreciate that. And I heard every word you said."

"But you're going to ignore every word I said," Ean stated.

"No. *We* are going to address every concern you have while we come up with a plan to rescue Tyler. Whether he really is in trouble or not, I can't, in good conscience, ignore his plea for help any more than I could one of yours."

"Yes, Alpha." Ean sighed heavily. "I suppose the best place to start is the layout of the pack lands."

Tanner smiled at Ean, a small sliver of relief slipping into Tanner's shoulders and feeding through to Luca. Just like that, the pecking order shifted without any real notice or fuss, and Tanner once again took over the meeting.

"Perfect. Thank you. Theran, will you grab pens, markers, and paper? Luca, can you grab the maps from your office? Vance, would you mind making us a snack? Ross can help you."

Those given jobs stood to leave the table. Matthias rose to his feet as well, a curious expression on his face as he stared at Ean, and then followed Luca upstairs. As they took the steps two at a time, Luca heard Ross start complaining.

"Only Deacon gets to suck me, Zombie Wolf. Keep your wolfy-vamp fangs to yourself."

"Fucking crazy," Matthias muttered from behind him and Luca smiled.

Chapter Seventeen

VANCE

Placing the plate of sliced meats, cheeses, and fruit on the table, Vance glanced over Theran's shoulder at the map that was currently the center of the conversation. Several locations were marked or circled. There were pages of notes and hand-drawn schematics scattered on the tabletop. Except for Ross, who was currently braiding and unbraiding Deacon's shoulder-length hair, the pack members were listening to Tanner describe his old familial pack's structure. In front of him, written on a large sheet of paper taped to the wall, was a list of names and what Vance assumed equated to each member's job within the pack.

When the conversation turned to breaching defenses and strategic maneuvering, Vance returned to the kitchen where things made sense to him. Sometimes he wished he had another Omega to talk to so he could get a sense of whether or not he was normal. He always felt like the odd one out when it came to matters of the pack, despite the fact he had no real interest in most of them. He wiped all the counters and washed the few dishes he'd used before heading upstairs to gather laundry. Vance always felt useful and succumbed to a strange kind of contentment when he was doing chores. He was deep in his own world, folding the clothing, when he heard his name yelled.

"What?" he asked as he looked up from the counter.

Ean leaned against the doorjamb with a smile on his face. "You were seriously focused on that shirt. I said your name, like, five times."

Vance ducked his head shyly. "Sorry." He set the folded shirt on top of the others and then gave Ean his full attention. "Are you Pack Beta now?" he asked.

"Yes," Ean answered, his smile growing. "Deacon officially stepped down at the beginning of the strategy meeting. Kind of felt like I had been set up to, well, step up, but it feels natural. You know?"

"Kind of like me doing what I do. Feels right."

"Yeah," Ean agreed, staring at Vance like he was trying to see into his soul.

Vance cleared his throat. "So, what's up? I'm used to Ross being the one sent to herd everyone in."

"We're going in tonight, and I was tasked with getting you up to speed...if you want to take part."

"Of course." Because every time he faced his fears, he was redeemed in his mother's eyes, at least in his mind.

"Okay. Come on, then. I'll show you where we need you to be and what we need you to do."

*

The rest of the day passed in relative quiet. The two couples who lived in the house had retreated to their respective rooms. Theran, Vance, and Ean played video games to pass the time. Matthias hadn't been seen all day, but everyone knew the dragon preferred the solitude of the library to being around the pack. He wasn't a member, after all. Vance wasn't even sure why he'd been included in the original announcement of Tyler's captivity. He hadn't taken part in the rescue planning.

Vance couldn't figure out what the older dragon's intentions were, other than perhaps taking the brief opportunity to set eyes on his mate. He certainly hadn't been shy about watching Ean, but he also hadn't been shy about walking away. Once darkness fell, Luca's librarian friend was the last thing on anyone's mind. According to plan, they broke into three groups. Deacon and Ross took Deacon's sedan, Luca and Tanner took Luca's Mercedes, while Theran, Vance, and Ean loaded into Theran's SUV.

At the agreed-upon fork in the road, Deacon turned right and Theran turned left. Luca pulled over to wait. Once they were in position, they would enter McBane Pack lands from each side while Luca drove Tanner right up to the front door. Tanner had provided guard schedules, entry points into the pack house, and given them the floor plan so they could get in and out of the basement quickly. Ean had bolt cutters in his bag, prepared for whatever type of chain was being used to bind Tyler. Deacon and Ross were tasked with distractions.

Their designated entry spot was a few hundred yards ahead, so Theran slowed the vehicle. He pulled into a copse of trees to remove the SUV from the line of sight of anyone coming down the road. They all three pulled out their phones. Theran and Vance tucked theirs into the glove compartment while Ean texted Tanner and Deacon to let them know they were in position. He then silenced his phone and they waited for their Alpha to give the go command.

"Tanner hasn't been home in a long time. How accurate do you think his guard schedules are?" Vance asked.

"He claims his father is a creature of habit and has become predictable. The old man certainly is hardheaded, given the way he keeps coming after us despite Tanner handing them their asses last time," Ean said, taking in their surroundings.

"Apple doesn't fall far from the tree," Theran said. Ean and Vance looked at him accusingly. "Tanner's as stubborn as his father is all I'm saying."

"I'm happy to say it's the only trait he shares with the old man," Ean said.

"He's very kind, thoughtful, and open-minded," Theran said.

"He would have to be to take on a wild dog pack led by an Elemental," Ean added.

"Hell! It takes a special person to take Ross in, crazy ass that he is," Vance muttered.

The nutty wolf was convinced Vance was becoming some weird vampire-wolf hybrid since his mating. He'd gone on about it nonstop while they prepared snacks for the strategy meeting. Vance admitted he'd wondered the same thing when he'd first met Sakima, but he knew better now. Sakima had educated the entire pack on that aspect of their mating while Vance had been unconscious and healing, but Ross was a dog with a bone, and he wouldn't let go. Theran chuckled and Vance glared at him.

"You love Ross and you know it, Zombie Wolf," Theran teased.

"Not you too," Vance grumbled.

He did love Ross. He loved all his pack mates. They were his dearest friends and only family. He'd be destroyed if he lost any of them. Ean's phone pinged with an incoming text. Theran and Vance turned to face him in the back seat. Ean nodded and tossed his phone to the seat.

"We're a go."

At the back of the SUV, they undressed and stowed their clothes in the cargo bay. They shifted and took a few minutes to acclimate to the unfamiliar surroundings, assimilating the foreign scents and sounds. It wouldn't be wise to get lost during the escape because none of them remembered where they parked.

This way, Ean said and headed into the underbrush lining the road. Theran and Vance followed while keeping watch for anything that might hinder their plan or require a last-minute change. Even something as minor and bothersome as a bear searching for food could become a problem for a wolf caught alone. Vance didn't smell anything threatening on the gentle breeze beyond the still-muted scent of the pack they were approaching.

This wind won't be good for Deacon and Ross, Theran said. Vance had been thinking the same thing as the pair was coming from upwind of the pack lands.

We're okay, Ross responded in his usual happy, everything-is-a-fun-game way. *There are horses over here, and we found some poop and rolled in it so now we smell like horse.*

Now we smell like shit, Deacon chimed in, sounding far less happy. *If I could have changed the direction of the wind without giving any of us away, I would have.*

A sense of laughter and levity bled through their bond—a much-needed release of nervous energy and pressure, brief as it was. The bond allowed them all to know where the others were; a necessary thing for wolf shifters when on the hunt. Each wolf needed to know where the others were to avoid injury. Sadly, the bond was just as effective when hunting their own kind. Ean slowed his pace as they approached the edge of the McBane Pack's compound. There were no fences or walls, no physical barrier at all. Tanner chose the entry points based off what he remembered of guard schedules and the paths each enforcer took during their rounds.

Pulling up to the main pack house, Luca informed them.

Vance found it odd to hear the dragon's voice in his head, but he was happy Luca was finally opening up to the pack. It gave him hope that one day Sakima would do the same. A lone wolf howl went up and was soon joined by others.

That's the alarm. Hold your positions, Tanner said. *And watch your backs.*

Vance's fur stood on end. He crouched low behind a thick tree as two rather large wolf shifters ran past them on their way to the main pack house. Judging from their size alone, he assumed the two men were guards—a position typically given to the largest and meanest wolves within a pack. While the small, weak, and timid became the pack caretakers; the Omegas like Vance. Once the men disappeared behind the barn a few hundred feet away and the area fell quiet, Ean rose to his feet. Vance and Theran followed his lead.

Out in the clearing they ran as quickly as they could while remaining as silent as possible. Houses and other small cabin-like buildings were scattered around in a haphazard manner, facing every direction, which increased their chances of being seen by someone. In the center of the clearing was a low fence surrounding a vegetable garden. Ean skirted around the fenced plot to the back of the main pack house, Vance and Theran sticking close to the Beta's heels. Vance could see why Tanner kept referring to this building as the "main" house. The structure was easily three times the size of any other building on the property and also the tallest, aside from the barn, thanks to the presence of a second floor. According to Tanner, it was the only house big enough to accommodate the entirety of the McBane pack at once.

Given his smaller wolf size, Vance had been the one chosen to sneak into the basement. Ean ran to the far end of the wall and took a sentry position at that corner while Theran stood watch at the other end. Vance's target was the small window set into the wall right at ground level about a foot from the back door. The doors and windows should be unlocked, if the McBane pack hadn't changed their ways since Tanner's expulsion, but old habits wouldn't matter if there was no one to be rescued. Lying on his stomach, Vance pressed his head to the glass so he could see inside.

The basement was stacked full of old, unused crap that made the room shadowed and crowded. The boxes and other miscellaneous items appeared to have been put there and forgotten, all neat and tidy as far as basements full of junk went. Vance cocked his head to the side. If it had been him being held against his will, he would have made a mess. Kicked boxes over, broken things. He certainly would have disturbed the layer of dust covering the floorboards. Nothing was disturbed and other than the voices floating to him from the front of the house, it was too quiet. Ean had suspected the whole thing was a lure to trap Tanner in enemy territory, and Vance was now certain his Beta had been right.

There's no one in the basement, Vance told the pack.

He rose to his feet and sniffed the air. Theran and Ean came to stand on either side of him as all three examined the village surrounding them. Apart from the guards he'd seen when the alarm was sounded, Vance hadn't seen, heard, or smelled anyone else. The anxiety the entire pack was feeling swelled through the bond. They were all on edge.

If Alpha McBane expected a fight like the last one, he may have evacuated everyone but the strongest, Ean said, answering the unspoken question of why the McBane pack lands were virtually a ghost town.

Implement the extraction plan, Tanner ordered.

Here it comes, Deacon warned as the wind kicked up.

I really didn't want to be right, Ean grumbled as the three of them ran back the way they'd come, Theran in front and Ean bringing up the rear.

You weren't, Tanner said.

Not entirely, Luca added.

Further discussion was cut off as Theran and Vance entered the tree line. Ean had barely reached the edge when a blur of motion sent him flying through the air. He landed with a shocked whine of pain, but Vance's attention was drawn to Theran as another blur knocked him into a nearby tree. Vance pinned his ears back to his head and flattened his body to the ground trying to figure out what was happening. Out in the grass clearing, Ean got to his feet and growled at the vampire standing in front of him. He snapped his jaws and growled as he circled the vampire male threateningly.

Vampires, Ean growled, as he let loose a particularly loud, angry bark.

What the hell? Deacon asked.

Another vampire appeared over Theran's prone body. Injured from hitting the tree trunk, Theran shook his head in an attempt to clear it. He didn't allow the pain to keep him down for long and was soon pushing to his feet prepared for a fight. Vance was frozen in fear, the memory of vampire fangs tearing through his side still excruciatingly fresh in his mind. With the memory came recognition. He didn't know which vampire was which, but he remembered the men from the club—Micai and Steffan.

The pack bond blasted open to a point Vance had never experienced before. The conversation between Tanner and his father could be heard by the entire pack, and they could all see what was happening through Tanner's eyes. The visual and auditory stimulation was unexpected and overwhelming, and the suddenness stunned Vance into dangerous inaction. Luca's cursing was joined by several *Oh, fuck*'s that filled

Vance's head painfully. Smoke puffed from Tanner's nose as he glared at his father. At least the older man had the intelligence to look concerned, even if he was able to hide the reaction seconds later. Tyler was on his knees in front of Ethan, chains around his wrists, blood and bruises covering his face and clothing.

"Vampires, Dad? You lecture me about my pack, but you conspired with vampires?" Tanner growled angrily, his voice deeper than usual.

"I do what's necessary to protect my own," Ethan said, lifting his chin defiantly.

"I was your own," Tanner yelled, power flashing through his veins and creating a weather storm of his own.

Tanner— Luca said through the bond.

Hold on, Deacon called, his voice ringing louder and clearer than the others. He was making sure everyone heard him over the cacophony of other sounds coming from everywhere at once. The bond slammed shut with such force Vance was left gasping for air. Whatever it was Deacon was planning, he hoped it would happen soon. The three of them didn't stand a chance against vampires. This hadn't been part of the plan, wasn't even a contingency they had considered.

What just happened? Are you safe? Sakima's voice was soft but drowned out the cacophony of noise surrounding Vance.

I don't know what to do, Vance told his mate.

He wanted to explain everything to Sakima, but there wasn't time. Why none of them had thought to include the vampire, he wasn't sure. They could definitely use a vampire fighting on their team right now. Remembering Sakima's special ability to see his memories, Vance pulled memories he thought were important to the front of his mind at a rapid-fire pace in an attempt to bring his mate up to speed. They weren't in order, and they made no sense, but he felt Sakima's understanding of the situation push into his mind.

I'm coming, Sakima said. The mating bond went silent, but Vance could still feel his mate there, staying with him.

Vance hunched low to the ground as Theran snapped his jaws and snarled at the vampire closest to him from his dazed position on the ground. Vance's heart seized in his chest as fingers dug into the scruff of his neck and then slid up to scratch behind his ears. Onmarie knelt beside him and leaned in close to his ear. She grabbed Vance's head in her hands and turned him to face where Ean and the other male vampire circled each other.

"He's a beautiful wolf, isn't he?" she asked. "Micai is only playing with him right now. You see, that wolf took something that doesn't belong to him so now he'll be destroyed. Vampires mate with vampires, and Sakima Hawke belongs with me."

I belong to you, pet, Sakima told him.

Vance whimpered, too afraid to move but fighting against his paralysis. He was Omega, but that didn't mean he was weak or incompetent. This simpering fear was his past; it wasn't his present. Black clouds formed in the sky above the houses in the near distance, rolling toward them at an unnatural pace. He hoped Deacon's storm would reach them before the three vamps decided to gang up on Ean. He'd heard of a lover's rejection driving human women to do some crazy things, but he'd naively thought paranormals were above that kind of petty jealousy. And she was going after the wrong wolf. Vance and Ean were similar in color as wolves so they were easily mistaken for each other to the untrained eye. Onmarie ruffled Vance's fur and then stood. She zipped across the short expanse of field to stand in front of Ean and was immediately joined by Steffan.

Vance! We have to get to Ean—

Theran's terrified voice cut through Vance's paralysis. He jumped up and ran to his friend's aid. He helped Theran to his feet as Deacon's storm finally rolled over them, pelting everyone with ice-cold rain and hail. Vance was thankful for the buffer his thick fur created against the slicing wind and ice, though the pounding against his injured ribs still hurt. Theran was unstable on his feet, but once all four paws were under him, he took off at a run.

Vance kept pace beside him until several dust devils erupted from the ground and burst into flames, dancing in chaotic circles across the ground and sending Theran and Vance in different directions to avoid getting singed. Ross's muddy, gunk-covered white wolf ran between two of the largest fire devils, leapt into the air, and latched his jaws onto Steffan's arm. Ross's weight and momentum pulled the vampire to the ground where Ross yanked on his arm in a twisted version of tug of war. Steffan screamed in pain as he tried to regain his feet, but Ross was tenacious, his jaws locked securely. Theran ran to Ross's aid, biting into the fallen vampire's ankle.

Latch onto a throat if you insist on engaging, Sakima snapped.

You're mad at me—

No, Sakima interrupted, but didn't elaborate more.

Micai held Ean off the ground, with one arm around his throat, protecting his face from Ean's snapping muzzle, and the other around his chest. Ean kicked all four paws in an attempt to throw the vampire off balance. Onmarie leaned in toward Ean's struggling body from the side, well clear of his flailing paws, and kissed the side of his nose before dragging her fangs down the side of his snout. Ean howled in pain as Onmaire licked at the blood welling from the wounds.

Vance launched himself at her, teeth aimed for the side of her throat. She spun and caught him midleap. He snapped at her neck, the tips of his canines ripping her skin. She screamed and slammed him into the ground. Pain exploded through his still-healing wounds. He could barely get enough air into his lungs to whine, let alone move. Vance remained still while the pain faded to a tolerable level, and then he slowly pushed to his feet. Onmarie had already written him off as any kind of threat, and he was perfectly aware he couldn't do any real damage to the vampire, but he wouldn't allow her to kill Ean, either.

Onmarie snapped her head to the side and Micai disappeared in a blur, Ean still in his grasp. She blew Vance a kiss before disappearing in a blur of her own. Ean's psyche disappeared from the bond, suggesting he'd been rendered unconscious. Vance ran after them, pushing through the blinding pain that seared through his body. As he reached the garden in the center of the compound, a wall of dust stopped him.

He turned his back to the swirling dirt, hunched low to the ground, and tucked his nose under his front paws. His mother had taught him to do this when he was a child to keep the dirt and debris out of his nose when they'd been caught out in the open during a dust storm near Phoenix. A dull thump sounded and the ground shook beneath him as something heavy landed near him.

Vance risked a peek between his front paws to see Luca's massive onyx dragon looming over him. Luca extended a claw and wrapped his talons around Vance's much smaller body. Despite the fact the dragon could have easily crushed Vance in his grip, the hold was gentle. Luca kept his talons spread far enough apart to avoid putting pressure on Vance's injuries. He lifted Vance off the ground with a pulse of his wings, adding more dirt and debris to the dust storm surrounding them as he took to the air. Vance flailed his legs and panic rushed through him, the pain of his injuries momentarily forgotten. He knew the creature holding him was Luca, but he'd never been picked up by a dragon before, never had his feet off the ground really, and he didn't like the sensation.

No, no, no. I can run, Vance protested.

Easy, Luca told him. *I won't drop you.*

Luca soared above the trees toward the SUV. Vance's anxiety and previous fear coalesced in his bladder. *I need to pee.*

Go ahead. I'll fly over Alpha McBane and his bloody fucking pack, Luca said, his laughter ringing through the pack bond as he let them all see his idea of drenching the asshole shifters in urine.

Vance added his own nervous laughter as the treetops flew beneath his paws at an alarming speed. At the SUV, Luca landed and placed Vance on the ground. Equilibrium shot, Vance wobbled on his feet as he breathed out a huge sigh of relief at being back on solid ground. The two shifted and opened the SUV to pull clothes out. Vance quickly took stock of his body. Massive bruising stretched across his entire right side, the raised white lines where Onmarie's fangs had ripped him open still visible through the mottling of skin. Luca watched the tree line for the rest of the pack as he donned jeans and shoved his feet into tennis shoes. He climbed behind the wheel, pulled the keys from the glove box, and started the engine.

"Open all the doors. We're going to blast out of here once they arrive," Luca called back to Vance.

Vance rushed to do as he was instructed. He felt his mate's presence a split second before Sakima appeared beside him. "You're injured again."

"I'm sorry," Vance rushed out. Sakima wasn't sharing his emotions through the mating bond so Vance had no idea how he felt. "I had to. He's—"

"Family," Sakima said. Vance nodded as Sakima pressed a gentle kiss to his lips. "I'm rather disappointed I missed all the mayhem, but I'm overjoyed to find you in relatively good condition."

Vance opened his mind to his mate, letting him see everything he'd seen, feel everything he felt, the regrets and mistakes he believed he'd made. He smiled at the love and understanding Sakima fed him in return. He'd fucked up by not including his mate in pack matters, but he was still getting used to having Sakima. They would figure it out.

"I'm sorry I worried you and took you away from your stripper poles and wet underwear contests," Vance whispered against Sakima's lips as small kisses were peppered on him. Sakima laughed and pulled him into a hug. Vance wrapped his arms around his mate's waist and breathed in his vampire's scent.

"Are you truly safe and well, my pet?"

"Yes. Minor injury, really. They took Ean, but I promise to include you in the search."

"I will hold you to that. I won't tolerate you placing yourself in harm's way without me at your side." Sakima kissed him again before disappearing as quickly as he'd appeared. A whispered goodbye floated through his mind.

"Everything good back there?" Luca asked, head hanging out the driver's window.

"Yes, but he's pack now. We should've included him."

Luca didn't have a chance to respond. Screaming, accompanied by the crunching of limbs and dried leaves, heralded the arrival of his pack mates. Ross still had his jaws locked on Steffan's forearm, hence the cause of the screams, as Theran, Ross, and Tanner rushed the injured and bleeding vampire to the SUV. Following close behind was a bloodied gold-and-white wolf. Tyler. At the cargo bay, Vance helped Theran shove Steffan into the vehicle, forcing Ross to release his hold finally. Steffan pulled his injured arm to his body and glared at Ross with his bloody muzzle. Theran and Ross jumped into the back after him, lying across his body in wolf form to keep him immobile. Vance slammed the hatch closed and then climbed into the back seat. Tyler jumped onto the seat beside him.

I'm clear, Deacon announced. *Meet you there.*

In the space between the SUV and the tree line, Tanner crouched as though preparing for an attack. Vance watched in fascination as his Alpha's fur became charcoal black and his form grew in size. Once the transformation was complete, Tanner released the loudest, angriest, and certainly the hottest roar Vance had ever witnessed, given the amount of flame that came from his mouth. The brush and trees caught fire, spreading quickly through the dry detritus. Yells erupted from the forest, suggesting the McBane pack had been close on their heels. Tanner turned, shifted, and leaped into the front seat. Luca was peeling away in a cloud of dust and gravel before Tanner's door was completely closed.

"What about your car?" Vance asked.

Luca, Tanner, and Tyler being in the SUV with them hadn't been part of the extraction plan. Then again, they hadn't exactly planned on being attacked by vampires, or Ean being kidnapped, or coming away with a captive of their own. Fear for Ean's life welled up inside him. It was his fault his friend was now at the mercy of a vengeful vampire; she'd been after Vance. In the front seat, Tanner glanced at Luca apologetically.

"He threw it into the pack house," Luca grumbled.

"You threw...the car?" Vance asked.

"I liked that car," Luca said, taking a moment to glare at Tanner.

The moment was poorly timed. Luca had taken his eyes off the road long enough to hit a pothole, jarring everyone painfully. The SUV was full of wounded men, so whimpers and grunts filled the cab.

Um...guys? Deacon's voice rang through the bond, silencing everyone. *I just found Ean in human form, naked, and unconscious on the side of the road.*

"Oh, thank god," Vance sighed and slumped against the seat in relief.

Ean was alive and safe. Vance hadn't realized how tense and terrified he'd been until that announcement. Now, he was deflated and worn out. Unfortunately, without his worry to occupy his mind, his pain was far more noticeable.

"What the hell?" Tanner muttered. "Why would they take Ean only to leave him on the road?"

"Mistaken identity," Steffan and Vance answered simultaneously.

Everyone glanced back at the vampire. Even Luca darted his gaze to the rearview mirror. No one said anything, but Steffan bared his fangs menacingly.

"They were all in wolf form and the two are similar in coloring. Onmarie doesn't want the Beta. She wants the Omega who stole Sakima from her."

Steffan held Vance's gaze. Vance narrowed his eyes, his anger over everything that had happened in the past several months rising to the surface and once again dulling his pain. He was tired of being attacked, tired of being afraid, and tired of being weak.

"Trade places with me," Vance said to Theran and Ross as he climbed over the seat into the cargo bay. Ross jumped into the back seat, snapping at Tyler until Theran jumped over and sat between them. Vance casually moved their belongings against the seat and then moved to the hatch. He popped the handle and let the door fly open.

"What are you doing?" Luca yelled.

They were driving at close to sixty miles an hour, the broken white lane demarcations slashing the blacktop at a hypnotic rate. Steffan watched Vance warily as Vance climbed over the reclining vampire's body. Vance gripped Steffan's shoulders and hooked his foot behind one of Steffan's knees. Leaning in dangerously close to bared vampire fangs, Vance let every ounce of his anger show in his eyes.

"Assuming he hasn't killed her yet, you tell that bitch Sakima is *mine*."

Vance rolled, bringing Steffan with him. Midway, without stopping his momentum, Vance shifted, shredding the linen pants he wore, and used all four paws to launch the vampire out the back of the SUV. Steffan hit the pavement with a sickening thud Vance found extremely satisfying. The fall wouldn't kill the vampire, but he took pleasure in knowing he'd at least caused some damage.

Vamp in the road, he warned Deacon who would be driving the same highway in a matter of minutes.

Can't promise I won't run him over, Deacon responded.

Vance didn't care what happened to Steffan, or if his message would be passed on to Onmarie. He'd deliver it himself if he had to. Vance shifted back to human, grabbed the cloth handle on the side of the door, and pulled it closed. When he turned around, he found four wolf shifters staring at him, and Luca casting him glances in the mirror.

"Sakima is mine," he repeated, as he got comfortable for the remainder of the drive.

Tanner smiled at him and turned back to the front. Luca huffed out a breath and then murmured, "Jesus." Tyler, still in wolf form, stared out the window. Theran gave him a thumbs-up while Ross peeked at him over the back of the seat, face framed by his hands, reminding Vance of a shy toddler. Vance leaned his head against the glass behind him and let the motion of the vehicle lull him into a light sleep.

Chapter Eighteen

SAKIMA

The club was packed. Sakima had reserved the largest table in the quietest corner he had for the pack celebration. While he had managed to divert the Coven's attention away from Tanner and toward the three rogue vampires who were now randomly attacking every wolf that even remotely resembled Vance's coloring, it didn't mean they were safe within Elysium's walls. Sakima's protests about the noise and crowd had fallen on deaf ears.

Deacon and the original four wolves of his pack had spent a lot of time at Elysium, and the club was the one place they wanted to go to celebrate the fact they had survived another McBane encounter. Sakima found that odd, but he hadn't wanted to tell Vance to stay away. It was well-known Elysium was a favorite hangout for Tanner and the others, and would probably be more suspicious if they stopped coming around. He was still amazed, given the frequency of Vance's nights out at Elysium, it had taken so long for him and Sakima to find each other.

In honor of the celebration, Sakima had the Full Moon appetizer, which comprised of raw steak and chicken pieces, sent to the table along with two servings of chips and salsa for Deacon. Every once in a while, Luca blew flames over his plate of bite-sized meats to cook them before eating them. Sakima had one of the waitresses taking entire bottles of tequila and scotch to the table, rather than waste time and energy having her run back and forth to the bar for shots.

Sakima was covering the tab anyway—a mating gift to his new "family" even though he refused to let Tanner bite him to bond him to the pack. Nothing unexpected had happened to the Alpha when Sakima and Vance had exchanged the mating bite. The older pack members, consisting of Sakima, Luca, Deacon, and Matthias, all believed it was because Tanner had not bitten him directly. It could also have been an anomaly, but they wouldn't know until the other wolves mated. After making his usual circuit around the club, checking on staff and guests alike, Sakima rejoined the pack table.

"What happened after you guys got home? Tyler just disappeared?" Deacon was asking.

"Yeah," Tanner answered and then threw back a shot of tequila. "All he said was that my dad beat him until he agreed to call me for help. We'd been close when we were kids, and he didn't want to hurt me, but he didn't want to betray his Alpha by helping me escape either. When I dragged him away with us, I fucked him over, or so he said."

"The hell you did," Luca boomed at Tanner's morose statement.

"Lone wolves don't usually survive," Ean said.

Ean glanced quickly at Ross, who was sitting on Deacon's lap, and then to Matthias who was brooding at the opposite end of the table before turning back to Tanner. Sakima watched Matthias's brow wrinkle and wondered if the old dragon was capable of any other expression. And he was oddly focused on everything Ean said or did.

"I told him about my last pack," Vance said. Sakima sat beside him and pulled his wolf into a hug.

Tanner grinned at him, more than a little tipsy. "Did you? That's sweet."

What it was, was Vance's Omega nature; the special instinct that pushed him to take care of everyone, even those not officially in his pack. Sakima felt Vance's small shrug against his chest.

"They were a good pack, certainly better than the McBanes. I didn't like being around them after my mom died, but...I hope he'll be happy with them. I know my mom was and they didn't frown on my Omega status."

Sakima absently rubbed his hand along Vance's arm as he glanced around the club, checking on the staff he could see from his seat at the table. Satisfied the serving staff were doing okay, he glanced at the bar and found Colby's gaze glued to him. Sakima tilted his head to the side in question. There was a customer trying to get Colby's attention. The bartender slid his gaze from Sakima to the man wanting a drink.

Colby turned on his trademark charm with a smile and sassy flip of his long, brown hair before pouring a Jack and Coke. He slid the drink across the bar with a flirtatious wink. When the man turned his back to walk away, Colby's smile dropped, and he turned a disapproving glare on Sakima. He didn't know what the boy's problem was, but if Colby thought he could stare at his boss, a vampire no less, in such a way, he had an education coming his way. Sakima's attention was pulled back to the pack discussion by the sound of his wolf's voice.

"Do you think Alpha McBane will leave us alone now? I mean…you put a car through his pack house and burned down half the compound with that fire…" Vance said.

Tanner's face twisted in a drunken scowl. "I don't like him being Alpha McBane when I'm also Alpha McBane. I don't want the name anymore. I want to be a Duray. We could make this the Duray Pack."

Now it was Luca's turn to scowl. "No. I'm good with you taking my name, but I don't want, or need, a pack named after me."

"We were Deacon's pack first. What about Linvale Pack?" Ean suggested, to which Ross squealed in delight and clapped his hands.

Deacon shook his head. "Everyone else refers to us as the Chevaliers. I say we own it."

"That will bring a lot of unwanted attention your way," Sakima told him. They already had the attention of a wolf pack, a dragon horde, and a vampire coven. Taking the Chevalier name would only make things worse for his companion and the pack.

"We already have unwanted attention," Deacon argued, while trying to keep a wiggling Ross from falling off his lap. The crazy wolf was attempting to dance to the music while remaining seated. The alcohol he'd ingested probably didn't help Deacon's cause.

"Take the name Chevalier, and I can guarantee your situation will get far worse," Sakima snapped. Vance casually turned his head and kissed Sakima's jaw. The action immediately eased his ire. No one had ever been capable of calming him as quickly as his beautiful wolf.

"I agree with Deacon," Ean said. "I say we own it."

"Should we vote?" Tanner asked from his position leaning heavily against Luca.

Everyone answered at the same time. Only Matthias and Sakima were firmly against the name change, but they weren't technically pack. And the pack had spoken.

"Chevalier Pack, it is," Tanner announced and lifted his shot glass in salute. The others did the same, clinked glasses, and then downed their drinks.

Sakima held Vance tighter against his body as worry reignited in his gut. He buried his nose in his lover's hair and then kissed Vance's temple.

He would simply have to protect Vance and the pack against the evils they had yet to meet. Vance smiled at him and in that instant, Sakima knew without a doubt his loyalties had shifted.

"I love you, but if you stay with me, will you be considered a rogue vampire?" Vance asked.

"Yes, but it will be okay," Sakima answered, nuzzling the shell of Vance's ear. "I love you, my pet."

Chapter Nineteen

COLBY

Leaves and tree limbs crunched beneath Colby's shoes as he trudged his way along the path. For the most part, the forest hid the fact a hiker was walking up the mountainside despite the dips and valleys of the pathway. Every once in a while, his socks or hair was snagged by a limb or a thorn. It had been a long time since he'd been surrounded by so much nature, and he found the foliate and bugs slightly annoying, though still preferable to the company of certain people. Colby sighed as he untangled yet another leaf from his hair. Because he was paying so much attention to that chore, he tripped over a small rock peeking above the dirt of the path.

Colby stumbled for a few feet before catching himself against a tree trunk. He'd never hated his mother as much as he did at this moment. No. That wasn't entirely true. Colby and his mother, the Grand Superior of Sorcerers, had been at each other's throats since he'd come out of her womb and set the delivery doctor's scrubs on fire. There had to be at least a dozen instances in which he hated her more than this moment, but this one was quickly rising to the top of the list.

His toe ached from where the tip had connected with the rock. He huffed out a breath as he conjured a minor healing spell and directed the magic into his foot. As the throbbing eased, Colby looked up to survey his surroundings and locked gazes with the most amazingly handsome man he'd seen in weeks. He'd not been at all stealthy, or even close to quiet, as he'd stumbled his way into this small clearing in the trees. The nearby river gurgled softly in the background as it flowed down to the man-made reservoir south of town.

The man was familiar, and it only took a moment for Colby to place him. This was one of the wolf shifters he was searching for. At the behest of the Grand Superior, Colby had been tasked with finding and reporting on the Chevalier Pack. So many rumors were circulating about the newly formed pack that no one really knew what to think. Colby had seen this shifter accompanied by several other paranormals at Elysium a few weeks before, but at that time, the idea they might be the famed Chevalier Pack had never crossed his mind.

If the new Chevaliers were as powerful as they were rumored to be, Colby only had one shot to incapacitate and subdue this shifter. He wasn't interested in doing any permanent harm to the gorgeous shifter, not yet anyway, but he had to do something to take the larger man down. A little paralyzing spell would do the trick. Colby initiated the magic flowing through his veins and pushed it into his palms.

This would be quick and easy as long as the shifter in front of him continued to be stunned by Colby's appearance. He brought his hands in front of him and started rolling the spell into a ball, feeling the magic radiate through his body in streaks, lancing out through the strands of his hair and turning his veins black against his pale skin. Colby's vision went black and white—the spell was ready.

The shifter took a step back and then crouched low to the ground, no doubt readying for an attack, but Colby was way ahead of him. The spell became almost palpable in his hands, ready to be unleashed, and then his world literally tilted.

"Don't—" the man said before he shifted into the most incredibly beautiful and achingly familiar brown-gray wolf.

Too late to stop the release of magic, Colby diverted the spell to a nearby tree where it exploded. His shock at seeing the wolf had turned the spell from one of minor inconvenience to one that could have killed the shifter if it had made contact. The wolf launched himself at Colby, hitting his shoulder and spinning him on his feet. Colby landed in a crouched position, flipped his long hair out of his face, and watched in fascination as the wolf he'd been having extremely lucid dreams about took off into the trees.

"Oh, holy fuck," Colby whispered.

Hearts of Magic

Chapter One

THERAN

Theran watched as the sorcerer flexed his fingers and twisted his wrists. His fingertips turned black, tendrils of darkness snaking up his arm in a sinister web as he focused all his magic into his hands. When he opened his eyes to focus on Theran, the orbs were solid black. The color bled through the man's long brown hair in streaks. Theran had never met a sorcerer, let alone seen one in action. He had hoped to never witness a sorcerer's power firsthand, but here he was, facing off with one. For the sorcerer, the timing was impeccable. For Theran, it couldn't have been worse.

He'd been caught away from the pack. Theran had decided on a walk along the riverbank, enjoying the temperate weather, lost in thought and unaware of how far he'd wandered. When he turned to head back to the rest of the pack, he saw a man standing behind him. The man was young and handsome. Dark hair hung down his back in soft waves, and intelligent caramel-colored eyes had taken in every inch of Theran in a warm caress before going cold. A tiny bell of alarm had rung in the back of Theran's mind, but he'd ignored the warning. It wasn't unusual to run into humans in the forest, albeit a joyfully rare occurrence. He'd thought this man was human at first glance.

Now, as Theran watched the sorcerer gather his power for an attack, that small bell of alarm became a blaring howl of fear inside his head. He struggled to wrap his mind around the fact someone so small and gorgeous could become something so terrifying in a matter of seconds. A gray mist formed in the sorcerer's palms, and Theran took a step back. The mist coalesced to become dark swirling clouds of magic, holding Theran's attention as he crouched lower to the ground. The sorcerer widened his stance, and Theran's eyes shot to the man's face.

"Don't—" Theran yelled and then shifted.

The transformation destroyed the clothing he'd been wearing and pulled on still-aching bones, but he couldn't be concerned with that right now. He lunged at the sorcerer in hopes of catching him off guard before he could make those clouds do whatever horribly painful thing they were meant to do. Theran's bulk collided with the sorcerer's shoulder, knocking him off-balance and sending those clouds of magic into a nearby tree rather than Theran's body. The spell nearly cut the tree in half, trunk splintering in all directions.

Theran had intended the hit to knock the smaller man to the ground, but in one fluid motion, the sorcerer spun into a crouch and stopped his momentum with both hands on the ground. He flipped his hair over his shoulder with a toss of his head and once again leveled his coal-black gaze onto Theran. If anyone asked him what he witnessed in that split second, he'd be hard-pressed to explain, the change was so swift. The sorcerer looked at Theran in confusion, and between one blink and the next, his eyes returned to their original caramel color before becoming oily black again. The slight interruption in magic rippled over the sorcerer's body like the aura from a heat wave. In that brief moment, Theran made a run for it.

The rest of the pack was downriver about a half mile, but in wolf form, he'd be able to close the distance swiftly, though not without some pain. Theran still felt the effects of being slammed into a tree by a vampire a couple of weeks ago—generally when exerting himself excessively. Despite the discomfort, he didn't slow his pace or look back to see if the sorcerer followed. He didn't know if magic would allow the man to catch up to him, but Theran truly hoped he could outrun anything the sorcerer might throw his way. He was intelligent enough to know he didn't stand a chance against a sorcerer alone, but there was strength in numbers. And when Tanner felt the need, the pack became a force to be reckoned with in its own right.

Laughter and conversation could faintly be heard over the thundering of his heart, and he skidded to a halt in the dirt and gravel lining the riverbank. This particular stand of rocks had become the pack's unofficial gathering point for hunts or simply enjoying the outdoors while meeting. Theran's sudden and frenzied entrance drew everyone's attention. Once his momentum ceased, he shifted. When seeking solitude, all the pack members would block the bond so no one else could intrude on his alone time. It hadn't occurred to Theran in those few short moments, while confronting the sorcerer, to drop the block. None of his pack members knew yet what he'd encountered; what could be coming for them if the sorcerer followed him. Theran rolled his neck and shoulders in an attempt to release some of the tension as he faced Tanner.

"Just got attacked by a sorcerer," he said between gulping breaths. His heart beat hard and fast, and not solely because of his run for safety. Something else tickled at his subconscious, making him uncomfortable. The sorcerer had looked vaguely familiar, but Theran couldn't place where he might have seen him before.

"Only one?" Luca asked from his perch on top of the rocks. "That's unusual."

"Is it?" Theran asked.

Deacon's nod drew his attention. Theran took one slow, deep breath in an attempt to bring his heart and lungs back to a normal rhythm.

"Sorcerers don't typically attack alone. They move in droves," Deacon said. Ross rubbed up against his mate's thigh in wolf form. Deacon lovingly smoothed his palm over Ross's dirty white head and ears. He must have been rolling in the dirt.

Theran shrugged. "Maybe because I was alone? He thought he had the upper hand?"

"No," Luca said. He rose to his feet and sniffed the air. "More likely he was a scout you stumbled upon, which is concerning. The Enclave hasn't had a known presence here in over fifty years."

"Scout or not, just one? Doesn't make sense," Deacon said. "One sorcerer might be a match for an ordinary pack of wolves, but *this* pack? Hell, the wolves aside, you or I alone could annihilate him."

"Yet, one sorcerer is lethal to a vampire."

Sakima appeared beside Luca on the rocks. The entire pack twitched in surprise, except for Vance who chuckled. Sakima and Vance had mated, but Sakima had yet to bond with the rest of the pack, so Vance was the only one who always knew where the vampire was. The pair certainly seemed to enjoy the vampire sneaking up on everyone. They all turned annoyed glares on Sakima, who offered only a fanged smile in response. As Sakima's words sank in, Vance's smile disappeared.

"You said *lethal*?" Vance asked, his amusement changing to distress.

Sakima gazed down at his wolf mate with affection. "Yes, lethal. Their magic, when inhaled by a vampire, attaches to the mutated DNA that makes us what we are and destroys it. The result is death." Vance's face lost all color. Within the blink of an eye, Sakima appeared at his side. Vance held on to his mate with a fierce grip while Sakima kissed his temple. "Shh, my pet. I will take precautions."

The wolves instinctively drew closer together in support and protection of their Omega.

"How does one inhale magic?" Tanner asked Sakima.

"They make clouds of it," Theran, remembering the misty stuff the sorcerer had conjured, answered before Sakima.

"Clouds?" Tanner, Ean, and Vance asked at once.

"Yes. He did this—" Theran mimicked the hand motions he'd seen the sorcerer make. "—and made clouds in his palms. He threw them at me but hit a tree instead. Blew it apart."

"Great," Ean said. "Exploding clouds of poisonous magic. Just what we need."

Ean picked up a rock near his feet and launched it across the river. His moods had grown increasingly dark over the past months, and he was quick to anger. By all appearances, Ean's decline had started when Matthias showed up at the pack house and only grew worse the longer the centuries-old dragon stuck around. The two were at each other's throats when they chose to speak to one another at all.

"Everyone back to the house. We need to be someplace defensible while we regroup, and the human neighbors will keep all paranormals on a level field. Luca, Sakima, Deacon, and I will meet with Matthias to figure out the best plan of action with this new development," Tanner said.

A blur of motion drew Theran's attention to where Sakima and Vance had been standing, but he only saw empty space. The vampire had a habit of whisking Vance away without notice. The rest of the pack began the hike up the trailhead to where the vehicles were parked. Luca held Tanner's hand as they walked side by side up the hill. Deacon fisted the white scruff of Ross's neck as he led him up the trail behind Tanner, leaving Theran and Ean to bring up the rear.

Ean took his time approaching Theran, heralding his reluctance to return to the house. He'd confessed to Theran once that he was uncomfortable in the pack house, which was the exact opposite of how it should be. Theran felt his friend's discomfort as if it were his own, but he had no idea what to do about it, especially when he didn't know exactly what caused it. He took comfort in the fact Ean at least hadn't talked about leaving the pack. He'd become Tanner's Beta recently and was flourishing in his role. Ean was a natural leader and, in any other pack, may have one day become Alpha.

"You should shift," Ean said as he finally joined Theran, and they started up the trail together. "Don't want to shock the little old lady across the street with your lily-white ass."

"You mean old lady McKinzey?" Theran scoffed. "She's more likely to snap a picture or cop a feel than be shocked."

Ean gave a slight smile at Theran's exaggerated shudder. He continued up the hill as Theran stopped to shift and then ran to catch up to his pack mate.

Chapter Two

COLBY

Colby observed the pack from his position on the other side of the river, hidden from view behind a shield of magic. He'd held his breath when the wolf shifter nearest the water threw the rock. It had missed hitting the shield by mere centimeters. Had it struck, the rock would have sent a shockwave through the magic that would have been visible and would have announced his presence. While Colby may have been one of the more powerful sorcerers, he was not so egotistical as to believe he stood a chance against this group of men. Not alone.

Confronting the pack wasn't on the agenda. He'd been sent to find out exactly what types of paranormals made up the new Chevalier Pack, and he now had the answer. What he would do with the information was another matter. Because he now knew far more than he'd anticipated. He'd known Sakima, the owner of Elysium and his boss, was intimately associated with a group of mixed paranormals, but he hadn't known those paranormals were the Chevalier Pack. Until now.

Another piece of new information he'd gathered in the past few minutes included the wolf shifter he'd been having dreams about, a faceless man who told him he was beautiful, one who protected him and called him mate, was no longer merely an image visiting him at night. The gorgeous gray-and-brown wolf was very much a reality, and the man was the very same one who'd captured his attention at the club a few weeks before.

He was bothered that his dream wolf would be part of the Chevalier Pack, especially on the heels of finding out he actually existed in the first place. The shock of seeing the man shift into the wolf right before his eyes had been enough to disrupt the flow of magic. Colby had lost control for a brief second, but it had been enough for the wolf to get away. Though he had no idea what he would have done, or said, had he managed to trap the shifter. One thing was certain: Colby would not have killed him or turned him over to the Enclave, which was what the Enclave would have required.

Colby wanted answers first. It seemed unlikely he would coincidentally cross paths with a wolf who was the exact replica of the one in his dreams. Something bigger was at work. This wolf shifter meant something, and Colby needed to know what. Keeping the shield erected around him, he watched the Chevalier Pack disappear farther up the trail. Colby couldn't tear his gaze away from the naked and immaculately built shifter as he once again morphed into the gray-brown wolf.

He'd been caught unprepared during the first shift, but this time Colby was ready, watching with rapt attention as the magic inherent in all paranormals extended outside the man's body and exchanged the human form for the wolf form. The change was swift, flawless, and immediate. Taken for granted by shifters, sorcerers could *see* the magic at work.

A few of the more powerful sorcerers, Colby among them, could interrupt the magic at the crucial point where one being split into two beings, and separate the human from the animal forever. The spell was called a severance and was unimaginably painful. The process always resulted in the death of one being, though no one, including the sorcerer, knew which one until the spell was completed. The magic involved was also dangerous to the sorcerer. The last one who'd succeeded in a severance had died of exhaustion the next day, drained of all magic and energy. No one had attempted it since.

Colby's dream wolf disappeared up the trail with the rest of the pack, and Colby took his first normal breath since stumbling upon the handsome man in the woods. He dropped the shield and stared at the spot he'd last seen the wolf. After committing a few more details of the shifter's appearance to memory, Colby headed back the way he'd come. He was scheduled to work the bar at Elysium later that night, where he would need to face Sakima while acting normal, as though his world hadn't become more complicated in the blink of an eye. He supposed it would be good practice for when he had to stand before the Enclave and lie.

During the thirty-minute hike out of the woods, Colby found himself obsessed with thoughts about the wolf shifter. He wasn't scheduled to meet with the Grand Superior of the Enclave until Monday, which gave him three days to figure out how to handle the situation. Nothing had to be solved now, so he let himself drift among the images and emotions swirling together in a way that made him hot and jittery. Colby wasn't overly sexual or romantic, but close proximity to the wolf shifter had triggered something in his psyche he hadn't felt in years. It wasn't something he missed, but now that he felt it again, he was thirsty for it, and he couldn't even identify what *it* was.

The man was just so big. His height and bulk had drawn Colby's attention at the club; that, and the fact Sakima, a typically solitary vampire, had taken up with so many other paranormal men. It had become clear rather quickly one of the wolf shifters was Sakima's boyfriend, and the other wolves were the boyfriend's pack. The shifter who'd snagged Colby's attention had been sitting across from Sakima in the circular booth tucked into a corner. Colby had initially thought the shifter was the Pack Alpha, given his size, but now he knew that wasn't true.

Colby was small, only standing at five eight in his bare feet, and thin. He blamed his magic for the high metabolism that kept him from building muscle and putting on weight. He'd been bullied quite a bit for his size when he was younger. As he got older, the teasing had started to include his homosexuality and his "feminine" appearance. Colby didn't think he looked feminine at all, despite his long hair, and he couldn't do a thing about his size or sexuality, so he'd developed a confrontational attitude and honed his sarcasm to keep people away. His disposition served him well for the most part, especially in his profession as a bartender. He had to be verbally combative when it came to fending off drunks with paranormal abilities.

His past was the main reason he gravitated toward bigger men. No one would mess with him if he was with someone stronger. He hadn't considered the man he was looking for would be anything other than a sorcerer, but he was oddly satisfied with the idea of a wolf shifter being his protector. Colby's boots crunched over the gravel lot as he approached his truck. He caught a glimpse of himself in the side mirror and stopped. He hadn't realized he was smiling until he'd seen proof of it in his reflection. He couldn't remember the last time he'd smiled without it being contrived.

Shaking himself, he unlocked the truck and climbed behind the wheel. As the engine rumbled to life, he imagined the big wolf in the cab with him. Colby had bought the large vehicle a year ago for no apparent reason other than the size made him feel safe. In light of recent events, he wondered if he had been subconsciously preparing for the wolf shifter. He synced his phone to the truck's radio and turned up the volume before pulling out of the lot. There were six hours before he had to be at work. A quick nap followed by a shower and change of clothes was next on the day's agenda.

Chapter Three

THERAN

The club had just opened and was still fairly empty. Within the next hour, the place would be packed and the noise level high enough normal conversation would be hindered. Theran and Ean arrived first. They claimed the large round booth in the back corner again since the table was the only one large enough for the entire pack. Theran was pleased they had a few minutes alone. He'd not had an opportunity to get Ean away from the other pack members long enough to ask about his recent depressed and increasingly volatile mood.

They slid into the booth and let the waiter who showed almost immediately know they would wait until the others arrived to place drink orders. Theran glanced at his friend to see what reaction he'd had to the handsome nymph, but Ean didn't even spare him a glance. Ean was slumped into the booth, staring at the table.

"What's going on with you, man? You've been moody as hell lately," Theran said.

Without lifting his eyes from the table, Ean answered, "Nothing."

Theran scooted closer until their shoulders touched. He leaned in and whispered into Ean's ear, "I call bullshit."

Ean sighed heavily. "This stays between us," he said, glancing at Theran through his lashes.

"Okay."

"It's Matthias…"

"I kind of already knew that," Theran said.

"No, you don't know." Ean scoffed. "He's my mate, but he's not interested."

"What?" Theran asked. He wasn't able to keep the surprise from his voice. Not only over the fact Ean and Matthias were mates, but also at Matthias's rejection. "How can he not be interested?" The idea seemed impossible.

"He's an ancient, prejudiced, egotistical, asshole of a dragon, is how," Ean grumbled.

"Oh," Theran said, because what else was there to say?

He'd not yet found his mate, now apparently the only member of the pack who hadn't, but he couldn't imagine the turmoil their Beta was going through at having found his mate, only to be rejected by him. Theran had never heard of such a thing happening before. The whole mate angle did explain Matthias's quick visit turning into an extended stay. The old dragon was around more often than not, and despite not being a member of the pack, he was present at every meeting. He didn't necessarily add anything of use to those meetings, and he had yet to take part in any of the confrontations they'd been through. He was just an oppressive figure who glared at everyone. Matthias's glares did have a tendency to be aimed at Ean.

Theran was about to ask Ean more about his situation, but was interrupted by none other than the dragon in question. Matthias sat at the end of the booth opposite them and stared with those dark-brown eyes that always appeared black against the backdrop of his silver hair. Ean didn't even acknowledge the dragon's presence. When the pretty nymph waiter returned to the table, Ean offered a flirtatious smile and ordered a bottle of cheap tequila. Ean was apparently tying one on tonight. Theran ordered water. He'd remain sober so he could keep an eye on his Beta and get him home to bed safely. He was the enforcer. It was his job to protect his pack mates, even if the ones being protected were the Pack Alpha and Beta themselves.

A moment later when the waiter returned, placing a shot glass and the bottle on the table, Ean turned on the charm. Matthias's eyes narrowed at Ean's overt flirting, but he said nothing. At least the dragon understood if he didn't claim Ean, then Ean would be with someone else. Despite all his failings, at least hypocrisy wasn't one of them. The whole situation was wrong as far as Theran was concerned. Thankfully, Ean's flirting was cut short when the rest of the pack arrived. Another minute more and smoke would have started puffing out of the old dragon's ears. He kept his silence, but Matthias looked pissed.

Luca shoved Matthias's shoulder in a suggestion to slide farther into the booth, but that would have resulted in Matthias and Ean sitting next to each other, so Matthias got up to go to the bar. Luca watched him leave, but said nothing. In a matter of minutes, the entire pack was tucked into the booth and drinks had been ordered. Vance sat at the end, glancing around the club. Theran reached across the table and rapped his fist on the wooden top to get Vance's attention. Vance looked at him, lifting a brow in question.

"He hasn't come down, yet," Theran told him.

The Omega wolf smiled at him, proving Theran had assumed correctly Vance was looking for his mate. Vance's gaze darted to Theran's shoulder as a soft touch brushed his arm. Theran glanced up at the cute, young phoenix male standing beside him.

"Excuse me. I don't want to interrupt, but are you free for a dance?"

The phoenix had a sweet voice and an adorable blush on his cheeks. He was much smaller than Theran, which he'd always preferred, and younger than Theran liked, but he could do one dance. Maybe offer a kiss at the end if things went well. He was a sucker for the pretty ones. Theran glanced back at Tanner in case he was about to start the meeting and received a small head jerk indicating he should go. Theran spun on the seat, smiled at the phoenix, and took his hand.

"Sure, cutie. I have time for you."

The phoenix's hand was warm, smooth, and light in Theran's palm as he led him onto the dance floor. Theran and Sakima shared a nodded greeting as they passed each other. Out on the floor, Theran pulled the smaller man into his arms and began moving to the music. A touch light as air rested on his biceps as the cutie followed Theran's lead. He pulled the phoenix tighter to his chest, amazed at the amount of heat he gave off. Theran leaned down to brush his lips across one pink-tipped ear.

"What's your name?" Theran asked.

The phoenix turned his head to speak against Theran's ear. "Cutie."

Theran chuckled. "Fair enough."

They danced a few more minutes, until one song bled into another. Cutie lifted onto his toes to plant a blistering hot kiss on Theran's lips. Other than the flush of warmth across his skin from the phoenix's natural heat, his body didn't respond at all. As adorable as the cutie was, nothing beyond the dance and kiss would happen between them. Cutie danced away toward a group of other phoenix males. Theran turned to head back to the pack table and froze. Standing right in front of him in a disturbing repeat of the forest was the sorcerer.

Except this time, they were surrounded by other paranormals, and no magic flowed through the other man. Despite the fact the sorcerer had tried to kill him, Theran found the man attractive. He ticked all of Theran's boxes. The sorcerer stepped closer, carrying a tray in his hand suggesting he was a waiter here. That explained why Theran had thought he looked familiar. They'd no doubt seen each other around the club in the past.

"I'm not alone," Theran told the sorcerer as he closed the distance between them.

"You never are, but they can't see you."

"I'm a wolf shifter, pretty boy. All I have to do is send out a telepathic SOS."

The sorcerer shrugged, stepping into Theran's personal space, close enough Theran could smell the smaller man's cologne. The subtle fragrance teased his nostrils and made his dick take notice. The background noise faded until all he really heard was this man's smooth voice. Damn, he really was an idiot when it came to smaller, gorgeous men, if even the one who'd attempted to kill him appealed to him.

"You can try, Poodle."

"Poodle?" Theran gritted out, affronted.

"What's your name?"

"My name? Are you in any way normal?"

"Depends on who you ask. I'll keep calling you Poodle, if you like."

"Theran, pack enforcer," he answered with a puff of his chest. "And you would be?"

"Colby," the sorcerer answered distractedly.

He was staring at Theran's muscular chest, so Theran took a deep breath, stretching his T-shirt tightly across his pecs. Colby licked his lips before snapping his eyes back to Theran's face. Why this man, who had attacked him just days before, would elicit such a primal response from him, Theran wasn't sure. At least the attraction was mutual. Colby was eating him alive with those gorgeous caramel eyes. Suddenly, Colby's eyes narrowed, and he moved fractionally closer. He was a good six inches shorter than Theran, but the power emanating from the smaller man couldn't be ignored.

"How are you doing it?" Colby asked. Theran tilted his head to the side, unsure what he meant by the question. "I'm a sorcerer, I know magic, but I can't figure out how you're getting into my head. Tell me."

Theran didn't know what Colby was talking about, but he could see the sorcerer was irritated. Unable to help himself while in a relatively safe place, he lifted his hand to the wavy brown hair hanging over Colby's shoulder and wrapped the long strands around his fingers. The hair was warm to the touch, which amazed Theran.

"Aw, Sweetness, all it took was one look, and now you can't stop thinking about me?"

"No," Colby snapped out. "You're...doing something. Stop it."

This conversation was fascinating to Theran. Colby was angry, heat wafting off him, but he was standing so close and seemed to be uncaring to the fact his hair was wrapped around Theran's hand. Colby wasn't the only one acting strangely; Theran was too. He knew he shouldn't trust the sorcerer, but something soul deep told him he could. Even the wolf inside him pushed Theran to cuddle up to the warmth created by Colby's magic. He'd never felt anything quite like it. Colby leaned in a bit before jumping back. He finally seemed to notice Theran's fingers tangled in his hair and knocked his arm away. Theran smiled and tucked his hands into his jeans pockets.

"What is wrong with you?" Colby asked. "You do remember I nearly blasted you to pieces a few days ago, right?"

Theran shrugged. "I don't think you'd attack me here. Too many witnesses. And I think you're—" Theran cut himself off when he realized he was about to tell Colby how incredibly handsome he was. "—smarter than that." Theran suppressed an eye roll. He sounded ridiculous, even to himself.

"I am," Colby said imperially as he pushed his hair back over his shoulder.

Theran was enthralled by the movement and Colby's self-confident posture. Sakima approached from behind Colby, drawing Theran's attention.

"Please stop monopolizing my bartender. He has work to do," Sakima said.

"Yeah, Poodle. Stop it." Colby walked away from them, and Theran laughed.

"Poodle?" Sakima asked, his expression a mixture of shock and mirth. "I feel like that should be addressed as inappropriate, but you don't seem offended."

"I'm not. It's fine." Theran headed back to the pack table with Sakima following. They each took a seat at the ends of the circular booth, facing each other.

"Have fun?" Tanner asked, and all eyes turned on Theran waiting for his answer.

"Yeah. Ran into Colby again, but this time he didn't try to kill me."

"What? Who?" several pack members asked at once.

Sakima's expression became ominous, and his fangs descended, eyes going stark white. "My bartender became violent with you? Unacceptable."

Theran suddenly realized he'd not lifted his block on the pack bond when he'd left the table with the cute little phoenix. He was the only one who knew what Colby was. He lifted a placating hand to the vampire. He didn't want Colby to get fired. And if what Sakima had said before about sorcerer magic being deadly to vampires was true, he didn't want Sakima confronting Colby.

"Yes and no. Don't fire him," Theran rushed to answer.

"What the hell is going on?" Luca asked, gaze bouncing between Theran and Sakima. Sakima leaned over the table toward Theran.

"I can't have an employee insulting and attacking patrons," Sakima told him.

"He didn't, not technically. He's the sorcerer from the woods the other day."

"The sorcerer who tried to blast you to pieces? *That* sorcerer?" Tanner asked, his eyes taking on an eerie red glow. That was new.

"Yes, but tonight he seemed more confused about me than hostile. He's really handsome when he's not going all witchy and lethal," Theran said as he glanced back toward the bar, hoping to catch a glimpse of Colby.

When Colby moved into view, placing a beer on the bar for someone, Theran couldn't stop himself from smiling. To think the attractive man had been working the bar the entire time Theran and the rest of the pack had been coming to Elysium. Or perhaps he hadn't, and that was why Theran hadn't run into him before. Theran's attention was pulled away from the sorcerer when Ross emerged from underneath the table and forced himself onto Theran's lap. It was a tight fit against the edge of the table, but Ross managed. Ross hadn't curled against Theran like this since mating with Deacon.

"Hi," Theran said, uncertain what was going on with his best friend.

"Our family is growing, and I'm happy for you," Ross told him.

"I don't understand."

"He said the same thing to me," Vance said. "Right after I mated with Sakima."

"Okay, but I'm not mated to anyone," Theran stated, though he thought that should have been common knowledge to everyone at the table.

"You will be," Ross announced. "He shares your aura."

Having apparently said his piece, Ross slid off Theran's lap and back under the table to reemerge at Deacon's side seconds later. Tanner's gaze moved to the bar and Colby while Ean and several other pairs of eyes locked onto Theran.

Finally, Sakima broke the surprised silence. "Colby is your mate?"

"I don't actually know," Theran admitted. "How did you know Vance was your mate?"

"He smelled like home," Sakima answered.

Vance smiled up at his mate. "Really? When you showed up in the backyard, I just knew. I don't know how I knew, though."

"What about you?" Theran asked Tanner.

The Alpha shrugged. "I didn't. I had no idea Luca was my mate, but I was instantly attracted to him."

Theran's gaze jumped to Luca. "I knew when he accidentally bonded to me."

Next, he glanced at Ean. He was dying to know how Ean and Matthias had found out they were mates, but the Beta threw back another shot, trying his best to ignore the conversation and his brooding mate. Only Tanner and Luca separated them. Theran imagined it must be extremely uncomfortable, painful really, to be so close to a mate who denied you.

Warmth infused Theran's body, and he looked back toward the bar where Colby was staring at him. Even across the expanse of the dance floor, dozens of people separating them, he felt the pull of those magical caramel eyes. Now that Ross had put the idea of Colby being his mate into his head, Theran could easily imagine a life spent with the gorgeous little sorcerer tucked into his arms. They may have had a rough start in the woods, but Theran would make sure all future interactions would be far more intimate and tactile.

"Do you think he knows we might be mates?" Theran asked, more to himself than the others. A thought occurred to him, and he smiled broadly when Colby once again locked gazes with him. "Oh," he breathed. "Maybe that's what he was talking about."

Colby's earlier claim that Theran was doing *something* to him could be the mating pull, yet unidentified by Colby. Theran couldn't pursue the sorcerer tonight—the pack had things to discuss—but he was already formulating a plan to be in Colby's business frequently. If it turned out they were mates, Theran *would* claim him.

Chapter Four

COLBY

Colby entered the dimly lit, windowless room and approached the U-shaped conference table inhabited by the Enclave Superiors. A spot on the floor marked where the summoned traditionally stopped. The distance was considered to be respectful of the power the Superiors wielded. Colby passed that point by a good five feet before stopping. He was young, but he was just as powerful, if not more so, than every one of the Enclave Superiors. Colby didn't hold any of them in the highest regard, and his decision to ignore their "respectful distance" limit announced his feelings. He'd always found their way of doing things to be antiquated and overly dramatic. Colby crossed his arms and sighed, content to wait them out.

"Colbarton Delavane—" the Grand Superior started.

"My name is Colby," he corrected, though the Grand Superior continued as if she'd not just been interrupted.

"Son of Iva and Drake Delavane—"

"Everyone knows who my parents are."

"You have been summoned by the Enclave in accordance with—"

"Oh my god, can we just get on with it? I have work in an hour," Colby interrupted again, louder this time. His voice echoed around the vast, otherwise empty, room. He actually had plenty of time to listen to her ceremonious babble, as he wasn't scheduled to work at all for the next two days, but he hated this nonsense.

The Grand Superior narrowed her eyes at him, and a collective grumble rose from the other Enclave members. His frequent interruptions and disregard to distance were one thing, but jabbing at the system by dismissing his mother's—the Grand Superior's—traditional speech of summoning was apparently one step too far. He took note of the misstep and waited silently. Colby had been a thorn in her side since the moment he was born and set the delivering doctor's scrubs on fire after he spanked his bottom to make him cry.

His birth was the first time someone had hit him to make him comply with their wishes. The last time anyone had dared, he was seventeen and had reduced the bully's car to ash. He'd been sanctioned by the Enclave for his actions, and it still grated him. Their message was clear: bullying was acceptable, but defending oneself was not. Colby had taken note of that, too, and made sure all other acts of revenge were done in a way no one knew for certain he was to blame. He'd learned both how to mask his sorcery so no one could identify him and how to render himself invisible. He loved hiding in plain sight and did so every night he worked at the club.

"Do not continue to disrespect your Superiors, or you will find yourself an outcast. You will become one of the lowest-ranking sorcerers, subject to whatever cruelties others choose to visit upon you, with no legal recourse," she warned.

Colby pinched his lips together. The Grand Superior—he'd long stopped referring to her as mother—probably believed his action to be acquiescence. The truth was that Colby was biting back a scoff and trying his damnedest not to roll his eyes. She truly believed her threat was...well...a threat. Colby found the idea of being cut free from the Enclave and their pomposity quite enticing. A smile tugged at the corners of Colby's mouth, but he refused to let her see how much her threat pleased him. If she knew that's what he wanted, she'd take it back.

"No more interruptions," she said, and Colby dipped his head in acceptance of her edict. He could play the game. "You were summoned because of your unfortunate association with the vampire, Sakima Hawke. Rumor has it your boss has joined the new Chevalier Pack. While I have my doubts that a wolf shifter would ever debase herself to such a thing as mating a vampire, this newest development must be looked into. You will continue to do this for us."

The holier-than-thou attitude rubbed every nerve in Colby's body the wrong way. He knew for a fact a male wolf shifter had taken Sakima as mate, but he'd burn in hell before he corrected her asinine assumptions. The small-mindedness was just as bad as the bullying and superiority complex. Colby stared at the Grand Superior, face blank, and waited. He wasn't entirely sure what she expected of him; perhaps that he would bow or offer gratitude? He glanced around the U-shaped table at each of the Superiors in attendance before returning his gaze to the Grand Superior. He raised one eyebrow.

"I will expect a report from you by the end of the week. You may go."

The dismissal was delivered with the air of royalty, and Colby snickered as he turned and left the Superior's chambers. He'd be delivering a report only when she decided to summon him again, or have him physically dragged back in. He certainly wouldn't be doing it voluntarily. Colby was playing with fire, and he was invigorated. With a wave of his hand, the double doors opened to the hallway, and he stepped through, not bothering to close them behind him as protocol dictated. Halfway down the hall, he heard the doors slam shut. He outright laughed as he exited the building and walked across the parking lot to his truck.

Colby had nowhere to be for the next two days, which he usually enjoyed, but this time he was twitchy, anxious, and restless. He was forgetting something; he should be somewhere or doing something specific, but he didn't know what. The entire situation was uncomfortable and confusing. As was becoming the usual over the past forty-eight hours, since running into Theran at the club, his mind drifted back to the big wolf. The man was everything Colby looked for in a partner—big, muscular, confident, and dangerous. Gorgeous.

He climbed into his truck, and then headed home on autopilot. The entire drive to his apartment, he daydreamed about a body much larger than his, holding him, surrounding him, protecting him. Theran's wolf form still haunted Colby's dreams every night, though now they were far more vivid. His memories mixing in his mind with his fantasies created one incredibly steamy package. Thanks to Theran touching his hair and moving in so close that night at the club, Colby not only saw his dream wolf, he felt him and smelled him too.

The shifter made Colby's dick twitch to attention, which was unusual. A damn near miracle, in fact, because he didn't experience sexual arousal the way other men did. As a teenager, his lack of response of any kind had become more ammunition for those who loved to torment him. In his mind, his impotence didn't matter because he preferred to bottom and pleasure his partners with his hands and mouth. His pleasure from sexual acts came from turning his lovers into babbling messes and then pushing them over the edge.

Every single one of those relationships had ended when the men started feeling inadequate because not only did Colby not come during sex, he didn't even get hard. The entire situation confused him. Especially now with Theran in the picture. Everything changed when the wolf shifter was present. Wherever Theran touched, a buzz would start beneath Colby's skin and then spread to his entire body. His cock included, something he'd never felt before. The response wasn't enough to make him hard, but usually he wouldn't react at all until he got to know the other person a whole lot better than he knew Theran.

Colby had a lot of experience with other beings attempting to exert their will on him. He knew what magic felt like, and he knew Theran wasn't pressing his wishes on him. Without questioning his actions, Colby drove past the entrance to his apartment complex and headed toward the forest where he'd first run into his wolf shifter. It was a long shot that Theran would even be there, but once the idea took root, there was no stopping Colby from looking for the beautiful furred animal. He tapped his fingers on the steering wheel in excitement, smiling as he turned up the music.

Chapter Five

THERAN

Theran ran. He pushed himself as hard and as fast as he could. Enforcers had to be big and strong, but they also needed to be fast and agile. His run was accomplishing two goals this time around. He was training, keeping his body in top form in order to protect the pack, and he was burning off his excess energy. It had been forty-eight hours since he'd met Colby at the club, but the anxiety and desire that erupted in him when the smaller man was around still burned strong. He needed serious relief. When masturbating in the shower hadn't put the fire out, Theran had decided a long, hard run might do the trick.

What he wouldn't give for just one kiss from the sorcerer. More than a kiss was the ultimate goal, but Theran didn't want to rush things. Colby seemed nervous and uncertain when it came to Theran. He hoped a few minutes spent alone with him would help dispel all of Colby's misgivings. He was certain of it, actually. The problem arose with getting Colby alone in the first place. The pack was always around, and there was no alone time to be had at Elysium. The place was constantly noisy and packed to capacity.

Colby's scent wafted over him in the wind, causing excitement to thrum through his veins and bringing him to a skidding halt. Colby's scent. *Can I identify my mate by scent already?* Theran pushed the question aside for a more pressing one. *Is Colby in the forest right now?* Theran didn't know why he would be, unless maybe he knew Theran was here. That was a thrilling thought.

Theran lifted his nose to sniff out the direction of his mate, caught his delicious scent, and ran toward it. Jumping over downed trees and dodging obstacles, Theran followed the unique smell. A few minutes later, he found the sorcerer sitting on one of the large boulders the pack used as a meeting spot. Colby's jeans and black turtleneck hung loosely on his body, the fit appearing to be for comfort rather than for attracting attention. Except it failed. Colby was heart-stoppingly handsome. His wavy, dark-brown hair blew gently around his face and hung down his back. Colby grabbed a handful of hair and held the strands against his shoulder as his pretty caramel eyes took Theran in.

Finding his mate here, in the spot his pack had claimed, filled Theran with joy. With his tail wagging, he gave a woof of greeting as he was filled with so many thoughts and desires. He wanted to hunt for his mate, bring him a nice dinner, but he also wanted to rub his body all over Colby to mark him with his scent. Theran took one step forward and woofed again. Colby was staring at him, virtually unmoving, and he was beginning to make Theran nervous. Perhaps Colby didn't know who he was, given he'd only been in wolf form in front of the sorcerer a very short time. Maybe Colby hadn't gotten a good look at him and didn't recognize him.

As Theran considered shifting, Colby rose to his feet and held his hand out, palm up. Theran approached, licked Colby's extended fingers, and then rubbed the side of his face into Colby's hand. He leaned in against Colby's arm so he could rub his head, neck, and shoulder. He adjusted on his paws to slide his rump and tail over Colby's thighs. In wolf form, every sense was heightened. Colby's scent surrounded him, the sorcerer's soft laugh music to his ears, and his touch was firm, but gentle, as he scratched over Theran's fur. The encounter was electric.

Colby buried his face in the scruff of Theran's neck and sighed into the fur. "What are you doing to me, Poodle?"

Theran wanted to say, "I'm not doing anything," but all that came out was a series of short barks and whines, making him sound like he was on the verge of howling. He certainly wanted to howl, because Colby did recognize him. And he was touching him, nuzzling into his fur and igniting Theran's blood. He couldn't believe only days before he'd been running for his life away from the sorcerer. Now, Theran wanted to mark him, mate him, and keep him safely hidden away for the rest of their lives. Wanting to shift so he could talk to Colby and maybe kiss him a few times, Theran took Colby's sleeve in his mouth and tugged in a nonverbal command to follow him up the trail to the parking lot.

"I parked at the other entrance," Colby told him.

Theran wasn't sure if that was some sort of invitation or just a statement, but it didn't matter. He wanted Colby to come with him to his SUV, where he'd stashed his clothes before shifting for his workout. He gave Colby's shirt another gentle tug. When the sorcerer started walking to the trailhead, Theran released his hold and ran ahead. He wanted to be shifted and dressed before Colby reached the lot to avoid any embarrassment. His mate was with him, and certain parts of him were at full attention.

At the top of the trail, he stepped behind a huge tree to shift. He scanned the lot and surrounding areas for any unwanted company, before running naked to the back door of his SUV and yanking it open. He grabbed a pair of jeans and bent down to step into them. A sharp intake of breath followed by a sighed "Sweet Goddess" had Theran yanking his pants up as rapidly as possible. He couldn't wipe the grin off his face though. He inhaled Colby's scent as he grabbed a pair of tennis shoes and slipped them onto his feet. The dirt and gravel didn't bother his paws, but his bare feet were a different story. Theran turned around to face a red-cheeked Colby. Damn, the man was adorable.

"Sorry, Sweetness. I thought I was farther ahead of you."

Colby swallowed hard as his gaze raked over Theran's bare chest and abs. "It's fine," he croaked.

"Like what you see?" Theran asked, huskily. Colby's heated gaze was doing all kinds of wicked things to him.

Colby cleared his throat and tossed his hair over his shoulder. "Nothing I haven't seen before. You're just more...chiseled, up close."

What an intriguing thing to say. "Up close? Kind of implies you've seen me from afar."

Colby's response was to side-eye him. His blush was too cute for Theran to ignore, so he stepped closer and ran his fingers through Colby's thick brown waves. "So warm," he murmured. He'd thought it had been a trick of his mind that night at the club, but Colby's hair was actually emanating heat. "It's like it has a heat source of its own."

"It's my magic. My temperature generally runs higher than other people's."

"Really?" Theran stepped into Colby's space and cupped Colby's jaw with his free hand. Being close like this filled his nostrils with Colby's scent, and he felt surrounded by the small man. Colby turned his face up to look into Theran's eyes, and Theran pressed their foreheads together.

"Wow," Theran whispered. "I never knew finding my mate would be so all-consuming. Every part of me wants you."

He smiled and was graced with the beauty of Colby's smile in return. "Yeah," Colby breathed. Then he jerked away, and the tires on Theran's SUV exploded. "Wait! What?"

Theran felt Colby's presence retreat farther, but he was shocked and fascinated his all-terrain tires were now shredded, hanging off the wheels in pieces.

"What just happened?" Theran asked, looking around the lot for anything that could have caused all four tires to suddenly burst in such a way. He turned to face Colby and found his mate's eyes wide with shock and the pink of his cheeks even more pronounced.

"I'm sorry. I didn't mean to, but you shouldn't say stuff like that. It's...cruel."

Theran pointed at his SUV and grinned. "You did that?" he asked. "Damn, Sweetness."

Of course, he'd already known his mate was a sorcerer, but to witness the effects of his magic again was awesome. Theran would have to shell out hard-earned money to pay for new tires, which wouldn't be cheap, and he didn't even care.

"You can't say things like that," Colby said louder, sounding a bit hysterical.

Theran tilted his head to the side in question because he didn't really know what he'd said that was upsetting Colby. He thought Colby's accidental show of power was neat. He wasn't mad, despite his destroyed tires. Colby took a few deep breaths as he visibly calmed himself. After one particularly large sigh, he peeked up at Theran through his lashes.

"You're clueless, aren't you, you big, handsome, dumb dog?"

Theran's smile was huge, and he puffed his chest a little. "You think I'm handsome?"

"Great Goddess, leave it to you to focus on *that*." Colby shook his head. "I just insulted you."

"Maybe, maybe not," Theran said.

He didn't think Colby was insulting him so much as employing a defense mechanism. Fate wouldn't have paired him with another paranormal who actually thought so little of him—he hoped. Theran looked his mate over, head to toe. Colby was small and pretty. If he'd been a wolf shifter, he would've been a prime target for teasing from the bigger, tougher wolves among Theran's familial pack. He had a feeling childhood was no different for sorcerer youngsters, but he would learn such things about his mate later. Right now, he'd managed to scare Colby.

"What's wrong, Sweetness? What did I do to upset you?"

Colby flipped his hair over his shoulder in a move Theran now realized was a mannerism uniquely Colby. "You said I was your mate," he answered softly.

"Because you are." Theran grinned. "Don't you feel it? The pull...the attraction...the chemistry?" He held Colby's gaze for a long moment until the urge to touch Colby became too much. "Can I kiss you?" he asked, not wanting to surprise Colby into blowing up the entire SUV.

"No!" Colby said, and stumbled backward toward the trailhead. "I...uh...have somewhere to be...'cause I need to be somewhere, so...bye." He turned around and rushed to the path. He glanced over his shoulder and yelled, "Sorry about your tires." He put his fingers to his mouth and blew into them, before disappearing into the trees.

Theran shook his head, disappointed he didn't get the kiss he'd wanted, but he couldn't stop the smile from spreading across his face. He turned to pull his cell phone from the back of the SUV to call for a tow and found his tires once again whole and undamaged. If he'd not seen the shredded rubber himself, he would never know anything had happened. Having a sorcerer for a mate was going to have its perks if Colby could put things together as easily as he blew them apart.

Chapter Six

COLBY

The remainder of the week passed in a mixed blur when Colby was working or daydreaming, and slow as molasses when he was at home doing his best not to think about Theran. He'd thought it was hard to banish the wolf from his mind *before* Theran had called him mate. Now, it was impossible. Colby had a whole new definition for the word obsessed, and it started with one hot wolf shifter. The entire situation was strange to him, and he didn't know how to handle his feelings. Colby didn't typically feel attraction the way others did, so the fact his brain wouldn't let Theran go was unusual and confusing.

He wiped the bar countertop with more force than necessary as he thought back on his reaction to Theran's announcement. He'd been an idiot, insulted the man, and had even blown up his tires. Colby couldn't imagine a worse way to take such news. He grew more embarrassed and angrier with every swipe of the rag, every memory that played repeatedly in his head like a broken record. He didn't hear the sorceress approach. "Excuse me, Mr. Delavane?"

The sound of the feminine voice cutting into his internal war was annoying.

"What?" he snapped and threw the rag down onto the mahogany bar top. Sakima wasted no expense when it came to his club. The sorceress lifted her chin defiantly at his tone.

"I am delivering a summons. Grand Superior demands your presence at Enclave Headquarters immediately."

Colby was in no mood for this right now. "Yeah? Well, no can do. I'm working." Technically, he wasn't on the clock. He was just trying to keep his mind distracted, but she didn't need to know that. Neither did his high and mighty mother. He really hoped this woman didn't take no for an answer. He was itching for a fight.

"You have no choice, and I think you know that," the sorceress told him.

"Which brings up a great point. If she wants me so bad, why doesn't she just teleport me where she wants, huh? She's so all-powerful...make me."

The woman narrowed her eyes at him, and Colby felt the swell of magic in the air. He'd initiated his own magic shield the second she spoke. He shouldn't be surprised she wasn't adept enough to mask her intentions. Most sorcerers, including his mother, didn't have half the ability Colby had. The air around the bar began to crackle with electricity; the magical aura only he seemed to be able to feel and see. The she-witch was honestly going to try teleporting him.

Colby extended an antitransitional field around his body and waited for the expression of disbelief to cross her face when she realized they were going nowhere. At least, not until he decided they were. She wasn't very powerful if she was broadcasting her intentions so damn loudly. Her eyebrows lowered over dark narrowed eyes. He smiled at her evilly.

"I said the Grand Superior could teleport me. Not you. Although, the only way she would succeed would be to take me by surprise, and that's hard for her to do. You see, I'm her son. I know all her tricks and all the ways to beat them."

Anger flushed the woman's cheeks. "Fine," she bit out. "I'll return without you and tell the Grand Superior she'd have better luck interrogating the wolf shifter."

Having been the victim of countless practical jokes and sucker punches in his youth, Colby didn't react to her words outwardly. Internally, however, he was screaming as fear for his handsome mate ran ice cold through his veins. One thing he knew for certain was he couldn't let on how much he cared, or the Enclave would use his feelings against him, but he needed to know what they knew.

"First, I never said I wouldn't go, only that I would decide when. Second, what wolf shifter? What could one of those animals possibly tell you?"

The sorceress shrugged. "I don't have that information. I'm not a Superior. But you were seen talking to a wolf shifter about a week ago. That shifter was then seen joining the alleged new Chevalier Pack in a booth here at the club."

"I work here. It's a bar catering to paranormals, and given I'm the bartender, I talk to everyone," Colby said.

He kept his voice calm, but he was desperate to pull the Enclave's attention away from Theran. The woman opened her mouth to reply, but Colby didn't allow her the opportunity. He initiated the teleportation spell in his palms, clapped his hands together, and appeared in the center of the U-shaped tables in the Superior's meeting room. He stared the Grand Superior in the eye. She stood a few short feet away from where he'd appeared. She looked angry, so he adopted a lackadaisical, carefree attitude. His sole purpose in life was to make her regret ever giving birth to him.

"Where is Dahlia?" Grand Superior asked.

"Who?" Colby asked, though he suspected she was referring to the sorceress sent to collect him.

The one he'd deliberately left behind in the bar trapped beneath a cloak of magic dampener. It would be about an hour before she managed to free herself. Colby briefly wondered what would happen if, or when, Sakima stumbled upon her. He was kind of depressed he'd miss that. Certain sorcerer magic was lethal to vampires, but Colby doubted Dahlia knew how to invoke it. Especially given how terrible she was at an elementary skill like masking the spell she was about to cast. Sakima would have her drained before she knew he was there.

Colby almost smiled—almost. Remembering he was here to protect Theran kept his mirth under control. He turned to the nearest table and dragged a fingertip along the shiny lacquered surface, ignoring the glares of the other Superiors. The Grand Superior huffed out an annoyed breath, but Colby ignored her as he slowly worked his finger down one long edge to the ninety-degree joint where he changed direction to continue his arc around the inside edge of the tables.

"You summoned me," Colby said. "Don't get all huffy when I show up."

"Your blatant disrespect and disregard for protocol will only be tolerated so long as you remain useful," she told him.

He didn't miss a step, but his heart skipped a beat. If Theran really was his mate, as he now suspected was true, Colby would be leaving the Enclave far sooner than the Grand Superior realized. Colby knew he was more powerful than most other sorcerers. He could protect Theran and the entire Chevalier Pack. Assuming he allowed things to progress that far. Colby's current plan was to convince the Enclave the pack was harmless, but it required he be their only source of information, which meant playing this ridiculous game.

"Understood," he said.

"Have you had any success with the task given to you?"

"I've watched suspected members from afar, made rudimentary contact, but haven't gotten a chance to engage."

"That's not what we've heard—"

"What you've heard," Colby interrupted, "is nothing more than me doing my job at the club and the patrons of that club mingling together." He turned to look his mother in the eye. "You're not going to get decent intel overnight and certainly not from gossipy partiers."

"You've had an entire week," she said.

Refusing to be pulled into a verbal sparring match, Colby stared at her unflinchingly. He'd gained the knowledge he'd wanted and was now prepared to leave.

"You have one more week, and only one, before I employ other options," she warned. Colby lifted a brow as the Grand Superior closed the distance between them. She kept her voice low in order to keep her words between them. "You forget how well I know you, little boy. Drag your feet on this task and things will get ugly."

Colby wasn't able to stop the grin spreading across his face. He'd never backed down from a challenge. Giving the Grand Superior and the Enclave information that was both believable and useless, while protecting Theran, was by far the biggest challenge of his life. Anger bled into his mother's eyes amongst the swirls of magic. Creating a whirlwind of smoke around his body, all for show, he teleported himself back to the bar.

Sakima sat on a barstool across the counter from where Colby appeared. The vampire picked up a peanut from a bowl and flung it at a very pissed off Dahlia. The peanut bounced off the dampening field to land on the floor among another dozen or so peanuts littering the floor. Apparently, Sakima had been at this awhile. Colby waggled his fingers at Dahlia in greeting. Sakima turned on the stool to face Colby, his ice-blue eyes questioning.

"I'll sweep that up once she's gone, boss," Colby said.

The two of them were in a precarious position at the moment. Everyone knew the vampire was part of the Chevalier Pack. It wouldn't do for Dahlia to report back to the Enclave that Colby was anything more than employee to the man, though Colby knew they would be more one day soon.

"And when will that be?" Sakima asked.

"As soon as possible," Colby answered, thinking of the moment he would officially mate with Theran and not completely understanding Sakima was on a different train of thought.

"Good. I don't want her here when we open. Now, who is she?"

Colby mentally shook himself, immensely grateful the answer he'd given was still relevant to Sakima's actual question. He needed to focus before he revealed too much in front of an Enclave lacky.

"A sorceress who thought she could force me into something I didn't want," Colby answered, ignoring Dahlia's ineffective kicks to the dampening field.

"Clearly someone who doesn't know you," Sakima said, glancing at Dahlia's useless attempts to gain freedom.

"Not even a little bit," Colby agreed. "But then, no one truly does."

Sakima held his gaze for a moment longer. "Once she's gone and you've swept up, come to my office. We need to go over inventory."

"You got it, boss."

Colby and Dahlia glared at each other as Sakima left. Colby knew the discussion with Sakima wouldn't be about anything work-related. Sakima didn't discuss the business aspects of Elysium. They would be discussing Dahlia's short-term imprisonment and Colby's sudden appearance behind the bar. Not once since working for Sakima had Colby ever practiced magic in front of him or anyone else while at the club. He did his best to be unidentifiable, in fact. And if Theran was as free with the term mate in reference to Colby when he was with his pack, Sakima already knew exactly who and what Colby was.

Moments later, after watching Dahlia fuss behind the dampener a few minutes longer, Colby released her. She turned on her heel, flashing him an ice-cold glare, and then stomped out of the club. Colby remained on the main floor until he was certain she wouldn't be returning. He rounded the bar, reached out a hand palm down, and then rotated his wrist until he was palm up. The peanuts levitated off the floor and hung in the air. He swept his arm across the front of his body, and the peanuts moved through the air to the other side of the bar. Once they hovered over the trash can, he dropped his hand, allowing the peanuts to fall. Cleanup was going to be so much faster now that his identity was known to Sakima. No more sweeping with a broom or wiping dried, spilled beer from the countertop after closing.

Colby crossed the club to the door marked Private. The entry led to a short hall where the storage room and Sakima's office were located. Sakima's door was open, so Colby walked in and sat opposite his boss. Sakima appeared to be working on the inventory, but Colby knew Sakima didn't actually need his help with it.

"Why was there a sorceress trapped in a bubble in the middle of my club?" Sakima asked without looking up from his spreadsheet. Colby had tried, on several occasions, to introduce the vampire to more modern means of record keeping, but Sakima preferred the old-fashioned handwritten method. To each their own, Colby figured.

"She was sent to collect me, but I decided I would go to the Enclave on my own terms," he answered. Sakima stopped writing and looked at him through his eyelashes, brows drawn. Someone was clearly in a mood. Colby sighed and stared at his jeans-clad knees. "I put her in a dampening field because she threatened Theran, and it made me angry."

Sakima's annoyed expression softened. "I can't blame you for protecting your mate."

As Colby suspected, Theran had announced their status to his pack. "I don't know about mates—"

"If you believe nothing else I say, believe this," Sakima interrupted. "When a wolf shifter claims you're his mate, you are."

Because Colby wanted so much to be someone's perfect match, he nodded his acceptance.

"Next question," Sakima said, eyes going near white and letting Colby know this was serious. "Is *my* mate safe?"

"For now," Colby answered. "The Enclave doesn't know who's in the pack or anything about them, actually."

"You're certain of that?"

"Yes. I'm the one giving them whatever information they do have, and I'm lying." Colby shrugged.

Sakima's eyes returned to their usual ice-blue color as he relaxed back into his chair. "Thank you."

"I'm doing it for purely selfish reasons."

"Perhaps...for the moment."

Colby didn't respond. As far as he was concerned, he was using the opportunity to stick it to his mother. Theran's safety was an important bonus. His mate might one day soon become the most important motivation but not right now. It was a matter of time before Colby himself was considered a member of the Chevalier Pack, but he would make sure everyone involved was safe first.

Chapter Seven

THERAN

Belly full, and exhausted from the hunt, Theran flopped face-first and fully dressed onto his mattress. Physically, he couldn't move a muscle. Mentally, his thoughts were restless, playing back memories from his life in a nonsensical mix of distant and not-so-distant past amidst his current hopes for a future with Colby. He was grateful he had won the toss for a room to himself when the pack moved into Luca's house. He'd almost had to share with Matthias, but the dragon preferred the couch in the library. Theran was just fine with that decision. He wondered how long it would be before Ean's big, empty bed had a dragon in it. Now that Vance was with Sakima at his loft above Elysium more often than not, Ean no longer had a roommate. Theran groaned out loud as his muscles protested the roll to his back. He stared at the ceiling. The sun was setting, casting shadows and streaks of light across the room that danced with the wind. The visual was mesmerizing and relaxing. As his racing mind slowed, his thoughts centered once again on his mate. What was his handsome little sorcerer doing right now? Was he obsessing over Theran with the same intensity as Theran obsessed over him? Could he possibly be that lucky?

A small smile pulled at Theran's lips as Colby's image formed in his mind. As though visualizing his mate had actually conjured the man, a fine silvery mist appeared above Theran, making the ceiling appear to be speckled with glitter. The mist coalesced into the shape of his sorcerer before solidifying into the man himself. Theran blinked several times while his brain struggled to catch up to what his eyes were seeing. Colby floated above him, looking down at him with his hair falling around his face like hot tendrils reaching out, begging to be touched.

"You can do some really cool shit," Theran said, awestruck.

"You'd be amazed by the things I can do," Colby told him.

"I'm already amazed." Theran lifted his arms toward Colby and motioned for him to lower himself. "Come here."

Colby descended slowly, his hair brushing Theran's chin seconds before his warm little body blanketed Theran's torso and thighs. Colby slid his palms across Theran's chest and then down his sides as he settled. Theran wrapped his arms around Colby's upper back and hugged him tight, sighing contentedly as Colby tucked his face into Theran's neck, nudging his nose against Theran's chin. His sorcerer was small, hot, and perfect. He fit in Theran's arms perfectly, cradled against his body so naturally. The fates knew what they were doing when they created his pretty little mate. Settling into the relaxed normality of the moment, Theran began gently rubbing Colby's back.

"How are you, Sweetness?" he asked softly, knowing his voice would rumble through his chest where Colby's ear was pressed.

"Better now," Colby murmured.

"Better than what?"

Colby snuggled in tighter. "Forget it, Poodle. Just hold me."

Theran chuckled and kissed the top of Colby's head, the heat from his hair seeping into the sensitive skin of Theran's lips. "So warm," he whispered.

"Mmm," Colby hummed. "So big and strong."

Theran held him, absentmindedly running his hands up and down Colby's spine, breathing in his scent. As a child, he'd been taught mates were the perfect match. Created to fill some need or void in each other. Theran believed that to be true, which meant Colby would fill some hole Theran didn't know he had, and he would do the same for Colby. And if Colby's murmured words about Theran's size were to be looked at in light of that belief, his sorcerer felt small and weak.

Where Colby got that idea would be learned as they got to know each other, but for now, Theran was happy to be anything, everything, Colby needed. He had no clue yet what role Colby would play for Theran. He'd never felt like he was missing anything...except for the pack bond to a true Alpha, but that had been remedied when Tanner became Pack Alpha. Pushing those thoughts aside, he focused on the fact Colby was curled in his arms, warm, relaxed, and content. No threat in the world could reach them in this moment. Theran slid his hand up Colby's spine to his head, where he threaded his fingers through Colby's hair and gently massaged his scalp.

"I'm a great listener, if you ever want to talk," Theran whispered, instinctively knowing things weren't right in his mate's world.

"I don't trust easily," Colby responded.

"Yes, you do," Theran argued. "We may be mates, but we're also virtual strangers, but here you are, in my arms, in my bed, in my pack house."

"This is...rare," Colby said so softly Theran barely heard the words.

"I'm honored you chose to trust me."

Colby grunted. He adjusted until he was completely on top of Theran, straddled his hips with his knees, and sat up. He danced those magical fingers over Theran's sternum to his navel. Theran swallowed, trying not to let his arousal surge unchecked beneath Colby's ass. Colby smirked down at him, no doubt feeling the pressure from Theran's stiffening cock.

"I can start if it makes it easier for you," Theran said in an attempt to take Colby's attention away from the rod poking at him. Despite the relaxed posture, teasing fingers, and sassy smirk, Theran saw the lines of stress etched around Colby's eyes and mouth. His mate had a lot on his mind. Colby's brows dipped.

"Start what?"

Theran so badly wanted to touch Colby, but he didn't want to scare him again, so he rested his palms on Colby's calves. His hands were big enough he could rub his thumbs on the edge of Colby's knees.

"My name is Theran Curley. I'm a security systems monitor at Luca's company, my favorite color is caramel, and I'm your gay wolf-shifter mate."

Colby studied him silently for a moment. "Colbarton Delavane, bartender at Elysium, gay asexual sorcerer." He narrowed his eyes, and his muscles stiffened beneath Theran's palms.

"You forgot your favorite color."

"I fo— Are you serious? I just said my full name and announced my sexuality, and all you say is I forgot my favorite color?"

"Tit for tat, Sweetness. I told you mine." Theran felt the need to keep this conversation safe and light because clearly Colby had caught some backlash for his name and sexuality in the past. Theran wasn't like all the other shitheads in Colby's life, and he was determined to prove it.

"Caramel isn't a color."

"Sure, it is." Theran reached up to brush a thumb beneath Colby's eye. "And it's a beautiful color," he whispered. They stared into each other's eyes for several seconds before Colby spoke.

"Silver." Colby pressed his cheek into Theran's palm, perfectly imitating a kitten seeking attention. He even came close to purring. "You're not normal."

Theran laughed. "Clearly, you haven't met Ross, or Tanner. Compared to them, I'm horribly boring."

"Come with me someplace quiet, somewhere we can be alone for a while," Colby blurted out.

Theran did a rapid mental assessment. They were already alone someplace quiet, but clearly Colby wasn't as comfortable being in the pack house as he appeared. Theran didn't have work until the next morning, and while he'd been exhausted when he'd come into the room, with his mate straddling his waist, he was now wide awake. The pack had hunted, eaten, and then each had gone his own way for the night. They didn't need an enforcer right now. Theran smiled and fisted Colby's hair.

"Okay, Sweetness."

Joy spread across Colby's face, making him even more beautiful, and Theran was instantly thankful he had said yes. Without warning, Colby bent and kissed him. Momentary surprise at the advance allowed Colby to take control of the kiss, and Theran was happy to let his mate lead this dance. His eyes drifted shut.

He lost himself in the warm press of Colby's lips, the cool wetness of his tongue as he licked across Theran's bottom lip, begging for entry. Theran opened his mouth, and Colby's tongue surged inside. The room tilted, and Theran felt like he was falling. He wrapped his arms around Colby's back and pulled him in tight. The moment was overwhelming. Dizzying. Amazing. Like kissing a live wire that sizzled and popped against him. Fucking perfect.

Slowly, Theran opened his eyes, cocooned by the fall of Colby's wavy hair. Colby brushed their noses together gently, then rose so he was once again sitting on Theran's pelvis. Then Theran noticed the change of scenery. Instead of his ugly white popcorn ceiling, this ceiling had exposed wooden beams. The top half of the walls were adorned with dark paneling, the bottom half exposed brick.

A fire burned in the empty brick-faced hearth across the room; one of Colby's magical additions. One wall was nothing but built-in bookshelves, currently bare. Colby continued to touch every part of Theran's body he could reach, fascinated with his physique. Theran sat up on what was nothing more than several layers of heavy comforters and pillows laid out on the worn wooden floor. He wrapped his arms around Colby's waist.

The curtains hanging on the windows were drawn, and aside from several boxes and cans of food sitting on the shelf above the sink, and one hot plate, the room was empty. It had the look and feel of a one-room cabin. The construction and setup reminded him of the cabin his pack had commandeered pre-Tanner. Other than being much smaller than the pack's cabin, this one smelled of wet dirt and Colby. His mate's scent was predominant and deliciously distracting.

"Will you always use magic to get us places?"

"No, I was in a hurry," Colby mumbled against Theran's neck, where he was nuzzling, pressing soft kisses into his skin.

Theran held Colby tightly as he lay back, and then rolled to put Colby beneath him. He kissed Colby gently and caressed his jawline.

"There's no rush, Colby. We're mates, and that means everything to wolves, to me. I'm not going anywhere."

Colby lowered his gaze, and his hands stilled over Theran's shoulder blades.

"And you just told me, literally minutes ago, that you were asexual. This doesn't have to happen. I won't pressure you into sex—" Theran's words were instantly cut off as Colby shook his head.

"Do not finish that sentence."

No matter what Theran did, he couldn't make his tongue work. He scowled down at his mate, certain his sudden inability to speak was his little sorcerer's magic at work. He growled and let his fangs drop to show his displeasure.

"Fuck, that's the sexiest sound I've ever heard, but unfortunately, you've already ruined what I had going on."

Theran tilted his head to the side. Colby's words suggested he wasn't turned on, but his facial expression said otherwise. His mate had done this before when they'd run into each other at the club: a moment where his actions and words were at odds. Perhaps Colby would always be this dichotomous. Colby leaned in and kissed him, running his tongue carefully over the sharp tips of Theran's canines. The sorcerer was giving mixed signals, so Theran chose to give him the lead and groaned when

Colby deepened the kiss, driving his tongue into Theran's mouth. Theran pulled Colby's body closer so he could feel every quiver skittering through his mate's smaller frame.

"What did you have going on?" Theran whispered against Colby's lips, when he broke the kiss for air.

"I felt...things," Colby answered haltingly.

Theran bobbed his eyebrows playfully and rolled his pelvis into Colby's ass. "I sure hope so."

"No. I mean, yes. I definitely feel you, but I was referring to me." Colby pushed Theran off him and then climbed off their makeshift bed. He reluctantly let Colby pull free of his embrace.

"I liked having you against me."

"Yes, well, my intelligence abandons me when I'm too close to you, so stay there."

Theran crossed his legs and made himself more comfortable on the layers of blankets. He'd meant what he'd said earlier—he wouldn't force Colby into anything he didn't want. Theran had never actually been around an asexual before and didn't quite know how to handle mating one, but they would figure it out together. Deciding to leave the sex question for another time, Theran stared at his mate's perfectly rounded ass and the wavy, brown hair that brushed the upper edge of it as Colby moved.

"What's your favorite food?" Colby asked, picking up a box of instant mashed potatoes and scrutinizing the contents.

"Beaver." Colby cast Theran a disbelieving glance over his shoulder. Theran smiled wolfishly. "But mac and cheese runs a close second."

"Mac and cheese," Colby muttered as he placed the box of potatoes back on the shelf.

"I'm a simple, rather cheap date," Theran said. "What's yours?"

"Steak with portobello sauce and garlic parmesan potatoes." Colby turned to face Theran and leaned against the sink. "I'm neither simple, nor cheap."

Theran smiled at his mate's flirty wink.

"I clearly won't be getting that here," Colby said as he glanced around the empty cabin. "And I didn't think ahead to the fact I needed to eat. This food is years old, so I need to make a quick grocery run. Stay here? I won't be long."

"Why can't I go with you?"

Colby returned to Theran, leaned down, and kissed him. Theran smiled into the sweet kiss, enjoying the way Colby's hair curtained down around them. "I won't be long, promise, and going alone will give me time to process everything."

"Okay, Sweetness. I'll wait here."

Chapter Eight

TANNER

Tanner stood tall, lifted his nose to the sky, and sent up the howl. Ean immediately joined in, followed in rapid succession by the other wolves. There were only four of them, but their numbers were masked by the fact Tanner started the second and third round of howls long before the echoes of the first had died down. If Theran were nearby, he'd pick up the song, compelled by a force greater than his own will. Tanner was concerned by the complete loss of Theran's bond to the pack. This was more than the occasional block each of them would erect for private moments. At least then, the connection could still be felt. This was a vast nothingness.

Tanner remembered all too well how he'd felt when the bond to his familial pack had snapped. Terrifyingly, Theran's sudden disappearance felt far too similar. The need to find his enforcer before bloodlust set in was felt at a cellular level. Ross was showing signs of improvement, which was encouraging, but Theran was much larger than the others and thereby much more dangerous if he wasn't firing on all cylinders. Tanner allowed the last vestige of the search howl to die away, keeping his ears perked for any response, no matter how distant or soft. Nothing. The silence was disturbing.

Should we continue west into the mountains, or run north along the foothills? Ean asked.

Tanner sniffed the air once again, trying to pick up the slightest hint of Theran's scent. Once again, nothing. He had no idea which way they should head because he couldn't find a trace of Theran anywhere. By the look of things, he'd simply disappeared into thin air right from his bedroom, which was where Ross and Matthias had both said he'd gone after the hunt. Once Theran's loss had been felt, the entire pack had congregated in the living room to formulate plans to find their missing pack mate.

Tanner had sent Luca and Deacon south along the foothills to check the camping grounds and forests in that direction. Sakima had rushed Vance back to the pack house before returning to Elysium. No one would have put it past Theran to seek out his mate there, despite it being Colby's night off. Matthias had unhelpfully suggested if Colby had whisked Theran away for some reason, finding him would be unlikely until the sorcerer chose to allow it. Ean then told him to go back to the library and stick his nose into a book, because he wasn't pack, and Theran was pack business.

If Ean had noticed the death glare Matthias leveled on him, he'd given no indication. Tanner knew he would need to deal with the animosity between the two sooner rather than later, as it seemed to worsen each day. The pack didn't need turmoil within its ranks. They had enough going on. Tanner asked Matthias to remain at the house in case Theran returned. The dragon had been instructed to call Deacon's cell phone if he happened to show. So far, there'd been no report of success from any of the others.

We can't go any farther north without risking running into the McBane Pack, Vance said.

A collective growl rumbled through the pack bond. They'd all had enough of the rival pack, and deliberately strolling into McBane Pack territory wasn't high on their list of fun things to do.

I'm not sure what to do, Tanner admitted. Perhaps showing weakness wasn't good for a Pack Alpha, but he was at a loss. He wasn't much of an Alpha anyway if he couldn't even find one lost wolf.

Maybe Drew came to his senses and called him home? Vance suggested timidly.

Who is Drew? Tanner asked.

Beta of Theran's familial pack. Drew was married, but his wife isn't his true mate. He and Theran had an affair, Vance told him.

Because Drew lied to him, and when it was announced Drew was next in line for Alpha, Theran left the pack, Ean added.

There was probably a lot more to the story than Vance and Ean knew, but Tanner didn't want to delve into Theran's past right now. He'd have that discussion with Theran once they found him. It didn't fit that Theran would return to an unavailable ex-boyfriend just as he'd found his mate.

He'll never go back. We're a family. He won't leave us, Ross said, far more coherent and steady than was his norm. *The witch got scared and hid him.*

So, Matthias was right? Tanner asked. Ean's rumbling growl was the only response. Why Tanner was willing to accept Ross's skewed view of things versus a much older and well-learned dragon scholar, he didn't know.

How do you know, babe? Deacon asked Ross. It was a good question Tanner hadn't thought to ask.

His room smelled pink and purple, Ross answered.

Tanner sighed. So much for coherent.

It's coming from that foothill to the north, Ross announced.

What is? Tanner and Deacon asked at the same time.

Pink, purple, and orange. We have to get to him. Orange is bad.

Can someone translate the Ross-speak for me? Tanner asked.

Well... Deacon hedged. *When he was slipping into bloodlust, he kept saying he was turning orange.*

Okay. Right or wrong, Tanner was running with that. *Deacon, you and Luca meet us here. We'll wait for you. Call Matthias and have him stick close to the house, just in case. Then, call Sakima and have him do the same at the club. We're heading north toward McBane lands.*

A round of agreement echoed through the bond as Vance and Ean flanked Tanner's sides. Ross came bouncing up to them like he was splashing through puddles only he could see. Given their recent conversation, Tanner believed the wolf probably did see things no one else saw. He would make an effort to have a conversation with Ross to learn how he viewed the world. Up to this point, Tanner had considered the crazy wolf shifter an invalid to be looked after, but Tanner was man enough to admit he might be wrong. If it turned out he was mistaken, he would learn about Ross and his unique abilities so he could turn what he'd originally assumed was the pack weakness into another Chevalier strength.

Chapter Nine

THERAN

Theran paced the small room, the pads of his paws landing softly on the wood-planked flooring. Every once in a while, he'd stop at the front door, whine, and paw at it. More than once, he had thrown his entire weight against it, hoping the flimsy-looking pine would break. The door splintered and bowed outward, but otherwise held firm. To take out his rising frustration, Theran pulled the cushion from the only chair in the room and destuffed it. Afterward, he lay on the floor chewing at the chair leg just to have something to do.

While there was a fireplace in the room, there was no wood inside the cabin, so he'd been forced to watch the fire that had been blazing hours before die out. He supposed a sorcerer like Colby wouldn't need wood to start a fire, if he even needed fire to warm the room, but Theran had gradually grown colder as the sun set. Shifting had offered the warmth of his fur, but it also brought forward the part of his psyche that was more wolf than man, and he did not like being caged up indoors. Where the man might have been able to reason away Colby's actions, the wolf could not.

Theran was incredibly unnerved by the fact he couldn't reach his pack. He hadn't noticed the bond was missing until he consciously dropped the block he'd had in place, and still felt nothing. He had the stupid idea the bond was like cell phone service and actually tried walking to different parts of the room to see if he could reconnect. He howled, but it was like yelling into a vacuum. The sound went nowhere. Everything was eerily silent.

This was what going crazy felt like; he was sure of it. Ross hadn't shared his experiences as he descended into bloodlust, assuming he was even aware as it happened, but Theran could easily understand the ridiculous thoughts Ross spouted and the constant, anxious movements he made. Theran approached the front door again, whined, and began clawing at the edges of the floorboards. He had a good chunk removed and was pawing a hole into the dirt beneath when he heard the knob turn. He backed away snarling and growling as the door swung inward.

Colby stood in the entryway holding a grocery bag. The scent of old, dead blood wafting to Theran suggested the bag held raw meat. He was hungry, but Colby and the food he carried were of little interest to him right now. The freedom on the other side of the door, the trees and open space he could see, held far more power over him. He bared his teeth and snapped his jaw as he moved to one side of the room.

Most people, especially humans, had the sense to move with him, keep him in front of them and offer as little resistance as possible as long as it meant the massive wolf didn't attack them. Colby wasn't most people. He stayed in the middle of the entryway blocking Theran's escape. He even dared take his eyes off the angry wolf to look down at the hole in the floor. He gave the room a cursory glance as he knelt on the splintered surface. He placed the bag on the floor next to him and then held out a hand, palm up, toward Theran.

"I'm sorry, Poodle. I didn't plan on being away from you so long," Colby said.

He kept his voice soft and his tone gentle. The words sounded sincere to Theran's ears, but Colby's eyes held no remorse or fear. He might have been away longer than expected, but he wasn't truly sorry about it. Theran growled as he approached Colby and the door. It looked like he was heading toward Colby's outstretched hand, but he was aiming for the door. Colby stared at Theran as his eyes turned black, the veins of his fingertips spiderwebbing down over his entire hand. Theran tucked his ears and tail. The only way he wanted to throw down with his mate was naked in a bed, but he wouldn't back down. Not this time.

"I'm good at hiding fear, and I rarely admit to feeling it, but you're scaring me," Colby whispered. "Please, Theran. Don't make me hurt you."

Theran lowered himself into a crouch and shifted. The loss of fur had him shivering instantly in the cold room, but he remained where he was. Scaring his mate hadn't been his intention. His only thought was of Colby standing between him and his freedom. Colby lowered his hand, his skin and eyes taking on their normal shades as he retracted his magic. He grabbed the grocery bag, stood up, and placed a hand on the door.

"No," Theran said, sternly. Colby froze with the door halfway closed and looked at Theran. "I'm a wolf, and I don't like being trapped. Leave it open."

"It doesn't matter if the door is open or closed. You still can't leave."

"I want to see the forest, smell the air."

Colby nodded and pushed the door open wider. "Okay. Is that why you were so destructive? Because you couldn't see out?"

Theran shrugged and rose to his feet. He returned to the bedding, which he'd left intact so far, and picked up his jeans. He pulled them on and fastened them as he walked to the door to look outside. He inhaled deeply and felt the wolf calm, the knots in his back and shoulders releasing. He felt marginally better being able to experience the wilderness outside, and he'd be lying if he said he didn't feel better having Colby back at his side where he belonged. Theran wanted to hug the man to him, nuzzle into his neck where the mating scent was the strongest, but his wolf had scared him, and Theran wanted to give Colby time to recover. He glanced up through the trees at the moon peeking through the clouds. It felt late.

"What time is it?"

"Just after eleven. Are you hungry?"

"No, Sweetness, I'm not. The pack hunted earlier this afternoon."

Colby nodded without looking at him. He grabbed a skillet and placed it on the hot plate. He turned the nob to high and began opening the steak packaging. The disgusting stench of old blood made Theran's nostrils twitch, but it would take more than that to keep him away from his mate. He approached slowly, giving Colby time to object.

"I'm sorry I scared you. My wolf was very close to the surface, and all he saw was you blocking our way out. I would never hurt you, Colby, and neither would he. At worst, we would have pushed you aside. I promise. It would kill me if anything happened to you."

Colby plopped the raw steak into the sizzling hot skillet. "You know what?" he said, as he turned to face Theran, and Theran prepared for the worst. "I believe you. I don't know why, because it sure as hell looked like you were about to kill me, but...I honestly believe you would never hurt me."

"Good," Theran murmured.

Colby returned his attention to the steak, moving the meat around in the skillet before flipping it. Theran smiled, leaned in, and kissed

Colby's temple. When Colby didn't object to the contact, Theran moved behind him and wrapped his arms around Colby's waist. Colby kept his attention on the food, but he leaned back against Theran's chest. He felt around his psyche for the pack bond, wanting desperately to tell Tanner and the others he was safe, but still found nothing.

"So, the magic you're using to keep me inside the cabin, does it also block my pack bond?" Colby stiffened in his arms, which was answer enough. "Okay. Well, just so you know, I can't be without a pack bond for long. Wolf shifters suffer from something called bloodlust—"

"I know. I won't let that happen," Colby said.

"Okay, but you should know, I was without a proper pack bond for at least a year before Tanner came along. By the time he showed, Ross was pretty much gone, and I was next in line to show symptoms. All this destruction and my demeanor toward you just now...that's all early bloodlust." He turned Colby in his arms and cupped his face. "Please, Colby, for your sake and mine, don't keep me here much longer."

"I'll try to move things along faster, but I won't take you back until I know you're safe."

"I think you have our roles mixed up, Sweetness." Theran smiled and brushed a thumb over Colby's bottom lip. "I'm the pack enforcer. I'm the guardian. I see to *your* safety."

Colby stared at Theran's mouth as he spoke and licked his lips. "Sure thing, Poodle. Whatever you say," he said distractedly.

Theran chuckled at how easy his mate's brain could be addled and then bent to kiss him, reveling at how fast the sorcerer melted in his arms. Their tongues dueled each other, each taking a turn dominating the other, until the smell of burning meat filled the air. Colby spun around with a curse and grabbed the skillet off the hot plate. Theran didn't see Colby doing anything unusual, but the smoke dissipated rapidly and the sizzling of the steak in the pan stopped immediately. Colby opened the one drawer to pull out a knife and fork.

"You may not be hungry, but I am," Colby told him before digging in like he was starving.

Theran wondered when he'd eaten last. In his estimation, his mate could stand to gain a few pounds. Given he'd destroyed the one chair in the cabin, Theran sat on the pile of blankets to wait for Colby to finish eating. Now that he could see outside through the front door, his nerves had settled somewhat. Colby cleaned his plate fairly quickly and then washed his dishes, leaving them in the sink to dry, before he finally turned to face Theran.

"So, what things are you working on that will keep me safe?" Theran asked.

"Diverting the Enclave's attention away from your pack. You're here in case I fail." Colby's usual demeanor changed, and then he added in a quieter tone, "She could kill you so easily."

"She who?"

Colby sighed and joined Theran on the blankets. He mimicked Theran's cross-legged position, his shins touching Theran's. Theran smiled at Colby's conscious desire to touch, but if he was to get through this conversation and figure out what was going on with his mate, then he needed to keep his hands to himself. He'd sit on them if he had to. Colby, bold as ever, stared Theran in the eye as he answered.

"My mother. She's Grand Superior of the Enclave and a self-centered, know-it-all witch hell-bent on proving her high-and-mightiness by going after the rumored all-powerful Chevalier Pack. Why are you smiling like that?"

"Self-centered, know-it-all witch," Theran repeated. "Sounds like you."

Colby grabbed his chest and gasped dramatically. "Damn, Poodle. It's like you know me."

Theran laughed. "I'm getting there, Sweetness."

"Anyway, once I've convinced her Tanner ain't all that, I'll take you back."

"Just tell them you kidnapped and tortured me until I spilled all the lackluster details about my pathetic wild-dog pack."

Colby quirked an eyebrow. "And what lackluster details would those be? Because she will ask."

Theran leaned in toward Colby, close enough for a kiss if he chose, and whispered, "We love to start rumors about our own abilities because we seriously suck at being wolves."

Colby's lips parted and he leaned closer to Theran, but if they kissed now, the conversation was over. He wasn't ready for that, so he backed away. Colby straightened and shook his head a little. His brows drew down, and Theran prepared for his mate's typical verbal strike.

"Sorcerer" was all he said.

"What?"

"I'm a sorcerer, not a witch. You called me a witch."

"That was three minutes ago, Sweetness," Theran said.

"Doesn't change anything. I'm still a sorcerer."

"Okay." Theran nodded. He'd call his mate a damn unicorn if it made him happy. "Is it because you're male?"

"No, it's because I'm fucking powerful. Witches are humans who think they know what magic is. Sorcerers *are* magic, and I own that shit."

Colby's eyes turned black just as his hair streaked with black strands, lifting on a nonexistent breeze. Theran smiled.

"Damn, you're beautiful when you go all...witchy," Theran said with a wink.

"I'm beautiful all the time," Colby responded in a voice octaves deeper than his usual. The grin Theran had been sporting disappeared as his jaw dropped in awe.

"Is there anything you can't do?"

Colby let the magic abate and shrugged. "Can't control minds or make myself taller."

"You sure about that?" Theran asked, his gaze suddenly taken with Colby's mouth as he spoke.

"Well, I'm still only five eight, so..."

"Yes, but you've got me panting after you like a dog in heat, so I think you got the mind control thing down."

"Will it hurt when you mate me?" Colby asked.

The change in topic from magic to sex was unexpected, but given the pull between them when they were close to each other, he wasn't all that surprised. Still, it took Theran a minute to switch the direction of his thoughts away from how pretty his mate's mouth was and how hot the skin of his shins was where their legs touched. For a man who rarely showed his true emotions, Colby was actually being quite forthright about how he felt. Theran didn't want to lie, but he didn't want to scare him either.

"Yes, but that's why we do the claiming bite during sex. Our brains turn the pain into pleasure when our bodies are flooded with postorgasmic endorphins. I'm sure there's a way to keep the pain level down for a non-sex mating. You can't be the first asexual to be mated."

"But you want to have sex with me."

The way Colby said it, Theran wasn't sure if Colby was asking a question or making a statement. "I'd love to, but—"

"Okay, then, let's do it."

Chapter Ten

COLBY

Nerves skittered beneath his skin like ants. Like an out-of-body experience, he heard his voice say words he never thought he'd say so soon, and he felt like he had no control. The only reason he allowed the unpleasant sensation was because he and his wolf-shifter mate were alone in a secluded cabin. Colby knew to his core Theran would never cause him harm or allow anyone else to hurt him. Personally, he had no interest in sex, but Theran had been truthful in expressing his desire. Colby wasn't accustomed to putting others first, but he wanted to with Theran. He wanted to be the only one to see to Theran's needs, and he was keenly interested in doing whatever was necessary to keep the mating bite from causing too much pain.

"We can find another way." Theran's voice cut through Colby's thoughts, but the words didn't make sense to him.

"What?"

Theran cupped Colby's face, and he practically melted into the bigger man's hands. He stared into his mate's earnest eyes and soaked in the warmth of his palms.

"Colby," Theran said, lips tugging into a grin. "Are you listening to me?"

A thumb brushed over Colby's bottom lip, and he swallowed hard. "Trying, but it's hard when you touch me like this."

"I'm hard when I touch you like this, but, please, listen to me when I say sex isn't necessary for us to mate and bond. Do you understand?"

"Being asexual doesn't mean I don't have sex. I've done it plenty of times," Colby said. "It just means I don't *have* to have it, and I don't get hard. Sex seems to be the way everyone expresses their attraction and affection, and I want that, so...I go with it."

"Okay," Theran said, looking a bit surprised.

"I want to have sex with you. I feel edgy and giddy, when I think about you being inside me."

"Okay," Theran repeated, this time with a smile.

"It's unusual for me, because I feel like if we don't have sex soon, I'll explode, but…"

"But, what?"

"My dick is still soft."

Theran held his gaze with a thoughtful expression. He lifted a hand and dragged a fingertip across Colby's forehead gently. "So, what you're telling me is that I need to romance your brain rather than your body," he said. "I can work with that."

Colby stared. No one had ever suggested that before.

"I bet you like to look at and touch your lover—"

Colby nodded. "Yes."

"—and enjoy some good strong dirty talk whispered in your ear."

"I don't know. No one has ever tried before. They just grabbed my dick and then got angry when I didn't respond to it."

"So, you don't like to be touched—"

"Yes, I do," Colby interrupted emphatically, afraid Theran would withdraw all physical contact. Theran pecked a kiss to his lips.

"Let me finish, Sweetness. You don't like to be touched *there*." Theran pointed to Colby's crotch. "Anything else I need to know before I throw you down on these blankets and have my wicked way with you?"

"I hate how out of control and overprotective I feel around you. I have this bone-deep attraction to you, and I want to be your mate, but I'm terrified once we claim each other, you'll be able to read my mind. My head's a fucked-up mess. I can't even control what I say or do around you." Colby shook his head and looked at his lap. He felt his hair dance across his back and shoulders as it fell forward to cascade around his face.

"That's important to you, isn't it? Being in control."

Colby glanced up at Theran through his lashes.

"I can give you that," Theran stated, tone thick with promise.

Colby tilted his head. He was an expert at expressing his emotions with a look. In this moment, it was doubt. He liked being in control. He also liked to bottom. With the type of man he was attracted to—a bigger, physically stronger man like Theran—Colby learned bottoming meant giving up his control to the larger man. He'd had only one experience in his past with a massive bear shifter who liked to be restrained where Colby was able to maintain the illusion of control, but none of his partners had satisfied the soul-deep need to be loved and accepted. He knew now that was because none of them were his destined mate. None of them were Theran. They weren't officially mated, but Colby didn't need to put his inner thoughts into words; Theran was able to figure it out simply by looking at him.

"You've been with the wrong kind of man, Sweetness. When you're ready—"

Colby surged forward and cut off Theran's words with a hungry kiss. The wolf caught him easily and lowered smoothly to his back, Colby sprawled on top of him again. Except, on top of his mate wasn't where he wanted to be. He wanted to be beneath him, surrounded by his strength. They both needed to be naked first. Planting his palms on Theran's muscled chest, Colby pushed himself upright.

The lust clouding Theran's eyes was overpowering, and Colby yanked his shirt off before diving back in for another taste. Theran cupped his ass with strong, gentle hands and squeezed. It felt good having his wolf's hands on his body, but he felt the familiar irritation gurgle in his gut that Theran, like every lover before him, would expect Colby to react. He broke the kiss on a small mewl of frustration and pushed to his feet. The pants had to come off.

He made short work of Theran's jeans, sliding them down his legs and tossing them across the room. Theran's cock, like the rest of the man, was thick and large, flaring into a red-tinged mushroom Colby desperately wanted to taste. Deciding to leave his own pants on to hide his lack of physical response, he knelt between Theran's thick thighs and laved his tongue up the underside of Theran's cock. Theran fisted the blankets at his hips, and his leg muscles tensed as he emitted a guttural groan that shuddered through his entire body. Sexy. Colby grinned.

Such satisfying knowledge that he could reduce his mate to nonsensical sounds with just one lick. Colby nudged Theran's legs farther apart and wrapped his lips around a testicle. He sucked gently on the orb before moving his attention to the other one. He nuzzled the sensitive skin where thigh met pelvis, taking in the scent of his wolf shifter, before nipping the skin between his teeth. Theran yelped in surprise and then growled Colby's name. He could get used to hearing his name said in such a way.

He wrapped his fingers around Theran's rigid shaft, amazed at the hot thickness, tugged once, and then took it into his mouth until the tip bumped the back of his throat. He relaxed his throat muscles, taking a moment to breathe and adjust, determined not to gag the first time he gave his handsome mate head. Precum oozed from the tip, and Colby closed his eyes. He wanted to remember everything: the stretch of his jaw, the solid weight on his tongue, the smell and flavor of Theran's arousal. His ass clenched at the idea of having such a massive cock sheathed within his body. Theran's fingers threading through his hair drew his attention. He looked up at Theran's lust-bright eyes as he slowly pulled his mouth up the length of his dick, sucking hard at the tip until it slipped from his lips with a soft pop.

Colby continued to pump his fist over Theran's rigid length as Theran sat up, pulled Colby to him, and latched his mouth onto the skin between Colby's ear and shoulder. He held Colby still with a hand at his waist and the other at the back of his head, fisted in the long tendrils of hair. His eyes closed again, this time in pure pleasure, when Theran sucked the tender skin into his mouth in a way Colby was certain would leave a mark. He loved the idea of this big wolf shifter marking him so primitively.

He gripped the pole of flesh in his hand tighter. Theran bit down on the skin in his mouth, twisted his strong torso, and Colby found himself on his back amid the layers of blankets, his gorgeous shifter pressing down on top of him. The sound that toppled from his lips was uncontrolled and wild and new. Colby wrapped his arms and legs around the bigger man and held him tightly. He dug his heels into the firm muscle at the back of Theran's thighs in an attempt to bring every inch of their bodies together. A strange itch emanated from beneath Theran's bite, making Colby want to squirm in his arms, but he found he couldn't move much, trapped in his embrace. Being restrained in such a way was wonderful and irritating at the same time. Theran lifted his head and brushed their noses together.

"Before I get all dominant and horny and do something you don't like, what do you want?"

"I want to make you feel good. And I want the mating bite, but I don't want it to hurt. And I want you to love me despite all my broken parts." Colby whispered the last, already afraid he'd said too much, revealed too many of his insecurities.

"And I want to be the one you never leave. For once in my life, I want to be the first choice, not the one who gets cast off as second best to someone richer, or smarter, or more influential," Theran said. He brushed a curl away from Colby's cheek and whispered, "You're no more broken than me."

"Fuck me," Colby blurted out, and Theran chuckled.

"You're quite eloquent too."

"Shut up, and get these pants off me, Poodle."

Still laughing, Theran pushed back onto his knees while Colby got to work unfastening his pants. Between the two of them, Colby was naked in a matter of seconds. Theran bent and started trailing kisses over one knee, and then the other, before moving up Colby's left thigh. He laved his tongue over the crease where thigh met pelvis before turning his attention to Colby's right leg. Colby rolled his eyes and sighed.

"It won't work," he said.

Theran finished dragging his tongue over the right crease before looking at Colby. "What won't work?"

"Doesn't matter what you do, I won't get hard."

Theran exhaled with a calming slowness. He studied Colby's face for a moment, rubbing Colby's hips and legs as he did so, before nodding once. "You won't be able to do it tonight, but one of these days you'll stop expecting me to be like your previous boyfriends. It *is* possible for me to make love to you and worship your body without expecting anything from you except pure enjoyment of the physical touch. Now, close your eyes and focus only on where you feel me touching you. Forget about your dick."

"Can't you just stick it in? That's what all the others...used to..." Colby let the words die on his tongue at Theran's narrowed gaze.

"I could, but I won't."

Colby threw both arms over his eyes. Hiding in the darkness seemed safer than continuing to stare into those gorgeous eyes. He knew in his gut he was disappointing his mate, but he didn't know how to fix it.

"I'm screwing this up already."

A long inhale was followed by a much longer exhale while Colby kept his face cocooned behind his arms. He wanted to cry in frustrated humiliation when he felt Theran lower himself onto the blankets beside him. "Fuck," he whispered to himself. Leave it to keen wolf hearing to pick up on it.

"We will, but not tonight. Maybe down the road a little farther when you've had a chance to get to know me better. Nothing I say to myself right now can convince me you're ready."

Colby risked a peek over one arm at the sincerity of Theran's tone. His pack enforcer wore his emotions on his sleeve. Colby admired him even more.

"I am ready," Colby insisted. "It's just hard to let go of the past when it seemed to repeat itself constantly. I'm struggling to believe you're different, despite the fact everything about you so far has been exactly that."

"I get it, believe me. I'm fighting insecurities of my own. I'm just damned determined not to let them infect my relationship with you. We're mates. And even though my pack has been blessed with finding theirs, it's not actually all that common. Most wolf pairings are love matches or power matches. Not true matings."

Colby rolled onto his side to face Theran and pressed a palm to the lightly furred muscles of his mate's chest and stomach. A deep urge to constantly be in physical contact with the man was overwhelming, so he gave into it. "Someone you cared about left you, didn't they?" he asked.

"Yes and no. He was never mine, and it took me a while to realize he never would be. He was the Beta of my familial pack, and he was married to the Pack Alpha's daughter. We had an affair." Theran shrugged nonchalantly, but Colby could tell by looking at him he was still hurt by it. Colby could play the nonchalant game.

"I've been bullied and belittled my whole life."

Theran smiled broadly as he twirled his fingers into the hair falling over Colby's shoulder. He tugged on the strands. "Did you squash their cars or incinerate their homework or shave their heads bald or..."

Colby laughed out loud. He couldn't help it. Everything about his mate made him feel good—about his past, his future, and his life in general.

"All of the above. Got it," Theran said, laughing.

Colby would normally be incensed by that, but he immediately recognized the difference between being laughed at and being laughed with. His already high opinion of his mate rose higher. One step further and he'd be in full hero worship. Instantly taking to the idea of worshiping Theran, Colby pushed him to his back and returned to his prior position between Theran's thighs. Before his lover could object, Colby had his semihard cock in his mouth. He groaned with desire as Theran stiffened against his tongue, and he raked his nails down Theran's chest to his abdomen.

Theran quivered in pleasure. Colby sucked on the head, dipping his tongue into the slit for a taste, before taking as much of his mate's length as he could. A few strokes later, Colby registered Theran's hands on his biceps, tugging at him firmly, but gently. Colby did his best impression of a growl without releasing his prize. Theran rewarded him with a flash of fang and a growl of his own.

"Don't stop; just turn around so I can taste you too."

Colby complied, spinning on the blankets until he was straddling Theran's neck. Their difference in height was made more obvious by the current position. Theran growled again as he was given a close-up view of Colby's flaccid cock. Colby had a moment of apprehension things would go as they always had, but was once again rewarded with the opposite. Theran wrapped his arms around Colby's thighs, gripped his butt cheeks, and pulled them apart to reveal Colby's pucker.

One slow, lingering swipe of Theran's tongue across Colby's anal bud sent shivers racing through Colby's veins. Not a single one of his past lovers had ever rimmed him. The sensation was overwhelming and amazing. When Theran had said he wanted a taste, Colby had assumed he'd take Colby's dick into his mouth, but no. Theran was different. He was *always* different, and Colby needed to start getting used to that. The sooner he stopped painting Theran with the brushes of his past, the better.

A tongue soon turned into a penetrating finger with quick licks to the base of Colby's balls. He'd never felt the dual sensations of a mouth sucking and licking his balls while a thick finger probed his ass. The fullness and pressure of Theran's finger in addition to the massaging of his scrotum by Theran's mouth and tongue resulted in a pleasant, yet irritating tingle at the base of Colby's spine. He tried to distract himself from the pleasurable discomfort by focusing his attention on giving his mate the best blow job of his life.

A few moments later, that pleasant tingle moved from Colby's lower back into his balls and rippled through his cock. He groaned and shuddered, but didn't stop his own ministrations to Theran's stiff rod.

Colby sucked hard as he slid his lips up Theran's shaft, his cheeks hollowing out. His head was grasped in a strong hand that held him steady, but didn't force him farther down, as the cock in his mouth erupted, shooting salty liquid onto Colby's tongue. The large body beneath him went limp, and the wonderfully amazing pressure in his ass eased as Theran pulled free.

Colby licked his mate clean before easing off him and sitting cross-legged on the blankets. He licked his lips as he stared at the boneless heap he'd turned his wolf shifter into, smiling at how blissed out the wolf appeared. As Colby leisurely examined his mate's body, he noticed a short, thin line of white fluid following the ridge of Theran's pecs. Colby couldn't comprehend what he was seeing as Theran dragged a finger through the small strip and brought it to his lips.

"Damn, Sweetness, you taste delicious all over," Theran said.

"I do?"

"Mm-hmm," Theran mumbled. "Your mouth is sweet, your skin has a spicy flavor, and your juice is the nectar of the gods."

"My juice? I came?" Colby asked. That had never happened before. He'd always assumed if he couldn't get hard, he couldn't orgasm. The small pool on Theran's chest suggested otherwise. He hadn't been aware of it happening. The puddle was tiny, nothing like the volume Theran gushed out, but still.

"Yes, you gorgeous, little witch. And I can't wait to make you do it again." Theran smiled at him wolfishly, and Colby was lost in the dancing, slightly feverish eyes of his mate.

"Sorcerer," Colby corrected breathlessly, still trying to process the fact he'd orgasmed.

A ripple through the magic shield he'd erected around the cabin sent chills over his naked skin. A dousing of cold water couldn't have yanked him from his moment of postsex bliss faster than an unknown passing into the sanctuary he'd created for Theran. He jumped up from the blankets and started yanking on his clothes.

"Get dressed, Poodle. No!" Colby changed his mind immediately, and Theran stopped midroll. "Shift. Someone's coming, and I think you're better off as a wolf."

Theran rolled to his hands and knees, shifted, and then shook out his fur. All that glorious brown-gray fur ruffling about hooked Colby's attention. He'd never get enough of seeing his dream wolf in living, breathing flesh. Problem was, now that Theran was no longer just a dream, he could be hurt, or killed, and Colby would be left in ruins. They walked to the open door as Colby allowed the cloaking spell to dissipate. With his wolf mate at his side, he stepped outside to greet their unexpected visitor.

Chapter Eleven

TANNER

Ross led the pack through the trees at a fierce pace. He moved with a certainty Tanner found unsettling, given they were chasing colors only Ross could see. The proximity to his father's pack lands was bothersome. It had only been a few short weeks since Tanner had thrown his mate's car through his father's pack house in a fit of rage. Luca had yet to forgive him for that despite the fact his car being destroyed gave the dragon reason to purchase a tricked-out Challenger Hellcat. "Can't let a vampire outdo me," Luca had told him, referring to Sakima's Dodge Viper, before quickly adding, "And you're not allowed anywhere near my girl."

Every step took them closer to McBane lands, and Tanner's gut twisted in anxiety. He was about to tell Ross to stop so they could decide what to do being so close to enemy territory, but Ross slowed down on his own. A tiny cabin came into view across a dry, shallow ravine. It had fallen into disrepair, as had the area surrounding it. A pine tree leaned precariously over the roof, looking as though a stiff wind would send it toppling into the small wooden structure tucked beneath its boughs.

No light was visible through the windows or the front door that hung at an odd angle. From all outward appearances, the cabin was deserted. The one thing that told Tanner what he saw might not be reality was Theran's scent wafting gently on the breeze. Their missing pack mate was inside. Ross lowered to his belly on the ground, staring at the cabin, ears flat against his skull.

Orange, orange, pink, purple. Too much orange.

Ean and Vance stopped at Ross's hindquarters while Tanner walked in front of him. If they were going to be speaking in rainbow, Tanner needed to learn the code. He gave a short woofing howl to see if Theran would respond. He was certain the wolf was inside the cabin, and apparently Ross was convinced as well, but if the sorcerer's magic could make the place look abandoned, what other illusions was he capable of creating? Deacon, Luca, and Sakima joined them a few minutes later. The entire pack had fanned out during the search, but the three nonwolf shifters had allowed Ross and the other wolves to lead the charge.

"Is he in there?" Deacon asked.

Yes, Tanner answered.

He's too orange. He can't be orange, Ross cried.

Deacon knelt at Ross's side and lovingly caressed one ear. Tanner's fur lifted and pulled beneath Luca's strong fingers as he stroked over Tanner's upper back.

Since taking over the pack, Tanner had learned Ross and Theran were best friends, rarely separated since meeting just after becoming lone wolves nearly two years ago. Theran had taken on the unofficial role as Ross's protector until Deacon came along, and then Vance and Ean when they joined Deacon's wild dog pack. The idea of Theran suffering bloodlust, even the beginning stages, clearly caused the other shifters varying degrees of pain. He didn't even know how close to bloodlust each of the wolves truly were, other than Ross, whose condition was obvious, and he realized just how much he still had to learn about his new pack.

Tanner blinked rapidly when the visage in front of him wavered and changed. The shallow ravine completely disappeared, a clear demarcation of where the magic began, and the cabin was no longer dark, nor abandoned. Light shone from behind the curtains and through the open door. In front of it stood Theran and Colby. Blessedly, the block keeping Theran and the pack from communicating lifted as well, and the anxiety the pack suffered from eased substantially.

Ross jumped to his feet, ran to Theran, and pounced. The two rolled around on the ground, playfully yipping and biting in enthusiastic greeting. Colby's solid black gaze never strayed from Tanner and the rest of the pack. Black veins spiderwebbed over his skin and streaked through his brown hair, magic lifting from his palms like a heat wave—a sorcerer prepared to fight.

Luca, Tanner said, looking up at his mate.

The dragon glanced at Tanner with a raised brow. Tanner tilted his head to the side.

"Seriously? Again?" Luca sighed. "Fine." He straightened his back and rolled his shoulders like he was about to do something more strenuous than simply allow Tanner to speak through him.

"We're not here to hurt you," Luca said for Tanner.

"As if you could," Colby responded, not letting his guard down despite the two wolves who had just playfully greeted each other. Theran shoved his head between Colby's thigh and arm, rubbing his snout against his mate's body. "Careful," Colby whispered as he pulled whatever magic was in his palm away from Theran.

Luca huffed a smoky breath. "You think you stand a chance against a dragon?"

"I'd rip the dragon right out of you before you even finished the shift," Colby said without hesitation.

Tanner tilted his head to the side. He'd never met a sorcerer before, so he wasn't sure if this was all bluster or was, in fact, something Colby could do.

Sakima scoffed from his position at the rear of the pack. "Only the most powerful of sorcerers can perform a severance, and the last one who successfully managed it ended up dying from the exertion."

"Try me." The smile that spread across Colby's face was evil, making Tanner all the more determined to bring Theran's mate to their side. This was not a man the pack needed as an enemy.

"What have we here?" came a deep voice from amongst the thick trees. All heads swiveled to see who the newest arrival was. Tanner immediately recognized the lead enforcer of his father's pack, Gerald. The born Beta wolf was in his prime: big, strong, and ruthless when the situation called for it.

"If I'm not mistaken"—Gerald's second-in-command, a Gamma named Tony, said—"the pack of abhorrent fairies has trespassed onto McBane lands again."

All five Chevalier wolves growled and snapped their jaws at the unwelcome intruders, and Luca emitted a dangerous-sounding growl. Tanner was fairly certain his father considered this land human territory, but there was really no point in arguing. Gerald and the other enforcers gathering behind him didn't care.

"Relax, little boy," Gerald said, locking his gaze onto Tanner. "You're not the Alpha I plan on taking down. Your father's reign as Alpha is coming to an end—"

Gerald's words were cut off as a tapestry of woven vines and roots rose from the ground, creating a wall between the Chevaliers and McBanes with shocking speed.

"We found Theran, so let's get moving," Deacon said from Tanner's right.

Tanner wanted to know what Gerald meant that his father's reign was ending, but he also knew he wouldn't get an answer right now. Colby's magic had effectively killed the opportunity.

Back to the vehicles, Tanner ordered.

In a blur of motion Tanner was growing accustomed to, Sakima swept in, lifted Vance into his arms, and sped away. They'd be back at the house long before the rest of the pack. Deacon and Luca took off at a run, four of the five wolves behind them, only to be swept up in a cloud of magic. When the cloud dissipated, the entire pack stood beside the cars. Colby crossed his arms over his chest and smirked at Tanner.

"You're welcome."

Chapter Twelve

COLBY

"I feel trapped," Colby murmured to Theran, who was seated beside him on the sofa. "Bad things happen when I feel trapped."

His mate placed his big hand on Colby's thigh and squeezed before kissing him on the temple. "You're perfectly safe. No one here will hurt you because you're mine. But, so we're clear, what kinds of bad things?"

"Depends on how threatened I feel," he answered as he glanced up at the two dragons approaching them. The great room was massive, but all the shifters in the house were bigger than him, including the Omega wolf. "The last idiot who cornered me ended up with two broken femurs and a dick the size of a cocktail wiener."

Colby lifted one eyebrow at the younger dragon who stood closest to him as the older one smirked at him from several feet away. Theran chuckled and pulled him against his big body with an arm around his shoulders. Despite trying to put on a fierce façade while in the company of strangers, Colby melted into his mate's warm embrace.

"I like you," Theran said, and Colby took a second to smile broadly at him before returning his scowl toward the dragons. Neither one had moved.

"We need to talk," the Alpha mate said.

"I could go a lifetime never speaking one word to you, actually."

The dragon shifter's eyes narrowed, and Theran pressed his lips against Colby's hair. "Play nice, Sweetness," he whispered.

"You want to rumble with us, little boy?"

"Luca," the Pack Alpha warned.

Colby smiled evilly as Theran jumped to his feet. He didn't step between Luca and Colby, but he was prepared. Colby slipped his fingers into the waistband of his mate's jeans in a subtle order for him not to engage. He was really only poking at the dragon for fun. He didn't actually plan on starting a fight with Theran's pack. He wouldn't back down if any of them started one, however. One of the other wolf shifters bounced onto the sofa and scooted up against Colby's side. He glanced at the man curiously.

"They won't really hurt you," he said. "You're too pretty and Theran is orange."

"Is he, now?" Colby asked.

"Ross, go into the backyard with the others," the Elemental said.

Ross stood and brushed his chest against Theran's as he passed. "Don't worry," he said. "He's a Mighty Mouse."

Colby watched the shifter leave the room, following the same path as the other two wolves several moments before. He was happy to have found his soul mate, but his damn pack was the strangest group of men he'd ever met. The Alpha walked up to Theran and clapped him on the shoulder.

"Come with me?"

"I won't leave him alone—"

"I can hold my own," Colby interrupted. He didn't like the idea of being separated from Theran, either, but not because he was afraid. It was simply the selfish reason of wanting to continue touching his man.

"Colby isn't in any danger. The old men just want to pick his brain and ask a favor," the Alpha said.

The comment was met with several scoffs and one growl. "You'll pay for that later, pup."

Theran glanced at Colby. "Will you be okay if I leave?"

"I'll be fine, Poodle. Go. And don't worry if you hear screams. They won't be mine."

Colby swatted Theran's jeans-clad butt and then waved as he and the Alpha joined the other wolves outside. When he glanced back at the dragons, Colby noticed the older one covering his mouth with his hand, belly jiggling in a way that looked suspiciously like laughter. The Elemental ran his hands through his shoulder-length hair. Sakima appeared beside Colby on the sofa with a whoosh of air that lifted small tendrils of hair from Colby's shoulder.

"Yeah," the Elemental said with a huff. "Good luck with this one."

He turned to take the stairs up to the second level, Luca following. Colby found it fascinating the pack would divide in such an odd way. He was also surprised the Pack Alpha wouldn't be a part of this conversation. The older dragon sat down in an armchair across the coffee table so he and Colby were facing each other. Sakima remained seated to Colby's left. This was the first time Colby and his boss had found themselves together outside of Elysium. Sakima and the dragon shared a look, and the dragon waved his hand.

"How much does the Enclave know?" Sakima asked without preamble. Colby had always appreciated that about his boss. Direct and to the point.

"More than they're letting on, I'm sure, but not enough to make a move is my guess," Colby answered.

"You guess," the dragon repeated.

"I don't know you," Colby said, holding the shifter's dark gaze.

"Matthias Caillamar."

The name tickled Colby's brain like a vague memory he couldn't quite latch on to. "Colby Delavane."

"I know who you are, sorcerer. It took a dragon's strength to pull you into the world. You were powerful even then, and rather...stubborn."

Apprehension warred with shock at that announcement. Colby had known his delivery was difficult, but he'd never once been told it involved other paranormals. No matter how hard he tried, he wasn't able to picture his mother allowing a shifter anywhere near her during such a vulnerable moment. Sakima tilted his head slightly.

"Prove it." Colby narrowed his eyes when Matthias chuckled.

"You drew power from me and set the doctor's sleeve on fire because he tapped your bottom."

"Why does this news not surprise me?" Sakima asked, glancing at Colby with a fanged grin. His boss had flashed those sharp tips at him so many times in the past the vision no longer elicited a reaction. Instead of answering, he winked at Sakima and then nodded once at Matthias.

"Now, back to the Enclave and what they may or may not know," Matthias prompted.

"I honestly don't know," Colby admitted. "I haven't told them anything of use, but I doubt I'm the only one watching you. The Grand Superior seems to be going off the rumor mill rather than fact, though."

"Good. That will work in our favor, considering all the new rumors we've started recently," Sakima said.

"I'm surprised she's listening to hearsay at all. Iva has never given much thought or care toward those she considers below her, especially shifters. I was brought in on Colby's birth by his father after the doctor voiced concerns about Iva's survivability. She was less than pleased," Matthias told them.

"Now I know where the lifelong hatred of me comes from," Colby stated. "I almost killed her."

"Pure jealousy. You've always been more powerful than your mother," Matthias said.

"Yeah. Why am I talking to the two of you instead of the Pack Alpha?" Colby asked, his curiosity over the odd situation finally growing to a level he couldn't ignore.

"Tanner is wisely deferring to his elders for this discussion," Sakima said.

"And we're the only two who were actually alive during the original Chevalier disaster," the dragon added on.

Colby shot Sakima a glance. "Elders, my ass. You're both just shy of ancient."

Sakima lifted one eyebrow and said, "Congratulations. You have just earned bathroom duty for the next week."

Colby chuckled. Every employee at Elysium hated bathroom duty, but at least his magic would make it faster and slightly less unpleasant. The teasing and acceptance felt good though. Colby finally felt like he belonged, and he would fight to keep that. And he would kill to keep Theran.

"Rumors alone won't be enough to turn Iva's attention away from this pack. Something or someone has convinced her Tanner and his pack are worth watching," Matthias said, bringing the conversation back on topic.

"That's why we wanted to speak to you. Because you can fix all of our problems without the paranormal world turning once again to annihilation," Sakima said.

"And how exactly am I supposed to do that?" Colby asked.

"Magic," Matthias answered.

Chapter Thirteen

THERAN

After the pack had located him at the cabin, and they all returned to the pack house in the dawn-tinted hours of the morning, everyone made their way to bed. Pleasure infused every cell of Theran's body when the pack's acceptance of Colby resulted in loaned sleep clothes and toiletries amid the absolute certainty Colby would be sleeping in Theran's bed. Everyone was at ease except for the sorcerer himself as he got ready for bed and then curled against Theran's side as though his heart rate wasn't beating at twice the normal rate. But, they both slept soundly and were the last to rise in the early afternoon hours the next day. The other pack members could be heard through the cracked window as they gathered outside.

Theran and Colby joined them after sharing a hot shower that included more touching and kissing than actual washing, but they managed to keep it short. Their late lunch was small by wolf standards, but Colby ate quite a bit, once again making Theran wonder about the last time his mate had a decent meal. Their conversation was lighthearted and comfortable, but Theran spent the entire meal wondering what had transpired with Colby after the wolves had been directed outside. They'd run mock hunting and attack drills until Tanner announced the conversation inside was over. Theran had returned to the living room sofa and his mate's side to find Colby distracted, lost in thought, but otherwise unharmed.

Now, he sat in Colby's overly large, silver truck waiting for him to emerge from the office building across the street. Colby had grown more agitated the closer they'd gotten to the building, but Theran had remained silent, choosing to wait his stubborn mate out rather than press an issue he might not be ready to discuss.

"Stay in the truck, and don't draw attention to yourself," Colby had instructed.

"Where are we?"

"Headquarters" had been Colby's only response as he killed the engine and got out.

That had been half an hour ago, and Theran was growing antsy. So antsy, in fact, he screamed and jumped in the seat high enough to bump his head when Colby materialized outside his window. Colby laughed as he circled the hood of the truck, Theran glaring at him the entire time, and climbed back inside. He tossed a small journal onto Theran's lap.

"You made that fun, Poodle."

"So pleased I could amuse you," Theran grumbled. His mate was going to be as bad as Sakima with the sudden appearances.

Colby's mirth died as a man close in age to Colby exited the building across the street.

"What was I thinking, bringing you here? I should have kept you locked away in the cabin like I'd planned." Colby shook his head and closed his eyes. "I'm so stupid," he whispered.

"No, you're not," Theran growled, earning a side glance from Colby.

The man looked around the lot until he found Colby's truck and began walking toward them. Colby cursed under his breath, and Theran glanced at him in time to see Colby's fingers twitching on the center console as though he were playing a piano.

"Don't speak and don't move," Colby said.

"Why?"

"Theran!"

Theran snapped his mouth shut at the warning in Colby's bitten reply. He was fascinated by the ease with which Colby affected his no-care-in-the-world bartender persona. Colby lowered the window and waited. Theran suffered a severe case of jealousy as the man sidled up to the driver's side door and leaned in a bit, smiling flirtatiously.

"Hey there, beautiful."

Colby shook his head slightly. "Relationship's over, Jude. Is there something you wanted?"

"We don't have to be over," Jude said.

The guy was completely clueless to Colby's disinterest and actually had the nerve to reach into the cab and touch his face. Despite the fact Colby was facing Jude, head turned away from Theran, he lifted his index finger from the seat. The reminder to remain still and silent was a spiked pill to swallow, but Theran did it.

"I have a meeting to get to, so can you get to the point of why you followed me out here?"

"I want you."

Jude pulled Colby into a kiss. Theran couldn't see how intimate the kiss was, thanks to Colby's hair obscuring his view, but when Jude pulled away, his expression said it all. Colby hadn't reciprocated, and it pissed him off.

"You know what? Screw this. There are hundreds of pretty little boys out there who will bend over for me and actually *get hard* by the simple thought of me fucking them."

Jude smacked the hood of the truck as he crossed the street to return to the office building. He yanked the front door open angrily and disappeared inside. Once Jude was out of sight, Colby grabbed a fistful of Theran's shirt and yanked him across the center console for a scorching-hot kiss. Unable to keep from touching his mate, Theran buried both hands in that glorious fall of rich brown hair and slid his tongue into Colby's mouth. Colby nipped and sucked at the appendage as he worked his hands under Theran's shirt. Having those nimble fingers dancing over his nipples made Theran painfully hard and he attempted to pull Colby over the console into his lap. Colby pulled away and dropped back into his seat, breathless.

"We need to go."

Colby straightened, put his seat belt on, and started the truck. As he pulled out of the lot and onto the road, Theran palmed his dick into a more comfortable position. Task done, he took in his mate's stiff posture and white-knuckled grip. Wanting to ease the stress Colby was feeling, he reached over and began massaging his head. The silence of the drive back to the pack house allowed Theran time to replay the interaction between Colby and Jude.

"He couldn't see me," Theran said out loud. The statement was completely out of context, blurted out midthought as it were, but Colby understood.

"No. He could've heard you though, and that particular spell causes heat-wave-type ripples with movement." Colby pressed his head back into Theran's palm. "It was the best I could do with a second's notice."

"You're amazing."

"A five-year-old can conjure a cloaking spell."

"Why do you do that?" Theran asked, tugging gently at the strands beneath his fingers. "Put yourself down." Colby didn't answer, so Theran continued. "I just don't get it. You know you're powerful; you've exhibited that power repeatedly, but then you turn around and say anyone can do it, which I don't think is true."

"Don't you ever question yourself?"

"On some things, sure. Everyone does. But when it comes to my strength, my speed, my fighting ability, anything to do with my position as pack enforcer, no. I'm naturally bigger, stronger, faster, meaner. That's just...*me*. And I own that shit." Theran smiled as he repeated Colby's own words, which earned him a smirk in return. Colby parked the truck along the curb across the street from the pack house just as Ean reached out to him.

We have company, Ean said.

Theran did a quick scan of the street but didn't see anything out of the ordinary. *Who?*

Pack Alpha Mariel Landon...and Drew.

Unaware of the bomb Ean had just dropped, Colby exited the truck and waited for Theran to join him on the sidewalk. Theran handed Colby the journal and then followed him, anxiety making his gut churn. As he entered the house, a familiar scent hit him, and he noticed the entire pack had congregated at the dining table. The conversation stopped as Colby approached the table and placed the journal in front of Matthias. Theran guided Colby into a chair and then crossed his arms over his chest. No one else appeared overly concerned about the female Alpha wolf or her Beta, but until Theran knew why they were here, he would remain standing, ready to do whatever was necessary to protect the pack.

What's going on? Theran asked.

Coup to overthrow Tanner's father, Vance answered.

Despite appearances, none of us are letting our guard down, Ean said. *Sit down, but stay ready.*

Theran did as his Beta instructed and sat in the chair beside Colby. Once he was seated, he locked gazes with Tanner for a brief moment, before the Alpha returned his attention to their surprise guests. Theran placed a hand on Colby's thigh, needing the connection to his mate to steady his nerves. It had been over a year since Drew had taken him to bed in yet another hotel miles from where any of their pack roamed, had sex with him, and then destroyed every dream Drew had fostered in

Theran's head about their future together. Drew's wife, Saline, was pregnant, putting Drew next in line for Pack Alpha after Saline's mother, Mariel, could no longer lead.

Theran glanced at his ex-boyfriend and found the man watching him. Drew dipped his head in greeting, but Theran didn't respond. Instead he slid his gaze down the table, taking in each of his pack mates in turn. As far as he knew, only the original wild dog pack knew what Drew had meant to him. When he locked gazes with Ross, his best friend raised one eyebrow, but Theran was rescued from having to answer the unspoken question.

"Theran Curly," Alpha Mariel said. "I wondered where you'd moved on to. Aside from being a member of the most disputed pack in the territory, are you well?"

"I'm great, thank you," he answered.

"And who is the sorcerer?" she asked.

Theran opened his mouth to answer, but Tanner beat him to it.

"Colby is Theran's mate. Together, they are the Chevalier Pack enforcers. Now, to get back to the original topic. So far, my father has failed at every attempt he's made to take us down. Why would this next time be any different?"

"He has recruited other paranormals to help him. Three vampires and a phoenix to date, and I've heard rumors he's reached out to the Eastern Plains dragon horde."

Theran caught the look Luca and Matthias shared before his attention was drawn back to his mate. Colby was staring daggers at Drew as he leaned heavily against Theran's side. Theran slid his arm around Colby's back, pulled him close, and nuzzled his temple.

"What's wrong, Sweetness?" Theran whispered.

"He's ogling what's mine," Colby murmured.

Theran smiled into Colby's hair before whispering, "Later."

"Thank you for the warning, but I won't go out looking for a fight," Tanner said. "Every encounter we've had with my father and his pack has been started by them. Why he feels the need to continue coming after us, I don't know, but I refuse to become the aggressor."

"As one Pack Alpha to another, I will respect your decision, though I have to say I feel it is a mistake to keep your pack isolated. You need alliances. Nothing breeds fear and fuels rumors like the unknown."

Alpha Mariel stood up, followed by Tanner, Ean, and Drew. Tanner and Mariel shook hands before he and Ean escorted their visitors to the front door. Theran squeezed Colby and then followed the others as was expected of the lead pack enforcer. He kept a respectful distance, but stayed close enough to be of assistance should his Alpha need him. The rest of the pack remained at the table. By all outward appearances, they didn't seem concerned with what was going on in the living room, but the pack bond was buzzing with alertness. Everyone was prepared.

While the Alphas exchanged a few more words on the front porch, Drew glanced over at Theran before his gaze slid to something, or more likely some*one*, behind him. Heat wrapped around Theran like a blanket seconds before he felt a finger slide down his spine. Colby stepped into the living room beside Theran. The magic wasn't visible, but Theran could feel the power pulsing off his mate in waves that gently rolled over him. Drew swallowed hard and then jerked his gaze back to Theran.

"Congratulations," the Beta said, before joining his Alpha on the porch.

Ean and Theran shared a smirk. Theran loved that Colby felt possessive of him, the way Tanner had included Colby in the pack dynamics, and that he now knew he no longer had any feelings whatsoever for Drew. He wasn't even sure what he'd found so alluring about the Beta. Tanner came back into the house, and they all returned to the dining room.

"Daddy dearest is amassing an army," Deacon said.

"Or at least trying to," Ean said.

"Mariel is right, though," Luca said. "We need alliances."

"We already have the groundwork to build from. Look at us," Deacon said, pointedly glancing at each pack member in the room. "We have five wolves from four different packs, a vampire, a dragon, a sorcerer, and an Elemental. If we all reach out to our own kind, we could make some fairly powerful friends."

"Or bring hell on earth to your front door," Matthias said.

"Why are you even here? You're not pack, and this is pack business," Ean snapped.

Matthias picked up the journal Colby had acquired and approached Ean. Despite his bigger size, Ean didn't back down. Anger and sexual tension snapped between them as Matthias leaned in until their noses were almost touching.

"Careful, little boy. Mess with the wrong forces, and you won't have a pack."

Matthias backed away and then left the room to return to the library upstairs.

"Mariel was right that we need alliances, but Matthias has a valid point, as well," Sakima said.

"I won't discount Matthias's warning, or yours," Tanner said to Sakima. "But I have to believe paranormals have evolved over the past four hundred years, and for my own sanity, I have to believe our pack is different. Yes, we took the Chevalier name, and, yes, we are interspecies, but we are not them. What's that old saying? There is no glory without sacrifice?"

No one answered. They all glanced around the room at one another, clearly thinking the same thing Theran was—where was the Alpha going with that line of thought?

"We sacrifice our comfort, we risk our safety, so in the future we can have our freedom. I propose we go old school, back to the time of our grandfathers, and we send out official communications to every pack, coven, horde, storm, and enclave in the state and surrounding territories announcing the formation of a new interspecies pack."

"That *is* going old school," Luca stated. "Those of us who are old enough to remember those days may find the traditional show of respect pleasing. The simple notification may not be enough to bring them to our side, but it might keep them from going against us."

"We should not dismiss our current strategy, however," Sakima said.

"You're certain the journal has useful information?" Tanner asked him.

Theran glanced at Colby. He knew Sakima and Matthias had asked him to retrieve the journal, but most of the pack had not been informed as to the why. Theran did know that because of the time period the Chevalier family had lived in, everything about them had been documented on paper, hence the tireless efforts of Luca and Matthias combing through books as old as dirt in search of information.

"Yes. That journal was kept by the only casualty of the allied forces. Her name was Alietta, and she was the most powerful sorceress of the time," Sakima answered.

"Explains a few things," Colby muttered, drawing everyone's attention. Sakima tilted his head in question when they locked gazes.

Colby clarified. "That journal is protected by an Excalibur spell and has a myth associated with it that rivals King Arthur. You know, only the worthy can pull the sword from the stone? Only the worthy can pick up the book. Kids have been daring one another to attempt it for decades, all unsuccessfully."

"But you picked it up, and I picked it up out in the truck, and Matthias took it upstairs with him," Theran pointed out.

Colby nodded and smiled sassily. "Like I said, I'm fucking powerful."

"You're a direct descendant of Alietta's, aren't you?" Sakima asked.

"I don't know," Colby admitted. "But I studied a lot of the old spells and incantations, the ones all the other students ignored because they weren't fun. I watched them when they tried to pick it up, studied the ways the spell reacted, so when I went in today, I knew exactly what spell was protecting the book and how to remove it."

"I've said it a dozen times, and I'll probably keep saying it—you are amazing." Theran pulled Colby into his arms and kissed his forehead. Once this meeting was over, he was going to worship the gorgeous little sorcerer.

Chapter Fourteen

COLBY

Music thumped, voices clashed, and the scent of alcohol and sweat filled the club, and Colby moved through on autopilot. He was constantly plagued by thoughts and memories of Theran and had to rely on his magic on more than one occasion when his distraction led to a cocktail being mixed wrong. His tips were beginning to suffer, even as the likelihood of him never having to pay rent again increased. He'd spent every night the past week at the pack house, sleeping in his mate's bed, held snuggly against Theran's massive body.

Like every other pack member, Theran had written a letter to his familial pack stating he was officially joining the new Chevalier Pack and accepting the position as lead enforcer. That letter, addressed to Alpha Mariel, would accompany Tanner's official notice of the Chevalier Pack formation. Sakima and Matthias had helped Tanner create the document in the traditional style, but word it in a way that was a respectful statement of fact, rather than a request for permission.

The official notification would go out to nearly three dozen paranormal factions, but their personal letters would only accompany those addressed to their respective "families." Even Deacon, Sakima, and Luca had provided one. Only Matthias and Colby had declined to announce their connection to the pack, each for their own reasons. Theran had been distressed by Colby's refusal but hadn't pushed for an explanation or pressured Colby to change his mind.

As if thoughts of the handsome wolf had conjured him, Theran's scent broke through the miasma to wrap Colby in comfort. Ignoring his mate for a moment, Colby finished the cocktail order he was working on, placed it on the bar for the waitress, and then deftly mixed Theran's favorite drink, as well as the pink concoction Ross favored. He turned around and placed the drinks in front of the men. Ross clapped his hands, bouncing on his feet, as Theran's gaze moved from the drink, to Ross, and finally to Colby.

"I get you knowing I was here, but how did you know he was?" Theran asked, jerking his head in Ross's direction.

"I...don't know," Colby answered. He'd moved on instinct, simply understanding that Ross was present, but it hadn't crossed his mind to question *how* he'd known.

Ross drank down half his glass before turning to Theran. "I bumped into your aura, and he felt it," he said.

"Oh, right," Theran said, nodding. "Because he and I share one."

"Exactly." Ross smiled broadly.

Colby had no idea what they were talking about, but clearly, they'd had the conversation before. He was still in work mode, such as it was recently, and immediately moved down the bar to the next customer who signaled for him. In much the same way he'd known about Ross's presence, he knew Theran would accept his disappearance as professionalism rather than abandonment. Feeling the comforting presence of his mate, Colby was able to lose himself to his work, and the time flew by.

"My, my, aren't you a pretty little thing," came a masculine purr from behind him, and Colby turned to find another of his ex-lovers leaning across the bar, smiling lasciviously at him.

"Taro," Colby acknowledged the lion shifter. "What can I get you?"

"Your tight, hot little body wrapped around my cock," Taro answered.

Colby spun, grabbed a glass, filled it with Guinness, and then placed the drink on the bar top. "Not on the menu and never will be. I'm taken. That'll be six dollars."

"I didn't order it."

"Then don't drink it."

Taro smiled as he slid a ten-dollar bill across the bar. Colby changed it out and held the remainder out to the lion.

"Keep it, kitten. Late wedding present. I'd heard you'd been mated but didn't believe it."

"What? Where did you hear that?"

Taro gestured around the club. "Talk around town is that a wolf claimed you. Not a dog person myself, but to each their own."

The lion lifted his glass in salute and then disappeared into the throng of clubbers. Colby stared at the spot Taro had occupied for long seconds in stunned silence. He couldn't remember a single instance when he'd told anyone about Theran or that he was soon to be mated to a wolf shifter, so where had the information come from? Then again, none of the pack were exactly quiet about who belonged to whom when they were at Elysium. Could be simple hearsay, or perhaps he and Theran weren't as good at keeping their relationship on the down low as Colby thought.

So many possibilities rushed through his head, and he was so focused on them that it took several seconds for him to realize there was black smoke rising from the dance floor. Given the paranormal world's comfort with flames, since several different species could create it, no one yelled fire, and there was no mad dash for the front door, unlike human clubs where chaos would surely have ensued by now. Colby rushed out from behind the bar and shoved his way through the crowd to see a pile of smoldering ash on the polished hardwood floor. Acting on instinct, he deployed a containment spell with a barely perceptible flick of his hand.

Sakima appeared in the center of the circle, turned to one of the club bouncers, a massive gryphon shifter named Ollie, and said something Colby didn't hear. Those nearest Ollie and Sakima obviously did, however, and had started across the dance floor toward the door before Ollie's booming voice announced the club would be closing early and to please leave in an orderly fashion. Colby watched all the open tabs leave before they'd paid and mourned the loss of those tips, but he was grateful this didn't happen often. Whoever the phoenix was, they'd come back in the next few hours, but the timing was unpredictable. The older the phoenix, the longer it took for them to come back from a spontaneous combustion, until one day, they simply didn't come back at all.

As the other bouncers saw to the mass exodus at the front door of the club, Colby noticed Theran and Ross waited about a foot behind him and Sakima. Taro was staring down at the heap of ash with a stricken expression, Ollie's hand on his shoulder. On the other side of the dance floor were three vampires. Another shifter of unknown type stood slightly behind them. His movements and features hinted at a bird of prey.

"We were just dancing...when he...I swear," Taro stuttered out, and Ollie rubbed his shoulders.

"Phoenix combust all the time. No one is blaming you," Ollie said.

Colby slid his gaze over to Sakima to see what his boss's response would be, but the vampire wasn't paying attention to Taro or Ollie; his focus was held completely by the five remaining patrons.

"Fancy meeting you boys again," said the female vampire. Her words seemed to snap something inside Theran because he immediately moved to stand right beside Colby. Ross stood on his other side. "Where's that gorgeous little Omega of yours, Sakima? Has the honeymoon ended so soon?"

One of the male vampires rubbed his arm as he stared at Ross, who licked his lips, looking every bit the hungry wolf.

"Onmarie, Steffan, Micai," Sakima said. "Have you not learned your lesson?"

Onmarie laughed, flipping her hair over her shoulder. "What lesson, lover mine? We were just here enjoying ourselves until lion-boy over there created a scene. It can be a dangerous thing getting a sweet little phoenix like Kyle all hot and bothered and then denying him. I do believe he'll be a little pissed when he reforms."

"I didn't deny him," Taro roared, his voice echoing through the relatively empty expanse of the club.

"Be a darling, Sakima, and sweep him up for me. We have a wolf pack of our own to get back to."

The smile Onmarie gave was full fanged and threatening. There was no doubt to the Chevalier Pack members present that Onmarie, her two vampire buddies, the phoenix that was currently ash on the floor, and perhaps the unknown shifter were the ones recruited by Tanner's father. Ignoring her comment about having a pack of her own, Sakima glanced at the smoking pile on the floor.

"No. Kyle's ashes stay where they are as decreed by the Elysium Licensing Agreement. All precautions will be taken to ensure a phoenix's ashes remain undisturbed until the phoenix reforms to decrease the risk of essential pieces being inadvertently separated from the rest," Sakima said.

"Well, lover, all it will take is a slight breeze to send poor Kyle's ashes skittering all across the floor," Onmarie said before she moved with vampiric speed to stand near the smoldering pile, pursed her lips, and blew.

Colby chuckled as her breath hit the containment spell keeping Kyle's ashes in place, the air dancing across the surface in pink and blue static shocks. Onmarie hissed when she realized her plan had been thwarted long before she'd even conceived it. Without warning, Taro's scream of rage turned into a roar as he shifted on the spot. One massive paw swiped out at the female vampire, claws barely scratching the surface of her shin as she moved away. The unknown shifter changed into a golden eagle and flew along the ceiling, out of the angry lion's reach.

Sakima sped to Onmarie's side to grab her arm, but she moved quickly too. The two became a blur of motion Colby couldn't keep track of. His attention was soon drawn to one of the male vampires who suddenly appeared in front of Ollie, catching the gryphon shifter off guard, but Ollie was a bouncer. His surprise lasted mere seconds. The vampire was fast and strong, but Ollie had sharp claws and mass. When the vampire attempted to twist Ollie's arm behind his back, Ollie spun, shifting midway, and took the vampire to the ground in one sweeping move. The entire encounter was over in the blink of an eye.

Stunned by the speed with which everything was happening, Colby hadn't been aware Theran and Ross had also shifted and were attempting to catch the third vampire. Taro crouched low to the ground, his eyes darting back and forth at the blur of motion that was Sakima and Onmarie. Unsure exactly what to do to help, Colby decided helping Sakima catch the vampire he was engaged with would be the best idea. Using Taro's line of sight as a gauge, Colby conjured a spell in the palm of his hand.

"Sakima, stop moving," Colby called out.

Sakima materialized and glanced at Colby. Not wasting a second more, Colby extended his arm and flung the spell at the hissing blur taunting Taro. Onmarie was suddenly frozen in place, face-to-face with a very angry lion. A white wolf Colby assumed was Ross, since it certainly wasn't Theran, bounded over to Ollie and tried to play with the gryphon. Ollie batted at the wolf with a wing like he was swatting at an annoying fly. Theran walked up beside Colby wearing an old pair of jeans that looked like they had come from the stash of donated clothes kept behind the bar. Taro roared and swiped a massive paw across the bubble keeping Onmarie in place.

"How'd you do that if you couldn't see her clearly?" Theran asked softly.

"She was being repetitive. I threw it a few feet ahead of where I thought she would be," Colby answered.

"Let us go or you'll be sorry," Onmarie threatened. "We're not alone anymore."

Sakima walked up to Taro, placed a calming hand on the lion's head, and regarded Onmarie thoughtfully. "Colby, do you perhaps have a truth spell in your repertoire?"

"Of course, but it's an active spell," Colby answered, though he hadn't used this particular one on anyone yet. He'd always been able to tell when someone was lying to him and had never cared enough in the past to learn what they were hiding. He'd been too lazy, and none of them had been important enough to use it on.

"What do you mean, active?" Theran asked.

"It means I can't just place it and let it do its thing. I have to actively maneuver it. It means I have to be in very close proximity." As Taro lay down beside the pile of ashes, which were already starting to knit together in the first stages of reformation, Colby approached Sakima and Onmarie. He got so close they were almost nose to nose. "I'm a sorcerer, vamp-girl. I could kill you with a whisper."

Fear spread across Onmarie's face as Colby's words hit home and sank in. He supposed until now she hadn't realized what he was. Now that she did know, this might actually go easier than expected.

"Honestly, I don't think a truth spell is needed," Colby said. "That Alpha last week—"

"Mariel," Theran supplied.

"Alpha Mariel said the McBane Pack had recruited three vampires and a phoenix. Doesn't take a genius to figure out who those particular individuals are. What I don't understand," Colby said, glancing at the gradually reforming phoenix. "If Kyle is supposedly an ally, why did you try to kill him?"

Onmarie sneered. "The second that lion announced they were mates, Kyle became dispensable."

"Why?" Sakima asked.

"They're different species," she answered. Her tone suggested that should have been obvious.

"Great. McBane is recruiting purists," Theran said.

Sakima nudged Colby aside, reached out, and wrapped his long fingers around Onmarie's throat. His eyes were white, fangs fully on display, and his anger was palpable. "If you ever set foot in my club or come anywhere near my mate and family, I will rip your throat out," he said, menacingly. "Get these two out of my sight."

Colby knew Sakima was speaking to him even though the vampire never looked away from the female in his grip. Using the same teleportation spell he'd used thousands of times in his life, Colby sent the two vampires to the top of Mount Evans with a clap of his hands. They would only be inconvenienced by an hour or so with their vampiric speed, but it felt good to piss them off.

"Ollie, first thing tomorrow, please inform all staff those particular three vampires are not to be allowed inside. Inform me immediately if they make the attempt."

The large gryphon nodded and trundled up to the bar, long tail and wings trailing the floor behind him. At the bar, he shifted and pulled out a pair of extra-large sweatpants, pulled them on, and then headed for the front door. Once the room was clear of the enemy, Taro turned his bright-gold gaze on Colby, and Colby could see the shifter's pain. The lion curled up as close to the ashes as he could and put his big head between his paws.

"So many pretty colors happen when mates meet," Ross said.

"What colors?" Colby asked, glancing at the wolf to his right.

"He sees auras and colors," Theran answered as he picked up the last of the shredded clothing from the floor. He approached Colby and slid his free arm around Colby's waist.

In that moment, Colby knew the small action was how Taro, and anyone else with eyes, knew Colby had been claimed by a wolf. The little looks and touches that had become second nature to them were a neon sign to everyone else. Colby resigned himself to the fact it was only a matter of time before he was brought before the Grand Superior for reprimand. Maybe he should have written the letter claiming allegiance to the Chevalier after all.

Sakima joined Colby, Theran, and Ross and spoke in a low voice. "Do you need to be here to lift the spell when Kyle reforms?" he asked.

Colby shook his head. "That particular spell keeps things out, but it won't keep them in. You noticed the smoke was still rising in the beginning? When he reforms, he'll just expand past the spell to the point it dissipates around him."

"Good. The three of you head back to the pack house. I've already warned Vance of Onmarie's return, so he can take precautions, but you can fill in any other details. I will stay here until the phoenix rises."

Chapter Fifteen

TANNER

A stack of reply letters sat on the desk in front of Tanner. So far, there was an even three-way split of those who accepted the Chevalier Pack, those who did not, and those who didn't care as long as they stayed on their "own lands." He'd hoped for better, but expected worse, so he could deal with the results as they stood. There were still two or three outstanding announcements, which was standard for this sort of thing, so he decided to place those few nonresponses into the Don't Care pile.

Even after years of watching his father run the McBane Pack, Tanner was surprised by the amount of work that went into keeping his pack together, alive, and sane. And there were only nine of them. He suspected growth to include at least one additional paranormal when Ean found his mate, maybe more if Matthias decided to stop hedging and joined them. He wasn't sure how he would handle a pack the size of his father's. As of now, Tanner had one official enforcer, one Beta, one Omega, and one Gamma who was completely out of his head. The non-wolf species added a unique layer to the pack, as well.

Fingering the journal Colby had procured for them, he wondered what it would be like to open his pack to any gay paranormal in the city who was in need of pack or family. He'd heard from Vance, and then later got the specifics from Theran, about the confrontation at Elysium. None of what he'd heard sat well with him. He'd extended an official offer to Taro and Kyle to join the Chevalier Pack, but had not yet received their response. Tanner had no idea how the phoenix's odyssey or lion's pride would react to their interspecies mating, and he wanted them to have an option for someplace safe to go. Not that his pack was exactly safe just yet. Tanner truly hoped Taro's pride would welcome the lion and his mate.

Tanner opened the journal and mindlessly flipped through the pages. He saw words that could have been anything—from spells and incantations to a diary of the woman's love life—for all he understood. He knew Sakima and Matthias had asked Colby to retrieve the journal because of certain information contained inside, but again, he didn't comprehend exactly what they were looking for. When the door to the library opened, he was overrun with the scent of his mate as Luca wrapped his arms around him from behind. Matthias walked around the desk and slid the journal from beneath Tanner's fingers.

"Perhaps someone wielding unusual power such as you do should not touch things that also wield unusual power," Matthias said. He took the journal with him as he sat on the sofa.

"My powers seem to be limited to just those of Deacon and Luca, so I'm not too concerned. Why did you want that book anyway? As Alpha, I think I should be in the loop."

"It contains a spell that could potentially remove your ability to steal dragon and Elemental powers. Colby would have to conjure it, of course, but I think it could be done. It would certainly be for the best if the spell does exist," Matthias said.

"I don't think so," Luca barked.

"You're letting your emotions interfere with your head. At least Sakima was clearheaded enough to know to put his heart in check," Matthias said.

"Of course, Sakima would be clearheaded; it's not Vance the spell will be fucking with," Luca said, his voice deep and booming in the small room.

It's okay, Luca, Tanner said.

No, it isn't, his mate argued.

Nothing will happen right now or without my consent, Tanner told him. "We'll think about it, talk it over," he said to Matthias. "For now, we need to focus on the immediate threat, which, of course, is once again my father. Any word from Taro and Kyle?"

"Nothing I've seen or heard," Luca said, still glaring at his old mentor. Matthias held the gaze unflinchingly.

Dragons, Tanner thought with a shake of his head. Luca smirked, suggesting he'd heard the comment. "So, three vampires and a hawk have joined my father at a time when he's being challenged by the Beta enforcer of his pack."

"Golden eagle, and I'd say daddy is getting desperate. If he's being challenged because he can't control you, then amassing power and overthrowing you may be his only option to remain Alpha," Luca suggested. He took a seat at the desk and pulled Tanner onto his lap.

"Or perhaps he's being challenged because he won't stop coming after you. Or perhaps it's because he's growing older, and the next generation thinks he's antiquated. Or, or, or, it could be anything," Matthias said. "What was the first thing I taught you as a hatchling?"

"Keep my mind open, and consider all options," Luca answered.

"But it doesn't really matter *why* my father is being challenged, only that he *is*," Tanner said. "It's an advantage. My enemy's enemy and all that."

"True, he's still a threat to us no matter his reasons," Luca agreed.

"Knowledge is power," Matthias murmured as he slid a palm over the cover of the journal, staring down at the worn leather with an expression Tanner couldn't quite identify. The older dragon was too experienced at hiding his thoughts and emotions. When he lifted his gaze to Tanner's, his dark eyes gave nothing away. "Knowing his reasons is as important as knowing his intentions since it gives you an insight into when, where, and how he will strike. If he wants to remain under the radar and not draw attention, he will keep the confrontation in a secluded area with small attacks. If he wants others to see his strength, it will be public with a large show of force. Why do you think the takedown of the original Chevalier family was so excessive? A point needed to be made. Fear needed to be instilled."

"It appears to have worked," Tanner said.

"And yet...here you are. Flaunting your power. Deliberately taking the Chevalier name."

"This started long before Luca and I ever mated, before I bit Deacon and took over the pack. This started because of a small-minded father's hatred of his son's sexuality. I fell in love, Matthias. I mated. I joined a pack. Do you think something that simple really deserves all of this?"

"Have you ever fallen in love?" Luca asked Matthias.

The old dragon didn't answer either of their questions. He stood up and left the library without a word, taking the mysterious journal with him. Tanner turned on Luca's lap so he could look his dragon in the eye.

"We have an ace in the hole, so to speak," Tanner said.

"And what would that be?"

"Kyle. I know neither he nor Taro have answered, but he was one of my father's recruits. Maybe he could tell us what the plans are."

Luca nodded and opened his mouth to speak, but he was interrupted before a word could be said.

"Your father isn't the only problem. What about the Enclave? They could still be a threat to Ther—, the pack."

Luca glanced at the doorway as Tanner spun to face Colby. "Have you notified them that you're joining us?" Tanner asked.

"No. I still don't feel that's a safe thing to do. Not because I'm afraid for me, but...if I'm on the inside, then I can keep their attention diverted."

"For how long?" Luca asked.

"They won't be put off for long, I'm sure," Tanner added. Colby glanced around the room as he thought about that. "I say we take a different approach with the Enclave."

"Different, how?" Colby asked, skeptically.

"Lie to them. With Sakima in the pack, Elysium is pretty much our domain. I say we use it. I say we start rumors of our own. Whisper in every ear willing to listen that I'm full of shit. I'm not powerful. I have no special abilities. It's all lies I tell to make myself seem special and more important than I am. I don't care what people think of me. I never have. All I care about is that the ones I love are safe and free to live their lives in peace."

Luca hugged him tighter and kissed the shell of his ear, but he didn't allow Luca to distract him. Not yet. He wanted to know what Colby's response would be. Matthias wasn't the only one in the house capable of hiding his thoughts. Hell, Colby had managed to hide the fact he was a sorcerer for over a year; no easy feat in a room full of paranormal beings with extraordinary powers.

"And you would have me tell the Enclave Superiors the same thing?" Colby asked.

"Yes."

A wicked smile spread across Colby's face. "My pleasure," he said before he turned and left the room.

Tanner turned back to Luca. "Let's reach out to the Stanton Pride again. See if Kyle is willing to speak to us."

"And if he isn't?" Luca asked.

Tanner sighed. "Yeah, one thing at a time, dragon."

"Whatever you say, pup."

Chapter Sixteen

COLBY

Colby sat on the sofa outside the Superior's meeting room. Every few seconds, he would send a probing spell pinging off the closed double doors. The Grand Superior had found a new spell to keep him from just popping in and out at his leisure, but it would only last so long. She had to know that. He'd broken through countless spells meant to keep him out over the years, and this one would be no different. Every time his magic bounced off the spell, he learned a little more about it. If she left him out here much longer, he wouldn't need her permission to enter. He'd be able to just counter the spell and walk in. Colby smiled as one heavy wooden door opened and one of the Superiors summoned him inside.

He entered the room and immediately felt the change in the atmosphere. A gentle hum of active magic filled the room, overlying everything. Colby stopped at the respectful distance this time because a wall of magic stopped him. The spell was rudimentary and easily dismantled by a child, but he allowed the spell to remain. Let the witch woman think she had him cowed. He glanced around the table at the other Superiors like he always did before glaring at the Grand Superior.

"Do you think I'm stupid, young man?" she asked.

"That's a loaded question," Colby said. "But generally speaking, no."

"I have eyes everywhere. I know you've been in frequent contact with members of the Chevalier Pack, despite your reports to the contrary."

"I reported to the contrary because I had no information. I've gotten close enough to them now that I can, without a doubt, tell you they are not what they've been rumored to be. They're actually fairly small and insignificant as far as packs go, and the so-called *Alpha* apparently has grandiose ideas about himself just because he's banging a dragon."

Colby shrugged and did his best to look bored. He didn't need the anxiety he was feeling to show on his face or in his posture. He also really hoped she hadn't discovered Alietta's journal was missing. Perhaps the Enclave believed the magic encasing the book would keep everyone away, and so they paid no mind to it. The spells inside the journal were quite advanced and impressive, and Colby couldn't wait to look through the pages again. He'd captured glimpses over Matthias's shoulder a couple of times, each instance making his itch to get his hands back on the book even stronger. The Enclave thought the Chevalier Pack was powerful now; what would they think when they learned Colby's mate was a member and of Colby's ability to wield such ancient power of his own?

"And what is this I hear about the McBane wolf pack recruiting other paranormals to protect themselves against the Chevalier?"

"Bullshit is what that is. One Alpha is the father of the other and hates that his son is gay and mated to another male. As for the paranormals he's recruiting, they're purists. They hate the interspecies mingling, nothing more."

Colby rolled his eyes. Sorcerers were the snobbiest, most high-and-mighty paranormal species he'd ever encountered, but as far as he knew, purism wasn't one of their faults. Personally, Colby had no tolerance for that way of thinking, and it had nothing to do with the fact his mate was a wolf shifter. He simply hated anyone who thought they could bully others for any reason.

"You expect me to believe that?" she asked.

Colby stared directly into the Grand Superior's eyes. "Do you expect me to believe you didn't already know that?"

She smiled haughtily and took several steps closer to him. "Do you think I don't know you've spent most of the past two weeks at the Chevalier pack house?"

Colby kept a straight face as she stepped even closer. He was the king of lies and deception; he could do this.

"Or how you've been seen in the arms of a wolf shifter living there."

The last came out more of a statement than a question. She wasn't asking him anything. She was directly pointing out everything she already knew for a fact, and Colby found himself in the very position he didn't want to be in. This was his reckoning; the fork in the road that would demarcate his life as before and after. He could tell a bald-faced lie and deny everything Theran was to him in order to save his own position in the Enclave, not that he held any real clout. Or he could admit everything, claim allegiance to the Chevalier Pack, and walk away from the Enclave forever. Rapidly assessing the active spells in the room, he noticed the one blocking the entryway earlier had not been reestablished.

He quietly conjured a spell that would enable him to move with the speed of a vampire and prepared himself for a rapid getaway. If this went badly, he wanted to be with Theran as soon as possible. Unable to hide the magic spreading through his body, changing his physical appearance for all to see, he looked at his mother with eyes he knew had gone black. He saw the black veins spiderwebbing from his fingertips up his arm.

"That wolf shifter is my mate, and I, too, am a member of the Chevalier Pack. They may not have been dangerous before, but they are now."

All the Superiors rose from their seats, and the magic in the room swelled as his mother merely lifted her chin and looked down her nose at him. He flashed an evil smile and, in the next breath, was gone from the room. Outside the building, as he was crossing the lot to his truck, Colby saw Jude crowding another young male sorcerer against Jude's royal-purple Mustang. The young sorcerer wasn't at all opposed to the position, given the amount of tongue Colby saw passing between the two. Wanting one last shot at revenge for the constant insults and insinuations Jude had thrown at him during their brief relationship, Colby bumped his shoulder as he sped past, sending Jude spinning down to the pavement.

Once Colby reached his truck, he erected the invisibility shield, sat in the driver's seat, and laughed until his stomach hurt. Some of it was relief, some happiness, but he was aware the majority of his mirth stemmed from hysteria. He'd just claimed his mate and renounced the Enclave to the Grand Superior's face. Never in his life had he spoken such heavy, honest words. Colby was finally free, as terrifying as the notion was, but he took comfort in knowing he wasn't alone. He had more family now than he ever had in the Enclave. He put the truck in Drive and headed back to the pack house. Colby no longer cared if the mating bite hurt; he wanted to be claimed more than his next breath, but the mating was put off once again by forces outside of his control.

Colby was halfway across the yard when Matthias opened the front door and stepped onto the porch. "Head for your abandoned cabin in the woods," he said.

"Why?" Though Colby had a feeling he already knew the answer.

"The pack accepted the request for a meeting with Alpha McBane's lead enforcer—Jeremy, Jared, what-the-fuck-ever his name is."

"I think it's Gerald," Colby supplied.

"Don't really give a shit," the older dragon said. "Just get your ass out there because nothing good will come of it." Matthias shook his head as he glared at the world in general. "Damned puppy is so determined to see the good in everyone," he muttered.

"Why aren't you out there?"

"I'm not a member of the pack."

"Neither am I," Colby told him, temporary as the statement might be.

Matthias scoffed. "Yeah, sure."

The dragon indicated the road to the forest with his chin, and Colby smiled. With a flourish of his hands, Colby teleported himself to the cabin and into the very situation Matthias had been worried about.

Chapter Seventeen

THERAN

Theran's gaze was drawn from the ring of swirling smoke and wind Tanner and Deacon had erected around the pack. A small opening appeared at the base of the maelstrom, and Colby calmly walked through. The entrance closed behind him with a flourish of his hands. Colby was in full sorcerer mode; veins, eyes, and fingertips the color of ink, hair streaked with black as it blew around him. He was a frightening, yet beautiful, sight to behold. Despite the entirety of Colby's eyes being black, Theran knew he was looking right at him, staring into Theran's eyes as he approached.

"I leave for two seconds..." Colby's deep sorcerer's voice boomed over the howling of the wind.

Luca thumped his tail to the ground, creating a small tremor. No one appeared concerned, despite the fact they had all taken their animal forms, and a battle waged on the other side of the wind wall. They were prepared, just in case the fight broke through their defenses. Ross was wriggling on his back in the grass with his tongue lolling out. Sakima knelt beside Vance, his arm over the wolf's side and fingers scratching his stomach. Theran trotted up to his gorgeous mate and rubbed his side against Colby's thighs in greeting. The warmth of Colby's fingers tunneling through his fur caused him to shiver with the cold that followed in their wake.

"You're not in danger?" Colby asked.

Sakima, tell him, please? Theran begged. He desperately wanted to speak to Colby himself, but that wouldn't be a possibility until they officially mated. Deacon glanced their way.

"For now, we're safe. The fight is between the McBane Alpha and his Beta enforcer. Our pack won't engage until the threat is directed at us."

Colby nodded and Theran licked his hand. Colby grabbed his snout and pulled his head up so they looked into each other's eyes. "Come with me," he whispered. The sorcerer walked to the cabin about a hundred feet away, just on the inside edge of their protective circle. Theran followed, happy to be at his mate's side, no matter the circumstances. Once inside the cabin, the black slowly faded from Colby's body to reveal the handsome man beneath the sorcerer. His caramel eyes sparkled, dark-brown hair falling down his back in waves.

Colby closed the distance between them to run his fingers through Theran's fur. Theran leaned into the touch, awestruck someone so much smaller than him could wield such immense power. Colby sighed before turning away. He snapped his fingers, and a pair of sweatpants appeared in front of Theran's paws. Theran gave a short woof and sat down.

"As beautiful as your wolf is, I can't have a conversation with you in that form. Please, shift."

The sorcerer kept his back turned as Theran shifted and picked up the sweatpants. He smiled at his man's attempt at decorum. Or perhaps he kept his back turned for a more primal reason.

"When we mate, you'll be able to talk to me in any form," Theran told him.

Colby grunted in response.

"Why the pants, Sweetness?" he asked as he pulled the sweats on.

"Like I said, we need to have a conversation. You in wolf form isn't conducive...yet, and you in human form naked...isn't conducive."

Theran stepped up behind Colby and wrapped his arms around the smaller man. He nibbled on Colby's earlobe, over his jaw, and down his neck. Colby let out a breathy moan.

"Please, stop," Colby whispered, though his voice lacked all conviction. He was saying the words, but he didn't mean them. Theran stopped the nibbling, but kept his arms locked tight.

"Theran—"

"Let me hold you, Colby. We've been apart too long."

Colby turned in his arms. "It's been a grand total of three hours."

The snarky attitude with which Colby spoke was easily ignored when he looped his arms over Theran's shoulders, nimble fingers dancing over the skin of Theran's neck to slide into his hair. Theran fisted a handful of Colby's thick waves. They were warm in his palm, heated by the sun and Colby's latent magic. Colby leaned forward with his face upturned, and Theran lowered his head, just in case Colby was aiming for a kiss. He settled for rubbing the tips of their noses together. Theran breathed in the scent of sage that always seemed to permeate from his mate, and sighed.

"You wanted to talk about something important enough to pull me from a fight," he murmured.

"You weren't fighting." Colby pulled back, desire and longing clear in his caramel-colored eyes. Colby slid his palms down Theran's neck, over his shoulders, and down over his chest before bringing them to rest just below his nipples. The touch was delicate, infuriatingly slow, and successfully short-circuited all of Theran's thought processes.

"So distracting," Colby muttered, gaze taking in as much of Theran's naked torso as possible.

"Yes." Theran cleared his throat. "Conversation."

"I did what Tanner asked. I told the Enclave he wasn't powerful at all, just full of himself. And..." Colby lifted his gaze back to Theran's face. Theran quirked a brow, wondering what might come of his little sorcerer's mouth next. "I told them you were my mate, and I was part of the pack."

Theran smiled and kissed the tip of Colby's nose even as concern bubbled up in his gut. "Will they be coming for us?"

"I don't know. I was so scared of how they'd react I made a very hasty exit. I'm sorry I didn't think to ask—"

Theran cut Colby's words off with a kiss. He didn't want or need apologies. Colby had accepted him and the pack, and that was all that mattered. With every mating that occurred, the pack grew stronger and more stable. Theran was more convinced now than ever before they would survive and be happy.

Colby joined the pack, Theran announced, even as he deepened the kiss with his mate, taking everything the little sorcerer wanted to give. *Knock on the cabin door if you need us.*

Several *Congratulations!* echoed in his head before he slid the block down on the pack bond. He wanted a few private moments with his man. Colby locked his arms around Theran's neck, wrapped one leg around Theran's waist, and then the other until Theran held the entirety of Colby's weight in his arms. His dick had been at full attention for several minutes and poked upward at Colby's bottom. Rolling his pelvis, Colby created the best friction against the head of his cock, and Theran groaned at the sensation.

Colby pulled out of the kiss, lips beautifully red and puffy from Theran's attention. "Mate me," Colby said, pressing in against him, their foreheads resting together. "Please," he whispered, soft breath ghosting over Theran's lips.

Theran kissed his mate as he walked to the blankets still piled in the center of the small single-room cabin. It seemed fitting he would claim his mate in the same place they'd experienced their first orgasms with each other. Theran lowered Colby to his back on the makeshift bed and ground their cocks together as he sucked Colby's tongue into his mouth. He pulled his arms from under Colby's body and worked his hands under Colby's shirt, lifting the fabric as he smoothed his palms up Colby's heaving, fevered chest. His handsome little sorcerer was on fire for him.

Lifting up, Theran made short work of removing his borrowed sweatpants and Colby's jeans, as Colby pulled his shirt over his head and tossed it aside. Theran was back between his mate's thighs as fast as he could manage, his big hand cupping one firm butt cheek. Colby arched his back on a moan as Theran squeezed the supple flesh, rubbing Colby's flaccid cock against his hardened shaft. He covered Colby's eyes with one hand as he dipped his index finger into the crack of Colby's ass to rub over his pucker. He pressed his weight down to keep Colby's movements restrained. Theran was not going to last if Colby kept rubbing on him, and he needed the mating to be good for Colby. He remembered Colby's fear of being bitten.

He leaned down to whisper over Colby's lips as he dipped the tip of his finger into Colby's hole. "So tight, Sweetness. I can't wait to sink into you."

Colby attempted to roll his hips downward, to drive himself farther onto Theran's finger, but Theran's weight prevented the movement. He pressed his lips to Colby's, so the sorcerer could feel his smile. He'd keep his hand over Colby's eyes the entire time, so he could focus on the sensations of his body and hopefully keep those self-deprecating thoughts at bay.

"So eager," he whispered. "This would go faster if we had lube."

Colby lifted a hand and rubbed his fingers into his palm. As he did, the digits grew slick with gel. Once he was satisfied with the amount, he presented his palm. Theran pulled his hand from Colby's ass to slide his fingers through the gel. He applied a generous amount to Colby's hole before guiding Colby's slicked hand to his cock. Colby wrapped his fingers around Theran's girth and squeezed as Theran reinserted his index finger into his ass. Remembering the potential threat right outside the cabin door, Theran sped up his preparations. He wanted to claim Colby with his dick buried as deeply as possible in his small, hot body as well as his teeth sinking into his delicious flesh. As he worked his mate's ass open, he whispered to him.

"You're a gorgeous little witch. Hot and tight and begging." Theran nipped at Colby's lower lip before trailing tiny love bites across his jaw to his earlobe. "Do you know what it will feel like when I slide into you?"

Colby panted in his arms, his only response to Theran's question a tightening of his fingers around Theran's shaft. Two fingers became three as Theran pumped them in and out of his mate's body.

"It will feel like nothing you've ever experienced before," Theran whispered. "I'll stretch you open, fuck you until you scream, and when I finally come inside you, I'll sink my teeth into your neck, and you'll know I'm the only man you'll ever want."

"You already are," Colby whispered back, breathlessly. He tugged on Theran's cock. "Please, Theran, now."

Theran pulled his fingers free and grabbed his cock, the knuckles brushing over Colby's. Colby released his hold on Theran to grab his own semierection. Theran slid his tongue into Colby's mouth as he pushed the head of his dick past Colby's spasming rim. They both grunted as he popped in and sank deeper into Colby's slick, welcoming heat. Colby wrapped his legs around Theran's waist and dragged his nails over Theran's shoulder blades, abandoning his own dick, as Theran's pelvis came flush against Colby's upturned butt. He was buried to the hilt inside his mate, and his wolf sighed in contentment. Colby moved beneath him, adjusting the fit and sending delightful tingles throughout Theran's body. Pure heaven.

"Fuck, Colby, you feel so damned good. Squeezing down on my cock, branding my body with your heat."

"Move...please," Colby panted. "Let me...I want to see."

Theran tightened his hand over Colby's eyes as he pulled out, stopping with the crown just inside the rim, and then pushed back in all the way. Colby grabbed his wrist, but Theran kept his grip over Colby's eyes. He'd let Colby see him as he was releasing inside him; he'd let him see the flash of fang before he claimed what was his once and for all. Until then, he wanted Colby to be awash in the physical sensation of their bodies connecting in such a primal way. Theran continued with the long, steady strokes until he couldn't take the sensation anymore. The need to pound into the smaller body beneath him was overwhelming, so he adjusted their bodies to make it easier for fast, hard movements. He buried his face in Colby's neck, grabbed his slim hip with one hand, and slammed into him.

Colby's heavy panting became desperate keening moans and gasps of pleasure as his legs tightened around Theran's thrusting hips and his nails dug into the straining muscles of Theran's shoulders. Soon the gasps and moans became words, and Colby's body arched beneath his powerful thrusts.

"Yes. Goddess, yes, right there. Fuck."

Theran's balls drew up. Nothing had ever felt as incredible as fucking this man and hearing just how much his mate enjoyed it. He was getting close to orgasm, and his fangs descended. Theran lifted his head from Colby's neck and slammed his cock into Colby's sweet little body a few more times. He studied Colby's body and the set of his mouth as he pounded into him. He knew the moment Colby was ready.

"Theran," Colby yelled as his body stiffened and then bowed beneath him.

Theran removed his hand from Colby's eyes and stared into the fevered, caramel orbs. He smiled around his fangs as his orgasm tickled down his spine. "You're mine, little witch," he said. One more hard thrust, and he erupted, his juices spurting into his mate's body, as he lowered his head to Colby's neck.

Colby bucked as Theran's fangs sank into the soft flesh where neck met shoulder and then he shuddered as Theran pulled a mark to the skin. The gentle bumping of minds and the itch of an incomplete mating pebbled the skin of Theran's back. He retracted his fangs and licked the new mating mark he'd created. A feeling of accomplishment and belonging filled him, but the itch for the reciprocating bite felt like ants beneath his skin. When he met Colby's gaze once again, the sorcerer opened his mouth to show his own set of fangs descending.

"Mine," he said.

Colby tightened his grip on Theran's body, everywhere, lifted his head to Theran's neck, and bit down. The sensation of the mating bond snapping into place sent another wave of pleasure racing through him, and he came a second time, still buried deeply in the heat of his mate. As the rush of the moment died down, Theran pulled himself free and rolled to his side to avoid potentially crushing his much smaller partner. Curiosity had Theran glancing over Colby's body, and the action did not go unnoticed.

"Nothing, sorry," Colby said.

Just curious, given the way you reacted under me, Theran said, testing out the new mating bond. Colby's eyebrows drew together, and he stared intently at Theran.

"That felt...strange," Colby said. "How do you do it?"

Theran was caught off guard by the question. He'd never been asked that before. "It's so natural for wolves, I've honestly never thought about it. I can feel you in my head, and when I want to talk to you, I just sort of *push* the thought at you." *You hear me?*

"Yes."

Push a thought toward me, toward that sensation in your head where you hear my voice coming from.

"Okay," Colby said, skeptically. *Sit, Ubu, sit.*

Oh, ha-ha. You're a funny little witch, aren't you?

Sorcerer. "And holy fuck, it worked." Colby sat bolt upright and Theran laughed. "Shift, Poodle. There's still a war being waged outside."

Theran rolled off the blankets into a crouch, so when he shifted, his wolf would be sitting. "After all this time, I doubt that shit's still going on."

Colby smiled as he pulled his clothing back on. Theran tilted his head at the cryptic expression and shifted. Even in wolf form, he wasn't able to read his mate's thoughts like the other wolves could do to each other through the pack bond. Since no one else he knew was mated to a sorcerer, Theran resigned himself to learning the ins and outs of Sorcerer Colbarton Delavane on his own. Colby opened the cabin door and flashed a beautiful smile over his shoulder at Theran. As he stepped out into the forest, his magic bled through his body, turning him into the terrifyingly gorgeous sorcerer Theran would forever be in awe of. Theran trotted out after him.

That was fast, Ean said as they rejoined the pack. Ross was still wiggling in the undergrowth on his back like a puppy. In fact, Theran noticed, no one had moved from their original spots at all. Luca's massive black dragon pulled an apple from a nearby tree and swallowed it whole, his spiked tail stirring up dirt and debris as it swiped across the ground behind him.

Fast, Theran repeated. *We were in there for nearly an hour.*

Five minutes, at best, Vance said as he leaned into Sakima's scratches.

Theran jerked his head to look at Colby. His wolf face couldn't express his shock, but his mind could, and he let Colby feel every bit of it. Colby glanced at him with a raised eyebrow.

"Time warp spell. Did you really think I would mate with you when all this was about to blow up?"

You did mate with me during all this, Theran pointed out.

Technically speaking, I suppose, Colby conceded. "It wasn't at the 'same time' exactly." Colby shrugged, and then his posture stiffened. "Incoming," he called out so the entire pack heard him.

Everyone jumped to attention just as three vampires, a golden eagle, and about two dozen wolves broke through the wind barrier. Deacon was the first to get hit as the golden eagle dived and caught his shoulder with sharp talons. Deacon screamed in pain, and a lightning bolt slashed to the ground, singeing the feather tips on one of the eagle's wings. Ross ran to his mate's aid and collided with a chocolate-brown wolf bigger than him by several dozen pounds. But size would never trump the bloodlust flowing through the white wolf's veins. He had a deep-seated need to kill, and this was the perfect outlet.

Theran joined Ean at Tanner's sides, flanking him as the Beta and enforcer were expected to do. He had only the barest sliver of concern over leaving Colby to fend for himself, the action going against his natural instinct to protect his mate. Black tendrils of magic snaking through the wall of swirling wind told him Colby was fine, so he focused on the vampire that materialized to Ean's left. Steffan.

Stupid vampires, Theran said. *How many times do we have to hand them their asses?*

Fire coming your way, Luca warned, as the white of Tanner's fur turned black, and he grew to twice his normal size.

Colby, fire, Theran yelled, hoping his sorcerer would be faster than Luca's flames. Both Ean and Theran flattened themselves to the ground as waves of heat blasted over them. Tanner didn't react at all to the increased temperature as he faced off with Steffan. So much activity had erupted around them, Theran had a difficult time keeping track of everyone. He could feel the entire pack in his head, save for Sakima, who no one could feel, but he knew the vampire was still with them through his connection to Vance.

On your feet, Poodle, before this heat singes your fur. Colby stepped in front of him, his hair whipping around behind him now solid black.

Run, Theran told Ean as he jumped to his feet and launched toward a nonfiery spot.

Colby shielded them until they cleared the smoke and fire. As they exited the haze, they found they were now behind Luca, and that deadly spiked tail of his was coming right at them. Ean leapt to the side, straight into Theran's shoulder, and they both went tumbling through the underbrush. Luca's tail swung within inches of their position and took out several McBane wolves who'd been right behind them.

Shit, where did they come from? Theran asked.

They're coming from everywhere, Ean answered. Sakima appeared beside them and lowered Vance to the ground.

"Keep him safe," the vampire said before disappearing back into the fray.

Theran took in Vance's shaking wolf and noticed blood welling from three scratch-type wounds on his haunches, and he wasn't putting weight on his right front paw.

What happened? Theran asked.

Eagle caught me, lifted me off the ground a good ten feet before he let go. Sakima caught me, but my leg hit a tree branch first.

Ean growled and took off into the melee. One second the Beta was running toward a group of wolves; the next he was swept off his feet by a blur of motion. Another damn vampire, Theran thought, as he prepared to run to Ean's aid, but the idea of leaving an injured Vance alone didn't sit well.

Colby, help Ean.

Thunder rumbled overhead, and the air became heavy with the threat of rain. Deacon drew a circle over his head with one arm, and a downpour ensued. The heavy rainfall would hinder the enemy's movements, but unfortunately, it had the same effect on the Chevalier Pack. Vance hunkered down near a tree where the thick branches somewhat protected him from the cold rain. It felt so wrong not to be in the middle of the fight. Theran struggled with aiding the rest of the pack or if his job as enforcer meant he protected the Omega. Ross came trotting up to them, snout, chest, and paws covered in blood, and his tongue lolling out. Happiness wafted off the crazy wolf as he joined them beneath the tree.

You're enjoying this far too much, Vance said. Ross didn't respond. He sat down beside Vance, tail wagging.

No more orange. Only purple and red.

Okay, Ross, Theran said, as he watched the fight rage on without one-third of their pack. Deciding there was no better protection for Vance than a wolf suffering bloodlust, Theran rushed back into the fight. Ross might be crazy, but Theran still trusted him more than most, and he knew Ross would protect Vance as best he could. *Stay with him, Ross.*

Theran leapt over Luca's tail and dodged between his big legs. Baring his teeth, he launched himself full force into a wolf about to jump at Tanner's back end. Tanner was still in his massive black form, eyes blood red, as he swiped one large paw at a blur of motion. One of the vampires was taunting the Alpha. The wolf Theran had knocked to the ground snarled as he pushed to his feet, and Theran went to crouch down in preparation for the attack, but he couldn't move. He shifted his gaze to Tanner and noticed the Alpha was also frozen in place.

What the hell is happening? Theran asked, uncertainty and fear leaking into his voice despite his valiant efforts to keep his emotions to himself.

The McBane Pack realized their compromised positions as well. He could see the malice spreading across their faces as they each moved into the best position to strike a death blow. A black-and-white wolf similar in markings to Tanner approached them. Thanks to Tanner's recognition feeding through the pack bond, everyone knew the wolf was Ethan McBane, despite never having seen him in wolf form. The Alpha actually had the audacity to shift into human form as he drew closer. It was a mistake that would probably cost the wolf shifter his life, because Theran felt a familiar nudge in his mind, and knew exactly what was going on. Ethan took in his son's frozen form before relief passed over his face.

"Finally," he said. "This whole unfortunate mess will be over, and your continued stain on the McBane family will be eradicated."

Tanner's pain and anger rippled through the entire pack, but Theran couldn't believe what he was hearing. Unless Alpha McBane had his own sorcerer or other magic-wielding paranormal on his side, there was no way he could believe their frozen state was due to something the McBane Pack had done. Theran didn't have any more time to think about it, though, because a thick gray cloud descended over everyone, blocking the sunlight and depleting Theran's ability to see anything clearly. His mind shot back to the first time he'd run into Colby in the woods and the little cloud of magic Colby had conjured in his hands.

You'll feel this, I'm afraid. Tell Sakima not to breathe, Colby told him.

Brace yourselves, and Sakima, hold your breath. This is Colby— Theran's words were cut off with a deafening boom, followed by a complete lack of sound before the world around him erupted in a white flash that pressed in on him from all sides, cutting off his ability to draw breath. He didn't think they needed to worry about Sakima taking a breath during this if Colby's magic felt this way to everyone. The white dissolved into black, and there was a pulse in the air before the dark cloud radiated away from them with another thunderous boom. As the magic dissipated, Theran began to feel faint because he still couldn't get air into his lungs. He watched in awe as Colby lowered from the sky, looking deadly and beautiful with his solid-black eyes, black-webbed skin, and black hair. Theran managed a quick, weak smile at his mate before losing consciousness.

Chapter Eighteen

COLBY

"He's waking up," Ross yelled, jolting Colby out of his catnap.

The wolf shifter hadn't left Theran's side since he'd passed out in the forest, which was slightly irritating to Colby. He was foolishly jealous of the other man, despite the fact Ross had been mated to Deacon for so long. Colby wanted to be the first one Theran saw when he opened his eyes. He needed to apologize to his mate for the accidental spell he'd put on him. Colby had intended to add an additional layer of protection to his wolf mate, not render him unconscious.

"Dude, get off me," Theran growled at Ross, his voice rough with sleep.

One thing Colby had learned over the past several weeks waking up beside his big, handsome mate was that Theran wasn't much of a morning person. He generally woke up quickly, and his mood improved, but immediately upon waking, he was cranky. Ross laughed, rolled off Theran and the bed, and then disappeared down the hall singing some song Colby had never heard. He walked to the bed and eased onto the mattress beside Theran. He gently caressed Theran's broad chest as his mate rubbed his eyes with the heels of his hands.

"What happened?" Theran asked, and Colby once again felt every emotion from the day before.

Colby swallowed thickly. "I wanted to protect you..." The scent of blood, the pained yips of wolves, the angry, fiery roar of a dragon, accompanied by his own fear and doubt, echoed in his head, and he closed his eyes. Theran's fingers gently touching his face, sliding up into the hair at his temple, silenced the phantom memories. When he opened his eyes again, he met Theran's loving gaze. Theran smiled at him sweetly.

"There's my pretty little witch," he murmured.

"Sorcerer," Colby corrected, but it sounded flat even to his own ears. He simply didn't care what Theran called him when it was said with such affection.

"I remember, fucking powerful." Theran smiled broadly at the repeated words before sobering again. "But seriously, what happened?"

Colby sighed. "I'm so sorry. I was conjuring the attack spell at the same time I was trying to put extra protection around you and accidentally sicced a constrictor spell on you instead. It's only meant to disable, not kill, so it dissipates the second the victim is rendered unconscious, but I am soooo sorry."

"I'm okay, Sweetness. I mean, knocking the pack enforcer unconscious probably wasn't the best thing to do right then, but... Is the rest of the pack safe?"

"Yes. We're all here. Only suffered minor injuries."

"Good." Theran caressed Colby's head, trailing down the length of his hair to his lower back. He tugged Colby forward so he lay sprawled across Theran's chest. This position was one of the shifter's favorites. "What about the McBane Pack? How did they fare with your magic?"

"Not as good. I aimed the actual blast over their heads, but that particular spell is poisonous to vampires so those three are dead. The eagle broke both wings because he was attempting to fly above the spell, and it knocked him into a tree. Not sure about the wolves, but I'm sure more than one probably died from injuries. Luca hit a couple with his tail, and that thing is downright lethal."

"What about the instigator—Tanner's father?"

"Was he the wolf in human form?"

"Yes."

"He was injured, but I don't know how badly. Other wolves dragged him away." Colby shrugged the one shoulder not impeded by Theran's embrace.

If he'd known Theran would put him through an interrogation, he would have paid better attention to who went down and how, but his focus had been on Theran's unconscious body, not whether the enemy suffered injury and/or death. Theran rubbed Colby's head for a few more minutes, relaxing Colby to the point he almost fell asleep. Theran's fingers tightened around his hair, and a kiss was pressed to the top of his head. Colby's upper body lifted and lowered as Theran gave a huge sigh.

"I'm being summoned," Theran said, softly.

"By whom?" Colby murmured. He was content to never move from the spot on his mate's broad chest.

Theran chuckled and rolled up to sitting, bringing Colby with him. "Tanner wants to see me."

"This will take some time to get used to."

"What will?" Theran asked as he stood up, grabbed jeans from the nearby dresser, and pulled them on.

"Not being on my own, not doing what I want when I want," Colby answered.

Theran bent and gave Colby a chaste kiss. Colby reached toward his face, but Theran straightened and Colby's fingers ended up sliding down bare chest. "You're definitely not on your own anymore, never will be again, but you *can* come and go as you please. I'm answerable to my Alpha, but you're not."

Colby jerked his gaze from Theran's delicious expanse of chest up to his eyes. Did he have it wrong? He thought once he'd left the Enclave in favor of the pack he'd become a part of it. "Am I not a member of the pack?"

"Of course you are. You're mine. But, you're a member by mating, not bonding. The Alpha would have to bite you for that, and we've determined that's not a safe thing for him to do given the circumstances. Sakima isn't a bonded member either."

"Oh."

Colby supposed that made sense. He most definitely did not want Tanner having access to his power. Sorcery of the magnitude Colby wielded was unimaginably dangerous to anyone not thoroughly trained in its use. He briefly wondered if Deacon would have allowed the bite if he'd known in advance his Elemental powers could be siphoned by the Alpha. As far as Colby knew, Tanner had yet to tap into the more destructive forces a powerful Elemental like Deacon had access to, and he hoped the Pack Alpha never learned how. Or that Deacon found a way to block access. The Chevalier Pack had enough fear and hate directed at them. Throw in an earthquake, volcano, or hurricane, and the entire paranormal world would descend on them.

Theran extended a hand. Colby slipped his fingers into his palm, enjoying the warmth and strength of his mate's grip, and allowed himself to be led into the hall. He didn't like having to leave the warmth of each other's embrace for a pack discussion, but he supposed he would have to get used to such things happening. Theran stopped at the open door across the hall, and Colby peeked around him to see Ean reading on his bed.

"You coming down?" Theran asked.

"Yeah. Be down in a minute. Just want to finish this page."

Theran nodded as he gently tugged Colby's hand to get him moving again. They found the rest of the pack outside in the backyard where they could enjoy the temperate weather. The mated couples were paired off, scattered around the patio and lawn. Theran found an empty lounge chair and sat, pulling Colby down onto his lap. Colby reclined against Theran's chest, sighing contentedly when Theran's muscular arms circled his waist. Now this he could get used to.

Matthias stepped out onto the patio and leaned a shoulder against one of the pillars. His dark brows lowered over even darker eyes as he scanned the pack. Colby was positive the dragon's only mood was grumpy, because since meeting Matthias, he'd never seen the older dragon be anything but disagreeable, especially when Ean was actively involved. Everyone picked up on their animosity, but no one commented on it.

"So, the two of you are officially mated?" Tanner asked. He and Luca were seated across from them, their fingers intertwined.

"Yes," Theran answered as Colby nodded, holding the Alpha's gaze.

"Congratulations. That's fantastic." Tanner's grin was infectious, and Colby found himself smiling back.

"What I find fantastic is that we learn once again you have no access to the sorcerer's power," Sakima said from his place on the grass, where he was stretched out beside Vance.

Tanner shrugged without breaking his focus on Colby. "Have you had a chance to talk to him?"

"No, you interrupted."

"What were you supposed to tell me?" Theran asked quietly, his lips pressed against the shell of Colby's ear.

Colby shifted on Theran's lap until he could comfortably look his mate in the eye without removing himself from Theran's embrace, which tightened as Colby spoke. "I've officially accepted the position of pack enforcer second to you," Colby finished.

Colby watched Theran's expression closely for any sign of disapproval. He was elated when all he received was a broad smile.

"With all due respect to my Alpha—" Theran started, making Colby's heart sink. Perhaps his mate wasn't as accepting as he first appeared. "—I think the pack would be better served if I was second to you. You *are* the all-powerful witch, after all."

"Sorcerer," Colby corrected, though he was smiling as he stared adoringly into Theran's sparkling eyes.

"I have no problem with Colby being lead enforcer as long as everyone is in agreement," Tanner stated.

"Lead enforcer *has* always been the strongest pack member," Vance said.

Colby glanced around at his new family as each of them accepted him, not only as one of them, but as the one who would ultimately be responsible for protecting them. He'd never been accepted so rapidly and openly, and he was humbled by it. Theran cupped his cheek and turned Colby's face back toward him for a lingering kiss.

"Now that we've settled—" Tanner began saying, only to be interrupted by Matthias.

"And where is your Pack Beta?" he asked. "Should he not have a say in this?"

Everyone stared at the older dragon for a moment before scanning the patio, gradually becoming aware Ean had yet to join them. Tanner broke the silence.

"Ean will accept what the majority has decided," Tanner told Matthias and then addressed the pack. "Next on the agenda is how to handle Gerald and his olive branch, such as it is."

"What?" Theran asked in surprise, jerking his bottom lip free of Colby's teeth.

Colby had been happily nibbling away at his mate's mouth, but now Theran's attention had been captured, and Colby would have to wait until the meeting ended to resume worshiping his wolf. Colby sighed and twisted on Theran's lap so he was once again facing Tanner, but it wasn't the Alpha who answered.

"Alpha McBane's former lead enforcer has reached out via messenger, asking for a temporary alliance to remove the Alpha from power," Deacon said. Ross sat on the back of Deacon's seat, knees over Deacon's shoulders, and combing his fingers through Deacon's shoulder-length hair. Colby found the wolf's calm behavior odd.

"Green can't be trusted," Ross said, never looking away from where his fingers slipped through Deacon's hair.

Theran tightened his embrace and straightened in the seat. "You can't seriously be considering that," he said.

"Actually, I am," Tanner told him.

"What does Ean say about this?" Theran asked.

"We're in disagreement."

"And everyone else?"

"Waiting to be swayed one way or the other," Luca said, glancing at his mate from the corner of his eye.

"Correct me if I'm wrong," Colby interjected. He'd been studying wolf packs but still had a lot to learn. Now that he was lead enforcer, his learning curve needed to make a steep incline. "Gerald's rank within the pack is Beta, but he's not Pack Beta like Ean."

"Right." Tanner nodded.

"He's already challenged Alpha McBane and lost. We learned that fact when the Alpha was the one to break through Deacon's defenses. If we accept Gerald's offer to join forces and make a challenge of our own, because you are also Alpha, if we win, won't that automatically make you the new Alpha of the McBane Pack and not Gerald?" Colby scowled at his own convoluted question. The thought had been so much clearer when it had first entered his head, but his mouth mucked it up. "Did that make sense at all?" he asked.

Tanner grinned. "It did, and you're right to a point. I can challenge my father and win, but until I actually bond the McBane Pack, I'm not their Alpha. They'll essentially be leaderless until someone claims the post of Pack Alpha."

"And that someone can be a Beta?" Colby asked.

"Yes, though typically they don't last. They don't bond the pack as tightly which leaves plenty of room for the born Alphas to muscle in," Tanner told him.

"It's what allowed me to be temporary Alpha to the wild dogs," Deacon said. "Until I could find a true Alpha to bond them."

"You're not even a wolf shifter," Colby said and then immediately felt stupid. Everyone already knew Deacon wasn't wolf, so pointing it out was ridiculous, but at the same time, Colby was immensely curious how something like that could happen. "How is that possible?"

"I don't actually think it is," Tanner said. "I think Deacon being Alpha was a combination of his mating bond to Ross and the pack bond Ross had to the others. I've come to believe Ross was the bond Alpha while Deacon acted as the Pack Alpha placeholder."

"Why do you believe that?" Luca asked.

"Time spent researching bloodlust. I wanted to find a cure. As I've been getting to know each of you, I'm learning your born rank. Ean is Beta. Vance is Omega. Theran is Gamma. But Ross? He was the tricky one. His pack rank suggests Gamma, but the more I study and learn and watch, the more I believe he's actually a born Alpha. I also believe the wild dog pack was suffering the beginnings of bloodlust not because they weren't properly bonded to an Alpha, but because the Alpha they were bonded to was already steep into bloodlust himself."

Everyone stared at Tanner, stunned by his suggestion. Colby didn't know enough about wolf packs yet to know if what Tanner was saying carried any weight, but judging from Theran's soft gasp and the minute tightening of his arms, Colby figured it must have.

"And as we're discussing bloodlust," Tanner added. "From the bits and pieces I can find on the original Chevalier Pack, I can't help but think many of the members with wolf DNA were suffering bloodlust. There's no suggestion anywhere they were actually a *pack*. They were a multigenerational family, and if the wild dog pack was infected through the bond, then why wouldn't they have been?"

"Seriously?" Theran asked. "Everything we're facing, all the hate and fear and attacks, are because a few wolves hundreds of years ago suffered bloodlust?"

A low growl echoed over the patio, and everyone turned to look at Matthias. The older dragon stared at Theran before sweeping his gaze back to Tanner. "I've said it before, and I will say it again: this is happening because you have powers you shouldn't have. Bloodlust does not account for that."

"Then what does?" Luca asked. "You know more than you're saying, old friend. What are you hiding?"

Colby's gaze bounced back and forth between the two dragons as they stared at each other, eyes locked in a silent showdown. He was lost on a few subject matters, but knew Theran would fill him in on all the details if he wanted. The journal he'd stolen from the Enclave dated back to the time of the Chevalier. Alietta had been alive then and may have written about the family. Colby opened his mouth to suggest they search through the journal for information but didn't get a chance.

"I'm not pack, so I have no reason to be here," Matthias said without breaking eye contact with Luca. After another brief second, he turned and walked back toward the house. "I'm going back to the library."

"Send Ean out if you see him," Tanner requested, a coy grin on his face.

"Why not just summon him through the bond like you did me?" Theran asked.

"The more opportunities I give them to talk to each other, the more opportunities they have to work out their issues and maybe find happiness. The sexual tension between them is reaching critical mass." Tanner clapped his hands loudly. "Now, back to this proposed truce. Do we take Gerald up on this offer and remove my father as a threat, or not?"

Colby twisted on Theran's lap and cupped his jaw. Theran looked him in the eye, smiled broadly, and then pecked him on the lips. He felt the gentle nudge into his brain that he was beginning to recognize as the mating bond.

What do you think, Sweetness? As lead pack enforcer, your opinion matters.

Nothing Colby had said in the past meant anything to anyone. The Enclave Superiors, his mother, past boyfriends—no one had cared much what he thought about anything. He was used to being ignored, discounted, and bullied when he spoke his feelings, so being taken seriously on such an important matter was terrifying.

What if I make the wrong decision and one of us gets hurt, or dies? What if they turn on me and kick me out? What will that mean for you? What if you're the one who gets hurt? I can't lose you.

Shh, Colby, sweetheart. You're powerful, smart, caring, and damned lethal in a fight. You earned the post of lead pack enforcer.

I'm terrified, Colby admitted and rested his forehead against Theran's, needing more skin-to-skin contact to draw on his mate's strength.

You don't have access to the pack bond, but trust me when I say we're all terrified. Especially Luca and Tanner because Tanner is the main target.

I'm not ready—

Maybe not, but you won't back down from the challenge.

Colby couldn't argue that point. Despite his small stature and lean frame, he'd spent his entire life taking on bigger, stronger opponents.

What do you think about this truce? Colby asked. He was in favor of staying out of the fray and letting Gerald fight his own battles. Why go looking for a fight when the fight was most likely to come looking for them?

One pack enforcer to another, Theran said, bumping noses with Colby affectionately. *I'm all for it. It's an opportunity to remove two threats at once. Because, quite frankly, I'm tired of Alpha McBane's constant threats.*

Colby nodded and then turned to face the Pack Alpha, and noticed the entire pack watching them.

"We voted while the two of you nuzzled," Tanner said.

"We were talking," Colby informed him. In response, Tanner smiled knowingly. Colby blew out a breath because what he was about to say went against his natural instinct. "We vote to align with Gerald."

"So did six others which is the majority. No matter which way Ean votes, the decision won't be swayed. I'll send word to Gerald tomorrow that the Chevalier Pack accepts his offer."

With that said, the pack broke into their usual couples, and each went their own way. Sakima helped Vance from the ground, scooped him into his arms, and then vanished in the blink of an eye. Deacon stood with Ross piggybacking and headed into the house behind Tanner and Luca, leaving Theran and Colby alone on the patio. Doubts and fears over words spoken, decisions made, and roles accepted rolled over Colby, threatening to drown him. He curled into Theran's strong embrace and tucked his face into his mate's neck.

"You may be the lead pack enforcer, but you're my mate first. And I will do anything, everything, to protect you. I promise you, Colby, I will be there for you whenever and however you need me. Forever."

Overwhelmed by emotion and unable to speak, Colby kissed Theran's neck and held him as tightly as he could. When he'd first dreamed of a beautiful wolf protecting him in a forest, he'd dismissed it. As the dreams began to happen more often, he had found them curious and tried to analyze what they meant. Never had Colby imagined he would end up mated to his dream wolf or that he'd find himself in the middle of a paranormal struggle for the right to exist. He was willing to fight for it, though. For Theran, his mate and the love of his life, Colby was willing to die.

Chapter Nineteen

EAN

Ean set his book down, finally giving in to Tanner's constant prodding to join the meeting. He didn't enjoy disagreeing with his Alpha and didn't much like that Tanner wanted to take their disagreement before the pack. He wasn't used to that sort of response. He was used to the Pack Alpha dictating decisions rather than placing them in the hands of the pack. Ean supposed he would get used to the new ways Tanner led. He let Tanner know he would be down to join them in a few and left his room.

Having a room to himself was something else he was getting used to. When they'd first become a pack, Ean had shared the room with Vance. Now, as the last unmated wolf in the pack house, he was the only one in a room by himself. Ean grumbled to himself over that fact. He didn't want to be unmated and alone, but Matthias was being an ass and adamantly refused to acknowledge he and Ean were mates. Everyone else had their mates by their sides, but Ean's was being a dick. Ean made a quick pit stop in the bathroom before heading toward the stairs.

He slowed as he approached the library, hoping to get a peek at Matthias. The dragon was amazing to look at. Tall with silver hair, dark eyes Ean could stare into forever, tattoos that covered almost every inch of chiseled muscle, and a presence that demanded respect. No matter where the dragon went, he couldn't be ignored. Ean was somewhat embarrassed by the amount of time he spent lurking in the hall, peeking around the doorframe to stare at the older dragon doing whatever it was he did on a daily basis. Matthias wasn't very social and hid himself away more often than not, but the dragon wasn't in the room this time.

Several books of differing age and condition lay open on the desktop. A map was folded on one corner, and a few scrolls hung precariously off one edge. Ean approached the desk and nudged the scrolls back onto the mahogany. The journal Colby had taken from the Enclave lay open in front of the chair. He'd noticed how Matthias treated the small book with reverence, and his curiosity had him flipping through the pages before he truly thought about his actions.

The majority of pages were written in a language Ean had never seen before; others were in English and recounted the author's daily life as far as Ean's quick perusal allowed him to interpret. For some reason, reading the journal without permission felt like an invasion of privacy, but at the same time, he had the distinct impression the book held far more within its pages than simple diary entries. That nagging suspicion was validated as he turned one last page. Ean stared at the page, slowly comprehending what he was seeing. His heart rate increased as understanding dawned.

This was it. This was what Luca and Tanner had been searching for since their little pack had formed. This was the answer to everything.

"What are you doing?"

Ean jerked his head up to find himself ensnared by the irritated scowl he'd come to both love and hate. He narrowed his eyes as Matthias stormed into the room and yanked the journal from Ean's hands. The dragon glanced at the page, snapped the book shut, and then glared at Ean. Ean pushed to his feet and glared right back. Matthias's deception hung heavy between them, and he was fighting to find the words to call his mate out. He wanted to scream, punch, cry, and all-out rage at the dragon he was meant to spend the rest of his life with, but it all failed him. He couldn't break the silence. He was at a loss.

"Information out of context, in the wrong hands, can be dangerous, little boy," Matthias said.

Ean's fury bubbled to the surface, but he attempted to swallow it. He really did. *You catch more bees with honey than vinegar,* his sister used to say.

"We have been searching for information on the Chevalier for months, and you were pretending to help while sitting on the answers the whole time. You've known everything from day one, but you've said *nothing,*" Ean bit out. "You've let us waste time spinning our wheels, left us to look like idiots, while *you knew everything,*" he yelled.

"Keep your voice down," Matthias growled.

"Or what?"

Ean moved around the desk, crowding into the dragon's personal space. He was at least half a head shorter, but that didn't stop him from squaring off with the older man. Ean had Matthias by the balls, and they both knew it.

"You gonna tattle, dragon? Not likely. Fates forbid you tell the truth and own up to your deceit."

Matthias's nostrils flared as he inhaled. He dipped his head and moved closer to Ean. Under different circumstances, Ean would have believed the actions to be amorous. Given all he'd just seen, he knew these were the actions of an enemy attempting to intimidate, and he refused to give in. More than anything, he wanted to feel the touch of Matthias's lips on his, feel powerful arms wrapped around him. Childish dreams.

"What do you want?" Matthias asked, voice deep and low.

You, Ean so desperately wanted to say. Instead, he asked, "What do I want...in exchange for my silence?"

Matthias glanced down at Ean's mouth before returning to his eyes and nodding.

Ean smiled smugly. "Claim me as your mate."

HEARTS OF DESTINY

Prologue

DURAY HORDE VAULT

After adjusting the stack of scrolls tucked beneath his arm, Matthias opened the door to the vaults and headed down the stairs. He had no idea what was contained in the newest additions to the horde library, but Sadie had insisted he take them, look through them, and archive them appropriately. The sheer number of scrolls he was carrying guaranteed weeks of sequestered reading, and he was looking forward to it. Matthias often disappeared for days within the vault stacks, and no one cared. He was moody and antisocial at the best of times and preferred his own company to that of other dragons.

At the back of the library, he dropped the scrolls unceremoniously on top of the desk he'd claimed as his, decades ago. Since no one came down to the vaults, no one had challenged his claim. As far as the horde was concerned, the vaults were Matthias's domain. The soft thump of little feet echoed in the cavernous space, dulled slightly by the papers and leather-bound tomes that filled the shelving. Matthias knew who those steps belonged to, and his disposition lightened a bit. Sadie's son had a thirst for knowledge that Matthias admired, even if it did mean his quiet sanctuary was invaded on a regular basis by the child.

"Hi, Matthias."

"What are you doing down here, Luca?"

The fledgling hefted a book that was nearly a third his size, and Matthias recognized it as an old human-written story about a witch. He wasn't sure it was an appropriate choice for a fledgling of just eight years to read, but he'd learned early on that Luca was not an ordinary little dragon. There was something special about him: something that reminded Matthias of the child he'd raised centuries before.

"Nothing in that book is factual," Matthias told the boy.

"That's good, because the witch ate the kids." Luca winced before turning around and disappearing into the shelving.

"Don't make me come behind you and straighten up," Matthias ordered, his voice carrying through the room despite him not raising it the slightest bit.

Twenty entirely-too-quiet minutes passed before Matthias rose from his chair to go check on Luca. He found the book the boy had brought back exactly where it should be, but Luca wasn't there. Returning to the main aisle, Matthias glanced down each row as he passed until he finally found Luca sitting on the floor with his back against the stone wall with a book opened across his little legs.

"This isn't a row you're allowed to be in," Matthias said, shocking the little boy who was clearly immersed in what he was reading.

Matthias squatted in front of him, closed the book, and willed the panic he felt explode in his chest to not show on his face as he pulled the book from Luca's grasp. He stood and placed the tome well above the boy's head. Luca was entirely too curious for his own good.

"But I liked that story," Luca complained. "It had a dragon married to a wolf, and I didn't know that could happen, and I want to see what happens next."

Matthias swallowed thickly. Luca thought he was reading a fictional story, but Matthias knew all too well that the Chevalier family had been real, and he'd be damned if he put the idea of interspecies matings into the head of the horde matriarch's son. Pushing the memory of his own interspecies mating to the back of his mind—because what did it matter anymore?—he looked down at the fledgling.

He steered the boy into a more appropriate area of the vaults to be explored and then returned to the tome he'd confiscated. Pulling it off the shelf, Matthias thumbed through page after page of his own historical account of the Chevalier, removed the most informative and thereby damaging chapters, and then replaced it on the shelf. Luca was only going to get older, taller, and more curious with age. Matthias wouldn't risk him finding the book again.

Later that night, after darkness had fallen and the compound had grown silent with slumber, Matthias burned one of the last firsthand accounts of the Chevalier—his own. Why he'd thought it was a good idea to put that horror down on paper, he'd never understand. Youthful folly. All that was left to do was locate and obtain Alietta's journal, the final remaining written history of the family and subsequent events Matthias had yet to destroy. For now, he was content knowing the only memory of the Chevalier that existed in the Duray Horde was now locked safely away inside his head; a place no amount of childhood curiosity could penetrate.

Chapter One

MATTHIAS

"Claim me as your mate."

Matthias stared at his defiant young mate. Brown eyes blazing, mouth set into a smug line, Ean looked directly into Matthias's eyes as he made his demand. Damn, he made a pretty picture. Ean may be the oldest of all the wolf shifters in the pack, but to a dragon pushing five hundred, he was still so young. Matthias wouldn't trade Ean's hot-headed temper for anything. Strong personalities such as Ean's turned him on, which meant he was constantly fighting his arousal. Crossing his arms over his chest, Alietta's journal securely in his hand, he watched Ean's eyes narrow as he took his time to respond.

"Is that truly what you want?" Matthias asked. "To be claimed under duress?"

Ean's defiance melted into distress; the heat in his eyes subsiding. Apparently, his pretty little wolf hadn't thought the demand completely through. Matthias, however, didn't want his past mistakes dangled in front of Tanner or the rest of the pack just yet. He still hadn't decided how he was going to handle the situation, and he needed Ean to keep his secret. At least for a little longer. The wolf shifter walked around the desk. Matthias thought he would head straight for the door, but instead, Ean stopped in front of him.

"Why don't you want me?" he asked.

The pain in Ean's voice stabbed Matthias through the heart. Taking a mate wasn't something he was ready to do, and tying someone so young and innocent to someone as damaged as him wasn't right, but Ean didn't know that. One day, he would. Ean may have thought he'd just discovered everything his pack was searching for, but the horrible truth had yet to be disclosed. Ean hadn't been far enough into the journal to truly understand Matthias's deceit. Something deep inside, probably his dragon who ached to be with his mate, wouldn't allow Matthias to leave Ean in such a state. He stepped closer to the wolf and lowered his head so their noses were nearly touching.

"I *do* want you, little boy," Matthias said.

Ean's features smoothed out, his lips parted, and he reached for Matthias, but Matthias stepped back, and Ean lowered his hand before making contact.

"Patience," Matthias said as he stepped around the desk. He needed the mahogany barrier between him and his mate to prevent himself from dragging the wolf to the floor.

Ean braced his hands on the desk. "I won't keep this information to myself for long, dragon. The pack deserves to know—"

"And they will," Matthias interrupted. "There are still things I need to prove before I lay it out for all to see. Past decisions, actions, ancient spells: the consequences have a way of taking on a life of their own when left unattended."

Ean sighed heavily and dipped his head. Matthias silently admired the wolf as Ean stared at the desktop between his hands, weighing his thoughts. Nothing was more attractive to Matthias than an intelligent man. He didn't always agree with Ean's actions, but the Pack Beta was a very smart man. Ean straightened and ran his fingers through his short brown hair before putting his hands on his hips.

"Fine," Ean said. "But, as I said, I won't keep quiet for long."

"Understood."

"Good. Now claim me as your mate."

"No."

Fire once again erupted in Ean's eyes as he glared at Matthias. It took everything he had not to smile at the wolf. Intelligent, strong-willed, and far too young. While Matthias was attracted to the boy, and occasionally entertained the idea of joining him in bed at night, he had no intention of ever claiming another mate. The idea of a second chance to get things right was a wondrous proposition, but Matthias knew he was unworthy of such a thing. Ean deserved better, but for the moment he didn't know it. Matthias was in no rush to show him either. Like the horrible person he knew himself to be, Matthias would let Ean continue to think he was just a stubborn old dragon, rather than the fucked-up mess he truly was.

"Why not?" Ean growled. "You said you wanted me."

"Wanting to pin you beneath me and fucking you is not the same as claiming you."

Ean's fangs descended as he emitted a second animalistic growl, and Matthias went hard in his pants. Ean was flashing his temper, which was a damn sexy sight. Completely unaware of Matthias's sexual arousal, Ean spun on his heel and stomped out of the library. He slammed the door shut behind him, blessedly leaving Matthias alone to deal with his turbulent thoughts and hard dick. Taking care of himself wasn't something he would be indulging in at the moment. He'd been doing that far too often of late, since unexpectedly meeting Ean several months before, and it was becoming more difficult. His hand simply wasn't what he or his dragon wanted.

Taking a seat in Luca's plush office chair, Matthias set the journal down and heaved a big sigh. He'd kept himself hidden away for centuries, first in the Duray Horde archives and recently up in Luca's private library, for this very reason. He didn't want to risk finding his true mate. If he had known coming to aid Luca, a young dragon he thought of as a son, would land him in the exact situation he'd spent the majority of his life trying to avoid, he would have left the damn fledgling to his own devices. Looking back, that's exactly what he should have done.

In the beginning, he had entertained the idea of walking away from Luca and his little interspecies pack. The longer he had stayed, though, the less likely it became he would ever leave. Alietta had been his lover, a sorceress he had thought was his mate, but after meeting Ean he knew what a true mate was. He could never walk away from Ean...not for long. Matthias would inevitably be drawn back to the handsome, young wolf shifter. His dragon would demand it. Given the amount of trouble Ean and his pack continued to get into, it was probably wise for Matthias to stay. Someone had to look out for the impetuous boy.

Chapter Two

EAN

Ean was hot, horny, and pissed as hell. He stomped down the stairs and then headed down the hallway toward Luca's first-floor office where he could feel Tanner's presence through the bond. He didn't understand why Matthias was being such a hardheaded asshole about mating with him, but the dragon was on his last nerve. It was becoming physically painful to be around his mate and continually be denied by him. None of the others had this problem with their mates. Deacon, Luca, Sakima, even Colby, had fought to be with the wolf shifter they were meant to be with. Ean was annoyed that it would be *his* mate who was reticent. He needed a break.

Knocking on the door out of courtesy more than requirement, Ean opened the door to Luca's office and stepped inside. Tanner was seated behind the desk while Luca stood behind him, massaging his head and shoulders. Ean would give anything to have Matthias treat him with such care. He could so easily imagine the older dragon's large hands on him, even in such a nonsexual manner. Because being mates meant finding his perfect partner. Luca kissed the top of Tanner's head as Ean sat across the desk from him.

"I'm going upstairs, force Matthias to help me do some more research," Luca said as he headed out the door.

Ean bit his tongue. He'd promised Matthias he wouldn't divulge his secret just yet. Though Ean had gotten nothing out of the deal, he wouldn't go against the promise he'd made to his mate.

"Took your time getting down here," Tanner said with a soft smile.

Ean recognized it as gentle teasing. Tanner wasn't actually angry with him for blowing off the meeting. Being in disagreement with his Pack Alpha was a new experience for him and he found it quite uncomfortable. The Alpha seemed to understand.

"Got caught up in a book," Ean said.

First it had been the mystery novel he was reading, but Alietta's journal had been intriguing and revealing. Ean still couldn't believe what he'd read in those pages, though he was aware those pages were out of context. Half of them weren't even written in English. He was acutely aware that the most revealing page, the one that told of Matthias, had been written by a different hand. Whoever had provided that final page in the journal had not been Alietta. Ean always loved a good mystery, and between that page and Matthias's refusal to claim him were two of the biggest mysteries Ean had ever faced. Tanner's voice pulled Ean from his thoughts.

"I'm sure you've heard the pack has decided to assist Gerald in the challenge against my father."

"I hadn't heard, actually." Ean sighed. It was his day for not hearing the words he wanted to hear. All in all, it was turning out to be a frustrating day.

"I'm sorry. I know you wanted a different decision, but the rest of the pack voted for it. They agree that taking the fight to my father rather than waiting for him to come to us is a faster way to end all this," Tanner said.

Ean nodded. He didn't agree, but he would do his job as Pack Beta all the same. "I'll meet with Theran and discuss strategy later today."

"Colby."

Ean tilted his head to the side in question. Tanner shrugged.

"Another unanimous decision you missed. Everyone, including Theran, voted Colby lead enforcer. Though I imagine where one goes, the other will follow, so you'll probably be meeting with both of them."

Ean shook his head. "I swear, that will be the last pack meeting I bail on."

Tanner laughed, but Ean didn't join him. He was immensely uncomfortable with Colby's rapid acceptance into such a position within the pack. Another pack decision he disagreed with. Ean looked at his hands in his lap and released his breath slowly.

"You can speak your mind, Ean. I count on you to keep me grounded."

"Thank you, Alpha. I'm concerned having Colby responsible for pack safety might not be the best idea. He killed three paranormals that we can confirm, maybe more. He has no qualms about taking life."

"He protected the pack, which is what an enforcer does."

"We're already feared and hated. When word gets out, and it will—I promise you that—the entire paranormal world will see us as unhinged and dangerous because now we've actually killed. We can't claim all we want is peace, love, and quiet existence anymore. And now you're telling me we're going on the offensive and taking part in the attempt to remove Alpha McBane from power? If the vampires, wolves, and sorcerers didn't vote for annihilation before, they will now."

"We can't be seen as weak, or it will never stop," Tanner said.

"I don't think we've ever been seen as weak. That's the problem, Alpha," Ean said, using the term of respect purposefully. He didn't want Tanner to think his Pack Beta was being insubordinate, but he had to say his piece.

Tanner sighed and leaned back into his leather chair. "Good arguments, as always, and I will take them into consideration when deciding our pack's next move."

Ean nodded, somewhat disbelieving. He couldn't shake the feeling Tanner had already made up his mind and Ean's words were ineffective in dissuading his Alpha, but time would reveal the outcome. The longer Tanner held his gaze, the more uncomfortable Ean grew. Tanner picked up on Ean's discomfort with ease and finally broke the silence.

"Are you doing okay, Ean?"

Ean wasn't sure how to answer that question without revealing too much of his own inner turmoil, which was probably exactly what Tanner was aiming for. So, he said nothing as he nodded and bit his lower lip.

"You seem to have a lot on your mind lately. You're my highest-ranking pack member; you're helping me lead, and I just want to make sure that you're thriving here. We haven't really had much of a chance to talk about things *not* pack related."

"I'm feeling a little off," Ean admitted. "I'm thinking a few days out of this house would do me some good though."

"Yes," Tanner agreed. "Everyone can feel the tension between you and Matthias. You make a valiant effort of blocking the bond, but we still have eyes...and ears. Will you confide in me?"

"Not yet. I have some things to deal with on my own first. I just need a few days away."

"I'm nervous about you being away from pack right now—"

"I'll stay with one of them," Ean interrupted.

Now that the idea of getting away from Matthias had entered his head and vomited from his mouth, he was eager to get moving. Maybe the constant ache in his chest that worsened each day, the nagging itch beneath his skin, would ease once he was away from the dragon. Ean couldn't accidentally spill secrets that way either. Ean relaxed his ever-vigilant hold on the pack bond so that he could send out his request.

Does anyone have a room I can stay in for a few nights?

Yes, Deacon answered immediately, though Ean had already known the ex-Pack Alpha had room. Deacon's three-bedroom apartment had been the first pack house and frequently saw the wild dog pack sleeping in the spare rooms.

Sakima and I have space, Vance said.

Us too, Theran piped in.

Ean considered the options his pack mates had given him. He'd always been able to count on them in a pinch, no matter the circumstances, and that hadn't changed after each of them had found their mates. The ache in Ean's chest grew, and he made his decision.

I'll stay with you, Theran. We need to talk strategy anyway.

Sounds good. You can come with us when we go later, Theran told him.

Thanks, Ean told his friend.

Tanner smiled at him. "Okay, then."

"Okay," Ean echoed.

Luca returned to the office with two steaming mugs of tea as Ean was leaving. They passed each other without a word, as was their usual. Luca's acceptance of the wild dogs had been forced in the beginning, and Ean still felt a bit of tension from the Alpha mate on occasion. Nothing like the tension that radiated off his own dragon mate upstairs though. Ean blocked the pack bond once again and hunted down Theran. He found him on the back patio, relaxing in a lounge chair with Colby on his lap. It had been easy asking for a place to stay and choosing Colby for his magical abilities when he wasn't looking at the sorcerer nuzzling into Theran's neck. Seeing the two newly mated lovers made him feel like an intruder. Ean turned to go back inside.

"You're not interrupting," Theran said, and Ean turned around to face him.

"I'm sorry I asked. I wasn't thinking..."

"And I wouldn't have offered if there was a problem with it." Theran pointed one finger skyward. "Becoming too difficult to be around?"

Ean nodded just once. Theran and Vance were the only two Ean had told about Matthias being his mate but refusing to claim Ean. Nothing had been said outright, but Ean was positive Ross knew too. The nutty wolf had an uncanny ability to pick out fated mates in a crowd, even before the two to be mated knew they were meant to be together. Ean was surprised and pleased that the wild dogs hadn't said anything yet. Not even to their own mates, for which he was grateful. He didn't want his failure to secure his own fated mate to be known by the entire pack. It seemed inevitable, but he wasn't ready to deal with that just yet.

"Go get a bag together," said Theran. "We'll head out in a bit."

Ean left the two lovers on the patio and rushed back to his borrowed bedroom.

Chapter Three

MATTHIAS

Matthias lay on the sofa, feet up on one armrest. He had an arm tucked behind his head while his other held Alietta's journal to his chest. The glass balcony doors stood open to allow the evening breeze inside. He stared at the clouds lazily moving across the dimming sky. The view was lovely and Matthias appeared to be relaxed, but his mind was a roiling storm of thoughts. It was how he always presented himself to the world. Calm, quiet, and peaceful on the outside while inside his head, a war raged.

Wrapped safely in his grip was the last remnant of his first lovemate, even as his current true mate was slipping through his fingers. There was no one to blame but himself. He'd never once been the kind of man a mate should be when it came to Ean. And he had never taken the time to explain to the beautiful wolf why he was reticent to claim him. So, the fact Ean had packed up what few belongings he had within the pack house and left was Matthias's own damn fault.

"Unhappy dragon. Maybe he needs to eat someone."

The unexpected voice snapped Mathias out of his thoughts. He rolled his head to the side to find the weird wolf, Ross, sitting cross-legged on the edge of the desk. Ross tilted his head to the side; a move Matthias had recently begun to associate with wolf behavior. All the wolf shifters did the same thing when they were confused or inquisitive.

Ross nodded. "You're mostly pink, though, so that's good. You have a little red and green, but that's your fault."

"Mmhmm."

Matthias held Ross's gaze, attempting to assess the wolf. Something about this particular shifter needled at Matthias's subconscious, and it was annoying. Like a fly that continually buzzed near his ear. He had the sense of familiarity, but where he would have run into a twenty-something-year-old wolf shifter when he'd not been outside the horde compound in nearly a century, he wasn't sure.

"When Colby works the magic in that book what will happen to the bond?"

Suspicious of the sudden clarity coming from a wolf who a moment before was speaking in code, Matthias lowered his feet to the floor and sat up on the sofa, facing Ross. He gazed into Ross's pale gray eyes. In this moment, the haze of crazy that usually coated them was gone and Matthias saw the intelligent, lucid man beneath. He'd never witnessed such a thing before though he had heard of it happening among humans who suffered dementia. One moment they'd be perfectly aware of the world and the next confused and unable to recognize those around them.

"You're a fascinating creature," Matthias said.

Ross smiled. "And you're avoiding the question."

Matthias grasped the journal and leaned forward, propping his elbows on his knees. "I don't know what will happen," he admitted. "But something needs to be done, or this little pack of yours will never be safe."

"Why do you care?"

Because I need Ean to be safe, Matthias thought, as he and Ross continued to stare at each other.

Matthias had the uneasy feeling he was being assessed quite thoroughly. If it weren't for the bloodlust pulsing through this wolf shifter's veins, Ross would be a force in his own right. Tanner was correct in believing Ross was a born Alpha. Matthias saw that quite clearly in this moment, though it was easy to miss when the bloodlust was running rampant.

"You should claim your mate if you love him so much," Ross said.

The comment shocked Matthias to his core. He sat up straight and eyed the shifter with open suspicion. Ross smiled and shrugged.

"The pink sparkles with silver when you think of him." After a moment of silence, Ross added, "If you have Colby magically suppress Tanner, you might also suppress the True Alpha bond and having something that strong suddenly disappear will be far more dangerous to Ean, to the pack as a whole, than the current threats we're facing." Ross glanced down at the book in Matthias's hands before returning to Matthias's face. "There's a reason that book was locked away. Just because we have it in our possession now, doesn't mean we should ever use it."

Ross closed his eyes and smiled broadly as he breathed in deeply, letting it out on a sigh. "My Deacon found me."

A solid knock sounded on the library door. Matthias creased his forehead as Deacon entered the room. The back and forth between crazy and lucid was odd, and the lucid moments dug in under Matthias's scales, creating an irritating itch. He hated admitting Ross might be right in his warnings. Matthias hadn't considered any of that when he'd first come up with the idea of Colby stealing the journal and removing Tanner's abilities magically. Being a dragon, the pack bond hadn't been a variable he'd even considered. He would think about it now though because suppressing Tanner wasn't worth any risk to Ean, no matter how trivial or small.

"What are you doing in here?" Deacon asked Ross as he approached his mate at the desk. Deacon glanced at Matthias, gave a quick nod of acknowledgment, and then returned his attention to Ross.

Ross wrapped his legs around Deacon's waist, placed his palms on Deacon's chest, and nipped at Deacon's chin. "Till death do us part," he mumbled, and then bit Deacon's neck hard enough it made Matthias wince. From the expression on Deacon's face, it hurt more than the Elemental would've liked too.

"Easy, love. I haven't had to sedate you in months, and I don't want to have to start again."

Ross released the bruised chunk of skin from between his teeth, and then fisted Deacon's shoulder-length locks. "I'm taking you with me," he growled.

"I know. You've told me."

Tendrils of electricity danced at the tips of Deacon's fingers, behind Ross's back. His voice was soft, his posture relaxed, but the Elemental was prepared to take his mate down if things turned violent. Apparently liking the verbal response, Ross looped his arms around Deacon's neck and tucked his face beneath Deacon's chin. The tiny lightning bolts dissipated, and Deacon held the wolf to his chest as he glanced over at Matthias. There were no words Matthias could think to say. The entirety of the past several minutes had been strange, and he wasn't quite sure what to do with any of it. Deacon lifted Ross off the desk and carried him out of the library, leaving Matthias with a mass of confusing and disturbing thoughts.

Chapter Four

EAN

Ean smiled drunkenly as Colby put what was probably his ninth, maybe tenth, tequila shot on the bar in front of his face. He'd lost the ability to sit up straight or even hold his head up about two shots before, but as long as he had friends nearby, he knew he could indulge to the point of passing out if he chose. And tonight, he very much wanted that wonderful oblivion.

He was so sick of the anger, depression, and pain. Ean had thought it was hard being in the same house as Matthias, but it turned out that was nothing compared to *not* being near his mate. He didn't get those quick sights of Matthias, or feel his looming presence when they were close to each other, couldn't smell him. All that surrounded Ean now was the aroma of sage that accompanied Colby's magic and the familiar scent of pack.

Lifting his head the minimal amount necessary to achieve the goal of swallowing, Ean poured the acidic liquid down his throat and then returned his chin to the comfy resting place on his forearm. Seconds later, the incredible scent of peat he'd come to love and hate wafted over him. Ean closed his eyes. He missed that scent.

"How much have you had to drink?" Matthias asked.

That deep, rich voice was much closer to Ean's ear than Ean expected. Luckily, the alcohol dulled his senses enough that he didn't jump away or rear back as he normally would have. He remained slumped over the bar in a miserable heap as his eyes blinked open.

"Nine, ten, I don't care." Ean shrugged.

Colby sidled up to the bar and pushed his long hair back over a shoulder as he slid another shot in front of Ean.

"This is number fifteen, actually," Colby said and then once again disappeared down the bar to another waiting patron.

"Don't worry about it," Theran said from Ean's other side. "Pack takes care of pack, or haven't you figured that out yet?"

"You call this taking care of pack?" Matthias rumbled. "Sitting there watching him drink himself stupid?"

Ean scoffed.

"I call it letting him dull the pain caused by the denial of his asshole mate," Theran snapped.

Shit. That's what I need to top off my night. Tanner finding out his enforcers got into a bar fight with a dragon because I'm on a bender. Ean attempted to push himself up and away from the bar. Everything would be fine if he could find his feet and square off with Matthias on his own like he usually did.

We're not getting into a bar fight, Theran said. *Just telling the old man how it is.*

Fuck. Said that out loud?

Ean snapped his head to the side to look at Theran and nearly fell over.

Not exactly.

Theran grabbed his biceps with one hand to help steady him. Two more strong hands grabbed his hips and squeezed. He knew who those hands belonged to, and he practically melted against the large body he felt close to his back. Pretending to tip backwards as though he lost his balance, Ean sought out a more solid touch. Matthias had never touched Ean before, and, damn it, the dragon's warmth was overpowering his inebriated brain. He wanted more.

Easy, there, Theran said.

Ean grinned at his friend. *I'm okay.*

Theran tilted his head to the side before jumping his gaze up over Ean's shoulder. After a moment of consideration and a good, hard assessment of Ean's condition, Theran nodded once and then left Ean alone with Matthias. At least, as alone as the two of them could be in a crowded club. Elysium was busy for a Thursday night and what Ean had originally thought was a good thing now annoyed him. He wanted Matthias alone, truly alone, away from everything and everyone. Ean wanted to get lost in his dragon mate.

Ean straightened and spun around to face Matthias. His shifter metabolism was already clearing the liquor from his system, though he was far from sober. He leaned forward so their chests pressed together, and Matthias wrapped an arm around Ean's waist. Heat flashed through Ean's body at the strong, tight grip, and he closed his eyes to hide the surge of desire when Matthias cupped his face. What he wouldn't give to have Matthias's lips press down on his right now. It was a simple thing he asked for, but knew he wouldn't get.

Wrapping his arms around Matthias's hips, Ean pressed his palms against the dragon's broad back. Matthias may be over four hundred years old, but he was built like a brick house. Solid muscle moved beneath the thin white T-shirt and black jeans. There was so much power locked up in a deliciously tall, tattooed physique. For the first time since meeting Matthias, Ean wondered what Matthias's dragon looked like.

Luca was a massive black dragon with lethally sharp spikes on his head and tail, which was the hallmark of an older dragon. Matthias's dragon would be majestic, no doubt. Ean groaned and opened his eyes to stare into the black depths of his mate's gaze. He didn't hear Matthias's growl, but he felt it in his chest and watched as silver swirled into his near-black eyes. Now that was a gorgeous sight.

Matthias cupped Ean's chin and lowered his head, their noses brushed across each other, their breath mingling. It wouldn't take much for Ean to kiss him. All he had to do was lift up on his toes a fraction of an inch and their mouths would connect. Ean moved in and up: a slow, slight move. His lips brushed Matthias's in a ghost of a touch when Matthias suddenly released his hold on Ean and stepped back. The movement was so fast and unexpected it left Ean wobbling on his feet. Matthias reached out a hand in attempt to help steady him, but Ean slapped it away.

"Why the fuck are you here, old man? Did you feel the need to torture me more?" Ean yelled. He felt tears welling in his eyes. Honest to god tears. He hadn't cried in years. Not since his parents had been shot and killed when he was ten. It pissed him off even more that he felt this situation was worth crying over. Matthias didn't deserve his tears. Ean jammed his palms into his eyes to keep the tears from falling.

"Goddamn alcohol," he grumbled. That had to be what was causing his unusual and overwhelming sadness.

"Torture was not my plan. I heard you were drunk and came to assess your safety, given recent events. I wouldn't have come at all if I'd known Theran and Colby were with you," Matthias said.

Ean couldn't look at the dragon. He was on the verge of a meltdown; he could feel it swimming just below the surface. "Go away, then."

Matthias's growl was the low, frustrated sound Ean had grown accustomed to hearing. It was a special sound the dragon seemed to save just for him. The only thing his mate had ever truly given him—his own special, rumbling growl. Matthias's scent dissipated among the crowd, and Ean lowered his hands. He had thought he'd waited long enough for Matthias to be out of sight at least, but he was wrong. Ean saw him at the other end of the bar, talking to Theran. Colby was behind the mahogany bar glaring. Nosy, interfering, infuriating dragon. Ean felt tired and depressed and wanted nothing more than bed, but Colby's shift didn't end until two in the morning, and it was only midnight.

Ean turned toward the dance floor, with the intention of passing the next couple of hours rubbing against hot, hard bodies that didn't push him away, and plowed right into a wall of muscle. He stepped back and then looked up, and up, until he met the golden eyes of Sakima's gryphon bouncer, Ollie. If Ean had had the good fortune to meet Ollie before setting eyes on Matthias, he might have ended up in bed with the man. He was tall, handsome, and muscled—everything Ean looked for in a partner.

"Are you okay?" Ollie asked.

Ean stared up at the gryphon shifter. He was most definitely not okay. He was drunk, depressed, and feeling a bit reckless, but he couldn't say that to the bouncer or he might be escorted out.

"Just looking for a dance partner and didn't see you there."

Ollie cocked one eyebrow. "I'm rather hard to miss."

Ean winced slightly. The big guy wasn't lying. Ollie stepped closer to Ean and then bent down to speak directly into his ear.

"Be a good little Chevalier wolf so I don't have to throw you out."

Ean swallowed hard and nodded. He waited until Ollie was a few feet away before he pushed onto the crowded dance floor and let himself go to the beat of the music within the heaving, sweaty mass of bodies.

Chapter Five

ROSS

Ross skipped and danced down the cinderblock-and-tile hallway of the abandoned elementary school, as much as a wolf could skip, anyway. On one particular hop a sharp ache radiated down into his paw, reminding him he'd been severely injured during the early days of the Chevalier Pack's creation. He'd seen his mate's handiwork swirling beautiful and violent in front of him and decided in his hazy brain that death by his lover's talented hand was a good way to go. The pain Deacon had suffered as a result hadn't been planned, but Ross hadn't been thinking as clearly in those days. He was getting better as time passed.

He couldn't say the same for his father. After Ross's mother died, Ross and his father suffered a rapid decline in their mental state. Her death had not been unexpected, but the consequences were. Their small, but strong, family bond had snapped, the ends tattered and frayed and forever irreparable. Certain connections in Ross's brain had broken. Ross and his father had gone their separate ways a few months later in search of a way to reclaim the bond.

Ross had found a weaker bond with Theran first, and then Deacon, followed by Vance and Ean. His father had taken to living in the gymnasium of the abandoned elementary school in a similarly abandoned mountain town. Crested Lake had been a bustling little town when Ross's parents met, but by the time Ross came along, it was slowly dying. His parents refused to leave and, looking at how their lives had turned out, Ross believed that to be a good thing.

Ross couldn't remember the last time he'd seen his father in animal form. He'd stopped shifting even before Ross's mother's health had declined. His father was still adrift in his madness. For Ross, bonding to Tanner had been a godsend. The True Alpha had given Ross the bond he needed to heal psychologically, at least a little bit, but he'd also given

Ross the outlet he needed because he couldn't get those broken parts in his head to work right.

A human roar of frustration echoed through the empty halls followed by a crash that brought Ross to a stop. It wasn't a new sound, but it seemed to be coming from a different part of the school than usual. He gave a few short yips.

"In the choir room," his father yelled from nearby. "I can't find my hat."

Ross turned down the hall and shifted. Dragging his fingertips along the metal bumps and ridges of the faded red lockers, he approached the room his father was in and peeked around the doorframe.

"Hi," Ross said.

As disheveled as always, hair not combed and sweatpants hanging loosely around his thin waist, Ross's father turned to face him.

"Have you seen my hat?"

"No."

"If you haven't seen it, then why am I even looking for it?"

Ross tilted his head to the side. "I'm not sure."

"No help at all," his father grumbled as he exited the room and headed down the hall toward the gym.

Ross followed at a more leisurely pace, snagging a pair of shorts he found on a chair that was inexplicably in the middle of the doorway into the gym. He pulled them on and then joined his father in the large room. His father's living conditions had worsened since Ross had last been to visit. He'd heard that could happen with advanced age, but he'd expected it would happen gradually over years, not in one short month. Ross pointed to a large pool of dried blood.

"What happened there?"

"When?" His father turned around, saw where Ross was pointing, and then waved it off. "Threw up. Dinner didn't sit well."

"You threw up blood?"

"Elk tore up my gut."

Ross nodded, because on the surface that made sense. On a deeper level, it didn't seem quite right, but that part of his brain couldn't form the thought properly enough for Ross to voice it. This was where having the bond to Tanner helped. Those deeper parts of his mind where coherent thought, intelligent action, and control resided could rise to the surface and get out into the world the way Ross wanted them to, but couldn't make happen anymore.

"Bones will do it every time. Eat slower," Ross said.

As he walked around the gymnasium, taking in the new items his father had compiled since his last visit, he thought back over his conversation with Matthias. For a change, he'd had little trouble articulating his deeper thoughts, but he'd yet to achieve the feat again.

"Are you really my son? You don't look quite right," his father said from the top of the half-extended bleachers.

"I'm not sure. Sometimes I feel like me and sometimes not." Ross picked up an old, yellowed book that was missing the cover. The pages were written in a language Ross couldn't read, but recognized. "Did you know a sorceress named Alietta?" he asked, and then tilted his head at his own strange, unexpected question. The handwriting in this book was definitely his mother's, not Alietta's.

"Heard the name. Didn't know her. She was something to my uncle."

Ross put the book back on the pile of junk where he'd found it. Other than his parents, Ross had never known any family. This was the first time he'd ever heard word of any extended family at all. His mother had explained that their little family was different than most and he'd accepted his secluded world at face value. It wasn't until he'd set off on his own that he'd realized how sheltered and naïve he was.

Thankfully, Ross had stumbled across Theran and his familial pack. When things had gone south between Theran and the Pack Beta, Drew, Ross hadn't thought twice about sticking close to Theran's side. Given all those previous decisions had led him to Deacon, and then to the rest of the wild dogs and Tanner, he was rather pleased with the way his life had played out so far.

Seeing that his father was surviving, despite the continued decline of his surroundings, which was expected in a ghost town, Ross gave into the pull to return to his pack.

"Take care, Dad," Ross said as he exited the gym into the school's hallway. He shucked the borrowed shorts and tossed them to the floor. He shifted and shook out his white fur. As he walked back out the way he came in, he heard his father's grumbling words.

"Don't know why you're asking me all the questions. Ask your uncle. I told you he knew. Always getting into stuff."

Ross decided once he got back to the pack house, he would investigate his own family tree a little in order to find his uncle. He didn't know how to find that sort of thing, but there were plenty of older and wiser men at home who could help him. A rabbit skittered across the cracked, overgrown parking lot a few feet ahead of him. Ross immediately gave chase, and all thoughts of uncles and family trees was lost to the thrill of the hunt.

Chapter Six

EAN

"You don't feel even a little bit hung over?" Colby asked for the third time since Ean had rolled out of bed.

"No," Ean answered...again.

Colby huffed as he returned his attention to his cereal. He'd been swirling it around in the bowl more than actually eating it. Theran chuckled.

"He's a little envious of our wolf shifter metabolism."

"Whatever," Colby mumbled.

"I'm cursing it, myself. I'd love to be able to hold onto the numbness for hours on end like humans do. Hell, half of them aren't even sober the next day, and that's just plain unfair," Ean said. "Us? If we don't keep drinking, we're back to feeling miserable within hours."

"I can guarantee humans feel miserable after binge drinking," Theran said, sipping his coffee while idly playing with Colby's hair.

"Sorcerers feel miserable after drinking as much as you did," Colby grumbled, glancing up at Ean through his lashes.

Ean smiled. Theran's mate really was a pretty little thing. It was probably good Ean wasn't the least bit attracted to the same kind of men as his friend, or Theran might feel the need to beat him to a pulp for the way Colby was looking at him right now.

"I'm sorry, Sweetness." Theran kissed Colby on the temple and then winked at Ean. "Since we have the Pack Beta with us, what do you say we go over the plans with him?"

"What plans?" Ean asked.

Colby got up and walked to the kitchen counter where he grabbed a rolled-up map. Ean had noticed it there the past two nights but had decided not to ask about it. He was a guest in Colby's home, and he didn't want to be nosy. Theran cleared the table of everything except their coffee, and Colby spread the map out. Inside the roll were the smaller hand-drawn maps of the McBane Pack lands Tanner had created for them before they set out to rescue his childhood friend, Tyler. Ean cleared his throat and took a massive gulp of coffee in an attempt to burn those unpleasant memories away. He'd been taken by vampires for a short time before they realized he wasn't the wolf they wanted.

"So, I kind of destroyed the cabin during the last scuffle," Colby said.

"Seems to be our thing, destroying cabins," Theran said as he retook his seat at the table. Ean grunted in agreement. Colby looked between the two of them before pushing the map closer to Ean.

"The area is still a good one for staging an offense. Especially with McBane lands bordering it, which I did not know when I took Theran there, by the way."

When neither Theran nor Ean responded, Colby pointed.

"The clearing is small, but it'll work. We keep ourselves behind this tree line, the McBanes will have to come through the clearing to get to us."

"I'm having déjà vu," Ean said.

This plan was exactly what they'd tried to do the very first time they'd stood against the McBane Pack. They'd thought they were in a defensible place then too. For the most part, they had been. Ross was the only one physically hurt, but it had dropped Tanner on the spot. Things had steadily escalated as time went on, though, and Ean didn't want to make the same mistakes twice. Ean listened to the entirety of the plan the enforcers had created without interruption, making notes in his head of what he liked or could tweak for the better, and the one thing he wanted to avoid.

"There it is," Theran said. "That's what we came up with. Now...poke holes in it."

Ean twirled his empty mug on the tabletop. "Only one hole, but it's a big one. I don't like the location. Otherwise, nicely done, Colby."

"Thank you," Colby said, dipping his head so his hair hid his face.

Theran pulled the smaller man between his legs and wrapped his arms around him. Bold and confident one second, meek and shy the next, Theran's little sorcerer was quite the contradiction. Another wave of sadness and anger hit Ean straight in the chest, knowing everyone in the pack had found their mates, had claimed and been claimed, and he remained alone, spurned.

"Want to hear my other plan?" Colby asked.

"Sure," Ean said without thought.

"No," Theran barked, drawing Ean's attention away from the map he'd been staring at.

"Obviously, my mate doesn't agree with it."

"Obviously," Ean agreed.

"Basically, I ask Alpha McBane for a meeting..." Colby said.

Theran growled.

"I go in, perform a severance, and come home. Done."

"I love how you left out all the problem spots," Theran said.

"Like going in alone?" Ean asked.

"Like performing a spell that historically has killed everyone who conjures it."

Ean leaned back and watched as the two mated enforcers glared at each other. It was good to know that being mated didn't mean perfect harmony. His jealousy wasn't as lethally sharp now.

"I've heard this word before: severance. What is it, exactly?"

"Dangerous," Theran snapped without looking away from Colby.

Colby pushed his hair away from his face and deliberately slid his gaze off Theran and onto Ean. "It's a spell that does exactly as the name implies. It severs the human from the animal and only one half will live."

"It basically removes everything that makes you a shifter," Theran added.

"Can you pick which half you want?' Ean asked, wondering if that was the answer to his problem. He wouldn't need the pack bond or suffer the effects of a mate who didn't want him if he made himself human. He wasn't sure how his wolf would fare though. A different kind of depression and fear hit him, then. The idea of living the rest of his life human with his wolf dead wasn't a pleasant one. He'd always remember his wolf half and mourn his loss, and he would never forget Matthias even if he was no longer pulled toward the dragon by forces too big for him to understand.

"No," Colby answered, pulling Ean out of his thoughts. "You can't choose which half survives and neither can the sorcerer."

"Why would you ask that?' Theran asked.

"Thought it might be the answer to all my problems," Ean answered.

"That's what I was afraid of, and it's not. Besides, I can't imagine either half of us would live long without the other. We're too integrated. This is what we are on a molecular level."

"I already came to that conclusion," Ean said.

"I can't even believe you considered it an option."

"Because Colby never denied you. None of your mates did. You guys have no idea what it feels like to be in the same house as your mate, see him every day, be surrounded by his scent, and have him constantly pushing you away."

Ean let Theran feel the emotions behind the words so that his pack mate could understand why Ean would think something as extreme as a severance seemed like a good idea. Theran winced but held Ean's gaze. After a moment of shared pain, Theran glanced at Colby, who grinned wickedly.

"Perhaps a severance is exactly what's needed," he said.

Theran shook his head vigorously.

"I'm not saying I'm actually going to do one, at least not on Ean."

Theran's responding growl was a deep, resonant warning.

"I'm saying if word of Ean undergoing a severance got back to Matthias, it might spur the old man into claiming him. Trust me, all the old guys in the pack know exactly what it is and what it means."

Wow. Manipulative, Ean said to Theran. Theran's gaze bounced back to Ean's. *I like it.*

Theran sighed and glanced back at his mate. "You won't do any magic even remotely associated with the actual spell...right?"

"Right," Colby agreed. "I can make it look really convincing though."

"Let's do it," Ean said.

He leaned back in his chair and allowed a genuine smile to spread across his face. It was just a matter of time now before he and Matthias were together the way they were meant to be. It was a gamble that the old dragon would hold such a manipulative act against him, but Ean was desperate. Every time he thought about Matthias or was in the same room with him, his wolf whined and clawed beneath the surface, desperate to be acknowledged by their mate. If this worked, Ean and his wolf would have what they wanted soon.

Chapter Seven

MATTHIAS

Dawn turned the sky above the mountains a gorgeous rainbow of colors. The mountains themselves a faded blue and white rising above the forest at their base and the trees scattered throughout the neighborhood. Matthias sat at the highest point of the roof, watching the majestic sight that heralded the beginning of a new day. This was his favorite thing to do—start the morning off watching the sunrise.

It was a different experience at the horde compound located in the heart of the mountains than it was east of the range, and it had nothing to do with location or how the sun rose. The experience here was unique because he didn't feel isolated and alone among Tanner's pack. Despite his attempts to remain separate, he was very much integrated. Ean's existence demanded it. In fact, Ean's existence demanded everything from Matthias—his presence, his attention, his protection, and his love.

Would Ean sit on the roof beside him every morning? Watching the sunrise every day with his young mate at his side would be wonderful. Except, he was fairly certain he'd chased the boy away. Ean had demanded Matthias claim him in exchange for keeping his secrets, but Matthias hadn't agreed, and yet, Ean kept his silence, which both confused and delighted him.

His wolf shifter was a lot like Alietta, but also so different. Nothing Matthias said or did turned her away from him either. Eventually, she had won his heart. They'd kept their status as mates very quiet, because while it was a different world four hundred years ago, it was also very much the same. Now, Matthias was faced with the same problem. His mate was a different species and same sex in a time when it wasn't completely accepted. Ean's entire existence fascinated him. Of all the people in the world, why was Ean his mate?

Movement from below drew his attention from the lightening sky above. He didn't see anyone in either of the yards, but he knew Luca was awake and moving. Not only did he know the younger dragon's scent after so many decades tutoring the boy, but they'd fallen into a sort of routine since Matthias's arrival several months back. Luca's deep timber reached Matthias's ears, soft in the quiet stillness of early morning.

"You up there, old man?"

Matthias sighed. He wasn't ready for the rest of the world to wake up. He wanted more peace and quiet to dwell on his situation and think about his mate. He stood up, stretched, and then made his way down the steeply sloped roof to the library balcony. The roof stopped about a foot short of the edge of the balcony, giving Matthias room to jump down.

"Good morning," Luca said when Matthias landed in front of him.

Luca leaned against the doorjamb, sipping his coffee, and appearing like he had no cares in the world. Matthias knew better. The well-being of the entire Chevalier Pack rested on the other dragon's shoulders. Matthias eyed the mug of coffee as he passed, entering the still-dark library.

"Morning," Matthias mumbled.

"Coffee on the desk," Luca told him without moving from his position at the door. "Temperature outside is nice for the moment."

"Yes," Matthias agreed. He picked up the mug of steaming hot brew and took a gulp. He wasn't sure why Luca was up so early or why he was making small talk. They'd always gotten along because neither of them was exceptionally big on the social niceties, so why now? "Something you wanted?" he asked.

Luca sighed and turned to face him. "I don't really know how to go about this, but being blunt has always worked between us, so I'll stick to that."

Matthias grunted in response as he gulped down half the coffee in his mug.

"I hate rumors. They're very rarely true."

Holy hell, Luca was driving him nuts with the hedging. "It's too early for this," Matthias grumbled.

"I've heard talk among the original four wild dogs suggesting they believe you're Ean's mate. I know when I introduced him to you a few months ago, I was convinced you were mates, but then you were at each other's throats." Luca shrugged.

Matthias eyed Luca over the rim of his mug as he emptied it. He placed the mug on the corner of the desk and then idly thumbed the edge of Alietta's journal. "I've heard the talk, as well."

Luca's gaze dropped to Matthias's hand. "That journal means something personal to you, doesn't it? There's more to you asking for it than just the idea it could help the pack."

Matthias was caught off guard by the question, and he wasn't sure how to answer, or if he even wanted to. So far, Ean had kept his silence despite Matthias's refusal to meet his demands. He fought a constant battle in his head over what to share, how much detail to give, or to simply ignore the questions all together. Matthias much preferred the simplicity of sequestering himself in the horde archives, or Luca's tiny library, to the relentless push and pull of his conscience.

The most terrifying thing was that Ean's presence, his very existence, made Matthias want to confess everything, get it off his chest and out of his head so that he could be free to pursue a future with his mate. Four-hundred-plus years of age and Matthias still felt like a fledgling in love for the first time every time he set eyes upon the young wolf. Matthias sighed, picked up the journal, and took a seat on the sofa.

Holding Luca's gaze, he said, "This journal contains everything we need to know about the Chevalier family, as well as several spells that may prove useful. Most of it is written in another language, of course."

Luca sat in the office chair behind the desk and stared at the floor. After a moment of quiet thought, he shook his head. "It's more than that. You and Sakima openly admit being alive during the original Chevalier takedown, but I can't shake the feeling you were both more involved."

Matthias took the statement to heart. Luca wasn't wrong. Despite being on the battlefield at the same time, Matthias and Sakima never crossed each other's paths. The vampires and sorcerers had been tasked with containment and killing those who attempted escape, while the dragons were given the task of infiltrating the Chevalier castle and destroying those inside. The Elementals had kept the winged Chevalier from taking to the sky and generally turned the entire scene into a wet, muddy mess. By the end of the fight, it had become a free-for-all bloodbath. Matthias and Sakima hadn't shared the specifics of their involvement, stopping with the admission to each other they'd been involved. War and the acts committed as a result were never something a soldier chose to speak about, even among the paranormal world.

"We were," Matthias said.

Luca nodded and puffed smoke from his nostrils. "Care to share the details?"

"I need to do a few things first."

Like talk to Sakima in more detail, decide how much they were truly willing to share, and most importantly, figure out how his involvement in a battle four hundred years ago would affect his mate in the present. The hairs on the back of Matthias's arms stood up, and he shot a glance at Luca as the air in the room became heavy. If he'd been outside, he'd suspect a storm was moving in. Looking toward the door he realized that's exactly what was happening. A dangerous storm was coming. Deacon walked into the library, lightning zapping between his fingertips and racing up his forearms. Something had the Elemental in rare, primal form.

"Deacon?" Luca said as he carefully adjusted his stance so he was facing Deacon.

Matthias followed Luca's lead, rising to his feet carefully so as not to provoke the Elemental further. Until they knew exactly what they were dealing with, proceeding with caution was wise. Deacon was a powerful Elemental who was already on edge. Deacon's clouded eyes latched onto Matthias. He narrowed them angrily, and the house shook. Matthias crossed his arms, holding the Elemental's gaze unwaveringly. He'd taken on the crazy Chevalier Elemental so this one didn't frighten him.

"What have you done, you stupid fucking dragon?" Deacon rumbled, small echoes of thunder filling the room.

"I suggest you be far more specific if you want an answer to that question," Matthias said.

"You denied him, rejected him, to the point that he has asked the sorcerer for a severance. He's going to destroy everything he is because of you."

The announcement hit Matthias in the gut with the power of a cannonball. He dropped his arms to his sides and straightened, fighting to get enough oxygen into his lungs to think straight. The only thought bouncing painfully in his head was *no, no, no. Not again.* Matthias shook his head dumbly.

"Who?" Luca asked, his confused glance jumping between Deacon and Matthias.

"Ean," Deacon answered.

This time when he spoke his voice was normal, and the lightning had dissipated. Blue eyes that were far clearer continued to watch Matthias as he struggled to regain his balance. Nothing the Elemental could have done physically would have knocked Matthias off his feet so completely as that one word—severance.

Chapter Eight

EAN

Ean sat on top of the largest rock at the pack's meeting spot listening to the river's steadily flowing water. The sight and sound never failed to relax Ean. He wasn't sure when he started to think of Tanner and the others that made up their pack as family, or when this little slice of wilderness began to feel like home, but at some point over the past several months it had. There were only two things standing in the way of Ean being perfectly happy—the McBane Pack with their hate-mongering, and one handsome, stubborn dragon.

Tree branches rustling and a cascade of small rocks drew Ean's attention to the path connecting their spot to the parking lot. Ross, in wolf form, came barreling down the hill at full speed. Ean had no idea where the white wolf was headed, but when Ross saw him on top of the rocks, he attempted to change directions. The wolf's momentum worked against him, and his feet scrabbled for purchase on the loose dirt as he skidded toward the water.

Ean shook his head and laughed. His friend was always playful and reckless and took joy in everything around him. Ean was envious of Ross's ability to take life with a grain of salt until he remembered exactly why Ross was the way he was. While the resultant carefree attitude was nice, the bloodlust that led to it was no laughing matter. Ross was still suicidal from time to time, though he did seem to be improving as time went on. Something else Ean was happy to see but didn't understand.

There was a lot in the world Ean didn't understand. His parents had been overtly traditional, much in the same way Tanner's father was. Wolves mated with wolves and kept to themselves. Intermingling with other paranormals was frowned upon, and living among humans was unheard of. The horror stories he'd been told by his parents and other pack elders were enough to keep even the most errant wolf pup under control when it came to humans.

The fact that his parents had been hunted and killed by humans when he was ten had kept Ean fearful for the entirety of his youth. It wasn't until his pack took on new members and he started hearing different stories that he started to grow curious. His sister, Bethany, had done her best raising him, and they'd been happy, but when she married one of the new pack enforcers, things changed. Joe wanted pups immediately, which meant the live-in adult brother needed to move on. And whenever Bethany wasn't around, Joe made it clear he didn't like Ean.

One of the new pack members was openly gay, and he helped Ean recognize and admit his own sexuality. While neither Joe nor Bethany were vocal with their disapproval, it was evident everywhere. Eventually, Ean left home because it was no longer a place he felt welcome or happy in. Ross whined and bumped Ean's shoulder, pulling him out of past memories. He had a chosen family now that he was willing to die for, and that was the truly important thing. Ean bumped his human nose with Ross's snout in greeting.

Do you miss your family? Ean asked.

I miss Mom a lot, Ross answered, sadness bleeding into the bond. It wasn't an emotion Ean was used to feeling from the white wolf.

I miss my mom too. Every day, Vance chimed in.

I think we all miss our families a little bit, added Theran.

Speak for yourselves, Tanner said with a chuckle. *I'd rather like to be away from my family long enough to begin to miss them, but Dad is making it kind of hard to care. Are you missing your family, Ean?*

I miss some things about them, but I'm happiest here, with all of you.

Now, to nail down your mate, and all will be good, Tanner said as he came down the path at a leisurely pace followed by Vance and Theran, all in human form, with Colby bringing up the rear.

Deacon was at the pack house for his part in this ridiculous and horribly manipulative plan of theirs. Ean desperately wanted it to work though. He knew he'd have to atone for this later, maybe grovel at his mate's feet for a while, but he'd decided being claimed, under any circumstance, was worth the cost. He was frustrated and angry with the dragon, but Ean wanted him more than anything else.

Hope you're ready. One charged-up dragon heading your way, Deacon warned through the pack bond.

Ean slid down the rock on his butt until his feet hit the ground. The water's edge was just a few feet away and despite the confrontation he knew was coming his way, the sound continued to relax him.

"Matthias is on his way," Theran said out loud for Colby's benefit.

The bonding process had taken on a new meaning for their pack. While Luca and Deacon were bonded to the pack through Tanner, Sakima and Colby were not. It had been strange at first to have Vance repeat bonded conversations out loud for Sakima's benefit, but now that Theran was doing it, too, it had become commonplace. Ean expected he would be doing the same for Matthias. Hopefully, very soon.

Colby clapped his hands and went "witchy," as Theran liked to say. Black streaked through Colby's long hair and spiderwebbed up his arms from his fingertips. The entirety of his eyes turned black, something that never failed to creep Ean out. Changing eye colors wasn't anything unusual in the paranormal world, but solid black was freaky.

"Let's do this," Colby said in a deep, resonating voice.

Ean knelt at his feet, back toward the water, and grinned up at the sorcerer. Colby was putting on quite the show and enjoying it given the broad smile on his face.

"You're evil, aren't you?" Ean asked.

Colby didn't have a chance to answer before Ean's world tilted.

Chapter Nine

MATTHIAS

Deacon's words rattled through his brain so loudly and painfully Matthias didn't think—he acted on pure instinct. He'd lost Alietta to Mariana Chevalier's severance four hundred years before. He refused to lose Ean the same way. Ignoring the jeans and T-shirt he wore, he leapt from the balcony, shifting as he fell. When he landed in the backyard, he was in full dragon form. In the back of his mind, he knew he was taking a risk of being seen by the humans in nearby houses, but hoped the early hour would keep exposure to a minimum. The little sorcerer could work his magic on them by erasing their memories instead of separating Ean from his wolf.

His talons barely touched the grass before he pulsed his wings and launched back into the air. Fog lifted from the ground behind him before swallowing him in a masking haze. Matthias would thank the Elemental later for his assistance hiding Matthias's dragon. He was grateful he'd crashed many of the pack meetings, or he wouldn't have known where the "meeting rock" Deacon mentioned was located. He headed toward the forest where the wolves liked to hunt. Despite how fast his wings could carry him, Matthias feared he would be too late. What had he been thinking, pushing his mate away? In this moment, it was difficult to remember all the great reasons he'd had for staying away because right now the only thing in the world that mattered was Ean's life, happiness, and safety—all things Matthias should have been seeing to the moment he'd set eyes on his handsome young mate.

Flying low over the trees, he aimed for the river, where he dipped even lower, below the canopy of the trees, so his massive dragon wasn't as visible. The outcropping of rocks the pack used as a congregation spot could be seen from his position above the river. Matthias saw the pack gathered around Ean in a semicircle, Ean's back to the river. He knelt at Colby's feet, so Matthias pumped his wings harder to close the distance faster. With his back turned, Ean didn't see Matthias coming, but the others watched as Matthias swooped in, legs extended.

The breeze created by his wings blew leaves and dirt across the ground and sent ripples cascading outward into the river. Matthias planted his back feet on the ground, wings outstretched, as he gently wrapped his front talons around Ean's body. He pulled the wolf shifter to his scaled chest. Once he was sure his mate was secure, Matthias pushed off the ground backward, flipped upright midair, and headed for the mountains. Knowing firsthand what the Duray Horde matriarch thought of Luca's wolf mate, Matthias refused to take Ean to the horde compound. Running through his options quickly, he decided on Whisper River Lodge and banked south. He felt Ean's grip tighten on his wrist.

"Land," he yelled. "Please, land."

They were still miles from Matthias's chosen destination, but he complied, descending steadily to the ground. He aimed for the rocky mountainside, just above the tree line, and touched down softly. Certain his mate couldn't escape easily, he released his hold on Ean, who promptly bent at the waist and vomited. The reaction was unexpected and concerned Matthias. He extended a wing to caress Ean's back gently as he heaved, careful not to cut the wolf with his talon tip. Ean wavered on his feet so Matthias pressed his snout to Ean's shoulder to help steady him, while using his wing on the other shoulder.

"Fuck. Tanner said flying long distances made wolves puke, but I didn't believe him."

Matthias emitted a warbling growl in response. His huffed breath ruffled Ean's hair. Ean pushed Matthias's head away, but didn't move from beneath his wing, allowing Matthias the small physical contact he rather suddenly needed. The idea his wolf mate had actually thought of causing himself harm in a way that would have resulted in his death, and possibly Colby's as well, had tipped the scale of his need for Ean to the point of action. How he'd once thought he could go without claiming this man, he had no idea.

At this moment, Matthias couldn't imagine his future without Ean in it. If he were honest with himself, he'd admit he had never planned on being anywhere other than where Ean was. Being nearby was the only way Matthias would be able to ensure his young mate's safety and see that Ean was happy. Ean deserved everything good in the world. Ean raked his hair back and walked several feet away before turning an angry glare on Matthias.

"What the fuck, dragon?" he growled.

Whisper River wasn't far, and Matthias didn't want to shift until he had Ean safely tucked away in one of the rooms—his room preferably. Only then would he return to human form to have this discussion with his mate. He turned and extended his tail toward Ean, glancing back over his wing as he nudged Ean with the scaled muscle about a foot above the lethally spiked tip. When Ean did nothing more than look down disdainfully, Matthias stepped back to wrap his tail around Ean's back and pull forward in nonverbal encouragement to climb onto his back. Ean turned his disgruntled expression to Matthias's face.

"One, you better be taking me home. Two, if I puke on you, it's your own damn fault."

Using Matthias's scales as handholds, Ean climbed up his tail, over his back, to settle on his shoulders, feet hooked beneath his wings where they met his body. Ean grumbled something Matthias couldn't make out as he flattened himself to Matthias's large body. Not wanting to waste another second, Matthias once again took flight. He most certainly was not going to take Ean home, not yet, but the young wolf had no way of knowing that until it was too late.

Chapter Ten

EAN

Matthias was majestic in dragon form. Head-to-toe silver, Matthias's scales glittered and shone in the bright morning sun, at times even reflecting rainbows on the ground. Six spikes protruded from his tail and two horns curled outward from his head. Even his eyes were a gorgeous, sparkling silver. Fucking beautiful creature.

Ean knew the dragon wasn't taking him home, and he was trying so hard to be angry about that, but he found it hard while straddling something so incredible. Even the height and motion of the flight didn't bother him when he was so focused on the movement of Matthias's leathery silver wings, or the play of muscle and scale beneath his hands. The experience of flying on Matthias's back was exhilarating and terrifying.

Twenty minutes after Ean's puking fit on the side of a cliff, Matthias began the descent toward a small clearing in the forest. As they drew closer to the ground, Ean saw an old, abandoned motel situated beside an overgrown dirt road. Train tracks hugged the mountain slope several hundred feet behind the building. Matthias touched down with a muted thump and lowered himself to the ground on his belly. Ean swung a leg over, scooted to Matthias's wing, and then slid down the soft leather to the ground.

He walked toward the rundown building, hands on hips, and took the area in. Despite its dilapidated state, the building was intact. The roof was tattering, but still in one piece, and all the doors and windows were still solid. The dirt road and clearing in front of the old motel sported weeds and small trees, suggesting it hadn't been traveled in quite some time. From where he stood, the railroad tracks appeared to be fairly new, and Ean guessed they were still in use.

Movement to his left drew his attention from the building and the surrounding wilderness. Matthias had shifted and was now walking into the building...naked. Ean swallowed hard as he stared. He couldn't do anything else. He'd never seen Matthias naked since the old dragon had never shifted in front of the pack before. Ean had thought Matthias was beautiful in dragon form, but it didn't hold a candle to Matthias naked in human form. Smooth skin covered in swirling Celtic-type tattoos, gloriously defined muscles, and firm ass made one think the man was in his prime, rather than pushing five centuries of life. When Matthias exited the building, he was partially dressed in ratty jeans torn at the knees and a flannel shirt he hadn't bothered to close over his lightly furred chest. Ean forced himself to look away.

"So"—Ean cleared his throat—"Where are we?"

"Whisper River Lodge."

"Doesn't exactly answer my question."

"Doesn't it?" Matthias crossed his arms over his chest, pulling the shirt tight across his shoulders and biceps, making Ean's mouth go dry.

"You know what I meant. Where in this state, in relation to the pack house, are we?" Ean clarified.

"Not the question you asked."

Ean sighed. The man was being obstinate on purpose, and Ean wasn't in the mood. He should've known better than to even ask, given how secretive Matthias was about everything else. Why should this have been any different?

"Usually places with names like Whisper River Lodge have actual rivers nearby, like Glacier Falls back home. There's actually waterfalls there."

Ean walked up to the building and peeked into one of the dingy windows. The room on the other side was cleaner than he expected. A small wood-framed bed was shoved into a corner, and a wooden dresser leaned against the wall at an angle, due to one pedestal missing. The mirror above the dresser looked to be little more than old polished metal.

"Whisper River used to run along the back side of the motel," Matthias said.

Ean startled at how close Matthias was to him. He straightened and glanced over his shoulder where Matthias stood, mere inches from him. All he had to do was extend his hand back a bit and he could brush his fingers over Matthias's thigh. Such a tempting thing to do now that he knew what was beneath the worn denim. He'd felt Matthias's dragon beneath his fingers, but he had yet to experience what the man felt like to touch. And, gods, how he wanted to touch his mate.

"This area was well traveled when I built the place. People would follow the river through the mountains to the western slope."

"How long ago was that?" Ean asked, remembering the large expanse of earth between the motel and the tracks. It looked to have been dried up for a while, and the furnishings in the room were decades older than what would be considered antique.

Matthias shrugged. "Seventeen seventy-eight. The route was abandoned in the first few years of the 1790s due to several random attacks by wolf shifters who felt humans were encroaching on their territory. I keep it in good, and slightly updated, repair in case I have need of it again." Matthias brushed his knuckles down the side of Ean's face and then under his chin. "So young and innocent," he murmured.

"Only when compared to some," Ean responded. He backed away from Matthias's touch. As much as he wanted Matthias's hands on him, and to reciprocate the act, Ean needed to know exactly what the dragon shifter was thinking. "Why did you grab me?"

"You're my mate, and you were attempting murder-suicide."

"No, I wasn't."

"Yes, you were. Severances are dangerous for all involved. That little sorcerer is far too egotistical for his own good. Colby would have died after casting the spell, and the part of you that survived, whether wolf or human, would have been ripped apart by Theran." Matthias walked a few feet away before turning on his heel and pinning Ean with a pained glare. "I've already lost one mate to that damn spell. I won't lose you too."

Shit. Guilt and jealousy flared in Ean's chest. It hurt knowing Matthias had a mate before him, though given the dragon's age, it wasn't surprising. He'd probably outlive Ean, too, but it still bothered him on a cellular level. The fact the previous mate had died in such a way partly explained Matthias's reluctance to claim Ean. He knew firsthand the pain of simply being separated from his mate. He couldn't begin to imagine the pain of outright loss Matthias must have felt. He'd been young when his parents died, and he didn't truly remember his emotions back then. Ean knew he'd have to tell Matthias soon that his severance was a hoax—a hoax that worked—but his curiosity and the need to soothe his mate's hurt were stronger than the guilt.

"I'm sorry. Will you tell me about him? What was his name?"

Matthias glanced around the surrounding area, hands on hips and breathing deeply as he paced. Uncertain what the dragon was thinking or what he should do, Ean took the time to admire his mate. Salt-and-pepper hair mostly gone salty and a full beard that was slowly streaking white like the hair on his head were the only signs of the dragon's advanced age. His entire body was still chiseled, tattooed muscle that showed no signs of weakening. Looking into Matthias's near-black eyes, anyone could see the centuries-old intelligence, and when the dragon's silver swirled in them, they were mesmerizing.

Ean's gaze slowly moved down Matthias's back to his rounded butt and powerful thighs. He now knew the intricate runic tattoos covering Matthias's arms extended over his upper body and continued down his back to his butt. He'd never allowed himself to look this long, and certainly never so blatantly. Matthias turned once again to pace back toward Ean, and given he'd been taking in the man's ass, he was now staring directly at Matthias's bared stomach. He took in the sight of Matthias's six pack before being hypnotized by the light dusting of dark hair visible below Matthias's navel and the waistband of the pants.

Ean reached out as that happy trail drew closer, nothing else on his mind but getting inside his mate's pants so he could trace that smattering of hair with his lips. Strong fingers gripped his chin and lifted his face as his palm connected with hot skin pulled tight over the defined muscle of Matthias's side. Ean now stared into the gorgeous dark eyes of his mate, and he tightened his grip on Matthias to steady himself.

"First time I've caught you eating me alive with your eyes."

"First time I've allowed myself the pleasure."

Silver bled into Matthias's eyes and a deep, sexy growl emanated from his chest that made Ean shiver. Ean stepped closer until their bodies touched, wrapped his arms around Matthias's waist beneath the shirt, and tilted his head back slightly. The close proximity forced Matthias to release his hold on Ean's chin. He wrapped his arms around Ean's back and pulled him flush against his chest. Ean was stunned when Matthias's lips pressed against his. When he'd tilted his head back, it was a silent request for a kiss, but given the numerous times Matthias had rejected him in the past, Ean hadn't expected the dragon to actually kiss him.

Ean moaned as he opened his mouth enough to trap Matthias's top lip between his teeth. He immediately released the hold when Matthias managed to get his own grip on Ean's bottom lip and pulled. The nips were small and gentle, but enough to give Ean's cock and temperature reason to rise. He pressed his burgeoning erection against a thick thigh and slid his palms up Matthias's back to his shoulders.

Matthias tilted his head to get a better fit as his tongue stroked into Ean's mouth, deepening their kiss. Matthias held Ean's head still with one hand while palming Ean's ass with the other, pulling him tighter against Matthias's thigh. Ean was so swept up in all the sensations being with his mate created that it took him a moment to realize Matthias was separating their bodies. In the next moment, he pulled out of the kiss, leaving Ean feeling fuzzy-headed and chilled. The dragon's body put off so much heat that being separated from it made the otherwise temperate weather seem cold. At a loss for words, Ean stared at Matthias questioningly.

"You asked me a question."

"I did?" Ean asked, wracking his brain for that memory.

"My previous mate was a female."

"Oh!" *That question,* Ean thought. He blinked a few times as he wrestled his fuzzed-out brain and raging hormones under control enough to have a somewhat coherent conversation.

"A sorceress."

"Okay."

"I learned days after the fact that she had died performing Mariana Chevalier's severance."

"Uh..."

"Her name was Alietta Strombler."

"Fuck," Ean breathed out.

Chapter Eleven

MATTHIAS

Ean's expression went from blissed-out to stone-cold sober in two seconds flat. Matthias had known the moment he started kissing the young wolf the timing was wrong. He'd been unable to stop himself when Ean presented himself so prettily. Now, he had to deal with the aftereffects of taking Ean to a scorching temp and then dowsing him with the frigid water of his past. To his surprise, Ean still held him around the waist, and Matthias was grateful for the small contact.

"Ean." Matthias traced the wolf shifter's jawline with the tip of his finger. "What are you thinking, little boy?"

"I'm not sure I am. That kiss fried my brain."

Matthias shook his head. He knew better. He could see the wheels turning behind Ean's eyes. It was one of the things about Ean that Matthias found attractive. He was always thinking. Matthias grabbed Ean's upper arms and pulled him closer, because he had to. Forces stronger than him were at play, and he was tired of fighting against them. Ean's gaze darted down to Matthias's mouth.

"Tell me what you're thinking, and I'll kiss you again," Matthias prodded.

Ean's eyelids slid closed on a slow blink and he sighed. "I'm thinking this explains why your name was mentioned in her journal and how she was able to detail exactly what your part in the Chevalier annihilation was. And I'm thinking we have a long conversation ahead of us, and that I won't like most of what I hear, but I want to know everything there is to know about you, good and bad. Problem is, I'm so damned horny right now I can barely think straight. You've been pushing me away for so long that I feel like I'm about to combust from being close to you. Please, Matthias, put me out of my misery. Claim me. We can push through the rest of this shit later. Together."

"Ean—"

"Please."

"I want nothing more than to claim my mate, here, in this place I hold dear." Matthias pressed their foreheads together. "But not while my secrets are still between us."

A pained expression twisted Ean's face, and he clenched his jaw, a frustrated growl rumbling in his chest. Matthias saw the explosion building, but he didn't want to fight with Ean anymore. Keeping his wolf mate on the offensive was no longer his primary goal. Making Ean feel cherished and wanted was. Matthias yanked Ean against his body by the grip he still had on his upper arms and took Ean's mouth in a fierce kiss he felt through his entire body.

Ean melted in his arms and Matthias took advantage of his wolf shifter's pliancy. He held Ean's body close, grabbed Ean's thigh and coaxed the wolf to wrap his legs around his waist. Once he had Ean's full weight in his arms, he carried Ean into the apartment at the back of the motel lobby. He was rather impressed he only stumbled once. It was difficult to focus on his feet while plundering Ean's mouth and taking in his mate's flavor.

He laid Ean down on the ancient wood-framed bed and covered him with his body. Comfortably nestled between Ean's thighs, his arms wrapped around his neck, fingers massaging the back of his head, Matthias finally felt at home. He hadn't been blessed with enough time before Alietta died to truly become intimate with her, to feel this connection. Customs were different four hundred years ago. Here, now, it was acceptable for him to take his mate sexually without claiming him. Matthias reveled in that freedom.

Matthias pulled away, breaking the kiss. Ean gave a sweet little whine through kiss-swollen lips and stared up at Matthias. His tongue flicked out over his bottom lip and Matthias followed the appendage across Ean's mouth with his thumb. Matthias was determined to take this moment slowly, to enjoy every look and sound Ean gave him. He'd been with others since Alietta, but they'd all been a means to an end, an outlet for built-up sexual need. This was Ean, his mate, and he would treat the young wolf like the miracle he was.

"Please, don't stop. I don't think I can take it if you leave me now."

Matthias's chest ached at the vulnerability in Ean's voice. "Leave? You're the only reason I'm still here. I had every intention of returning home that first day I arrived at Luca's, but then you walked into the room, and everything changed."

"But you pushed me away."

"You're a ray of sunshine, and I'm an abyss of misery. You deserve better."

Ean cocked an eyebrow. "You wouldn't be miserable if you'd accepted me the minute you realized I was your mate."

"Maybe." Matthias chuckled. "Let me explore you."

Matthias pecked Ean on the lips before pushing up to his knees. He dragged his hands down Ean's clothed chest, over the rough denim covering his thighs, and then back up under his T-shirt. Ean's skin was hot to the touch. He bent to pepper kisses over the newly exposed skin of Ean's stomach and chest as he rucked up the shirt. Ean wasn't idle beneath Matthias. He ran his hands over every inch of tattooed skin he could reach.

"Let's get this off," Matthias muttered as he fisted the hem of the T-shirt bunched up around Ean's neck.

Ean sat up as best he could with his legs still draped around Matthias's waist. Matthias pulled the shirt off and dropped it to the floor beside the bed. Ean dragged his nails down Matthias's chest as he flopped back on the mattress.

"You are so fucking hot. Do the tattoos continue down your legs?" Ean asked.

"What? You mean you didn't look when I shifted?"

"As much as I dared. Only got to that sweet divot above your ass before you were out of sight. I think I remember seeing tats on your legs…"

"I see."

Matthias stared at Ean as he pushed off the hard mattress to stand at the foot of the bed. Ean propped himself up on his elbows as he held Matthias's gaze. It only lasted until Matthias slipped his thumbs into the waistband of his ripped jeans and pushed them down his legs. Ean's gaze followed the descent with rapt attention. Matthias released his hold on the pants at his knees and allowed the fabric to fall. Being naked in front of others was nothing new for shifters, but this was Ean. His mate. Matthias could practically feel the heat of the wolf's eyes as they took in his form, lingering noticeably longer on Matthias's erect cock.

Ean's gaze popped up to Matthias's face, and he bit his bottom lip before lying back and quickly removing his jeans. Now it was Matthias's turn to stare. He'd seen Ean after shifts, but he'd always averted his gaze.

He didn't have the right to look at his mate's body when he was actively denying him. Now, he took in Ean's magnificent physique with the same slow deliberate pace Ean had used on him. Only a quarter-size birthmark on the front of Ean's left hip broke the expanse of smooth skin. Ean's long, semi-hard dick rested on his right thigh. He was aroused, but not yet fully erect. Matthias would change that soon. Ean bent his knees and spread his legs as he beckoned for Matthias to move between them with the crook of a finger.

Rather than return to his original position, Matthias eased himself onto the bed between Ean's legs so that his boy's cock was at his lips. He kissed the base of the shaft before laving his tongue up the underside to the tip where he circled the entire head lazily. Ean tunneled his fingers into Matthias's hair and fisted the strands. Such a strong reaction to a simple touch told Matthias his young shifter was going to be excessively responsive.

Overcome with the urge to see Ean lose his well-crafted veneer of in-control, unshakable Beta, Matthias engulfed Ean's entire length in one swift motion. The wolf shifter's rich flavor coated his tongue, and he was instantly addicted. The soft gasp followed by a deep groan sent shivers down Matthias's spine. He tightened his lips around the pole of flesh, humming as he worked it with his mouth.

"Damn, damn, damn." Ean shuddered beneath him, making Matthias smile.

Matthias palmed Ean's balls and rolled them in his hand. He extended his middle finger and brushed the tip over Ean's pucker. Ean bucked his hips with a small shout.

"No, no, no. Can't take it. Gonna blow."

Those words were music to Matthias's ears. He wanted nothing more than to push his mate over the edge, give him a pleasure he'd never known, and maybe tip the scales in Matthias's favor for when his secrets came to light. His dragon purred when the first drop of fluid leaked from the cock tip. Continuing his ministrations with Ean's scrotum and ass, he wrapped his other hand around the base of Ean's cock and squeezed.

"Matthias," Ean cried out, launching to a near-sitting position.

His grip tightened in Matthias's hair as the first spurt of semen shot into the back of Matthias's throat. He was annoyed it hadn't hit his tongue, so he pulled off until just the tip was resting on his tongue. He pumped his fist up and down Ean's shaft in the hopes of coaxing more of the wolf's essence into his mouth. Ean dropped onto his back, releasing his hold on Matthias's hair in favor of digging his claws into the mattress as his hips pumped upward.

Sensing his little wolf needed a bit more stimulation, Matthias slipped his finger into Ean's ass and was rewarded with a full orgasm. Ean's hips stuttered in their movement, and his whole body shook as he released into Matthias's mouth. He swallowed it down greedily, sucking on the tip to get as much out of his mate as he could, and eased his finger free of the tight clasp of Ean's sphincter. He took one long, final swipe of his tongue over Ean's shaft before resting his chin on Ean's hip and smiling up at him.

"Delicious little boy," Matthias rumbled.

"Fuck. Sorry I didn't last long. Haven't had a blow job in years." Ean's chest was rosy and heaving as he tried to catch his breath. His face was flushed, beads of sweat dotted his forehead, and a light sheen of sweat covered his body.

"Are you being serious, right now?"

"Yes. Just haven't met anyone in the past few years I wanted to have sex with," Ean told him.

"What about all the guys you flirted with at Elysium?" Matthias asked.

Ean had certainly turned on the charm whenever the pack had a meeting at the club. Matthias watched in silent anger as any number of other men touched his mate while dancing, ogled him from across the room, or flat out kissed him on the dance floor. He would always spend the remainder of the night sitting in Luca's library fighting mad over the situation he himself had caused. He had no choice but to watch and know his mate was finding pleasure elsewhere.

"Never went anywhere. Didn't want any of them. I wanted you, but you were being an asshole, so I...tried to hurt you. Wanted you to feel the pain I felt."

"Well...first: if I'd wanted you to last, you would have."

Matthias didn't need to see Ean's eye roll to know it happened. It was one of Ean's favorite reactions to just about anything Matthias said. Matthias rubbed one of Ean's thighs, hand slipping up over his hip to his ribs. Ean reached down and lightly scraped his nails over Matthias's bicep.

"Second: I felt the pain, even without your overt flirting with other men. It hurt every time I denied you, but I thought I was doing the right thing."

Ean pushed to a sitting position and scooted across the bed to rest his back against the wall. Matthias followed, unwilling to stay in a place where he couldn't touch his mate. He sat cross-legged next to Ean's outstretched legs and rested a hand on Ean's ankle, happy that Ean didn't pull away from his touch.

"The right thing would have been to acknowledge I was your mate and claim me."

"You say that now. But when you know the truth—

"I saw the journal, remember?" Ean interrupted. "I know you went into the Chevalier castle. I know you helped destroy them."

"When you know the *whole* truth about me... I truly hope you'll understand. And forgive."

Ean sucked in a breath and then blew it out as he averted his eyes to the bedding where he fiddled with a loose thread on the blanket. Matthias tilted his head as he considered his mate's reaction. The bond between them was strengthening, and Matthias felt Ean's sadness and guilt.

Chapter Twelve

EAN

"I hope you forgive me too," Ean said. He continued to pull on the loose thread because he couldn't bring himself to look at his dragon.

"What do you need to be forgiven for?" Matthias asked. He grabbed Ean's jaw and forced Ean to look at him. "What could you have possibly done?"

Ean stared into his mate's dark eyes. The urge to run his fingers through Matthias's hair had him reaching for Matthias before he was truly aware of his action. He brushed his fingers over Matthias's ear and then down his bearded jaw to caress the mouth that had just brought him pleasure. All he could hope for was that Matthias's secrets were darker than the lie Ean had told. It was a selfish desire, but he'd finally moved in the right direction with his mate. He didn't want to go back to their previous animosity.

Matthias leaned forward to peck a kiss on Ean's lips. "I can see you're upset, and I can feel the emotion. Tell me."

"We lied. *I* lied. The severance was a hoax. We weren't going to go through with it."

Matthias dropped his hand from Ean's face and sat back, dark brows furrowed. "Why would you fake something like that?"

"I needed you. I was in physical pain, and I felt like I was losing my mind. I'm sorry I manipulated you like that, but I didn't know what else to do."

Ean glanced down at his ankle where Matthias still held him. He hadn't severed physical contact completely, and Ean held onto that small slice of good.

"When you said you were in pain earlier, I took that to mean emotional pain, but not being with me caused you physical pain?"

"Yes. My chest always felt tight, like my ribcage was being crushed. Wolves don't fare well separated from their mates."

Matthias pressed his palm against Ean's chest as he gently squeezed Ean's ankle. Ean's heart rate picked up at the unexpected contact, and his dick twitched to attention.

"I knew being away from pack could cause problems, but I didn't know it was hurting you to be away from me. How are you now?"

"I'm better. The moment you rescued me the pain started to ease."

"Rescued," Matthias repeated with a quirk of a brow.

Ean smiled shyly. "My knight in shining silver armor."

Matthias scoffed, making Ean chuckle. Ean lifted his legs, twisted on the bed, and placed one leg on each side of Matthias's hips. Ean wrapped his arms around Matthias's neck, staring into his dark eyes swirling with silver, as he scooted forward until his butt rested against Matthias's shins. Matthias reached around to cup Ean's butt in his hands and lifted Ean into his lap. Both of their cocks were erect, trapped together between their stomachs, as Ean took the initiative and kissed Matthias.

The dragon opened his mouth to allow Ean's tongue inside, and Ean immediately accepted the silent offer. He moaned into the kiss as his mate's flavor, mixed with his own earlier release, filled his mouth. He rocked his hips in an attempt to get friction against his cock and gasped into Matthias's mouth as the grip on his ass tightened. The sting of slightly sharpened nails digging into his butt flesh bordered on painful, and he loved it. It meant Matthias was losing his control right along with Ean.

Matthias launched to his knees, lifting Ean with him, and then laid Ean back on the bed. He slid one hand around Ean's thigh and then lifted Ean's leg over his shoulder. He grinned wickedly as he sucked two fingers in his mouth before pressing the tips against Ean's pucker.

"Open up, my little wolf. Let me in."

Deciding to be facetious and goad his dragon for old times' sake, Ean grinned evilly and narrowed his eyes. "Make me," he growled.

Matthias leaned in until they were nose to nose and whispered, "Challenge accepted."

Matthias pressed the tips of his fingers against Ean's hole and massaged the ring of muscle. Ean fought the sensation, attempting to remain tightly closed as long as he could. Matthias pushed and rubbed against the pucker until eventually Ean relaxed enough to allow both fingers to slip inside. Matthias continued to kiss and nip at Ean's mouth and neck as he worked his fingers in, turning Ean into a gasping, moaning wreck. Matthias jiggled his fingers, and Ean attempted to squeeze his legs together, lifting his pelvis off the mattress.

Precum pebbled at the slit of his cock and he grabbed the base, squeezing it tightly to slow his roll toward orgasm. He refused to come again without Matthias inside him, and he was enjoying the preparation. He tightened down around Matthias's fingers in an attempt to create resistance. Matthias growled. Without warning, he pulled his fingers free from Ean's hold, grabbed both Ean's legs behind the knees, and pushed them up toward Ean's neck.

Matthias sealed his mouth over Ean's pucker and speared him with his tongue. Ean's fangs dropped with a shout as he slapped his hands down onto the mattress and dug his claws in. Matthias alternated between kisses, licks, and stabs of his tongue, working Ean to a fever pitch and holding him there on the edge. Ean was relaxing beneath Matthias's ministrations whether he was ready to or not. Ean grabbed Matthias's elbow where it rested alongside his thigh.

"I'm ready. Please," Ean groaned.

Matthias stared into Ean's eyes as he licked over his pucker, laving his tongue up over Ean's scrotum and then up the underside of Ean's cock. He flicked his tongue over the slit, taking the pearl of cum into his mouth.

"If I keep eating your ass, will you come for me?"

"I could, but I don't want to come again without you. I want you inside me."

Matthias lowered Ean's body to the bed and jumped off. Ean stared at his mate in confusion as the dragon went to a small table by the door, pulled open the rickety-looking drawer, and grabbed something. When Matthias turned around to return to the bed, Ean lost his breath. Apparently, Matthias had lube hidden in that old table because he was actively slicking his cock as he approached Ean. Ean's mouth went dry and he had to swallow several times to get the lump in his throat to clear. Watching Matthias get himself ready was one of the sexiest things Ean had ever seen.

Ean spread his legs and pulled his knees to his chest, offering unobstructed access to his body as Matthias climbed back onto the bed. Matthias eased back between Ean's spread thighs and placed the tip of his dick against Ean's entrance. He rocked back and forth, his cock nudging against Ean in a teasing, frustrating way. Ean glared at his mate.

"Shove it in, old man. I'm not going to break." He punctuated the demand with a growl.

Matthias's eyes went completely silver, and he gave a fanged smile before doing exactly what Ean wanted. He buried himself to the hilt in one firm, steady push. Ean sucked in air as he worked to relax and stretch around Matthias's girth. Matthias covered Ean with his body and kissed him sweetly.

"Look at you, little boy," Matthias murmured between kisses. He caressed Ean's hair lovingly. "Taking me so good. Hot and tight around me."

"Feels incredible." Ean grabbed Matthias's ass cheeks and squeezed. "Now fuck me."

"Fair warning," Matthias said, pulling his cock out until Ean felt the mushroom head tug at his sphincter. "I won't last long. Taking everything I have not to spill inside you right now."

Ean nodded. "I'm good with fast and hard." He closed his eyes and arched his back as much as he could with his dragon pressed down on top of him. Matthias pushed back inside his body at the same maddeningly slow pace.

"Mmm," Matthias grumbled, and then he whispered directly into Ean's ear. "Hold on, little boy. This is going to be rough."

"Finally," Ean breathed.

Matthias pulled Ean's arms above his head, placed both wrists in one hand, and pushed them down onto the mattress. He put his other hand on the wall above Ean's head, and took the sex to the next level. Matthias slammed into him, rocking the entire bed and knocking it against the wall. Ean hooked his ankles over Matthias's thighs and turned into a gasping, moaning puddle of goo.

This wasn't the sweet and slow buildup they had started with. This was a rough, desperate fucking between two men who'd been denied too long. In a strange mix of too soon and not soon enough, Ean's balls tightened. Every thrust caused Matthias's stomach to slide up and down Ean's hard shaft, pushing him closer and closer to orgasm. Ean watched Matthias's face as he drew closer to his own release. The man was gorgeous as he smiled down at Ean.

"Come with me, boy."

"Not enough. Need more direct stimulation."

Matthias straightened, releasing his hold on Ean's wrists in favor of grabbing his hip in one hand and his cock in the other. All without a hitch in his thrusts. The change in angle combined with Matthias's firm grip drove Ean to the edge much faster than he expected. Ean's entire body stiffened as he crested the peak and came with a cry. His orgasm raced through him, painting his stomach and chest in white ribbons of fluid.

"Goddamn, thought you were tight before," Matthias grunted. He released Ean's cock, grabbed his hips, and pounded into Ean. "Oh, fuck, yes."

Matthias's thrusts became erratic, his breathing hitched, and Ean knew he was close. Just a little more and his dragon would come inside him. Ean raked his nails over Matthias's nipples as he squeezed down on Matthias's cock. The dragon roared as he slammed in to the hilt and stilled. Matthias's entire body shuddered as he came. Ean's fangs distended as he fought the urge to sit up and claim his mate. It would be so easy. Matthias's eyes were closed, and he wouldn't know until Ean's canines sank into his neck. Ean felt a bond to Matthias already, incomplete as it was. For now, that bond would have to be enough.

"Bite me," Ean said. "You don't have to claim me, but bite me."

Matthias bent down and sank his teeth into Ean's shoulder. It was a little too far away from his neck for it to be a claiming, but the sharp teeth digging into his flesh pushed him into another, smaller, orgasm. Unable to hold back, Ean bared his own fangs and bit into the nearest piece of flesh he could reach. Matthias shuddered and growled so low in his chest it resembled a purr. The new bond was still weak, but Ean knew the sound wasn't anger because Ean bit back. He'd been careful to miss the mating site. This mewling sound was happiness and comfort. They were mates, and Matthias had finally accepted him.

Chapter Thirteen

MATTHIAS

The early morning air was brisk. Temperature didn't bother Matthias, thanks to his innate dragon heat, but it was definitely something Ean felt—at least in human form. Matthias had woken in the dark of night, and he used the time to prepare a wonderful start to the next day. He'd taken blankets and bottles of water above the timberline and laid them out near a rocky outcrop.

He'd then shifted and set out on the hunt for breakfast. The bobcat had been injured and hadn't stood a chance against Matthias's dragon. After dropping off their meal near the blankets, he hurried back to the motel to wake Ean. There were plenty of predators moving about the night who would make short work of stealing the bobcat if he didn't get Ean up and moving quickly.

Ean was stretched out on his stomach, the covers bunched up around his waist. Matthias trailed soft kisses up the exposed contours of Ean's spine and nuzzled behind his ear. He sucked the lobe between his lips, closing his eyes as the flavor of his sleepy mate covered his tongue. Ean moaned in his sleep but otherwise remained still so Matthias continued his kisses onto Ean's neck and shoulders. Ean rolled to his side and rubbed his eyes.

"Time's it?" he muttered.

"Sunrise in ten," Matthias told him. He pushed the covers off Ean's lower body. "Come with me, now."

"Where? Too early to be up."

Despite his complaint that it was too early, Ean sat up and swung his legs off the bed. He shivered when his bare feet hit the cold wood floorboards.

"You should shift. We're going outside, and it's cold this morning. I predict snow in the next few days."

Ean nodded, still visibly drowsy. He shifted and shook out his fur. Matthias squatted so they were face-to-face and ran his fingers through Ean's thick gray fur. He scratched behind one ear, and Ean pressed his head into Matthias's palm, seeking out a harder caress. Without warning, Ean dropped to his chest, butt and tail wagging in the air. Remaining in the same crouched position, Ean skittered to one side and woofed. Matthias smiled at his mate's sudden playfulness, though he didn't know what brought it on. Perhaps it was the cold air that had snapped Ean awake so quickly.

"Let's go."

Matthias straightened and headed out the door into the early morning quiet. He jumped a bit when an ice-cold nose pressed into the crease where butt cheek met thigh and he glared down at the wolf. Ean bolted away to run a wide circle around Matthias, tail down and butt tucked as his paws kicked up dirt and leaves. Matthias shook his head at Ean's puppy-like antics before he, too, shifted.

Their timberline picnic area was only accessible from the motel by a flight straight up the mountain. He huffed out a smoky breath when Ean jumped on his tail, far closer to the deadly spikes than Matthias would have liked, humped a couple of times against his scales like a dog in heat before running off again. Matthias would seriously have to rethink waking Ean up early if this insane energy was going to be the result.

Matthias lowered his sizable bulk to the ground and waited. When Ean came ripping past his snout, Matthias reached out and snagged him. Ean yelped in surprise and wiggled in his grasp, but Matthias launched into the sky. Only moments later, he landed at the outcropping, pleased to find their breakfast hadn't been stolen. He put Ean on the ground, watching his mate hack and gag. In human form, it might have been dry heaving. As a wolf, it looked like he was trying to cough up a hairball.

On the walk to the blankets, Matthias shifted. He swatted Ean away when the wolf ran in front of him and pressed that damned cold nose against his dick. Ean woofed and took off again to run another wide circle—this time around the outcropping of rocks. The queasy stomach from the flight straight up the mountainside obviously hadn't lasted long.

"I'm an old dragon, you little shit," Matthias grumbled as he sat on the blanket he'd laid out on the ground. He leaned against the massive rock behind him. "I like to start the day off quiet and lazy, watching the sunrise, and what do the fates do? They pair me with an excessively energized puppy."

Matthias looked around but didn't see Ean. He sighed as he realized his mate had taken off somewhere and he was talking to himself.

"I'm cold." Matthias looked up and saw Ean peeking down at him from on top of the boulder. "The activity warms me up. Are you going to eat that?"

"No. Bobcat's for you, but in a bit. Come back down here with me for a few minutes."

Ean smiled and disappeared from view. When he came around the rocks to join Matthias, he was once again in wolf form.

"Shift and come here." Matthias uncrossed his ankles and patted the blanket between his knees.

Ean shifted and crawled to where Matthias had indicated. Matthias helped him get situated where he wanted him. Ean's back was pressed to his chest, body snug between his legs. Matthias shook out the thick wool blanket he'd had folded beside him and covered them with it. He wrapped his arms around Ean and rested his chin on Ean's shoulder. The sun was just beginning to rise over the eastern plains, the dark sky brightening, the world below still cast in blue shadow.

"Warm enough?" Matthias murmured.

"Yeah," Ean sighed. "Is this what you do every morning when you disappear?"

Matthias glanced at Ean who bit his lower lip before looking back.

"I kind of noticed you were missing right around sunrise once or twice." Ean swallowed and then whispered, "Every morning, actually."

Matthias smiled and pressed their heads together. "I shouldn't be surprised my mate would notice something like that, but I am. Want to know something I noticed that will surprise you?"

"Okay."

"You steal all the pretzels and peanut butter and hide them in your room."

Ean smiled. "Don't knock the combo until you try it. It's delicious. Don't tell Vance, though, or he'll start raiding my room rather than buying more."

Matthias chuckled and held Ean tighter. "I won't. Personally, I like this combo: you in my arms, the quiet morning, beautiful sunrise." Matthias sniffed the air. "Snow definitely on the way."

They fell silent as the sun slowly rose. The few clouds in the sky turned pink and purple as the sky was painted in shades of blue and gold.

A contented happiness descended over Matthias, a feeling that everything was right in his world. How he'd managed to deny himself this connection and love for so many months, he had no idea. Matthias didn't remember the last time he'd felt so whole. If he'd felt it with Alietta, the memory had long since faded. He wished the same could be said of the Chevalier annihilation, but unfortunately that war still raged in his head. A war that would soon soil the beautiful innocence he held in his arms right now. He kissed the shell of Ean's ear and forced himself to focus on the present.

Chapter Fourteen

EAN

The past three days had been amazing. Ean had skipped work to extend his weekend one more day. He wanted more time alone with his mate, preferably several weeks, but the world didn't stop just because Matthias had finally come around. Ean couldn't ignore his station as Pack Beta either. Tanner had been understanding and accommodating, but Ean knew they needed to discuss the pack's next move. So, he forced Matthias to rent a car in the nearest town to drive them home. Ean would not be flying again if he could help it. His stomach couldn't take it. They returned the car at a lot near Luca's office building, and Ean reached out to the pack for a ride.

"Have a good weekend?" Luca asked as they climbed into the Hellcat.

Ean squeezed into the back, allowing his larger mate to have the front seat. Luca peeled out, and Ean fisted the seat belt across his chest as his stomach lurched into his throat.

"Remind me of this drive the next time I refuse to fly with you," Ean told Matthias.

Matthias turned in his seat to put a hand on Ean's knee. "Are you feeling sick?"

Ean nodded.

"Don't you dare throw up in my girl," Luca barked, catching Ean's gaze in the rearview mirror.

"Don't drive like a fucking maniac, and I won't. I need to have a conversation with Tanner about allowing you anywhere near a hemi."

"Hey! Leave my sweet boy out of this. Matthias, control your mate."

Matthias responded with a chuckle and a squeeze of Ean's knee. Ean grabbed his mate's hand and didn't let go until the vehicle stopped. Matthias assisted him out of the car, draped an arm over his shoulders, and pulled him tight against his body. As they walked up to the house at a lazy pace, Matthias pressed a kiss into Ean's hair. Ross met them at the door.

"Your dragon looks happy," Ross said to Ean before turning his attention to Matthias. "Did you finally eat someone?"

"Yes. You could say that, you crazy motherfucker," Matthias answered.

Ean blushed furiously at the reminder of Matthias's skilled tongue on his cock and his resultant orgasm in Matthias's mouth. Ross clapped and bounced on his toes, a huge grin on his face, as Matthias led Ean through the door into the house. Ean held his mate's hand while the entire pack congratulated him. In less than a year, his little wild dog pack had gone from the verge of bloodlust to properly bonded and mated.

"I have something to take care of," Matthias whispered and then kissed the shell of his ear. "Colby, can I have a word?" he asked, heading up the stairs.

"No," Colby and Theran responded together.

Matthias stopped halfway up the stairs and looked down at them.

Colby eyed him suspiciously. "Why?" Colby asked.

"I'd like to discuss a memory-sharing spell. Nothing more. Meet me in the library." With that, Matthias disappeared into the upstairs hallway.

"Okay. Stay, Poodle." Colby patted Theran's chest and darted upstairs.

"If you'll excuse me, pet. I'd like to be part of that conversation," Sakima told Vance. Vance nodded, they kissed, and then Sakima disappeared with a blur of motion.

"Interesting," Tanner muttered. He and Luca moved into the kitchen and put their heads together, having a private conversation through their bond.

Deacon sat on the sofa, flipping through a magazine. Ean smiled at his closest friends as they formed a circle in front of the living room fireplace. It had been Theran, Ross, Vance, and Ean for about a year before Deacon came along, plus another year before Tanner walked into their lives.

"Less than a year. Can you believe it?" Vance asked, softly.

"I always believed Deacon would find us a pack, but all of us finding our mates? I never expected that," Theran answered.

"Was it finding them that is unexpected, or that none of them is a wolf shifter?" Ross asked, sounding more like his usual self than he had in fourteen months.

"Honestly?" Ean said, running his fingers through his hair. "Everything that's happened since the Alpha bonded us has been unexpected."

"Agreed. Still, we're a real pack, we're all mated, and Ross seems to be getting better every day," Theran said, clapping a hand on Ross's shoulder. "I say that calls for a celebratory drink."

"Should we wait until we defeat the McBane Pack?" Vance asked.

"Hell no," Theran answered, pulling Vance into a side hug. "This is a celebration of us and our men and the incredible fact that we found them. The haters can take a back seat for tonight."

"I still have the bottle of Laphroaig my Deacon gave me for my birthday," Ross chimed in. "It's in our room."

Ross turned and ran up the stairs. Theran and Vance followed close behind. Deacon looked up from his magazine.

"We're having a drink to celebrate," Ean told him as he approached the bottom of the stairs more slowly. "Want to join us?"

Deacon smiled, but shook his head. "Enjoy yourselves."

"Ean," Tanner called from the kitchen, "let's talk during breakfast tomorrow. A lot has happened in the past few days."

"Sure thing, Alpha. Thank you."

Ean took the stairs two at a time, eager to join his friends. He appreciated their Alpha was allowing them the night to be together when so much was going on and he didn't want to waste a moment of it. Most of the time they spent together now was with the entire pack so he was excited to have some alone time with Vance, Theran, and Ross. Ean wouldn't trade any of their mates for anything in the world, but it was going to be nice getting back to their base friendship for a night.

He grinned like an idiot as he passed the door to the library and heard the low murmur of voices. He couldn't make out what was being said, but it didn't matter. Matthias was one of them, and it filled him with happiness. Ean practically skipped down the remainder of the hallway.

Chapter Fifteen

MATTHIAS

Matthias lounged back on the library sofa and listened to the boys getting rowdy down the hall. The occasional ruckus and sound of laughter lit Matthias up from the inside. The change in Ean since Matthias had snatched him from the riverside was staggering in its intensity. Deep black to the brightest white overnight. The pack had split in two and each group was having its own gathering.

The wolves were in the back bedroom, Tanner having been invited to join them about an hour ago. The mates, as they'd started referring to themselves, had congregated in the library, where Luca had poured them all snifters of scotch. Of them all, Colby was the youngest, but the bartender had proven early on he was more than capable of keeping up with the "old men" in the room. Matthias glanced around at the occupants of the library—two dragons, an elemental, a vampire, and a sorcerer.

"Fuck," Matthias breathed. "The last time I was in a room with so many different species it was to discuss the destruction of the entire Chevalier family. Never in my wildest imagination..." He shook his head and took a large swallow of scotch, reveling in the slight acidic burn.

"I can't say the same. Elysium has broken down many barriers among paranormals, at least those in the LGBT community," Sakima said. "Having said that, I do agree with keeping the Chevalier family where they are—dead, buried, and nearly forgotten."

"If my mate wasn't being targeted because of them, I would agree. Hell, I wouldn't even know about them if Tanner hadn't channeled my powers and drawn notice," Luca said from the office chair.

Deacon sat across from him. Colby sat cross-legged on the floor, leaning back against the sofa Matthias was stretched out on. Sakima stood at the door to the balcony, occasionally looking out into the cloud-covered night. The snow falling in the high country had yet to make it down the mountains to the city, but the nights were noticeably colder.

"Arden, my Coven leader, was concerned over the blood moon," Sakima said, eyeing the sky. "The belief is that it makes wolf shifters stronger, thereby making our Alpha stronger than he already is. If that is true, we need to get the McBane Pack out of the picture or perhaps take ourselves to an undisclosed location to wait it out."

"I vote for option one so we can be done with them," Deacon said.

"But if option two becomes necessary, I have a place we can go that's very much off the beaten path," Matthias said.

"What I wouldn't give to take the fight to them. I hate waiting for them to make the damn moves," Deacon grumbled.

Luca swiveled in his chair to face the Elemental. "But Tanner is right to make the decision for Gerald to make the first move against the McBanes. If we, the non-wolves in this room, attack a wolf pack without provocation, our own governing bodies would be forced into action, and that is precisely what we *don't* want."

"I'm feeling awfully provoked," Colby mumbled. He was staring at the ball of magic he was swirling in the palm of his hand.

"Be careful with that," Sakima said, glancing down at the milky-white cloud. "I'm not ready to leave Vance just yet."

"Not dangerous. I'm conjuring the memory spell," Colby said. "Never done it before, so I'm practicing."

Raucous laughter and raised voices filtered down the hall, making Matthias smile. Glancing around the room, he noticed the others were doing the same. Hearing their mates enjoying themselves was a welcome sound. Until he'd snatched his mate from the river, Matthias didn't have one single memory of Ean's laughter. And this night was his first memory of all five wolves being rambunctious and rowdy together. Even when they met at Elysium, at least one of them was in a mood—usually Ean.

Matthias sat up, swinging one leg over Colby's head so the sorcerer was between his knees. He stood and stepped over the sorcerer on his way to the desk where he'd placed Alietta's journal. He picked it up, opened it to the page he wanted, and handed it to Luca. The younger dragon took it, eyeing Matthias curiously.

"The binding spell I want Colby to use on Tanner," Matthias said. Luca dropped the book to the desk with a thump and narrowed his eyes. "I've seen it used before. It's not harmful to the recipient," Matthias assured him.

"Not that we're aware of, anyway. A lot of the spells you're asking me to conjure are ancient and haven't been cast in recent memory," Colby said. Matthias sat on the sofa and thumped Colby's ear. "Don't test me, old man."

"Long term use can be detrimental, but for one year, no harm will come of it. But first, the memory share."

"Give me another day or two to perfect it," Colby said.

A wolf howl echoed through the night-shrouded neighborhood outside, rapidly joined by several others. Everyone in the library rose to their feet as the door down the hall opened. The Chevalier wolves came down the hall and stopped at the door. Tanner looked into the library, the other wolves behind him, and stared at Luca.

"This isn't going to be good," Tanner said, before he and the other wolves headed down the stairs. The mates followed behind silently.

The entire pack congregated in the foyer at the foot of the stairs. Matthias leaned against the railing. Ean raked over Matthias's entire body with his eyes and then looked away with a sigh. Matthias smirked at his young wolf's attraction, even in tense moments like these. Tanner stood facing the door, waiting. Several minutes later footsteps were heard on the porch followed by a knock on the door. Tanner approached the door and opened it to Gerald, accompanied by eight to ten other wolves.

"We were having a good night," Ean said.

Gerald narrowed his eyes at the Beta and Matthias straightened. Truce or not, if Gerald made a move toward Ean, Matthias would rip him apart.

"Why are you here, Gerald?" Tanner asked.

The McBane enforcer slid his eyes from Ean to Tanner. "Protocol required that we wait until your father was healed to challenge his Pack Alpha status. He's appropriately healed, but he's not at his best. The blood moon rises next Sunday, and we take over the pack then."

"I would advise against that," Sakima said, sharing a quick glance with Matthias.

"I agree," said Matthias.

Making a move for power on the night of the blood moon was a terrible idea. It would work out fine as far as Gerald and the other wolves were concerned, but the Chevalier Pack, with the additional multispecies powers their Alpha possessed, would be flirting with disaster if they attempted to fight on the blood moon.

"And I'm considering other options," Tanner said.

Matthias didn't see any outward reaction to that announcement, but he wondered if the pack bond was alive with the same surprise he felt. Last he'd heard, Tanner had decided to assist Gerald with his endeavor to overthrow the McBane Pack Alpha. Matthias looked at Ean who stood unflinchingly beside his Alpha. Had his sweet boy managed to change Tanner's mind? Gerald took a step toward Tanner, irritation clear on his face. Ean, Theran, and Colby each took an answering step closer to their Alpha. The move didn't go unnoticed by Gerald or his cohorts.

"What do you mean, other options?" Gerald bit out.

Tanner shrugged nonchalantly. "Sometimes the enemy of my enemy isn't always my friend. And let's be honest with each other, for once. You don't approve of me any more than my father does, so, should you actually succeed in overthrowing him, what's going to stop you from coming after 'the abhorrent fairies,' as Tony so lovingly referred to us?"

Gerald responded with a low, barely audible growl.

"Exactly," Tanner said. "When I've had ample time to consider all of my pack's options, I'll contact you. Should you decide to make a move before then, you're on your own."

With growls and nasty glares, Gerald and his followers turned on their heels, shifted, and took off into the cold winter night. Matthias glanced at each member of the Chevalier Pack. That had been an interesting and unexpected conversation to witness.

Chapter Sixteen

EAN

Everyone held their positions until Tanner turned the deadbolt on the front door, and then they all expressed their confusion. Ean, of course, was the loudest, considering he was the only one who originally opposed the idea of a truce with the McBane Pack enforcer.

"What just happened, Tanner?" Ean asked and then corrected himself. "I'm sorry. What just happened, Alpha?"

Tanner faced him and shook his head. "Calling me Tanner is acceptable," he said, and Ean dipped his head in acknowledgment. "And what just happened is me changing my mind. This whole thing is making me uncomfortable. Yes, we now have allies. Yes, our pack is being acknowledged by other governing bodies, even if we're not being accepted."

"But?" Luca asked from his position at the foot of the stairs.

"I can't trust my own parents or anyone in the pack I grew up with—people who knew me and actually liked me until I came out as gay. How am I supposed to trust complete strangers I've never met?"

Tanner's sadness was felt through the bond. Ean didn't know about the non-wolves of the pack, but every single one of the wolf shifters understood their Alpha's pain. They all knew what it felt like to be alone and adrift in a world where no one wanted them.

"I don't suppose you can," Luca mumbled and held his mate's gaze for a long moment.

Vance smiled at Tanner as he took Sakima's hand. "We're your family now, and we have your back."

"No matter what," Ross chimed in.

"All the way," Theran said with a smile as he pulled Colby into his arms.

Tanner chuckled and locked gazes with Ean. Ean smiled mischievously and said, "To infinity and beyond."

"Good grief," Tanner said with a roll of his eyes, accompanied by the groans and mutterings of his pack mates.

Theran playfully punched him in the arm. "Dude, that was just bad."

Ean shrugged and laughed with the rest of them. He was still a little buzzed from their indulgence of Laphroaig, and the humor felt good after such an unexpected, tense confrontation. At least Gerald hadn't made the interaction physical. He didn't know about the five mates who'd been congregated in the library, but he was damned certain the five wolves were inebriated enough to skew a fight with Gerald in favor of his small platoon of shifters.

"Damn, I'm tired," Vance said and then yawned.

"Same," Ean said, momentarily catching Matthias's gaze.

"Scotch will do that, pet," Sakima added.

"Listen," Tanner said, and everyone turned their attention to him. "I know everyone has their own places, but I think it would be best if we all stayed together until this whole thing with my father is resolved."

"Do we have room?" Deacon asked. "There are a lot more of us now."

"Yes, if Ean is willing to join Matthias in the library," Luca answered.

"It's only a double mattress, but we could make it work," Matthias said.

Ean creased his brow. His dragon did, indeed, sleep in the library, but it had never once occurred to him how that was possible. "There's a bed in there? I've never seen one. I thought you slept on the sofa, or something."

"Murphy bed," was all Matthias said.

"Tomorrow, everyone can head to their respective homes and pack some things, but for now, let's all get to bed. I don't know what it is, but things feel off to me."

"Yeah," Theran agreed, hugging Colby tighter. "Maybe it's the blood moon, maybe it's the alcohol..."

"Maybe it's the fact we're looking at the potential end to all our problems," Vance added.

After a long moment of quiet, Luca broke the silence. "Come on, pup. Bedtime."

He held out a hand and beckoned Tanner to him. The Alpha pair led the way up the stairs, followed by Sakima and Vance, and then Deacon and Ross. Theran and Colby brought up the rear, leaving Ean in the foyer. Matthias held his position on the stairs, staring down at Ean.

Ean lifted one finger, indicating he'd be a minute, and then moved around the downstairs living area making sure windows and doors were locked up tight. He doubted anyone would be stupid enough to break into the house, especially if they knew who was inside, but the McBane Pack had proven, on more than one occasion, just how brazen they could be. Back in the foyer, he found Matthias had disappeared. Ean shut the overhead light off and then headed up the stairs to the library. He flipped the hallway light off and entered the cozy room, closing the door behind him.

Matthias had moved the sofa down the wall, in front of bookshelves rather than its usual place beneath a large painting Ean hadn't paid much attention to before. Matthias grabbed one corner of the frame and pulled it away from the wall, except the entire wall descended toward the floor to reveal a thin, full-size mattress. Ean had heard of Murphy beds, but he'd never seen one before.

"Wow. That's kind of cool."

Matthias grabbed the metal rod laying across the foot of the bed and flipped it down underneath where he set it on the floor. Ean pointed at it.

"That's what holds up the foot of the bed?"

"Yes, and as you can see, it's rather flimsy, so there will be no vigorous, acrobatic sex tonight."

Ean scoffed. "Excuse me, hello?"

Matthias stopped making the bed to look at Ean, who waved his hand at all the other furniture in the room.

"What?" Matthias asked, glancing around.

"We have options, oh, dragon mine. Don't try telling me you've never screwed on anything other than a bed. I won't believe it."

Matthias stared at Ean through lowered lids. "You'd be shocked by some of the places I've had sex," he said, as he returned to tucking the sheets.

"No, I wouldn't," Ean said.

He crossed the room and picked up the blanket tossed over the arm of a chair, and then helped Matthias spread it over the bed. Ean chuckled at how domestic he felt making a bed with his mate. There was an underlying uneasiness he couldn't identify, but it didn't detract from the overall comfort being with Matthias gave him. Ean stretched and rolled his shoulders, then his neck and hips, trying to relieve the sensation.

Matthias watched him from across the bed, hands on his hips and those amazing muscles pulled tight. Ean took a few seconds to look over his dragon mate and memorize the moment. It had taken them so long to get to this point, he didn't want to forget one thing about it. The mate pull had been there from the moment Ean set eyes on Matthias, but it grew stronger every day they were together, but not mated. He really needed Matthias to claim him soon before he went nuts from wanting.

"You're already feeling it, aren't you?" Matthias asked.

"I've always felt it," Ean answered, still stuck on his desire to be mated and claimed. "You're the one being difficult."

"I was referring to the blood moon and its effects."

"Oh."

Ean shrugged and then started getting undressed for bed. He'd packed up all his things when he'd moved in with Theran and Colby so he was going to have to sleep naked. Everyone except Tanner and Luca, and possibly Matthias, were in the same boat. They'd all be wearing the same clothes when they met up again in the morning because none of them had planned to stay at the pack house for the night.

"I was blaming you for the discomfort, but now that you mentioned the blood moon, I do think that's what's causing this...anxiety." Ean moved his spine side to side with an audible pop and then sat down on the bed gently. The bar holding it above the floor really didn't look like it would hold Matthias's weight, let alone Matthias's and his. "Are we going to suddenly wake up on the floor when this thing gives out? The two of us together aren't exactly light."

Matthias smiled as he pulled his shirt off and then shrugged. "Guess we'll see."

Ean eased himself down onto the bed and then settled the covers over his legs. Matthias tossed his shirt onto the desk and then, bracing his hands on the mattress, leaned over to kiss Ean's mouth.

"Mmm," he hummed before nipping at Ean's lower lip.

His dragon had a thing for his bottom lip, not that he was complaining, really. Ean smiled up at his mate. Maybe it was his reclined position, or the alcohol he'd ingested earlier, but Ean was suddenly very tired, and he fought to keep his eyes open long enough to watch Matthias strip completely. Nothing was hotter than his dragon mate naked.

"What happened to your desire to be fucked on every available surface?" Matthias mumbled against Ean's throat before he planted an open-mouthed kiss to Ean's jugular.

Ean moaned and tipped his head back slightly on the pillow. "Don't know. Lying down made me sleepy, I guess."

Matthias trailed laughing kisses and nips over Ean's neck, shoulders, and chest before standing so he could finish undressing. He stared into Ean's eyes as he undid his jeans and slid them down his legs. Ean's eyes were drawn to the naked, tattooed skin of Matthias's thighs, and then the rounded firmness of his butt as Matthias tossed the jeans onto the desk with his shirt.

"You look...just...so amazing," Ean said, struggling with the words to express how gorgeous his mate was to him. He wiggled on the bed, trying to get comfortable.

"You're quite handsome yourself. I've heard that wolf shifters don't feel the pull as much in animal form."

"You heard correctly."

"Go ahead and shift so you can rest."

Tired and uncomfortable, Ean rolled off the bed to the floor for the shift. *Is anyone else feeling this?* Ean asked the pack. *I feel it every year, but it feels stronger this time.*

I think it's our unusual pack dynamics, Tanner answered.

Good call denying Gerald tonight. Put in a fight right now, we'd all be loose cannons, Theran said.

This must be why Matthias wants to bind Tanner before the blood moon can take full effect, Luca said.

Ean looked up at Matthias who was sitting on the bed watching him. The dragon lifted his brows. "Is this why you want to bind Tanner? Because you knew how bad this was going to be?" Ean asked, unable to keep the accusation from his voice. He was getting tired of Matthias keeping secrets from him.

Matthias simply nodded, and for whatever reason, that irritated Ean further. He shifted and growled at his mate, voicing his displeasure. At least he felt better in wolf form.

Matthias knew. He admitted it. If you all shift, it feels better.

Acknowledgment followed by several good nights filled the pack bond before each of them withdrew in order to sleep. Ean circled the rug before flopping on the floor and glaring at Matthias. The dragon shook his head and sighed. Twisting to the side of the bed, he shut the lamp off and plunged the room into near darkness. The night sky glowed orange with the promise of snow, bathing Matthias and the bed in a soft golden hue.

"I know you're upset with me. I can feel it." Matthias's soft tone filled the quiet room and Ean lifted his head to watch his mate roll on the bed to face him. "But I'd still like you to be in the bed with me. Please?"

He rubbed the mattress where Ean had been lying moments before, and Ean found he didn't have it inside him to be apart from his mate, no matter how annoyed he was. Ean jumped onto the mattress and curled up. Matthias spooned behind him and dragged Ean back against him with one strong arm. He rubbed Ean's chest and ribs while nuzzling into the fluff behind his ears.

"I've been single for centuries, little boy," Matthias whispered. "Give me time to adjust to having you."

Taking that to heart, Ean's ire settled, and he whined his acceptance. It wasn't just Matthias making him feel this way, and he knew it. Other strong, outside factors played a part as well. Ean gradually fell asleep, surrounded by Matthias's strong arms and natural dragon heat. Moments later, Ean's eyes snapped open when raised voices filled the hall. He shifted to his human form and grabbed his phone off the floor to see the time. What felt like moments had actually been hours. They'd turned in around eleven the night before, but it was now just after five in the morning.

"What in bloody hell?" Matthias grumbled from behind him.

"I don't know," Ean said flopping back onto the bed.

"Do you have any idea how bad this is? I've been in that room. I know the kind of power they possess," Colby shouted. Each word became louder and clearer as he came down the hall, closer to the library.

"Would you please calm down?" Theran said, his voice much calmer than his mate's.

"Don't tell me to calm down," Colby snapped back.

A knock sounded on the library door. "Ean, Matthias," Luca called out. "Meet us downstairs. We have a problem."

"Stop being a dragon downer. This will be fun," Ean heard Ross say as he passed.

He and Matthias both groaned as they rolled off the mattress to get dressed.

Chapter Seventeen

MATTHIAS

As Matthias entered the dining room behind Ean, he became aware of two things simultaneously. The conversation bordering on argument was well underway, and the tension filling the room was tangible. Whatever had happened had tipped the scales toward fight mode, and each individual's power was snapping at the surface of their control. It appeared Colby was closest to the edge, which Matthias found concerning. Usually, the sorcerer was cool and confident, overly so at times.

"Are none of you listening to me? This is the worst idea ever. Have you met my mother?"

"Yes," Matthias said, calmly and loudly so as to be heard over the din of side conversation taking place. When the room grew quiet, he added, "Iva and I are acquainted. What's going on?"

Tanner crossed his arms over his chest. "Colby received an email this morning from the Grand Superior of the Enclave with the instruction to pass it on to the Chevalier Pack Alpha."

"Which I did under the assumption that the Alpha would put more thought into his response," Colby said. Theran put a hand over Colby's mouth and whispered something in his ear.

"Dare I ask?" Ean said.

"We, as a pack, have been asked to attend a tribunal at the Enclave," Tanner answered. "Apparently, the largest of the Enclaves, Covens, Hordes, and Packs in the area want to set eyes on us so they can assess the truth behind the rumors. And they're *insisting* it take place today."

"Sounds like a lot of fun," Vance said, sarcastically, from his place in Sakima's arms.

"Sounds dangerous," Deacon said.

"Yes, it does," Ean agreed. "Nine of us surrounded by god knows how many of them? We could be walking into our own annihilation."

"Ten and, no, we won't," Matthias said.

"What?" Tanner asked, as Ean spun to look at Matthias.

"Ean said nine, but there are ten of us." Matthias held Ean's gaze as his words slowly began to make sense to the young wolf, making him smile. He'd known that openly accepting Ean and stating his intent to be a part of his wolf's pack would be met with joy. Though, Matthias would have liked to make the statement under different circumstances.

Tanner nodded and smiled as well. "Glad you finally decided to join the pack," he said. "But how do you know we won't be walking into our own execution?"

"Because you're not the first Chevalier, and this is not the first tribunal to be held," Sakima answered.

Matthias glanced at the vampire, the only other one in the room who'd already been through one tribunal.

"The original Chevalier were brought before two different tribunals forty years apart. They were given a chance to answer for their actions and time to change their ways. After the second tribunal was ignored, and they continued as they had been, it was determined an intervention was required and their destruction was ordered," Matthias told them.

"We will be given the same courtesy," Sakima added. "We will be given the chance to show them who and what we are, and we will be allowed to leave unharmed."

"But," Matthias interjected. "You will need to present as harmless and powerless as we want them to believe you are," he said to Tanner.

"Meaning, what, exactly?" Luca asked, brows drawn tight.

"Colby needs to bind him—"

"Absolutely not," Luca practically roared.

"Or at the very least suppress his abilities," Matthias finished calmly. Rising to Luca's ire would only result in a fight between the two dragons, and there wasn't enough room in the house for that. He'd known what to expect from Luca at the suggestion, but Ean's reaction was unexpected.

"Are you kidding? You want us to walk into a room full of paranormals, who despise and fear us, completely defenseless?" Ean asked, once again giving Matthias that annoyed glare he'd grown accustomed to receiving.

Like always, seeing the young Beta wolf's temper turned him on, but now wasn't the time. He narrowed his eyes and let his dragon bleed into them.

"Don't give me that look," Ean growled.

"Then listen to reason," Matthias growled back. Ean adjusted his stance, preparing to square off with him, but Tanner interrupted before they could really get going.

"Colby, what exactly would go into binding me?" Tanner asked.

"Nothing, really. It's quick, painless, short-term, but I'm not sure it'll work, because we don't know exactly how you're doing it. My answer to that situation is for you to simply not siphon power off Luca or Deacon while you're in the room. If no one here can identify the magic taking place, I seriously doubt the Grand Superior can."

"And I'm guessing she'll be able to detect a binding spell?" Tanner asked.

"If I'm not able to mask it, possibly. Yes. Certain sorcerers, like me, have that ability."

"Okay. I'll just not tap into Luca and Deacon, then," Tanner said with finality. "Now to my next question: Why is this happening now?"

"The blood moon," Sakima answered. "Arden, my Coven leader, was quite concerned about what your power would be when the blood moon rose."

Matthias held his tongue as the conversation continued. Tanner's decision wasn't what he thought best, but he wasn't officially a bound member of the pack and certainly wasn't the Alpha of the pack. He would always voice his thoughts and opinions, even if they continued to start fights with his young mate. The tribunal wasn't anything he was overtly worried about, but it did push up his plans. Time was no longer on his side, and the memory share needed to happen sooner, rather than later.

Chapter Eighteen

EAN

Ean was going to piss his pants. He was certain of it. After three life-or-death encounters with the McBane Pack, he'd thought the tribunal would be nothing. He was wrong. Walking into the Enclave headquarters and feeling the sorcery that filled the halls had made him nervous. Now, entering the Superior's chambers, that nervousness turned to fear that coalesced in his bladder because they were outnumbered by at least five to one.

Everyone stay on your guard, but don't do anything that can be taken as a threat, Tanner said.

And stay close together. Don't let them separate us, Ean added, and everyone sent their agreement through the bond. He heard Theran and Vance whisper the orders to their mates. He really hoped Matthias's keen hearing allowed him to hear the whispered words since he wasn't able to tell the dragon himself.

Tanner entered first, followed by Ean to his right and Luca to his left. They were followed by Theran and Colby, then Deacon and Ross, and lastly Vance and Sakima. Matthias was the last to enter, and having his mate so far away from him physically made his skin itch. If they were going to die, he wanted his dragon mate at his side, like everyone else had theirs. Ean understood the formation and the deliberate distribution of power it provided, but he hated it.

"Stop there," the woman at the head of the tables said.

Tanner and Ean both glanced down to the floor to the see the line Colby had told them existed. The superiors had truly carved a mark into the floor where they deemed was an acceptable and respectful distance for those summoned to stand. Ean swallowed down the nervous giggle he felt at seeing it and distracted himself by looking around the room.

Six tables were set in a large U-shape. At one table to the left sat the vampires. The next table up were the wolves, represented by the Landon

Pack. Ean breathed a bit easier seeing at least one ally in the room. The top of the U comprised of two tables that held the sorcerers; the Grand Superior stood between the two tables. At one of the tables to the right sat the dragons. The final table on the right, closest to Ean, was empty. His curiosity about which paranormal should be seated there was short-lived thanks to the Grand Superior.

"Deacon Linvale," she said. "I am no longer surprised at the resounding silence from the local Elemental Storm. Shall we take your stance with the Chevalier as an announcement of your Storm's allegiance to them?"

"More than an allegiance. My mate and I are members of the Chevalier Pack," Deacon announced to the room.

Ean looked to his former Alpha in shock, as did the rest of the pack. Apparently, Matthias wasn't the only one in the pack keeping secrets.

"And the other heads of your Storm?" the Grand Superior asked.

"Have been informed that this pack is no more powerful than any other and poses no danger to anyone," Deacon answered. "The Plains Storm has no interest in these proceedings."

The Grand Superior glanced over the pack before she settled her gaze on Tanner. "You're the Alpha?"

Tanner nodded.

"The heads of state you will speak to are Arden, of the Springs Coven; Mariel, Alpha of the Landon Pack; Sadie, of the Mountain Horde; and I am Iva Delavane, Grand Superior of the Midwest Enclave. I'm sure you are more than aware of who we are, though, given those among your entourage."

"Yes," Tanner confirmed. "Mariel is Theran's former Pack Alpha. Sadie is my mate's mother. Arden is Sakima's former Coven leader. And you are my lead enforcer's mother."

Iva huffed at that last part. "Where is the rest of your pack, Alpha? I specifically asked that *all* members attend this tribunal."

"This is the entire Chevalier Pack," Tanner answered, voice strong and steady.

Iva laughed. "There are only ten of you? Is such a low number even worthy of the term pack?" she asked, looking to Alpha Mariel.

Mariel turned her attention from Tanner to the Grand Superior. "Packs are not defined by size, Iva, but by the bond the Alpha creates among the members."

"Fine." Iva straightened her shoulders and regrouped. "Holding a tribunal seems ridiculous to me, now, but protocol requires we complete the process. I will say, however, that this entire thing could have been avoided had *my son* been more forthcoming with information regarding the Chevalier Pack in the first place."

"Excuse me?" Colby said from behind Ean. "You're not putting this on me. It's not my fault you never thought to ask how big the pack was. All you were concerned about was how powerful they were."

"Honestly," said the female dragon, Sadie. "How much power can such a small number truly wield?"

"I must admit the reports of the Chevalier Pack have been wildly exaggerated. I had expected a much larger number and far more power," said the male vampire, Arden. "As it stands, aside from the Elemental and the young sorcerer, I feel no more power than is typical for each of our species."

"Perhaps, but I think we can all agree that the reports of the Chevalier Alpha's unique and slightly unbelievable ability to use power not his own must be addressed," Iva said.

"Especially with the blood moon looming in the near future," Arden added, proving Sakima's earlier words that the Coven leader was concerned about that fact above all else.

"If the Chevalier are no more powerful than their individual bloodlines, I see no reason the blood moon would be an issue. It will, of course, make the wolf shifters in the pack a bit more erratic, temperamental, and cranky, but it has no other effect whatsoever," Mariel stated. She grinned at Tanner before adding, "They will be more of a problem for their mates than anyone else."

Ean glanced back and forth as each person took a turn speaking. It was an odd feeling to be talked about when you were present, but it seemed they weren't going to need to say much in their defense. The arguments were being made for them simply because they weren't a large enough pack to be perceived as a threat. Strangely, for once, Ean didn't mind being viewed as weak if it got them out of this tribunal alive and unharmed.

"I'm bored and hungry," Ross's voice suddenly rang out.

Ross, be quiet, said Ean, followed by a *shush, baby,* from Deacon.

"I want rabbit," Ross said, ignoring both his mate and his Beta.

Ean didn't have to look to know that Matthias moved from the back of the formation to stand on the opposite side of Ross, effectively boxing the errant wolf into the middle of the pack. Even though they'd yet to claim each other, they were able to feel the other's emotions and have a general sense of where the other was in a room. When Ean had mentioned it to Tanner, he'd received the confirmation that the Alpha and his dragon mate had had a similar experience. Ean and Luca shared a quick glance and then focused on Tanner who seemed unfazed by the unplanned interruption.

"Apologies. This meeting wasn't exactly in our plans for the day, and we're due for a hunt."

"Unfortunately," Iva said, clasping her hands together in front of her. "There is only one way to proceed with the next topic of discussion given the likelihood that you will lie."

"What—" Tanner's words were interrupted by a flash of magic.

"Deacon," Colby yelled and the cloud of magic surrounding the pack was electrified with bolts of lightning.

Ean spun to see Colby's hair and eyes had gone completely black, veins spiderwebbing over the skin of his arms. Sakima had vamped out, eyes nearly completely white and fangs distended. Deacon's eyes had gone from their usual light blue to a stormy dark gray-blue. It wasn't often that they saw the Elemental in such a primal state.

"What the hell?" Tanner yelled over the sound of gale-force wind. "I thought you said they wouldn't attack," he said, staring directly at Matthias.

"It's not an attack," Matthias yelled back. "It's a test. She's trying to force you to tap into powers that aren't yours to prove you can."

"Don't shift, don't siphon off Luca or Deacon," Colby said, voice deeper than usual. "When I feel their magic stop hitting against mine, I'll drop the bubble. They're only feeling me and Deacon right now. We need to keep it that way." A few seconds later, he added, "Barrier coming down."

Deacon withdrew his power just as Colby allowed the spell he'd cast to drop. When the room came back into view, everyone was exactly as they had been moments before, as though nothing had happened. Tanner's irritation rippled through the pack bond.

"What the hell was that?" Tanner growled. "You brought us here to attack us?"

"Hardly," Sadie said. Tanner turned his glare to his mate's mother. "Had we simply asked if you could tap into dragon, vampire, or sorcerer power, you would, of course, have said no. We needed to see for ourselves that you were nothing more than wolf."

"Right. Because my father's word carries more weight than mine," Tanner bit out.

"Why do you call yourselves the Chevalier Pack?" Arden asked.

"We're an interspecies pack, nothing more." Tanner shrugged.

"Explain the car being thrown into the McBane's pack house," Iva demanded.

"I lost my temper," Luca growled.

"And your mate growing into a large black wolf that breathes fire?" Sadie asked.

"Me," answered Colby and Deacon simultaneously. Surprise rocked through the pack bond, but everyone managed not to react outwardly.

"Excuse me, little boy?" Iva said, jaw tight and eyes narrowed.

"Seriously? A wolf shifter with the power to grow, change color, and breathe fire? Either the entire McBane Pack was high on hallucinogens, or it was a spell, *mother*. I changed his appearance and Deacon created the fire, because that's what sorcerers and Elementals do."

Tanner picked up on the lie with ease and continued. "As you pointed out earlier, we're a small pack. Our best defense is instilling fear. Given where we now find ourselves, I'd say that strategy worked."

Iva huffed out a breath and then shared a silent glance with Arden before moving to Mariel, and then to Sadie. No one said anything or moved from their seats, but apparently a decision had been made. Ean watched as all three leaders rose to their feet with Iva.

"You're free to go, Alpha, but know that we'll be watching and listening, ready to intervene should it become necessary," Iva announced imperially.

Ean suppressed an eyeroll. He understood Colby's annoyance with his mother. Ean couldn't imagine spending a lifetime with this woman. Tanner turned to leave the room and Ean followed, looking into Matthias's eyes as he passed. Once they were all outside near the vehicles, Colby sagged against the door of his truck. Theran was immediately at his side taking the sorcerer into his arms. As Ean glanced around at the other wolves of the pack, each of them was taking comfort in their mate's arms. Before the small seed of jealousy could blossom, Matthias had him wrapped in a strong embrace, chests pressed together.

"That went well," Matthias said, and eight heads jerked around to look at him in shock.

Sakima chuckled.

"That was considered a good meeting?" Tanner asked.

"I felt like puking and shitting myself at the same time," Colby said.

"I nearly peed my pants, if that makes you feel better," Ean told the sorcerer.

"Doesn't matter how you felt. All that mattered was how you acted and reacted. You passed their test, and they'll basically leave you alone now," Matthias said and kissed Ean's creased forehead.

"I don't know about anyone else, but I'm tired of all the secrets and being caught off guard," Ean said, staring directly into Matthias's eyes. "Everyone is doing their own thing, and I like to think it's all to protect us as a pack, and yes, so far it has worked out, but we should all be aligning our efforts. We all deserve to know what's being done so we can prepare for any unforeseen consequences. This could have gone sideways so damn easily because we didn't know about Deacon and we didn't expect the "test" attack, or that Colby was going to claim responsibility for Tanner's additional shifting ability. We have got to be smarter than this."

Ean had been speaking directly to Matthias, momentarily forgetting about the rest of the pack as he lost himself in the beautiful, silver-swirling eyes of his mate. Tanner's laughter pulled him back to reality, and he turned to look at his Alpha.

"You'll make a great Alpha one day, should you ever have the desire," Tanner told Ean. "And I agree. Reconvene at the house, and we'll go from there."

Chapter Nineteen

MATTHIAS

It had been a long afternoon. The pack had quite the heart-to-heart once they returned to the house, and the discussion had lasted hours.

Deacon wasn't just an elder advisor for the Plains Storm; he was the *top* elder of the Storm. He'd been quietly diverting the attention of the Elementals from the moment Tanner had first pulled power from him and blown out the side of Luca's office building.

Colby had been fibbing his way through every meeting he'd had with his mother, just because he could, and apparently enjoyed seeing how long he could string her along before she lost patience with him. After running into Theran in the woods and realizing they were mates, his motives had become more personal.

Sakima had been called to stand before his Coven leader on a near-monthly basis to give report on the pack he'd found himself a part of. Arden hadn't been overtly condescending or hateful toward the new Chevalier Pack. According to Sakima, the information Arden asked after seemed more like the vampire was feeding his own curiosity than gathering intel for an attack.

Now, it was Matthias's turn to clear the air. Except, Matthias's secrets couldn't be revealed fully in mere conversation. Once Colby assured them he was comfortable conjuring the memory-share spell, and that he could do so safely, the pack moved from the dining table to the large open floor of the living room.

Matthias stared into Ean's beautiful eyes as their fingers laced together, completing the magic circle. He couldn't remember a time when he'd been this nervous. If this spell worked the way it was supposed to, and Colby was powerful enough to hold it the length of time necessary for the entire memory to play out, his young wolf mate would be getting a firsthand look at Matthias's dark side, his biggest regret, and the deepest loss he'd ever felt. He hoped Ean was strong enough to overcome the largest barrier between them. Once this was over, Matthias would either claim Ean as his mate, or lose him forever.

Colby's murmured words filled the room as tendrils of smoky white and gold began swirling up from the floor in the center of the circle. The arc gradually widened until it surrounded the entire pack, blocking out all view of the room they stood in. One cloudy tendril swirled in the center before bending and curling its way toward Matthias where it caressed his forehead with a ghostly touch. Given the havoc this tendril of magic was about to wreak, it was far too soft and gentle.

Without warning, a flash erupted from the center of the circle. Matthias squeezed his eyes shut against the brightness. When he opened them again, he was in the last place he ever wanted to be again—in the middle of a war zone. Dragons were in the air. Vampires zipped around the perimeter, stopping every so often to engage a frightened villager. A wolf's howl lifted into the air and was quickly joined by others. The Chevalier family castle was in flames, and there on the drawbridge was Alietta.

Matthias had one task, and he knew what he needed to do. Aware that the rest of the pack was with him in his head, seeing all of it for the first time, Matthias approached his mate. He and Alietta had only recently met and were still in the get-to-know-you stage of their pairing, but the mating pull between them was strong. She smiled at him sadly as he approached her, stopping a few inches short of taking her in his arms.

"Why the tears?"

"Children," she answered. "So many children, and so young..."

"We knew that before we started, love."

Alietta nodded and blew out a breath.

"Just keep their powers as muted as you can while I'm in there. That's all I ask," Matthias said.

"Yes, I will."

With that, Matthias moved past his sorceress and entered the castle. Most of the flames were in the back of the large estate, not that they would have bothered him, but the smoke could be a problem when unobstructed sight was needed. As he walked down the long hallways in search of hybrids who might be hiding inside, he felt Ean's surprise and despair flowing gently over him. It was a strange sensation to be reliving an age-old memory and still be aware of the present. The sensation was comforting in an otherwise horrible situation.

Matthias glanced into each room as he passed, noting the entire first floor was empty. He took the servant staircase to the second floor where smoke was just beginning to fill the long hall. A man was in the hall, and he turned to face Matthias, hair blowing in a nonexistent wind. The smoke in the hall began swirling, centralizing to create a whirlwind that blasted its way toward Matthias, who responded by shifting his eyes and initiating the dragon sight that would allow him to see clearly.

The Elemental was erratic in his movements and decisions, but Matthias was able to partially shift, extending his wings to trap the man against a wall. Matthias grabbed the Elemental's neck in his hands and squeezed, gritting his teeth through the pain of electrical shocks zinging through his forearms. Eventually, the man stilled, arms dropping to his sides and eyes rolling back in his head. Matthias released his grip and turned his back on the man before his body had even hit the stone floor.

In the first room he came to, he found one of the hybrid females folding a blanket on the bed. It seemed an odd thing to be doing at such a time, but Matthias figured it was her insanity at play. All the Chevalier hybrids were crazy and dangerous; prone to hallucinations, suicidal and homicidal acts, and took enjoyment from torturing humans before making a meal of them.

The female straightened and turned to face him. She flashed fangs, announcing her vampire nature right before she appeared in front of Matthias. She was small and unskilled, but fierce. Matthias took quite a few scrapes from the tips of her fangs before he was able to snap her neck. The hybrid fell to the stone floor in a lifeless heap, Matthias's blood fresh on her lips. He knelt as he stared at her.

He'd acted without thought, but now that he had time to take it all in, remorse set in. As did the realization that unlike the man in the hall, this hybrid was small and unskilled because she was still a child. Probably around twelve or thirteen years of age, if he guessed correctly. Alietta had warned him, and he'd thought he was ready. He scrubbed a hand down his face and rose to leave the room. There would be time later for him to process the shame and horror of taking a child's life. Right now, he had a job to complete.

A small cry stopped him at the door, and he whipped around to face the bed. The hybrid girl hadn't been folding a blanket as Matthias had first assumed. She had been swaddling a baby. He stared down at the child, a war waging between his brain that told him to kill the hybrid and move on, and his heart that told him killing a newborn was morally wrong. Matthias reached out with the intent to smother the baby but, instead, lifted the child into his arms. The baby's eyes swirled with the telltale sign of a dragon. Matthias had no way of knowing what other blood flowed in the baby's veins, but he was a dragon shifter for certain.

Knowing the smoke filling the room and hallway wouldn't bother a baby dragon, Matthias carried the child out of the room. He took the back stairs he'd come up only moments before to the main level. He hoped with the chaos outside, no one would notice him slipping out the back door of the castle. He kept close to the wall, deep in the cloud of smoke as he worked his way toward the small abandoned hut tucked just inside the tree line of the forest.

Wanting to show Ean only what was important, Matthias jumped over the next several decades of keeping the dragon hybrid hidden, raising him to be the best dragon he could, and went right to the memory of taking the young man to a sorcerer. Roland had taken to living alone in the mountains, outside the Enclave's reach.

"My, my, what a surprise this is," the sorcerer said after he opened the door.

"Roland," Matthias said, dipping his head in greeting. "This is my nephew, Remy."

Remy waved at Roland as the sorcerer looked him over and then returned his attention to Matthias.

"Nephew, yes," Roland said, words heavy with disbelief. "Suppose you best come in."

Roland disappeared inside the mountain cabin. Matthias placed a hand at the back of Remy's neck and pushed the fledgling inside ahead of him. They followed Roland to a room at the back. Books, glassware, and herbs filled the room in a sort of organized chaos. Roland walked directly to a bookshelf and began pulling things down, placing them on the battered wood table in the center of the room. Matthias had the eerie feeling Roland already knew why he'd brought Remy here.

"You know, don't you?" Matthias asked.

"That your nephew is more than he should be?" Roland glanced over his shoulder at Remy. "I imagine I know more than you, which is why you're here, isn't it?"

"Yes. I need to know what's in his blood."

Roland tossed a blanket on the floor and pointed at it. "Sit there, young man."

Remy and Matthias shared a glance before Matthias shrugged. "Go ahead." Remy sat on the blanket, rearranging it beneath him until he was comfortable. Matthias joined Roland at the bookcase.

"This won't hurt him, will it?" he whispered.

"I doubt much of anything will hurt that man," Roland whispered back. "What happened to make you bring him here?"

"He got angry and zapped me."

"Zapped? As in channeled electricity?"

"Yes. I should probably tell you...he's a Chevalier hybrid. Newborn when I found him. I couldn't kill him."

"Do you know which pair conceived him?"

"No." Matthias sighed as he remembered the circumstances surrounding Remy's discovery. "I encountered an Elemental hybrid in the hall and the child protecting him had vampire in her."

Roland grunted. "Family like the Chevalier that doesn't mean much. Could be siblings and still have different abilities. The mixing of blood should never have happened. That's why they were eradicated... supposedly. And yet, here one sits, in my house."

"I know what I'm asking—"

"Once we know what he is," Roland interrupted. "I will conjure a binding spell. He's been raised as a dragon so he should continue to be one. If he carries Elemental or vampire, or anything else for that matter, the binding spell will make those powers inaccessible."

Matthias glanced at Remy. He still sat on the blanket, drawing invisible shapes on the floor. Remy was nearing his fiftieth year of age, still a fledgling by dragon standards, but all those years had been spent alone with Matthias. He had no real social skills, given Matthias never took him where other paranormals might question his existence or guess who and what he was. Until now.

"Binding spells require constant and frequent restoration," Matthias muttered as he stared at the young man he'd raised. He'd never told Remy who he was, where he came from, or what he was. For his part, the fledgling believed himself to be 100 percent dragon shifter.

"Yes. You need to make a choice," Roland said. "Tell him what he is, and teach him the skills necessary to use his powers wisely, and inform him why it is of vital importance he remains sequestered."

"Or?"

"You relinquish him to me. I live a secluded life here. It would be nice to have the company of a young male, and it would be easier to restore the spell whenever it appears to be weakening if he's here."

The Chevalier were still too fresh in everyone's minds for Remy to be safe in the open, and Matthias was having a harder time keeping the young dragon hidden on horde lands as he grew older, bigger, and more curious about the outside world. Remy's life was more important than Matthias's need to alleviate his guilt and loss. Alietta had died the day after he took Remy. He'd been so concerned with saving the newborn that he'd abandoned his mate on the battlefield, and later learned she'd made a life-ending decision.

Alietta had performed a severance on the matriarch of the Chevalier family, and the exhaustion had taken her life. As far as he'd known, the Chevalier were falling so there'd been no need to put herself at risk like that. Matthias often wondered if she'd known what he'd done; that perhaps she'd performed a spell she knew might kill her because of the betrayal she'd felt at his desertion. The proposition of leaving Remy in Roland's care created an ache in Matthias's chest, but it was the best option. Matthias nodded his agreement.

Feeling drained and more exhausted than he could ever remember, Matthias allowed the memory to fade. As the past melted away, and Colby retracted the spell, he closed his eyes. Weakness slammed into him, and he felt his body give out. A short rest sounded amazing before facing Ean's contempt. He was unconscious before he even hit the floor.

Chapter Twenty

EAN

Ean released his grip on Matthias and Deacon so he could wipe the tears from his eyes. That had been one hell of a trip, and glancing around the circle at the rest of the pack, it was clear the memory share had left everyone reeling. He wondered if the others had felt the depth of Matthias's emotions the same way he did, or if it was more real for him because of the mate situation. Either way, his dragon had been through a lot of turmoil internally and Ean finally understood why Matthias was so reluctant to claim him. Matthias didn't feel worthy.

Some of Matthias's actions that day were atrocious, but overall, as far as Ean was concerned, Matthias was also heroic. His inner battle proved he was, at his core, a good and honorable man. Ean was proud to call him mate, and he was going to do everything in his power to prove it to the stubborn, old dragon. He saw Matthias going down from his peripheral vision and turned in time to help ease him to the floor a little more gently.

"Matthias?" Ean prodded as he cradled the dragon's head.

Ross crawled over to them on hands and knees, tears on his cheeks and a soft smile on his lips. It was odd to see Ross in human form curling up against Matthias's side, resting his head on Matthias's stomach. It was an action he typically did while in wolf form. Ross stared at Matthias's face with unconcealed reverence. Ean and Deacon shared a glance at Ross's strange behavior. Deacon knelt by his mate's feet and touched his knee.

"Ross, baby," Deacon said.

"He's gold and shiny," Ross said.

"Gold?" Ean asked Deacon, who shook his head.

"I know pink is love, orange could be crazy, red is anger, and I think purple might be jealousy, but I don't know gold," Deacon told him.

"He saved us. When he wakes up, I'll take him home," Ross said.

"Um...okay," Ean said, because what else was there?

"Sounds good, baby. Until then, why don't we let Ean take care of his mate?" Deacon asked, as he slid his arms beneath Ross's body.

"Shiny and pretty," was all Ross said as Deacon lifted him into his arms and carried him upstairs.

"I think everyone could use some time to assimilate what we've learned," Tanner said. "We'll meet back here in a couple of hours to discuss everything and figure out how to move forward. Sound good?"

Everyone murmured their agreement and broke off into their respective pairs. Ean returned his attention to Matthias who was slowly coming to. Matthias looked up at Ean briefly before rolling to his side and pushing himself to a seated position. He sighed heavily and scrubbed his hands down his face before he spun on his butt to face Ean, expression resigned. Ean closed the distance between them by scooting until his knees touched Matthias's shins. He placed his palms on Matthias's forearms where they rested across his lap.

"You're an amazing man," Ean said.

"Did you not see everything I tried to show you?"

"Love, bravery, fear, remorse, compassion, grief, guilt. Feel free to let me know if I missed anything," Ean answered.

"I killed two people, one of them a child, both too young to die."

"And then you put yourself at risk to save Remy. You raised him as best you could. I felt that. You gave him the best chance at life that you could without exposing him. Matthias," Ean said, crawling into his mate's lap, "four hundred years is a long time to beat yourself up, to hide in libraries, and to pretend you're happy being alone."

"Ean," Matthias whispered against Ean's lips as Ean leaned in close for a kiss.

"I forgive you, and I'm proud to call you mate," Ean whispered back. "Can you forgive me the killing I've done while fighting the McBane Pack? Because I'm sure there's been at least one who's died by my wolf."

Matthias grabbed Ean's face with both hands and pressed their foreheads together. It was odd trying to look into the dragon's swirling silver gaze from this position but Ean did his best.

"If you killed, it was self-defense. You do whatever it takes to stay safe, no matter what, every time. By the gods, little boy, I need you to be safe."

"I thought the idea was to stay safe without killing, so we don't actually become the Chevalier and end up in front of a tribunal again."

"They killed for sport. That's why they had to be stopped."

"And don't you ever forget that," Ean said. "They killed for sport. You killed to stop them."

"Okay, little boy, okay," Matthias murmured.

Ean ignored the placation and kissed him. He poured everything he felt into the kiss and took comfort from Matthias's strong embrace around his back, holding him firmly against his dragon's chest. Matthias leaned back and then rolled, lowering Ean's back to the floor. Ean groaned into Matthias's mouth as the dragon deepened the kiss, licking his tongue across Ean's and settling his weight between Ean's thighs. Heat, strength, and affection surrounded Ean, and he grabbed hold of it, never wanting the moment to end. But, as seemed to be their luck, the moment did end. And it did so with the usual Chevalier Pack flair. Footsteps thundered from overhead and then down the stairs.

"Ross," Deacon yelled.

Matthias broke the kiss and rolled off Ean just as Ross jumped over the last few stairs and landed with a thud at the base, butt naked. Ean barely had time to register what his friend was doing before Ross threw open the front door. Deacon was still only halfway down the stairs.

"Ross, get back here," he yelled. The rest of the pack appeared behind Deacon at the top of the stairs.

"Come on, dragon. Let's go home," Ross yelled as he ran out the door.

Deacon ran outside after him but came back in almost immediately. "Damn it, he shifted."

Matthias had managed to get to his feet and was helping Ean up from the floor as Deacon rushed past them. The rest of the pack joined them in the living room. Deacon returned from the kitchen with his car keys.

"Where is he going?" Ean asked.

"Home, wherever the hell that is," Deacon answered. "Has he ever told you where he comes from?"

"No, he hasn't told me," Ean admitted. "Theran?"

"I've asked and gotten strange answers I could never make sense of," Theran answered. Par for the course as far as talking to Ross about anything was concerned.

"The pack bond will allow us to follow him. Ean, Theran, Vance, and I will shift. We can follow through yards and forests or whatever else he decides to charge through. The rest of you follow us in the cars. Colby, drive Theran's SUV. He has spare clothes for us in the back."

Ean immediately stripped, blew Matthias a kiss, and ran out the door behind his pack mates. Memories of a time when chasing Ross like this had been the norm resurfaced in his mind. Images of a time when they questioned how long it would be before they went insane, or if they'd ever find an Alpha and a pack that would accept them. They'd found an Alpha, but what followed was the creation of the pack they'd always dreamed of. Ean was once again fueled by the fire of indignation that anyone thought they had the right to tell him, or his pack mates, how to live or who to love.

He's headed to our hunting spot, Tanner told them as they took the corner at the end of the street. As they reached the parking area at the edge of the forest, Tanner took their usual path down to the river, then banked hard west. As the terrain began to climb, Tanner stopped and looked southward.

Ross, where are you going? Tanner asked.

Home. He needs to know, Ross answered cryptically. Tanner's ears twitched.

Will you tell us where home is, buddy? Theran asked, but no answer came.

Fine. Southwest, it is, the Alpha said.

Tanner pushed the information to Deacon, who was driving Sakima and Matthias, and Luca, who was accompanying Colby. Ean was grateful Deacon and Luca had thought ahead enough to each be in a vehicle with those who were not bonded to the pack. It would have been possible to communicate directions between individual mates, but it saved time doing it all in one blast.

Ean's legs burned by the time Tanner slowed his pace. They approached the edge of the forest where it met a cracked and broken paved road. An old wood sign with peeling paint announced they were approaching the town of Crested Lake. The population number at the bottom had been scratched out and re-carved multiple times by what looked like claws. The final number carved into the sign was the number one.

Population of one? Vance asked. *That's not freaky at all.*

We'll wait here for the others, Tanner announced.

A few seconds later, Ross came trotting down the center of the road to join them, tongue lolling out to the side. Ean took comfort that the crazy wolf was as winded as they were from that run. The white wolf rubbed his head beneath Tanner's chin before flopping down on his side in submission when Tanner's response was a deep growl. Ean and the others flattened their ears at the dominant sound and remained where they were.

It had been a long time since they'd been part of a proper pack, and Ross's insanity made it harder for him to remember the dynamics, but he wouldn't learn if they continued to intervene and protect him. Ean was pleased Tanner had accepted them despite Ross in the first place, and he'd been excessively patient with the wolf over the past months, but everyone had their limits. Tanner lay on the side of the road, and after quick looks at each other, the other three did the same. Ross took the action as forgiveness and started wiggling on his back in the dirt.

An hour later, after the rest of the pack arrived in the vehicles, the wolves shifted and dressed. Choosing to leave the cars parked at the edge of town near the sign, they all walked into Crested Lake together. Ross, hand securely held by Deacon, lead the way.

Chapter Twenty-One

ROSS

"Well, this is a bit creepy," Colby said. He moved closer to Theran's side as he glanced at the boarded-up bank they were walking past.

"I think it's cool," Tanner said from across the road where he was peeking into the crusty window of an empty shop. The pastel-painted metal sign hanging above the entry identified the shop as Beau's Ice Cream. "I like this town. Luca, buy me this town."

Luca scoffed. "Sure thing, pup. I'll do that."

Tanner ignored his mate's sarcasm and continued down the street. "Did you like living here, Ross?"

"It's home," Ross answered as he led the pack down Crested Lake's Main Street.

He held Deacon's hand and smiled. When he'd struck out on his own years before, he'd never dreamed he would one day be bringing his mate and pack, his family, to his childhood home. He was so excited for everyone to meet his dad and for his dad to see that Ross was not only doing fine, he was thriving. Ross looked behind him, searching out Matthias. The older dragon had withdrawn and grown quiet the deeper into Crested Lake they'd gotten. He was walking down the center line, holding Ean's hand, and staring straight ahead.

"When did you last visit here?" Ross asked him.

"Twenty-six," Matthias answered.

"Was it like this twenty-six years ago?" Ean asked.

Matthias huffed and lifted Ean's hand to his lips for a kiss. "I meant 1926, and no. It was still a thriving community then."

"You used to live here, Ross?" Tanner asked as he rejoined them in the center of the street. "When did it become a ghost town?"

"There was only a gas station and general store when I was really young. By the time I turned twelve, it was just us here. After my mom died, I left, so it's just been my dad for years."

"So, he's the population of one? That's really sad," said Vance.

"You will never be alone, my pet," Sakima said, picking up on the Omega wolf's underlying worry. Vance smiled at his mate.

"Dad prefers it. He's never been big on other people. That's Matthias's fault."

"How so?" Ean asked.

Ross smiled at the Beta before turning away. The school was at the end of Main Street, and they were almost there. Ean would get his answer when the rest of the pack did, though, Ross imagined all of them had some idea who his father was by now. Matthias most certainly did, given his strained expression.

"Your mother's name was Olivia," Matthias said.

"Yep."

"And the bloodlust, such as it is, started after she died."

"It did."

"What?" Ean and Tanner asked simultaneously.

"It's not true bloodlust Ross is suffering from. It's the repercussions of the binding spell dissipating upon his mother's death," Matthias said.

"His mother was a sorceress?" Colby asked.

Ross smiled as shock followed by understanding rolled through the pack bond. Seconds later, Matthias proved the blossoming beliefs.

"And his father is Remy Chevalier. This explains everything." Matthias stopped walking, and the entire pack stopped with him. Ross turned around to face Matthias when Deacon tugged at his hand. He smiled broadly when Matthias met his gaze. He was so excited and happy to have his family all in one place, and he made sure the entire pack could feel it through the bond.

"Exactly *what* does it explain?" Tanner asked.

"Everything. Ross is a hybrid of dragon, wolf, and Elemental from Remy, and sorcerer from Olivia, who was a direct descendant of Roland Bartovic. Great grand-daughter or something like that. Additionally, Ross is mated to an Elemental. He's using his sorcerer abilities to channel all his powers through the True Alpha bond with you. All these things you can do are because of him. That's also why the bloodlust is improving. He was going crazy because when Olivia died, he suddenly had access to powers he had no idea what to do with, but now he has an entire multispecies pack in which to disseminate those powers. I imagine Remy is suffering the same psychological trauma."

"Worse," Ross told him. "He's not healthy. Something is wrong with his stomach, I think."

"Wait a second. Ross," Deacon said, turning Ross to face him.

Ross smiled and stared lovingly into his mate's troubled blue eyes. He never grew tired of those eyes. He especially loved the color change when Deacon went full Elemental, clear and bright became dark and stormy, and it was a beautiful sight. He reached up and caressed Deacon's furrowed brow. He didn't know what was causing his Deacon distress, but he wanted to soothe it away.

"Did you know you had all this DNA in you? All this power?"

"No." Ross wrapped his arms around Deacon's waist and rested his head on Deacon's chest. "My mom always said I was special, but I just thought I was crazy."

Deacon hugged him, and Ross snuggled deeper into his mate's embrace. He loved being held by Deacon. He was tall, muscular, and powerful, and Ross felt safest with him.

"What can we do for him?" Deacon asked, his voice reverberating beneath Ross's ear. He suspected the question was asked of Matthias, since he was the one who answered.

"I don't know right this second. He's getting better now that he has a pack, and as it was wisely pointed out to me by my mate, I don't know what a long-term binding spell will do to the pack bond. Given that it's a multispecies pack with various abilities, he can virtually hide in plain sight. That's basically what he's been doing anyway, so I suggest, for now, we continue on as we are."

"How the hell did he fly under the radar of the highest-ranking sorceress in the region?" Tanner asked, to which Colby scoffed. Tanner smiled.

"My guess? As it stands now, all of his powers have a representation in this pack. He exhibits nothing out of the ordinary for those he's surrounded by, so he simply didn't stand out," Matthias answered.

"So, if it's Ross and not Tanner, Sakima and I can be bonded to the pack, like everyone else?" Colby asked.

Ross turned his head enough to see Theran give his mate a loving smile. Colby missed it because he was looking at Matthias, hope shining in his eyes. Ross was drawn to the colors surrounding his best friend and the sorcerer. Just like Vance and Sakima before, and Luca and Tanner before them, Theran's and Colby's auras were shifting, mingling, and joining.

He slid his gaze to Matthias and then to Ean. Their auras were similar in color, reaching for each other, but still individual and distinct. The other couples in the pack had joined far more quickly, but they'd also been far more willing from the start. Matthias had pushed Ean away. The pack members all understood why now, but it was still a journey for Ean and Matthias to get back to where they had been when they'd first met.

Straightening and stepping back from Deacon, Ross looked toward the school still a few hundred feet away, and waved. He felt his father's presence, the barest brush of contact in his mind, just as his father came running across the lot. He skidded to a halt on the pavement of the road with a half woof-half howl and stared directly at Matthias.

"Surprise," Ross said. Unable to contain his excitement, he bounced on his toes and laughed. Ean's poor old dragon looked completely befuddled.

Chapter Twenty-Two

MATTHIAS

Matthias stared at the brown and white wolf with confusion. He felt he should know the shifter, but he didn't recognize them. The same could not be said of the wolf, however. The animal stared at him with clear recognition.

"Hi, Dad," Ross said.

"Oh my god," Matthias whispered, but Ean heard him and moved closer so their arms pressed together. He gave Matthias's hand a gentle squeeze and Matthias clamped down, seeking an anchor in the storm of his mind. His feet felt cemented to the spot and his chest burned from the slow, measured breaths he was forcing himself to take.

"What's wrong? It's Remy, isn't it?" Ean whispered.

Matthias nodded and swallowed thickly. He wasn't sure he could speak, but he pushed through the lump in his throat and made the attempt. "Yes," he rasped. "But he's in wolf form. I knew Olivia was full-blood sorceress, and for Ross to be a wolf shifter, Remy had to have the DNA, but..." Matthias shook his head, still holding Remy's bright-green gaze. "I've never seen it. He always took dragon form while I was raising him. Always."

"Monkey see, monkey do," Ean offered, drawing Matthias's gaze away from Remy. "You're a dragon, he saw you shift to dragon from the time he was a baby, so that's the form he learned to take. He's obviously learned how to use his wolf shifter ability since then."

"That's a scary thought. If he's learned one ability, he may have learned them all."

"And that's bad, I assume," Ean said.

"In an abandoned town? Perhaps not."

Matthias dipped his head to whisper directly into Ean's ear. At this particular moment, he deeply regretted not giving Ean the mating bite so they could communicate privately. He'd just have to be careful of the supernatural hearing that surrounded them.

"Believe me when I say that he's far more dangerous than Ross, despite the increased mixed blood Ross carries because Remy knows how to use his powers. And he's far crazier than Ross could ever be."

"Why?" Ean asked, barely audible to even Matthias's heightened hearing.

"Because he knew how to use a lot of his powers before he was bound, and then he was cut off from those powers for centuries. To have them suddenly return in conjunction with the loss of his mate has pushed him over the edge." Matthias sighed heavily and rested his forehead against Ean's. Sadness at the situation overwhelmed him as he said, "Look into his eyes, Ean. There's no coming back from that. There's no saving him."

"Uncle Matthias."

"Remy," Matthias said as he lifted his head from Ean's.

Matthias took in Remy's human appearance. He looked ill and frail, barely more than skin and bones. He'd probably taken to shifting to wolf form simply because shifting to dragon would have taxed his gaunt physique. Remy muttered to himself, volume growing steadily until Matthias could pick up on the words he was saying.

"Uncle, uncle, a lying uncle but not mine. A monkey's uncle, that's what you are. And now's not a good time. It's a bad time. Olivia isn't back yet, and there are too many visitors. Too many. Eating all the food. They're eating too much food. Not enough food." Remy's agitation escalated with each sentence he uttered, and he started pacing. He stopped in front of Deacon and wagged a finger at him. "Olivia's not here, and my boy needs protection. Are you going to protect my boy? They're big and mean. Hateful creatures. All of them. They followed him so you need to protect him."

"Anyone else getting the bad feeling that he's not talking about us?" Ean asked, but the answer was clear. Tanner and Theran were already scanning the immediate area for threats, assessing all the places an enemy could be hiding. The pack instinctually moved closer, tightening their ranks.

"I'm getting so tired of this," Vance said, and everyone grumbled their agreement.

Matthias hadn't taken part in any of the previous skirmishes and watching the pack dynamic in the face of a threat was new. He had no idea what his "job" within the pack would be during a fight, if he was even being considered part of the pack at all yet. He'd accompanied them to the tribunal, but the circumstances had been vastly different, at least in his mind. Out in the open as they were, no rituals or protocols dictating what could or could not be done, Matthias felt threatened, so he knew the others did.

"Can't be here. Not here. Too many places and it's not safe."

Remy was babbling, but the words made sense in a strange way, given the circumstances. Similar to Ross hours earlier, Remy shifted without a word and took off at a run toward the elementary school. Ross pulled free of Deacon's grip and ran after his father, Deacon following just a few steps behind. The rest of the pack looked to Tanner for direction.

"Yeah, okay," he said, gaze darting up and down the empty street, taking in all the abandoned shops. "His fear is a bit infectious. Everyone inside the school."

Sakima lifted Vance into his arms and disappeared in a blur. Colby grabbed Theran and then, they too disappeared.

"Guess we're running," Luca said. He glanced at Tanner, and then they, Matthias, and Ean ran toward the school.

They barely made it halfway across the parking lot.

Chapter Twenty-Three

EAN

"Luca!" Matthias yelled.

Heat erupted around Ean, but he barely had time to register the flames in front of him before he was slammed to the ground by a massive silver dragon's clawed foot. The air whooshed out of his lungs as Matthias settled his weight on top of him. Between the inferno and the dragon's bulk, Ean wasn't sure if he was going to be burned alive or crushed to death. Nothing made sense to his brain. He couldn't see, was only able to take the shallowest of breaths, and everything he did hear was muffled by Matthias's body.

He'd been caught off guard. He hadn't noticed a threat and wasn't aware of Matthias shifting until it was done. He felt like an idiot for not taking Remy's and Tanner's assessments of the situation more seriously. Ean admitted to himself now, in the dark, hot cocoon of his mate's scales, that he'd rationalized everything to the point he'd given himself a false sense of security. He'd allowed himself to become complacent and that was unacceptable.

What the hell? Ean asked.

There's a huge ball of flame on top of you, Vance told him.

I'm being suffocated, Ean said.

Stop complaining. We're protecting you, Luca told him.

Anyone have eyes on where the flames are originating? Tanner asked. *While I love this big-ass dragon to death, I'd like to stop being crushed by him.*

Elemental or sorcerer about halfway down the street behind you, Theran answered. *Shit! School just got blasted and is on fire. We gotta run.*

Follow me, Ross said. *I can get us out. The gym at the back has a door outside.*

Ean felt Matthias's muscles flex with the barest movement. Seconds later, Matthias's weight lifted off him just as his lungs were beginning to scream for more oxygen. More out of instinct than conscious thought, as soon as he was able, Ean shifted, shredding the clothing he was wearing. It was one of the hazards of being a shifter. Clothing didn't last long. He shook out his fur and then came face-to-face with his beautiful, silver-scaled, dragon mate. The stench of burned meat reached Ean's nose, making him shake his head in disgust. Luca's black dragon lifted from his hunched position nearby, freeing Tanner from beneath him.

Tanner shifted into his larger black wolf and howled. The answering howls of the other Chevalier wolves echoed from behind the school.

We're heading back to you and we're bringing friends, Theran said, tone thick with sarcasm over the word "friends."

The four Chevalier wolves ran around the corner of the school toward them followed a few seconds later by several McBane wolves. It was pathetic that Ean could now recognize half of Tanner's familial pack, but he'd fought them fang-to-fang so many times, he now knew them on sight.

About to get wet and windy, Deacon warned.

Clouds formed rapidly overhead and then pelted everything in a deluge of wind and rain. The fire burning on the roof and front wall of the school hissed, but continued to burn. The clouds and rain coalesced into a waterspout that whirled around the edge of the parking lot, roaming in and out of the forest to the side and back of the elementary school. Ean had no idea where Deacon was, but he was manipulating the rain tornado in a clear chase.

Two hawks emerged from the curling smoke and dive-bombed Theran. One gripped his tail in sharp talons while the other attempted to grab hold of the scruff at the back of his neck. The front doors of the school blasted off their hinges and a lethal-looking Colby stepped through the flames. He extended his arm to the side and released a cloud of magic that sent the hawks tumbling to the ground. Theran yipped in pain as the hawk behind him was pushed away, pulling him along by his tail. Ean ran to his friend's aid, grabbing the bird by the neck and clamping his jaw down until the bird went limp.

Thanks. Fuckers cut me.

Are you okay? Ean asked.

Yeah. Bleeding has already stopped. Let's take these assholes down once and for all, Theran said, and then he ran to his mate's side.

Colby wasn't in need of help, Ean noticed. None of them really were. It felt odd seeing the enemy equal in numbers to the Chevalier Pack. Ean thanked Deacon's tornado for that. It had probably chased the majority of McBane wolves away. And who knew exactly what kind of magic Colby was throwing their way. The fog of magic he'd just sent into the forest was a sickly yellow-green in color. After the spell dissipated, so did Deacon's storm.

Ean glanced right as Luca swung his spiked tail and took out three wolves aiming for Vance who was, surprisingly, without Sakima. Ean did a quick search for Matthias and found him on the other side of the lot, sending bolts of flame followed by slashing that dangerously spiked tail at a female Elemental who threw everything from ice balls to lightning bolts at him. Two of the buildings in the immediate vicinity were burning, sending dark swirls of smoke into the air. The school behind them was now completely engulfed in flame. Part of the roof where Colby had blasted his way out was hanging at a precarious angle. Ean ran toward Matthias, intent on helping his mate fight, when Sakima appeared behind the Elemental female, yanked her head to the side, and sank his fangs into her neck.

A flash of movement to Ean's side drew his attention, but not quickly enough. A vampire he'd never seen before grabbed him. Ean yelped as his forward momentum was abruptly halted by the strong vampire grip. He flailed uselessly as sharp fangs sank past his fur into flesh. Ean attempted to wriggle free, but the vamp had a solid hold around his body and fighting caused pain to shoot down his back and legs. Since struggling wasn't getting him anywhere, he did the exact opposite. Ean relaxed every muscle in his body and went limp in the vampire's grip. The result was exactly what he'd hoped. The vampire thought he'd lost consciousness and dropped Ean's body to the ground. Ean felt exhausted and nauseated, but as far as he could tell his injuries weren't life-threatening.

Ean peeked through lowered lashes and found his attacker staring down at him, blood trickling down his chin. Ean didn't feel exceptionally weak so he couldn't have lost that much blood. The vamp didn't look quite right to Ean, and then it registered with him that it was the vampire's own blood he was seeing flowing from that fanged mouth. The vamp's body dropped to the ground with a thud revealing the vampire's cause of death standing behind him. After forming their little wild dog pack and being introduced to Elysium by Deacon, Ean had thought he'd seen just about every paranormal there was, but he'd never seen anything like the creature in front of him.

Uncertainty and fear froze Ean to the spot as the thing moved closer to him. One eye was brown, the other an odd mix of green and gold. It was covered in brown and white fur with horns protruding from the top of its skull and another rose from the tip of his bushy tail, which was covered in blood. The snout was canine in shape, but the fangs in its mouth definitely were not. It walked toward Ean on four furry, clawed feet.

"When will you learn?" Colby's deep, magic-heavy voice boomed, drawing everyone's attention, friend and enemy alike.

A ring of magic radiated outward from where he stood. The spell rolled over the Chevalier Pack members without incident, but it knocked the few remaining McBanes and their helpers off their feet with explosive force. Ean was fascinated to know how that particular spell worked, because it didn't touch the creature in front of him. Luca breathed flames at the heels of a few wolves who were able to get back on their feet quickly. A wave of nausea hit Ean and he rolled onto his stomach to vomit. Matthias roared as he lumbered over to them, but it seemed to be more of a concerned sound than anger.

Ean's stomach rolled again and he swallowed convulsively trying to keep things down. His neck and shoulder ached. Ean swore he would kill the next vampire to ever touch him. He was cool with Sakima, and he knew it was wrong to hate, but the emotion filled his veins as he vomited again. Matthias eased his incredible bulk to the ground beside Ean and gently lowered his head over Ean's back. The dragon emitted a warbling sound similar to a purr.

Why is no one worried about this thing standing over me? Ean asked.

It's my dad, Ross said.

Ross limped over to Ean on three legs. The fourth, he kept pulled up against his chest. The leg he'd injured during their first confrontation with the McBanes had never completely healed, but now it hung at an odd angle, suggesting it had been broken again.

And that is my *dad,* Tanner said, growling at the haggard-looking man being dragged along in Deacon's grasp.

Ethan McBane had grown a beard, his hair a bit longer and messy, and he held a cane in a white-knuckled grip. He glared at them with hateful, angry eyes. Ean was surprised the Alpha wasn't spouting obscenities and hurling threats. He was usually so vocal. Senior was still in human form and fully dressed, suggesting he'd never shifted. He was far weaker than they imagined if Deacon's hold on his upper arm was enough to control him. Or maybe not, Ean thought as Colby got closer to the Alpha and puffed another spell into the wolf shifter's face.

"He'll be paralyzed for hours," Colby said.

"Good." Deacon released his hold on the Alpha, uncaring of where the shifter landed as he crumpled to the ground. Deacon knelt at Ross's side and began to assess his leg injury.

"We should kill him," Colby said.

"No," Sakima said. "We'll take him before your mother. She's the commanding force behind the tribunal. He'll answer to the same governing bodies for his actions as we had to, except I don't think his trial will end as well as ours did."

"Pathetic excuse for an Alpha," Colby grumbled, clearly annoyed by the fact the shifter was being allowed to live. Theran rubbed his body against Colby's legs, distracting the sorcerer.

Sakima glanced at the dead vampire, Vance's tawny-colored wolf sitting at Sakima's side staring up at him. "We also need to inform the Grand Superior of McBane's Purist recruits. They may continue to be a problem for us with or without the Alpha's fearmongering."

Remy moved closer to Ean and Matthias, and then pressed his misshapen snout against Ean's ribs with a strangled-sounding whine. Ean was feeling much better, grateful for the accelerated healing rate of wolf shifters, and he pushed to sitting. He lifted his nose to the sky and stretched his sore muscles. Matthias reared up with a terrifying roar that raised the fur on Ean's back and the entire pack jerked around to face him. A six-foot-long spike of ice had punctured the more tender meat of Matthias's side just below his wing, behind his front leg. Ean imagined in human form, his mate would be sporting a nasty wound in his upper rib area. Remy emitted a sound that made Ean's ears hurt, and he folded them down on his head to muffle the sound as much as possible.

Matthias twisted with a roar, attempting to blast the spike of ice with fire, but only hit the outer end. Luca moved closer and hit the base of the ice with his own flame, cauterizing the wound in the process. While Matthias and Luca were focused on his wound, Remy launched over Ean's body, darted between the two huge dragons, and aimed those lethal horns on his head at the female Elemental. At some point, unnoticed by everyone, she'd regained consciousness and created a nasty piece of ice to launch. Ean's anger spiked because the bitch had aimed for *his mate* and had *injured* him.

Ean took off after Remy. He was weak and his stomach still rolled, but he would take this Elemental bitch down for what she had dared do. It had been a mistake to assume Sakima had killed the woman, but it wasn't a mistake Ean would make twice. While the Elemental was distracted, pelting Remy with sharp spears of ice, Ean went for the bitch's throat. His fangs ripped into the soft tissue of her neck and sank into her jugular vein, but not before she managed to send a spear directly into Remy's abdomen. Unfazed by the injury, Remy slashed at her chest with his dragon-wolf claws. When the Elemental fell to the ground this time, Ean was certain her injuries would keep her down. With the immediate threat removed, Ean did a quick check of Remy. The dragon-wolf hybrid pushed Ean's nose away from him.

"I'm fine, Beta," Remy said in a very human voice.

Ean took a frightened step back. That kind of thing shouldn't be possible, but Remy did it. Shifters weren't meant to speak human words from their animal mouths. Talk about unnatural. No wonder the original Chevalier family had been so feared.

Convinced Remy would be fine, and really not wanting to be anywhere near the strange hybrid, Ean ran back to his mate. A few dozen feet from Matthias, Ean shifted so he could talk to him. A large black burn marred Matthias's gorgeous silver scales from where his wound had been cauterized by dragon flame. It was hard to tell while he was in dragon form, but Matthias appeared angry more than hurt. Ean held his hands up toward Matthias, and his dragon lowered his head to rest in Ean's palms.

"You're okay?" Ean asked, staring into big silver eyes.

Matthias nodded and huffed small puffs of smoke at Ean's chest.

"Good, because I'm not ready to lose you."

Matthias gave a soft, warbling roar.

"Now, claim me, you damn stubborn dragon."

Chapter Twenty-Four

MATTHIAS

Three-hundred-forty-eight years. That's how long it had been since Matthias last set foot inside Roland Bartovic's cabin. Three hundred thirty-two since he'd created a temporary home, holed up in the natural cave about a mile up the mountain from the cabin. After fifty years of raising Remy from infancy, he'd found it hard to leave the hybrid shifter in the care of someone else, even a long-time acquaintance like Roland. He'd found the cave during a snowstorm after a few nights sleeping under the stars in dragon form, which was always a risky thing to do, even back then. The cave had been home for nearly a decade as he'd kept an eye on Roland and Remy. Once he was convinced the two would be all right together, that Remy would thrive in his new home, Matthias had left the area.

Ean had hesitantly agreed to allow Matthias to fly them the short distance to the cave, but as was Ean's usual response to being airborne, he vomited as soon as he slid off Matthias's back. Matthias wondered if his young wolf mate would ever be able to handle flying or if he would be forever sickened by it. He was only moderately encouraged by the fact Ean's puking fits seemed to shorten with each trip.

"I'm cold, old man. You need to do something to warm me up before my dick shrivels to nothing."

Ean wrapped his arms around himself and shivered. Deacon had suggested returning to the vehicles for clothing, which the others had readily agreed to, but Ean had refused. Matthias agreed with the Beta's logic. Any clothing they donned would be removed again soon enough, so why waste time. Remy, who looked far more injured than he acted, had pointed out the old hotel at the far edge of town for the pack to use. The west wing had collapsed, but the east wing appeared to be structurally sound. With Tanner's decision that the pack would stay in Crested Lake for the duration of the blood moon, still four days away, the pack headed east to the vehicles, and Matthias took Ean west into the forest farther up the mountain.

At the entrance to the cave, Matthias grabbed a claw-full of twigs and branches, and then hobbled on three legs into the cave. He felt ridiculous, but his dragon strength made taking the needed supplies inside easier and faster than the multiple trips it would have taken him in human form. Ean followed him in, eyeing Matthias with a lifted brow and giggling. When Matthias set the branches on the ground and blasted the bundle and the rocky cave floor with flame, starting a fire to warm the enclosed space, Ean outright laughed.

"Not the kind of heat I was hoping for."

Ean slid his palm over Matthias's neck scales, over his jaw to rest on his cheek before he pecked a soft kiss on Matthias's nose just above his nostrils. Matthias stared into Ean's glittering brown eyes. How he ever thought he'd be able to resist his gorgeous mate was beyond him at this moment. Ean had pushed for their mating almost from the moment they'd met, and Matthias had wanted to, but he'd let his ugly past and deep-seated fears keep him away. No longer.

Matthias shifted and pulled Ean against him, taking his mouth in a kiss that unloaded every emotion Matthias had been suppressing since Ean had come through the library door nearly nine months prior. He slid his tongue into Ean's mouth where they dueled for dominance. Matthias would never get tired of feeling Ean pressed against him or the flavor of his mate filling his mouth. He lifted Ean into his arms and admitted that even when they'd made love before, he'd been holding a big piece of himself back.

Almost losing Ean twice—first to a spell and then to a vampire—followed by facing his own mortality for a brief moment, Matthias was done wasting time. Ean wrapped his legs around Matthias's waist, redistributing his weight in a way that allowed Matthias to cup a butt cheek with one hand. The moan that escaped from Ean's mouth made Matthias desperate for more. He stepped closer to the fire until he felt the smooth, warm rock surface beneath his feet and then lowered Ean onto his back. Matthias chuckled at Ean's full-body shiver, earning himself a punch to the shoulder and Ean's signature glare.

"Not funny, old man. I was cold, and I wasn't expecting this rock to be warm."

"I blasted it with fire."

"I know—"

Ean's words changed to a moan as Matthias circled a nipple with his tongue, working it to a taut peak before biting it gently. Ean's hips bucked up, his thigh brushing over the still-fresh wound in Matthias's side. Matthias sucked in a pained breath.

"Oh fuck. I'm so sorry."

"I'm fine."

"This was a bad idea. You're hurt. What was I thinking?"

"We're doing this."

"Matthias—"

"I'm claiming you. Right here. Right now." Matthias slid his arm beneath Ean's knee and placed Ean's leg over his shoulder. "We'll just keep this right here where it can't do any harm." Matthias squeezed Ean's thigh as he kissed his inner knee. "Besides, this spreads you open so prettily."

Matthias sucked a finger into his mouth and then pressed the tip to Ean's pucker. He teased the opening with circular motions, enjoying the noises his young mate was making. Every so often, he would add pressure, feeling Ean's tight ring clenching and relaxing beneath his ministrations.

"Do you know why Sakima calls Vance his destined companion?" Matthias asked. Ean lowered his brows. "It's because vampires believe that destiny has created that one perfect mate for them, and they're willing to wait a lifetime to meet them. Sorcerers and Elementals believe in gods and goddesses, wolves have fate, but whatever you choose to call it, I now wholeheartedly believe in it."

"Good?" Ean breathed out.

Matthias brought his fingers back to his mouth, wet two, and then went back to Ean's hole. He eased them past Ean's tight rim and watched as Ean's features smoothed out in bliss.

"Destiny knew what it was doing with us, little boy. Knew it would take hundreds of years for me to become the kind of dragon that could understand you and the unusual situation you're in, to accept you. I believe I had to experience the Chevalier catastrophe, lose Alietta to a severance, and raise Remy in order to grow into the dragon you would one day love."

Ean writhed on the ground as Matthias pumped his fingers into him. He grabbed the base of his cock with one hand and squeezed. With the other hand, he grabbed the back of Matthias's neck and pulled him down into a hot kiss.

"I do love you," Ean whispered against Matthias's lips. "I think I always have, or your rejection wouldn't have hurt so much."

"Maybe. No longer matters."

"No, it doesn't. Enough talking, dragon. Fuck me."

"Mmm, little boy," Matthias growled. "I'm going to do so much more than that."

Hope shimmered in Ean's eyes, and Matthias was determined to see it come to reality. Pulling his fingers free, he wet his cock with saliva and then carefully penetrated Ean's ass. Lube would have worked best, but he'd been shortsighted as far as that was concerned. What he wouldn't give right now to have Colby's magical ability to conjure things out of thin air, but they would make it work. Ean bit down on his lower lip, digging his nails into the meat of Matthias's forearms, until Matthias was fully encased by Ean's body. Matthias wanted to spend the rest of his life being surrounded by Ean's tight, hot silkiness, listening to the sexy sounds Ean made, and enduring his young wolf's stubborn, angry glares. Ean's face gradually relaxed, and the tight grip he had on Matthias's cock eased, signaling he'd adjusted to Matthias's entry.

Matthias sealed his mouth over Ean's, swallowing his moans of pleasure as Matthias started moving inside him. Their previous sexual encounters had been a slow, steady build to the crest in comparison to this moment. Matthias felt incapable of going slow. Ean deserved to be taken care of and cherished, but Matthias's dragon was determined to claim their mate, and Matthias was helpless against the desire. Ean wasn't upset by the force or pace of their mating, either, by the way he responded to each of Matthias's thrusts. Using the leg over Matthias's shoulder, he lifted his hips upward into every forward push Matthias made. Sharp claws pricked into Matthias's skin and Ean nipped at his lips with distended fangs as they both raced toward orgasm. Matthias trailed hot, wet kisses over Ean's jaw down to his neck.

"Come for me, angel," Matthias murmured against the damp skin of Ean's throat.

"Yeah, harder," Ean grunted.

Matthias shortened his thrusts. He pushed in balls deep and began pumping into Ean with as much force as he dared. He knew the moment Ean reached the precipice from the increased grip around his cock as Ean bore down. His little wolf shuddered beneath him with the force of the orgasm rocketing through him. Liquid heat pooled between their bodies where Ean's cock was trapped between them. Matthias prepared himself, knowing his wolf shifter would claim him while the endorphins from his orgasm were still high. When Ean sank his fangs into the meat of his neck, he wasn't surprised. What did surprise him was the force of the orgasm that blasted through his body as the incomplete bond to his mate lit up his brain and set fire to his veins. Instinct took over. Matthias's fangs dropped and, while still pumping his release into Ean's body, he bit down on Ean's neck and claimed his mate.

"Yes!" Ean said and then sucked Matthias's earlobe between his lips. *Finally. Took you long enough, old man.*

"Mmhmm," Matthias mumbled. *Be sweet, little boy.*

He trailed lazy kisses over Ean's neck and jaw, and gave a few small, final thrusts before pulling out and flopping to his back on the cold ground. The cold against his overheated skin was a welcome relief. Ean rolled to his side and scooted up against Matthias's uninjured side. Matthias draped an arm over his back to hold him close. He was hot, but he wanted to keep touching his mate. While his mind had been occupied with other things, the wound in his side had gone largely unnoticed. Now, it throbbed.

You're feverish.

It's the healing process. I just need to rest.

Ean snuggled in closer and rested his head on Matthias's chest.

Ean, my little wolf?

Yeah.

"I've always loved you too."

*

Morning dawned with newly fallen snow and heartbreaking news. Remy had taken a turn for the worse. His wounds hadn't started healing like they should have, and the bleeding never stopped. Ross had woken everyone through the bond early that morning when he noticed his father was missing from the hotel room he'd claimed. Ean had shaken Matthias awake and given him the news. Their little search party had found Remy's body curled up next to Olivia's gravestone beneath a thin blanket of snow.

Using fire with a little magical help from Colby, Matthias and Luca were able to thaw the ground enough to bury Remy beside his wife. Matthias had stood at Ross's side for hours until the young wolf was ready to leave his parents. While Matthias was pained by Remy's passing, the dragon-wolf-elemental hybrid had lived a long life.

"Did I do the right thing, bringing your father here, leaving him with Roland?"

"He was happy most of his life. He wasn't lonely. He had my mom and her family. He had me," Ross said.

"Four hundred years is a solid long life," Matthias said, trying to convince himself Remy's death wasn't untimely.

"A life he wouldn't have had at all if not for you. Never would have met my mom. I wouldn't even exist if it weren't for you, so thank you for that."

Matthias glanced around the snow-covered landscape as they leisurely walked to the other end of town where the rest of the Chevalier Pack waited for them at the hotel. "Destiny. Got to love her," he mumbled.

"Yes. She brought me my Deacon. And Luca, and Sakima, and Colby. And Ean snagged my long-lost uncle." Ross grinned at Matthias.

Matthias smiled back and nodded. "That he did."

Chapter Twenty-Five

MATTHIAS

Matthias wandered through the old cabin. Not much had changed in the past three-hundred-plus years, and it boggled his mind. Roland's apothecary looked much the way it had when Matthias brought, and then subsequently left, Remy to his care. The floors were still packed dirt. Many of the bottles, mortars, and pestles still sat on the shelves amid tattered leather-bound books.

"Wow," Ean breathed as he followed Matthias into the room.

"Roland's stash," Matthias said, waving his arm at the wall of shelving.

"Spell-making stuff? Don't let Colby see this."

"Colby is the *only* sorcerer I will allow in this room," Matthias said. "He's young, impetuous, and arrogant at times, but he's powerful, and despite his blatant lack of respect for certain people, he has great respect for the power contained within himself and these four walls. It's my *nephew* I'd prefer to keep out of this room."

"Ross will be fine. Colby's been working with him the past couple of days. It's been quite amusing to watch. Ross's brain is like a herd of cats, all of them going in different directions, some hiding, some climbing the curtains, some puking on the carpet, and there's Colby in the middle of it, trying to teach them how to sit, stay, and shut up."

"There's an image," Matthias muttered. "But everyone seems to be able to handle his spurts of insanity, so I have to agree with you that he'll be fine."

"The pack is growing on you, isn't it?"

Matthias offered his mate a small smile. "They've proven themselves to be good, honorable men."

"We have our moments."

Matthias laughed with his mate as he circled the desk and started rifling through papers.

"So, is this a trip down memory lane, or are you looking for something specific?"

"The deed to the town," Matthias answered. "Roland owned half this mountain back in the day. Crested Lake is built on land that was once his. Sorcerer like him"—Matthias shook his head—"wouldn't have sold the land. He would've given developers permission to build on it though. He also would've made sure his descendants did the same."

"Are you fucking kidding me? His descendants? Are you telling me Ross owns this whole damn town?" Ean practically shrieked the questions.

Matthias laughed, rubbing at his ear. "Tone, my boy. Going to deafen me."

"Holy shit," Ean breathed and then added, "that solves our problem. Luca doesn't have to buy the town for Tanner if Ross already owns it. Except I don't think Ross knows that, because he would've said something during the hunt this morning when Tanner brought it up."

Matthias stopped searching and stared at his mate. Only part of what Ean had just said made sense to him. "What are you talking about?"

"Tanner made the suggestion to move the pack here to Crested Lake. New start, new place far away from *Daddy McBane*. The rest of the wolves agreed, and we were each tasked with talking to our mates about it. Tanner is going to ask Luca to buy the town for him, again."

"When were you planning to discuss it with me?" Matthias asked. He laced his words with an annoyance he didn't actually feel, just so he could rile his sweet little mate and maybe see a bit of that fire he loved so much. He wasn't disappointed.

"Technically, I just did, old man, Keeper of All Secrets."

Ean's eyes flashed and his nostrils flared, making Matthias hard in a heartbeat. Damn, Ean was beautiful when he got flustered. Matthias narrowed his eyes and stood; palms flat on the desk in front of him. He locked onto Ean's heated gaze through his lashes.

"You want to rumble with me, little boy?" he growled.

The heat in Ean's eyes went from annoyed to aroused with a blink. "Yes."

Matthias couldn't look away from Ean's pretty brown eyes, and now that they were officially mated, he found he never wanted to say no. He'd spent nearly a year denying Ean, and he'd made a vow to Ean that it would never happen again. This moment was no different. Matthias moved around the desk with deliberate steps. Feeling his intent through their bond, Ean ran out of the room. The blood moon would rise in just a few hours. As the week had progressed, the wolves had grown more antsy, irritable, and voracious in their sex drives, and Ean had taken to playing hide and seek, the adult version.

Matthias counted to five. It was only fair to give the little wolf a head start. As he left the room, he glanced around at the shelving along the walls. The deed was here. He knew it. It was only a matter of time until he found it. Pushing that task to the back of his mind, he gave in to the dragon's desire for his mate. He ran outside into the cold, snow-covered forest and shifted. The chase was on.

Epilogue

CRESTED LAKE

Tanner sat on the porch and inhaled the cool morning air. Snow still clung to the grassy areas but was slowly melting. With fifty-degree temperatures and sunshine expected for the rest of the week, it would soon be gone. He suspected there would be a few more spring snowstorms, as was typical for their area, but the warmer weather would be welcome.

The roar of Luca's Hellcat could be heard long before he could be seen, and Tanner smiled as the rumble drew nearer. Now that they were no longer making the twice-daily trip to and from the office, Luca took every opportunity to drive his charged-up baby every time the need arose. Today, he was bringing a new mixed-species couple to visit Tanner. Anyone who wanted to move to Crested Lake had to meet with the Pack Alpha to get approval.

Tanner's trust of strangers had been pushed too far, and he was excessively picky about who he let into his town, and near his pack. If anyone deserved to be left in peace to live out their lives, it was the Chevalier Ten, as the town's growing population had taken to calling them. Everyone in the town considered themselves to be a part of the Chevalier Pack, despite the fact Tanner would never officially bond any of them. They were pack by choice. Upon moving to Crested Lake, Tanner had opened their proverbial gates to anyone who found themselves in the same situation Tanner had, alone and hated.

Luca parked the sports car in the driveway with a familiar blue crew-cab truck following close behind. Tanner stared at his mate as he exited the car. He'd never get over how hot his dragon was, and he'd never stop loving the man. Tanner's attention was pulled back to the truck as three shifters climbed out. Tyler leaned on the hood of his truck and nodded a greeting that Tanner reciprocated. Tanner smiled broadly when he saw who was climbing from the back seat of the truck. No wonder Luca had needed Tyler's help, the massive gryphon shifter would never have fit in the Hellcat.

Tanner pushed to his feet and met the newcomers halfway down the sidewalk. "Ollie, it's good to see you." Tanner shook hands with Elysium's bouncer. "What brings you here?"

Ollie smiled and stepped aside to reveal a much smaller man. The gryphon shifter put an arm around the man's shoulders and pulled him against his much larger frame. Tanner knew the two were mates, simply from the care Ollie demonstrated with the action.

"This is Lincoln. He's a lynx shifter, and he's my mate. His family is in Canada still, but when he told them he was mated to a male gryphon, they threatened him. I can protect him when I'm with him"—Ollie looked down at Lincoln lovingly—"but I can't be with him every second." Turning his attention back to Tanner, Ollie added, "I want to know he's someplace safe when I have to leave him. I need him to be safe."

"Everyone living in Crested Lake can understand that feeling," Luca said from Tanner's side. He draped an arm over Tanner's shoulders and kissed his temple. "We all have the intense desire to protect our mates."

"You're both more than welcome here," Tanner said. "We still have plenty of housing available. Tyler is one of Crested Lake's real estate agents. He can drive you to see whatever property is on the market right now. We're still in the process of renovating and rebuilding, as you can imagine."

The last McBane attack on the Chevalier Pack was well-known to paranormals statewide. Turned out the favorite pastime of Purists was bragging. In the attempt to take down Tanner, his father had pushed the local governing bodies a bit too far and, as Sakima had suspected would happen, found himself the subject of a tribunal. The paranormal equivalent of a restraining order had been awarded to Tanner and his pack so long as they honored the agreement themselves. When Ross had gifted him with the deed to the town of Crested Lake on the pack's one-year anniversary, they were all ready for the new start.

"Thank you," Ollie said "We appreciate the hospitality."

He squeezed his mate gently and then turned to head back to the truck. Lincoln stayed where he was, glancing back and forth between Luca and Tanner with his distinctly feline gold and yellow eyes. Ollie stopped to wait for the lynx shifter, still within reach of the smaller man.

"How many different paranormals live here?" Lincoln asked, his voice naturally soft.

"Not sure," Tanner admitted. "Never thought to count, but I'd hazard a guess of around a dozen, give or take."

"And all of them are...like us?" Lincoln averted his eyes shyly. Ollie cupped the lynx's chin and lifted his face so he could look into golden eyes.

"It's not a dirty word, my little kitten. You can say it out loud, especially here. I promise you're in a safe place."

"Gay," Lincoln whispered, staring up at his huge gryphon mate. "Are they all gay?"

If Lincoln was this shy and insecure, it made sense his mate was so much larger, confident, and fearless.

"Yes," Tyler answered, drawing everyone's attention to him. Tanner smiled. Tyler had never been excessively chatty, and generally remained silent until he had something he felt was important enough to say. "Everyone in Crested Lake is gay, bi, ace, poly, or some combination of the aforementioned."

Ollie nodded and then pecked a kiss to Lincoln's lips. "Come on. Let's get you back in the truck so we can go house hunting, yeah?"

"Yeah," Lincoln answered breathlessly. "Will we be part of the Chevalier Pack when we move here?" he asked Ollie, never taking his adoring gaze off the big man.

"No, not officially, but we'll be part of the Crested Lake community. The pack is required to stay small, but their town can be as large as they like," Ollie answered.

Lincoln continued to stare up at Ollie with clear affection as he was led to the rear door of the truck. While Ollie assisted his lynx into the truck, Tyler approached Tanner. The only outward sign the wolf shifter was disturbed was the slight tension around his eyes. A lifetime of friendship allowed Tanner to recognize it immediately.

"What's wrong?" Tanner asked, keeping his voice down so it didn't carry.

"There's been a tiger shifter sniffing around the edge of town. I just wanted you to know that he's mine." Tyler sighed with a roll of his eyes. "*One* of mine."

"Okay." Tanner smiled at his friend. "Out of curiosity, what's the other one?"

Tyler winced. "Bald eagle. I mean...what the hell?"

"Canine, feline, and avian," Luca said. "That's definitely an interesting combination."

"Yeah," Tyler scoffed. "Interesting."

When the Chevalier Pack had moved to Crested Lake and Tanner sent out the official notification to all the paranormal governing bodies once again, Tyler had been one of the first to show up at his door. He'd spent hours talking to Tanner about his own, admittedly unique, mate situation. Tyler had not one mate, but two. According to Tyler, his mates were coworkers at a car rental shop in the city about forty-five minutes east of Crested Lake, and, apparently, they couldn't stand each other. Tanner couldn't imagine feeling the way he felt about Luca times two, especially when the two didn't get along.

Tyler walked back to his truck and climbed inside. Tanner waved as the truck pulled away from the curb and disappeared down the tree-lined street. "How many does that make now?" Tanner asked.

"Officially, with Ollie and Lincoln, population will be sixteen. If Taro and his brothers finally move here and the two wolf shifter families decide to move here and open the school, we'd be at twenty-seven," Luca answered.

"Twenty-eight. Taro won't move here without his phoenix, Kyle."

"True," Luca agreed. "And if Sakima, Vance, and Deacon are successful in turning that old mansion near the hot springs into an LGBT resort and night club, we're likely to see some serious growth."

Tanner nodded. He and Luca were speaking in hypothetical terms, but to the marrow of his bones he knew the future they imagined was guaranteed. The Chevalier Pack had big ideas, determination, and backing by centuries-old money thanks to Luca, Sakima, and Matthias. Crested Lake was destined to become everything they'd dreamed. Glancing around the neighborhood and then at their own modest home, Tanner was struck by how far they'd come in the past fifteen or so months.

"From the verge of bloodlust, alone and afraid, to...*this*," Tanner muttered. He was speaking more to himself than anything, but Luca responded by wrapping his arms around Tanner's waist.

"The moment you walked into my office for the interview, I knew you were different, special, and I had to keep you close to me. You've done nothing but prove me right. You're amazing, pup."

For Your Drinking Pleasure

LUCA'S CHOICE
Dragon's Blood Cocktail
    Ingredients:
        1 tablespoon - red and green sugar crystals
        ¼ teaspoon - cayenne pepper
        1 ½ ounces - vodka
        1 ounce - coconut rum
        ½ ounce - Midori
        ¼ ounce - lime juice
        2 dashes - Fee's aromatic bitters
        Add pinch - powdered sugar (if desired)
        2 ounces - ginger ale (a strong one like Reed's)
        ¼ ounce - grenadine
    Instructions:
        Chill a margarita glass
        Mix the sugar crystals and cayenne pepper
        Wipe a line of egg white or syrup around the top of the glass
        Roll it in the sugar mixture
        Mix the vodka, rum, Midori, lime juice, bitters, and powdered
            sugar with 6 ice cubes in a shaker
        Strain the vodka mixture into the chilled glass
        Pour in the ginger ale
        Slowly pour in the grenadine

TANNER'S CHOICE
Wolf's Bite Shot
    Ingredients:
        ¼ ounce - Lucid Absinthe
        ½ ounce - Midori Melon liqueur
        1 ounce - pineapple juice
        Splash - lemon-lime soda
        Dash - grenadine

Instructions:

Gather ingredients

Combine the liquors and juice in a cocktail shaker filled with ice

Shake vigorously and strain into a tall shot glass

Top with splash of lemon-lime soda

Add a drizzle of grenadine

Serve and enjoy

SAKIMA'S CHOICE

Vampire's Kiss

Ingredients:

2 oz raspberry vodka

2 oz Chambord raspberry liquor (black raspberry liquor)

2 oz cranberry juice

Instructions:

Put ice and water in martini glass, to chill

Put all ingredients in cocktail shaker with ice and shake the heck
out of it

Dump ice/water from glass

Strain into martini glass and enjoy!

VANCE'S CHOICE

Lone Wolf Cocktail

Ingredients:

1.5 oz white rum

0.5 oz Southern Comfort

0.5 oz triple sec

0.25 oz lemon juice

Instructions:

Fill a shaker half full with ice cubes.

Pour all ingredients into shaker and shake well.

Fill highball glass almost full of ice cubes and strain drink into
glass.

Garnish with a maraschino cherry and serve.

COLBY'S CHOICE
Witches' Brew
(except I'm a sorcerer, but what-the-fuck-ever)
Ingredients:
Green Appletini Drink Mix with Caramel Rimmer
6 ounces of light rum
1 cup of water
4 cups of ice cubes
12 maraschino cherries
3 tsp maraschino cherry juice
Instructions:
Rim 6 martini glasses with rimmer packet according to package directions.
Prepare Green Appletini Drink Mix according to package directions.
Place 2 cherries in the bottom of each glass. Pour drink in glasses. Drizzle ½ tsp. cherry juice over each cocktail.

THERAN'S CHOICE
The Wolf
Ingredients:
6 slices of fresh jalapenos
1 ounce of simple syrup
3 ounces of Lunazul Tequila
1 ounce of orange juice
1 ounce of lime juice
Ice
Instructions:
Muddle together 3 jalapeno slices and the simple syrup until the jalapenos are broken down
Add in the Tequila, orange juice, lime juice, ice, and then stir.
Garnish with remaining jalapeno slices.

MATTHIAS'S CHOICE
Dragon's Heart
    Ingredients:
        3 lime wedges
        ¾ oz elderflower cordial
        5 dashes Angostura Bitters
        1 ½ oz rum
        ¾ oz mezcal
        ½ oz ginger liqueur
        1 ½ oz blood orange juice
        Garnish: Blood orange slice
    Instructions:
        In a cocktail shaker, add lime wedges, elderflower cordial, and
            3 drops of bitters. Muddle well.
        Fill the shaker with ice and add the rum, mezcal, ginger liqueur,
            and blood orange juice.
        Shake vigorously.
        Strain into chilled cocktail glass.
        Garnish with 2 drops of Angostura Bitters and a blood orange
            slice.

EAN'S CHOICE
The Gray Wolf
    Ingredients:
        2 oz Japanese whiskey (preferably Hibiki Harmony)
        ¼ oz demerara syrup (2:1 sugar:water)
        ½ tsp Benedictine
        ½ tsp plum vinegar
        1 dash Angostura Bitters
        Garnish: Express grapefruit peel
    Instructions:
        Combine all ingredients in a mixing glass over ice and stir until
            chilled.
        Strain into a rocks glass over ice
        Express grapefruit peel and discard

DEACON'S CHOICE
Glow in the Dark Bomb Shot
   Ingredients:
       ¾ oz melon liqueur
       ¾ oz blue raspberry vodka
       1 oz triple sec
       Tonic water
   Instructions:
       Pour melon liqueur into base of one shot glass and top with a
           splash of tonic water.
       Pour blue raspberry vodka into base of a second shot glass and
           top with a splash of tonic water.
       Set shots aside.
       Pour triple sec into base of pint glass and add tonic water.
       To shoot – drop one shot glass into the pint and then the other.

ROSS'S CHOICE
The Big Bad Wolf
   Ingredients:
       1/3 glass Curacao
       2/3 glass Old Mr. Boston Apricot Nectar
       1 egg yolk
       1 spoonful Grenadine
   Instructions:
       Shake well with cracked ice and strain into 4 oz cocktail glass.
       Serve.

Acknowledgements

I've heard, on numerous occasions, that writing is a solitary art. While I may sit alone at my desk, lost in the many fantastic and romantic worlds my imagination creates, it takes a village to make my novels a reality.

So, thank you to all the interesting people and places that exist outside my front door for the inspiration you provide.

Thank you to my editor, BJ, and my beta reader, Pat, for helping me keep my writing clean, catching all those missed words, and constantly fixing my comma problem. Punctuation is my nemesis.

Thank you to the copy editor and proofreader for helping me polish my shiny new baby, and to Natasha Snow for decorating it so beautifully.

Last, but by no means the least, thank you to my readers for sharing this journey with me. I write because I enjoy it, but I absolutely love being able to share these stories with you.

About the Author

Kay lives in Colorado with her husband and their animal children. Family is important to her, so there are weekly visits to her parents and frequent text messages with her brothers. She has a severe addiction to coffee and Mexican food. She loves to read and write and can easily become consumed by it for hours, much to the dismay of the husband and dogs. On occasion, she can be convinced to venture out into the world of the living.

Email: kaydohertyauthor@gmail.com

Facebook: www.facebook.com/kaydohertyauthor

Twitter: @kdohertyauthor

Website: www.kaydohertybooks.com

Other NineStar books by this author

Blind Date

Only You

Sugar Cookies & Mistletoe

Also Available from NineStar Press

Connect with NineStar Press

www.ninestarpress.com

www.facebook.com/ninestarpress

www.facebook.com/groups/NineStarNiche

www.twitter.com/ninestarpress

www.tumblr.com/blog/ninestarpress

www.ingramcontent.com/pod-product-compliance
Lightning Source LLC
Chambersburg PA
CBHW061205190726
48288CB00001B/62